The LORD is my shepherd, I shall not be in want.
  He makes me lie down in green pastures,
he leads me beside quiet waters,
  he restores my soul.
He guides me in paths of righteousness
  for his name's sake.
Even though I walk
  through the valley of the shadow of death,
I will fear no evil,
  for you are with me;
your rod and your staff,
  they comfort me.

You prepare a table before me
  in the presence of my enemies.
You anoint my head with oil;
  my cup overflows.
Surely goodness and love will follow me
  all the days of my life,
and I will dwell in the house of the LORD
  forever.

(Psalm 23 NIV)

THE JERUSALEM JOURNEYS

Valley of the Shadow

John H. Timmerman

INTERVARSITY PRESS
DOWNERS GROVE, ILLINOIS 60515

© 1994 by John H. Timmerman

All rights reserved. No part of this book may be reproduced in any form without written permission from InterVarsity Press, P.O. Box 1400, Downers Grove, Illinois 60515.

InterVarsity Press® is the book-publishing division of InterVarsity Christian Fellowship®, a student movement active on campus at hundreds of universities, colleges and schools of nursing in the United States of America, and a member movement of the International Fellowship of Evangelical Students. For information about local and regional activities, write Public Relations Dept., InterVarsity Christian Fellowship, 6400 Schroeder Rd., P.O. Box 7895, Madison, WI 53707-7895.

Cover illustration: John Walker
ISBN 0-8308-1677-1

Printed in the United States of America ∞

For Woody and Mary Vanden Bosch
with appreciation,
for they act justly,
and love mercy,
and walk humbly with our God

PART ONE
THE CAPITAL CITY

CHAPTER ONE

I knew what was coming.

When I saw him in those long black robes I had grown to despise, shoulders squared back so that he peered down the length of his face with cold eyes like chips of ebony stone, I knew why he was here. And what my answer would be.

And what the consequences would be.

He simply stood there, like a long, thin fence post staked to the earth, draped in a black silk robe with the hood thrown back so that the sun glinted across his thinning hair. He stood as if daring me to show myself.

I rose from my desk at the window and watched him. He may not have been able to see me standing within the shadows of the house, but even at this distance—he waited by the gate of the fence that Taletha had erected to keep the sheep from her flowers—I could see him clearly. Even the sunken cheeks in that angular face.

But especially those eyes. They dug into the house, shadows or not, and gripped me like a vise.

The pen trembled in my hand, and I threw it down angrily, noticing too late the dull ink splotch it left across the parchment.

Well, I would get it over with.

* * *

I walked to the door and stood there a moment, half-hidden in the shadows. Let him see me standing. Let *him* approach *me*.

I sensed a slight movement to my right, by the coop where Taletha kept her doves and pigeons.

She had built the bird coop under the shade of some oak trees, tall branching trees that caught and quenched the sun in layers of trembling leaves. I hadn't liked the idea at all and had told her why.

"Birds stink in a coop," I pointed out.

"Some do," she observed.

"They attract predators. Especially when they're cooped. You know, the foxes?"

"The dog will keep them away." She responded with that whimsical half-smile, her face averted slightly as if looking out upon the finished coop she already saw in her mind. As if she were saying to herself, "I know what I want, but I'll humor him anyway." As if! Taletha always did what she wanted—like the day she had returned from town leading the five sheep and the tough little goat. It was her business. Now her flock of sheep dotted the far hillside of the farm, kept under the care of Liske, the son of our friends Manasseh and Meridivel.

Liske had helped her build the bird coop. While I sat writing.

"If the fox gets one," she had said, "that's okay. Because I'm going to give them away, anyway."

"Give them away?"

"They will be for the people who can't afford the temple sacrifice," she said with an edge of iron to her voice. "Or those who have to squeeze out pennies they can't afford to appease the lawgivers." Anger surfaced through her words.

"Well, then," I had said, "why didn't you tell me?"

"Husband, I just did."

I knew there would be trouble, here in this land where religion had its price. The visit was not unexpected, then. I was just glad that Taletha was visiting in town with Meridivel, that Liske was up in the hills with the sheep.

The flicker of motion I had seen took the shape of two men moving through the oaks. There would be one or two more, I guessed. Probably at the other side of the house. He wouldn't have come by himself.

The lawgiver hadn't moved an inch. A finger of wind flicked the hem of his robe. I could hear the faintest silken rustling.

Get it over with.

I stepped through the door to the gravel path.

I heard a wrenching noise by the coop. Wood breaking. I whirled to the right and saw one of them—his guards—rip the door loose.

The guard was a big man, the sleeves of his red tunic pushed up over thick arms. He glanced my way, and I saw that a scar cut across his cheekbone, freezing his lips into a permanent snarl. He held the door as if admiring his handiwork, then tossed it aside. The other guard knocked out the delicate pieces of papyrus Taletha had knit over the windows. A dove whirled out, confused by the sudden freedom. There was another crack of splintering wood. Then a storm of pigeons flapped out of the door and window. Their heavy wings beat the air. They scattered wildly, loose feathers flaking off into the hot sky, then gathered round in a frantic oblong pack and arrowed toward the hills.

Beyond that first step past the doorway, I went no further. The two emerged from the oaks. Laughing, one brushed a fresh splat of bird droppings off his shoulder. Sensing others beside the house, I turned toward them. I was wrong—four more waited alongside the house, held on an invisible leash of the lawgiver's orders. They would make no move unless told to. Six in all.

More than enough to handle one man, by himself, out in the country.

I turned back to the lawgiver and smiled. "Just the few of us, Priest."

His cold glare riveted me. He ignored the insult. He said nothing, simply studying me the way one does a peculiar insect.

And why not? I am still the man from outside. Ever so. I have learned to live with it. "Next time," I said softly, "let me know, and I'll try to have dinner prepared. Something nice for you. Fried pig, maybe."

One of the guards growled. The lawgiver's dark eyes flashed a command, and the man fell silent.

"Or perhaps locust. Did I ever tell you, Lawgiver, how once, dying of hunger in the desert, I had to eat them? Locusts. Oh, I have eaten many forbidden things."

The guards moved forward at the contempt in my voice. But I held the lawgiver's eyes.

"To stay alive, man. Just to stay alive. Once I even ate something you know all about."

The lawgiver arched an eyebrow.

"Yes," I paused, "a thick, slimy slug, Lawgiver. A parasite. Now get off my land!"

He stepped toward me, moving like a gliding shadow, body rigid. His silk robes hissed in the air. When he stood six feet away, he spoke, and his voice was as flat and cold as the river bottom.

"I did not come for dinner, violator."

"What then? More taxes? I pay more than I make already."

His lips twitched in a faint sneer. "Nor am I interested in your money. But," he added, "a lot of land comes with a price. Those who pretend to greatness should be prepared to pay the cost."

"That is profound," I snapped. "I own my land, free and clear. I pay every cent of my taxes to the civil government. I owe you"—I matched the flatness of his own voice—"nothing. Now get off this land I own."

"Or?" he looked amused. One of the guards snorted.

He stepped closer, and the guards closed around. They were not military guards, I knew. The farthest thing from it. I had seen their sort at work before. They were thugs, recruited from seaside docks, the dangerous parts of a city, even from prisons. I sensed their blood lust.

"Don't start something you can't stop," I said to the lawgiver. But the threat was meaningless. He knew—had known—that I would be alone. He would never permit violence in a public place. But here? Where the land stood empty? It would be his word against mine. Lawgiver versus infidel, the foreigner. And the guards? He would deny ever knowing them. No official ties there. He would claim to have *stopped* them, if it came to that. But here we were alone.

"Precisely what I wanted to talk to you about," said the lawgiver. "Starting things that you can't stop. Things that should stop, Elhrain," he said. "Pigeons and doves, for example. You give them away to people to make their sacrifice. This is unacceptable."

"Then don't demand something the people can't give."

"As I said, everything has a price."

Standing this close to him, I studied his features carefully. They looked carved out of wax, like a death mask. Black eyes peering from that lean face gave the only sign of life. His lips barely moved when he spoke. A deathgiver.

I had been threatened before and by more powerful men. Still, I felt a sudden chill tremble through me.

"Your birds will no longer be honored," he said. "This is just a warning. The people will buy from the temple stock, at the temple price."

"Perhaps I'll give them the money."

"That would not be wise. Nor are your wife's activities wise."

Fear crept through my anger. "What do you mean?" My voice caught.
"She is off seeing a friend."

The lawgiver chuckled coldly, his lips a thin line. "You really don't
know, do you? You ignorant fool. All these 'trips' she takes? Trading wool
from that pitiful flock of sheep? Haven't you wondered about it, man?"

I couldn't think of anything to say. Truly, I did not know what Taletha
did on her time away. I had never wondered about it. Taletha would often
be off to visit her friends in Noke. It was understandable, living out here
in the hills. She needed more company than I gave her. At times she would
be gone for a week or more to the capital, most often traveling with old
Zophar the innkeeper on one of his many business deals.

The lawgiver probed my doubt. "So, while you hide out here, your wife
travels. Business deals? Do you really think so, Elhrain? Perhaps she just
needs an excuse. Perhaps there is a younger man?"

I flinched, and the guards tightened their circle about me. Eager. Ready.

He laughed aloud. "Why not? You're an old man, Elhrain. An ugly old
mongrel. It's your misfortune that you married a younger woman, and
one so very beautiful. Besides, she has been seen in the company of a well-
known prostitute. What do you think of that?"

I think I knew whom he meant. "Former prostitute," I murmured.
There was too much uncertainty in my voice.

"Hah! Yes, and leopards change their spots, don't they? Believe me,
Elhrain. Our eyes and ears are everywhere."

He sensed my bewilderment, attacked it like a predator. "I think," he
said slowly, "it is time to teach the foreigner a lesson."

He stepped back, lifted one hand to signal, flicked his lean wrist toward
me. Even then, in one of those moments when time seems to stand still,
I noted that the pale flesh of his arm was virtually hairless. He lived in
shadows, this lawgiver.

Then the guards' feet shuffled and closed in like a pack of animals,
predatory and vicious. I braced myself, arms loose, legs spread.

I am no longer a young man, now past my fiftieth year. But they have been years spent in survival, fighting for life against the brutalities of the desert in the face of the meat-eating sun. I have survived. If I had to take a beating, I was determined to set a price for it.

The guards welcomed the sign of resistance. They crowded in a carefully choreographed dance of destruction. One feinted. I whirled toward him.

From the other side a blow that felt like a mule's kick landed to my stomach. I doubled over, flailing with one hand to ward off another blow. Too late, and too many of them. A blow glanced across my cheek, into the eye socket, flinging me backward into the doorway. Then they were on me, feet kicking out, smashing into my body. I doubled over, letting the blows land on legs and backside, trying to protect myself while thinking hopelessly, *I'm too old!*

I thought the cry of outrage was my own. But then it seemed apart from me, rising from the direction of the riverbank that wound behind the oak trees.

I huddled backward over the threshold, trying to crawl into the house. Only the tight confines of the doorway saved me. I felt a sudden lance of pain in an old wound at my ankle as one attacker stumbled over me.

A shape suddenly materialized behind them, red and huge, obscured against the sun. A pair of large, sun-reddened arms reached for one set of shoulders. Massive hands clamped down, lifting the guard bodily out of the way.

The thugs were turning. One collapsed toward me as a rock-hard fist smashed into his jaw.

I staggered to my feet. Manasseh's massive shoulders stood between me and the guards now. He stood there alone, shoulders hunched, legs bent, those huge carpenter's hands raised in fists as thick and dangerous as thunder. One guard darted forward. In a whirl Manasseh seized his arm, spun the man and flung him back at the others like a battering ram. Three lay sprawled in the dust.

Manasseh stood there alone, staring down the retreating guards.

"Get out," he hissed, his fury like an acid flung at them. They stepped back warily, inching toward their leader who still stood rigidly inside the gate. The thin blade of a smile twisted his lips.

"Well done, carpenter," he said. "Perhaps," he paused, staring disdainfully at the guards, "we will meet again soon." He turned, and the guards followed him like dogs. One glanced back and shook a fist. The scar on his face shone white with anger.

A snarl came from Manasseh. I laid a hand on his shoulder. The bulged muscles were as tense and hard as hewn rock.

"Easy, friend," I said. "And thanks."

Manasseh relaxed, as if physically shaking off the presence of the lawgiver. He spat an oath, then straightened. Suddenly he boomed a huge laugh.

"Not so bad, eh? For a couple of old men?"

I touched the swelling of my left eye. "Too old for this," I said. "How did you show up at the right time?"

Manasseh walked back into the kitchen, panting heavily. He found a flagon of wine—brewed from my own vines—and sat heavily on a chair that creaked under his weight. Why couldn't the man stick with a bench?

He took a long, noisy swallow, wiping his mouth with the back of his hand. "I was delivering a table to that new couple on the edge of town," he said between heaves of breath. "I saw the man, the lawgiver, turn up the road. He was riding a horse. Must have picketed it down the road a ways. For sure he wouldn't walk all this way and get his pretty robe dirty. When I saw the guards following, I had to see what he was up to. I left my wagon down in the willow grove by the river and circled behind its bank. Just in time, too, it looks like." He took a long pull from the flagon, nearly draining it.

I tried to smile, although my lips felt like they were full of gravel. "Now what provoked that, I wonder?"

Manasseh rolled his eyes. "What provoked that? You provoke everyone, my friend."

"Giving away doves?"

"Maybe what you called him last time you were in Noke."

I had to think for a minute. "Ah, you mean when I visited old Napthali. How would I know this lawgiver would be at the temple? He is around a bit too much lately. He belongs in Jerusalem, not out here."

"Maybe he didn't like it when you told him you paid less attention to his laws than to a flea under a donkey's tail." Manasseh broke out laughing.

"I was being polite, Manasseh."

"Yes. But then you had to ask him why he crawled out from under the

15

donkey's tail to bother the people. Oh, yes. Napthali told me all about it." Manasseh sat grinning. He had *enjoyed* the fight.

"You make the best wine in the land, Elhrain. Just not enough of it."

"Thanks." I touched the swollen eye, felt a new surge of anger. "I'll have Liske bring you some more the next time he goes to town." I taunted him. "Liske must have milked the goats this morning. If you're still thirsty, I'm sure I can get you some fresh goat milk."

He waved his hand as if dismissing a poison. A weary grin crept across his wide lips. "You look like a mess," he said casually. Then he shook his large head, like an old bear. "Ah, yes. Liske. How is he doing? Never see my son anymore."

"He does well, Manasseh. A good boy. Good with the sheep especially. But also with the vines."

Manasseh sighed. "Well, he's not a carpenter, that's for sure."

Manasseh's good-hearted banter switched off like a pinched candle. He laid one meaty hand upon my forearm. I looked at it for a moment, startled. That red-hued, bear-paw flesh, ruffed with gritty reddish hair, lay against my ebony blackness, the flesh tracked with old scars. His hand clamped involuntarily, as if his powerful muscles were but clumsily controlled. He must have seen me wince in expectation, for he released his grip in an instant, withdrawing his hand.

I held his eyes with my own. "Yes?" I asked.

He shook his head, a red ring of embarrassment visibly rising up his face. "It's nothing."

"Okay. Then I better get busy fixing the coop."

He banged a fist against the table. "That's just it," he bellowed. Little drops of sweat popped out on his red forehead.

"Listen," he said. "Stop and think. What if I had not seen them? What would have happened?"

I smiled. But it was to calm him. My own heart still felt the fear. "But you came at the right time, my friend."

"Yes. This time." He took a deep breath. "Listen. You would have been beaten within an inch of your life. And—"

"It wouldn't be the first time," I interrupted.

"Right. But not at your age. You're . . . how old? Fifty? Fifty-five?"

"Probably."

"You're not sure?"

"I haven't counted recently."

"And Taletha. Look, she's not a girl anymore. She's involved, you understand. Leave it to the young ones, Elhrain. Let it go. At fifty-five, or whatever you are, a man deserves some peace, right?"

"So I'm an old man, Manasseh? Fit to go to pasture with the goats? Crawl around the grapevines?"

"Something like that. I didn't mean . . ."

I held up a hand. "You listen, friend. I want you to understand something. See, when Taletha and I arrived here—out of the desert, man!— we were coming *home*. At least for Taletha. It was her home. And I, her husband."

"I was at your wedding."

"I know, I know. But not at my side in the desert. Not when a southern king, a great bloated sack of evil named Kurdash, wanted to squeeze out my life like . . ." I found my fist raised and clenched. "Like some insect. Taletha was there. At my side. And I am not going to desert her now. Not her hope for a home."

"No one's asking you to do that," he muttered. "But I am afraid, especially for her. She's involved in things she doesn't understand."

"I understand," I said coldly. "I understand that these lawgivers," I waved my hand at the empty doorway, half expecting to see him standing there, "are killing the people's joy. Look, Manasseh. There's plenty about religion I don't understand, especially the religion of your people, but—"

"But," he exploded, "our religion is our life, man. It is in all the sacred texts."

"Have you read them all?"

Manasseh looked bewildered. "No. Of course not. The lawgivers . . . ah, I see."

"Right. The lawgivers can twist the religion any way they want. And by twisting it, how do you know they aren't turning people *from* the very God you serve?"

"Ach!" Manasseh muttered and waved the talk away. "All I'm saying, my friend, is be careful. Leave it for the young ones. You're too old for this."

I started to laugh until a sharp pain in my ribs stopped me. "I'll be careful, Manasseh. All we do is give a few birds to the poor. To meet the demands of religion."

He held me with a level gaze, his beefy shoulders hunched. "I would hate to have anything happen to you."

"Thank you, Manasseh."

I became aware of evening shadows darkening the room.

Manasseh peered past me, through the doorway, across the violet land. I followed his gaze. The trees stood in a misty haze rising from the stream, their leaves hanging heavily in the windless air. Beyond them the pasture land rolled toward the hills, their sides cut in dark green lattices at the grapevines. It was a beautiful land, more my home than I sometimes realized.

It's going to rain, I thought, as I watched the haze thicken to a veil over the land, softening the glare of the setting sun to a crimson wash.

He stood. "I have to go," he muttered. His eyes met my own. For a moment I thought he wanted to embrace me and, despite the sharp pain in my ribs, I would have welcomed it. But his gaze moved past me, through the open door, down the road.

"What's this?" he asked.

I followed his glance. Far down the road I saw figures moving in a wagon. The first I recognized even at this distance. It was Taletha, her thin body sitting erect and defiant in the seat as she rode along. But two others huddled behind her, a man and a woman, I thought, although it was hard to tell at this distance. They held their hoods across their faces and kept low in the wagon bed. As if ready to hide. Or run. Seeking shadows.

Behind them the sun balled up into a red disk, lowering over the western hills.

Manasseh and I walked out to meet them. Seeing us, Taletha jumped from the wagon and broke into a run, and I remember thinking, *She is still a young girl. Forever young.* But then I saw her expression as the two travelers climbed down behind her and stood uncertainly by the shelter of the oak trees. Drawing near to us, she turned and motioned them forward. Her face, when she looked at me, was hard as flint. Anger simmered under the surface.

"Perhaps you remember Tomit and Althea," she said.

"Yes, and good evening, wife," I said.

"They need shelter. Now."

"Well, our house is open."

"No! They are after them. We have to hide them. Quickly."

18

They? Who? Didn't Taletha see my bruises?

Tomit and Althea approached us warily. I did remember them. They were from the village. When we first arrived, it had been Althea who told us about the Messiah, the man that had so obsessed Taletha, the one that had drawn us to the capital city, the one who walked before us to a bloody crucifixion.

Tomit. Looking into his face as he drew aside the hood, I winced.

I hardly recognized him. Eyes swollen shut. His nose knocked askew and packed with sheep's wool to stop the bleeding. The broken lips, engorged with swelling.

Althea too?

She drew her hood aside in the courtesy of greeting me, and I breathed a sigh of relief.

"Yes, of course," I said. "Where?"

I found myself bewildered, depending upon Taletha. Once again.

She didn't hesitate. "In the hills past the sheep folds. There are some caves worn in the rocks. High up in the hills. I've been there with the sheep. There is one they can use as shelter. Liske knows of it."

Manasseh started in surprise.

"Okay," I said. "Let me get some things together for them, and you can tell me about it."

Taletha shook her head. She was already walking past me, as if she had tarried long enough.

"There's no time," she said. "And I already have provisions in the cave."

I followed, trying to understand. She had expected it! Knew it was coming. What was going on here? I looked at Manasseh. He shrugged.

"Wait a minute," I said.

Taletha whirled. "I said we don't have time, husband. Even now—"

"No. Not that. I mean, by all means hurry. But, Tomit and Althea . . ."

Their backs were to me. They paused by the corner of the house, waiting for Taletha to lead the way.

Taletha's face was like sculpted marble, tense but resolute. I walked up to her and touched her cheek. "Taletha, let me help."

Looking up at me, she noticed my bruised face. Suddenly she sagged against me, arms around me. It felt like my ribs were grinding on each other, but I winced and held her tight.

"Oh, husband." Her body trembled and tears came. "I'm sorry."

"Nothing to be sorry for. Except that I don't know enough."

"I know. I wanted to protect you."

I was thinking of what I could say. Something about withholding knowledge never being a protection. About it always being dangerous. If I had learned anything in fifty-nine years—not fifty-five—it was when to shut up.

I held her and let the tension break with her tears.

"Manasseh will take care of them," I said.

Manasseh nodded. "In the house?"

I nodded my approval, and he immediately went to the couple. It was evening. The lawgiver and his men were gone. Surely we could pause and eat, and move out under cover of darkness. I wanted to cry out, "Slow down!" I needed to understand.

"Taletha?" I spoke into the black waves of her hair as she leaned against my chest. The setting sun fired those strange red highlights in its darkness.

"Yes." She whispered. "I need you, husband."

"I need you too, Taletha. But about Althea and Tomit. I thought I remembered a child, a daughter. Where is she?"

Taletha held tighter to me, her fear a palpable thing. My ribs groaned and I bit my lips.

She released me, and the anger in her eyes unnerved me. It was the fierce predatory look of the protective mother. In Taletha—who had no children of her own. "They have her," she hissed. "She is missing."

Again I wondered, *They? Who?*

But then Taletha was pulling on my hand, urging me to the house. "We have to get them into hiding," she said. "Now!"

* * *

I understood her urgency, not for Tomit and Althea alone, but for the child.

Yes, that would strike Taletha, as surely as it struck the parents, Althea and Tomit. If there is such a thing as a mothering instinct, then it was a fierce vitality in Taletha. I remembered picking her up in Noke a few weeks earlier, after she had been visiting friends while I took care of some supplies. Meridivel, Manasseh's wife, had directed me to the village temple.

In the muddy foreyard played six small children. They played with the wild abandon of youth—mud splattering their arms and faces, stuck in clumps in their hair, one with a dirty streak across his face where he had backhanded a runny nose. They squatted around their own little mud village, its raggedy little buildings in disarray. It was their very own village: in their eyes, the mud lumps noble with palaces and shining turrets.

Squatting with them, the hem of her dress carefully tucked up from the muck, was Taletha. She shone with excitement, pointing with praise at a child's lumpy tower threatening collapse at any second. She said something I could not hear, and the children hooted with laughter. The boy with the runny nose toppled back, landing on his seat in a puddle. New waves of laughter rocked the children. Taletha stood up and, grasping the boy's muddy hand, lifted him upright.

She turned from the group with a huge smile, wiping her muddy hands on each other to scrape the muck loose.

My heart yearned for her. Taletha's dearest dream, I knew, was to have children. There were none. I sometimes wondered if her causes were not just an abstract substitute. No. That isn't correct. She could not be other than what she was. But I sensed this desire in her for children at such moments, or at night when we lay spent in the comfort of our bed and reflection settled on her, as if she were breathing the silent question, Why not me?

CHAPTER TWO

Rain slanted across the pasture, driven by a steady wind that smelled of the sea. The gray sky lowered dismally, stretching ragged filaments of cloud over the hills. The sheep stood pensive and forlorn, their eyes blinking, hindquarters turned to the wind. Water streamed from their woolly hides. Their odor was warm and reassuring in the cold, relentless rain.

A dreary day. A day for sitting by the fire, letting the orange tongues of flame tell old stories. Perhaps there would be bread in the oven, the whole house filled with the scent of its yeasty rising.

On another day. Not today when the rain slanted against our cloaks, swirled into eyes that blinked, like the sheep, large relentless tears. The soil sucked at my sandals, laden heavily with muck. Pools stood here and there in the pasture.

I noted, as we climbed to the vineyards, where some heavy grapevines had broken loose from a trellis. I would have to get them up. The grapes would spoil, lying against the wet soil. On another day I would do that.

"We should keep to the rocks," Manasseh said.

I nodded, and rain fell from my hood onto my face.

"In the hills," he added, "they will be looking for trails."

Past the grapevines the gentle hillside soon turned to rock. We wound through increasingly rugged passes, outcroppings of rock dripping water, the stone underfoot slick with rivulets. The wind blew harder here in the hills, knifing the skin with lancets of rain. Both of us were panting hard, sweat mixing with the rain on our bodies as we climbed.

When I stumbled for the second time, Manasseh stopped in the shelter of an overhang. He leaned against the rock, watching the rain spin past our shelter. He flung off the hood of his woolen cloak and shook his head like a dog, the red hair spraying water.

There was no laughter in his eyes today.

"No sense stopping," I said. "We'll just get wet again."

He turned to me. Manasseh was one of those men who seldom looked into another's eyes. I think it was shyness on his part. When he did so, it was an effort of will, and requested something. He looked at me in that way now.

"I think you should turn back," he said.

I was going to laugh at first. Did he think I went out walking in cold rain for the fun of it? Instead, I asked him why.

"Stinking wet here," he said matter-of-factly. "I feel like I'm walking through a swamp."

"Don't complain."

"I know. It makes the grapes grow." Manasseh looked downhill at my tangled vines.

"That isn't what I meant. I feel I can never get enough water. Even today. There's something in me . . . always thirsty."

"It's strange, Elhrain. We're friends . . ."

"True, Manasseh. That we are."

"But you've never told me . . ."

"About the past? Leave it alone. The past is past."

"No. It isn't, Elhrain. You can't do that. The past is everything that we are. Now. Here."

"True. But I don't have to talk about it."

"Of course not. But there's always that mystery. Just now you said there's always something in you that thirsts."

"Always thirsty."

"Same thing."

"Manasseh, I was born in the desert."

"I know that."

"Then know this—when you have lost your way in the desert, as Tale-

23

tha and I have, the sun parches your body from the flesh inward. You feel like a piece of fruit left out in the sun, the dryness, layer by layer, eating in, attacking. And the wind. There's always the wind in the desert, Manasseh. Sometimes it's the worst torment because it drives the sand like tiny needles into your flesh. The skin itself feels sandy. Sometimes I don't believe I have it all out yet. It is a bitter curse, Manasseh, to have survived the desert. For you never really survive."

Manasseh continued to look past me, watching the drip of water from the ridge of rock now. I leaned out, catching the drops in my mouth, rain gusting across my face.

"You never really survive," I repeated after swallowing. "That's what I meant. I left something of myself in the desert."

"Or the desert's still in you," he added.

"True. I learn to live with it. But the desert is all around us, even here, Manasseh."

He shook his head slowly, dismissing riddles. I wished it were that easy for me. Maybe I *should* tell him about it. But where would I begin?

* * *

Planning with the Magi to find this Messiah had seemed to me, at the time, a quest of pure madness.

I was the unbeliever, wanting nothing to do with quests or kings.

Nonetheless, I had reluctantly set out with them, if only because I had nowhere else to go. I had known little about my own ancestry—my mother was dead and my father unknown. So I left, with the only two people who were precious to me, Haggai and Doval, my young foster son and daughter.

But then came that horror in the desert, outlaws attacking the Magi's caravan, Haggai's body lying at the opening of my tent, the disappearance of young Doval—she whom I loved with all my soul. And that seemed all I had. My body wasted and ruined with wounds, left in the desert. To the mercy—as Balthazzar, the leading Magus, had said—of the gods. The devils rather. The demons of wrath and outrage did indeed keep me alive. Those and the remarkable appearance—perhaps there was a God after all—of the Roman legionnaire Lycurgus, who found and delivered me. The Magi had deserted me. Thereby stripped of a future hope, I retreated to the past. To search for myself.

My quest led me far to the south, through strange lands and strange years; for every new land was a rediscovery of old lands and every new year was a going back in time, rediscovering myself. The years passed and brought me closer to my past but no nearer my home.

Kush, fabled land of gold and glory, was a kingdom in decline and upheaval when I arrived. There again the demons that assailed me were assuaged by a person—Taletha, who came to mean all the world to me. Together we fled that land, in a last, desperate attempt to restore order to the kingdom by placing her adoptive brother, Eldrad, in power. Whether it succeeded I know not, for those were desperate hours during which we fled, together, for our very lives.

Once more, to the south. There, among the primitive life of the Beshali, deep in the jungle, I would gladly have stayed all my days. Among them there were no kings, no lords, no gods, and so there was nothing for me to rage against. Only the quiet patterns of a simple life. And even though the drought, carried on the back of the desert like an avenging horseman, infiltrated and drove back the jungle, we could easily have moved ahead of it.

Except for Taletha.

She had grown restless, as if the relief from treachery and struggle had permitted a small spark to kindle in her, to grow and flame into hardness and purpose. She would go no further south. Worse, she wanted to go home. She had no idea where home lay, only a strange, unsettled feeling, harbored in that tiny spark now flared to incandescence, that it lay north—across the desert.

Once more we plunged into its fiery heart, daring the appalling dryness of this land of demons that was the desert, in search of a home.

We found it. And so much more. We found the Messiah whom the Magi had sought so many years before. But we found him now, not at the moment of birth, not at the moment of glory, but at the moment of his death.

So we settled in this new land that Taletha called home, and I learned to make it a home. I retreated to my farm, tending the sheep and grapevines in a desultory way, mainly letting Liske have his way with them. I did a few chores to convince myself I was needed, if only by the doves and the sheep. Mostly I wrote, trying to order the past by scratching it out on the parchments by the glittering light of an oil lamp.

How could I tell Manasseh these things? It was an exorcism of old demons that would not leave me alone.

And despite all the things I had seen in this new land we now called home, I didn't understand them. I wondered if I *had* to understand in order to believe. Would believing, merely assenting, grant understanding? Could it be that simple, or that hard?

I had proof. I had seen this man! Had seen this Messiah, touched him, had even, in those weird final hours, attempted to carry his cross to the place of his death. *I helped kill him.* And he had named me: he knew me. If he were the Messiah, if I were to accept his authority, I also had to confess that *I* killed him. I, who had sworn off all killing.

Oh, I had proof. Even without the testimony of that physician, now involved in the cause, even without the testimonies of others, I had seen it. Touched him. Heard him. It was all true—this Messiah my brother Magi had sought indeed had lived.

But I had believed that the seeking itself was madness and destruction. I couldn't reorder the past. It lived in me and nearly drove me wild. Unable to speak of it, I sat at the desk penning words on parchment, retelling the story as proof against madness. I had proof, but to *believe* the conclusions to which that proof led—there was the chasm I had never completely crossed. For that chasm was my own heart, and every moment of the past that had made me.

I, who had found a home, am unhomed. Still the desert's child. It lived within me.

Is it any wonder that I am always thirsty?

* * *

Manasseh broke my reverie. He was pulling his hood back over that woolly mane of reddish-gray hair when he looked me in the eye. A signal, I knew.

"I think you should turn back," he repeated. His voice was firm.

I stood there.

"I don't know what you have endured. Or why. Or its effects. I can never know them fully, even if you told me every detail. But because of that . . . you should not get involved."

"Because I am the outsider," I said, meeting his gaze with a rise of anger.

"No. Or yes, only in that you don't realize the full cost."

"I am involved, remember? Taletha happens to be my wife." I paused. "Oh . . . I see. This is her homeland."

"To be sure it is. But Taletha has chosen this. Freely chosen. And she wants to protect you."

"From what! I need no protection."

"Don't be rash, Elhrain. For these last years you have hidden yourself away on your farm—"

"I haven't been hiding! I've been writing."

He smiled with disdain. "Perhaps they amount to the same thing. But Taletha has become deeply committed to our cause."

"*What* cause?"

"The cause of the Messiah."

"He's dead."

"No. That's not true. But I don't have time to explain now. Listen. Let me tell you one thing. Then you decide." He paused.

I nodded.

"Very well. Tomit and Althea are hiding in the cave. They are preparing to escape. With good reason. They are being hunted down for their work in the cause."

"I know that! I saw them just two nights ago."

"They were beaten."

"I said I saw them."

"Think, man! They were missing Sarah!"

"Yes. That's right. Their daughter," I whispered. In the reaches of my mind echoed another name, another daughter: Doval. At that moment Tomit and Althea's loss seemed overwhelming; the loss had been my own also.

"Right. Taken."

"Why?"

"As a sign, of course. You see, this same Messiah healed her when she was dying as an infant."

"Who would do such a thing? Why?"

He didn't answer my question, because the answer was obvious: to destroy a people's hope, to frighten them beyond belief. Take their children, and you rob them of all that is most precious to them. You rob their hope.

"You see the problem," Manasseh said as if reading my thoughts. "And now you don't know if you want in. I don't know if I want you in. We can trust no one anymore."

"You can't . . ."

He laid his hand on my shoulder and squeezed. His eyes glared with a terrible ferocity, and I wondered what this man, whom I named my friend, was capable of.

"No," he said. "I am not accusing. The point is . . . we must have *utter* certainty. Don't join us unless you are willing to risk everything at a time when we can trust no one."

"Why hasn't Taletha told me?"

"I told you. You've suffered enough. She wanted to spare you."

"Man, that woman walked by my side through the desert. How could I not—"

"Saying no would be the easiest thing in the world."

"And I *cannot* say it. I owe it to her."

"Come only if you owe it to yourself, Elhrain. Nothing less will do."

"I . . . I had a girl . . . like a daughter . . ."

"I know about that."

"How?"

"Come only if you owe it to yourself, Elhrain. Not Taletha. Not Doval."

I cringed at her name, as if struck by a fist inside my heart.

"No!" he shouted at me. "Only for yourself."

I brushed past him, knocking his arm aside, and walked out to the trail. To the cave. Thunder lashed the rocky hillsides, and it seemed to echo, on and on, inside me.

CHAPTER THREE

I n this part of the country a ridge of stony hills rises between the gentle farmland and the plain toward the Great Sea. The hills are a sort of wall against sea-bred storms. Seaward of the wall, near the coast, the land is rough, rocky soil, a bad land for farming. It's a land of wild stony places, open to the tempests that churn in black fury from the sea's heart. Where the rocky hills arch down to the sea in long, curving spines, they protect stretches of flat plain and create natural harbors for seaports. Small villages dot the coastline; their people are fishermen, tough and wise in the ways of the weather.

From this side of the hills, whose protected reaches tumble away to the east in rolling, green-carpeted countryside, dotted with farms and vineyards and sheepfolds, people often trade with their western neighbors. Salted fish for a young lamb or several flagons of wine or baskets of grain.

But always the separation of the hills is there. The villagers call them mountains. Perhaps they are; their strange passes jut high above the land. But I remember mountains that tore into clouds, and so call these hills.

Centuries of wind and rain had carved out stony caves in these hills. In times past, they may have served as a handy inn for a weary traveler, or for a shepherd, far from his main flock, seeking lost sheep and needing a night's rest and protection. The debris of old campfires littered such caves. They were many and well hidden. Now they served as a refuge for those fleeing persecution, for those whose lives were in danger.

The traders on the coast served more than one task for us now. They were, I discovered, essential to the transport of the refugees. Arrangements were made with coastal traders for transport to safe havens at seaside villages, where a group of people would harbor them and give them new lives, or to places over the sea itself to new lands. While awaiting such arrangements, people were fairly secure in the caves, even though troops patrolled the hills. The caves were countless, and, if need be, pilgrims could be shuttled from one spot to another ahead of the troops.

So Tomit and Althea waited. Liske acted as their eyes and ears. His wandering through the hills keeping Taletha's flock of sheep had become commonplace. He knew the hills like his own flock. By name he called his sheep; by name he knew the hiding places.

Liske struck me as an odd boy. I'm not certain why. He had not shared five minutes of talk with me during all the time he had worked for us. For Taletha, rather. They were her sheep; Liske her hiring. He was at home with the sheep, living long days in the pastures and hills bordering our farm, sometimes moving the sheep in a common herd with others from neighboring farms. When he returned to our home, he slept in a little lean-to, closer to the sheep than to us, and helped himself to food from our larder.

I do know that Manasseh was bitterly disappointed in his son's failure to follow the carpentry work. He was their only child, after all. Still, Liske seemed happy in what he was doing, and Manasseh and Meridivel seemed to accept it in time. Withdrawn and shy was this boy Liske. A boy of the hills and sheep and wild places. His old dog was his closest friend.

When Liske had come running to the house early that morning he had looked the most frightened boy in the world.

* * *

He came running across the pasture, his feet kicking up clots of mud from the still sodden fields. It had been raining without end since the night Tomit and Althea fled to the hills. We took it as a good thing; it would make tracking impossible.

He burst into the kitchen without knocking and stood there, mud slacking off his legs onto the floor, heaving for breath so desperately he could not talk.

Taletha forced him to take a drink of water. His eyes whirled about wildly. His whole body trembled. Liske was not a handsome lad at the best of moments. Now his face was flushed and contorted by fear, his mouth jerking at words, his eyes darting like two small birds caught in a net.

Taletha caught his face in both hands and held him still. Slowly his panic eased. Then he shouted, a cry of pain, "They're gone!"

Again the uncontrollable spasms racked him. Taletha cupped his face, willing control into him. "Who?" she whispered.

"The . . . people."

"Did you see anything? Tracks? Soldiers?"

Liske shook his head wildly. He stood for a moment. "They're just gone," he shouted. "It's not my fault!" He spun from her grasp and went running back across the pasture, away from the hills.

I stood up.

"Where are you going?" she asked.

"To look."

She shook her head. "I believe him. If there were no tracks they haven't been taken. They fled."

"Why?"

She stared at me for a moment. Her calm stare turned steely. Angry. "Sarah," she said. "They have gone seeking her, and they don't stand a chance. We've had people searching the desert already."

"You think she is there . . . in the desert?"

"That's where we lost track of them. We had better contact the others."

"What others?"

Her gaze turned blank again. "Those who are involved," she said. "You don't have to come."

"Right." I couldn't keep my own anger down. "Only those who are involved." I grabbed a cape from the door and flung it over my shoulders. I grabbed a walking stick by the entrance.

"Where are you going, Elhrain?"

"To check the hills," I replied angrily.

"Don't. There may be soldiers there. Enemies."

"Then heaven help them," I snapped.

"At least wait for Manasseh," she pleaded. "Help me hitch up the wagon. I have to let the others know."

*　*　*

Manasseh and I found nothing in the hills. No sign of trespassers. No sign of Tomit and Althea. Nothing.

I had waited for him, waited while the rain drummed down, obliterating any hope for a sign. If Tomit and Althea had gone searching for Sarah, instead of waiting for safe passage to the coast, they could not have picked a better time to hide their departure.

I couldn't blame them for looking, hopeless as their chances would be in the desert. *What parent wouldn't do the same?* I thought bitterly.

It was late evening when Manasseh and I returned, herding the scattered sheep into the fold. I was surprised to see Liske standing there. I went to him and squeezed his shoulder. "Don't worry," I said. "See to the sheep." He nodded.

Manasseh spoke not a word to his son. I wanted to lash out at him, to tell him to comfort the lad, but it was none of my business.

*　*　*

We rode in Manasseh's wagon through darkness and drizzling rain toward Noke. "I think you should join us," Manasseh said after a time.

"Oh? I'm invited, then?"

He noted the anger in my voice. "For one thing, it may be dangerous to stay out here. Alone."

"Let them come, then. This is *my* house."

I thought of Liske back at the farm with the sheep. I asked Manasseh if Liske should also come back.

He shook his head. "He's happy there."

"Yes, and right now he is very scared."

Manasseh shrugged. "What does he know about it?" he asked.

"About Tomit and Althea? Only that they disappeared. He thinks it is his fault."

"Is it?"

"What do you mean? Of course not. Liske has this feeling that he has to be perfect. And he is nearly perfect taking care of the sheep. But he feels he has to take care of everything."

32

"Could anyone have gotten to him?"

I didn't respond. I studied the broad, muscled shoulders of this man hunched over his reins. The ox plodded along the muddy road, kicking up clots the size of small plates. I didn't want to intrude. What did I know of fathers and sons? Yet, remembering the fear that paralyzed Liske this morning, I felt a protective instinct surge inside me. The way one would feel seeing a trapped animal.

"The enemy?" asked Manasseh. "Could they have gotten information from him?"

"I suppose they could. But I don't think they did. I agree with Taletha; I think Tomit and Althea went looking for their daughter."

Manasseh grunted. "Probably," he said. Then, as if reflecting, he said, "Liske is not a bright boy."

"What do you mean? Because he isn't a carpenter? Doing what his father wants him to do?"

Manasseh sighed. "No, I've come to terms with that. I think. But he's easily taken advantage of. He could have given information without knowing it."

"As long, Manasseh, as you don't take advantage of him."

He spun in his seat, his face flushed angrily. "Me! Watch your tongue, Elhrain."

My own anger rose. "Yes, you. With your everlasting plotting and planning. Let the boy be what he is."

Manasseh snapped the reins like whips, and the startled ox lunged clumsily down the road. We traveled in silence the rest of the way to the village. The sky was fully dark when we spotted thin lights of lamps through distant windows.

As we pulled into the village, Manasseh let the ox slow to a dull plod. Manasseh was not a man who spoke easily in the best of times; he buried his emotions under layers, hoping they would be safely tucked away. He jerked at the reins suddenly, bringing the wagon to a halt and half-turned toward me.

"I wish," he said, "that Liske had been around when the Messiah was here!" He leaned over the side of the wagon and spat, as if to say, "That's the end of the matter."

"Why is that?" I asked.

"Maybe he could have been cured. Healed, you know. But, no. He was off somewhere, playing with his dog. Imagine that. Everyone in the village—from miles around!—crowded into the town square, and Liske's off dawdling somewhere." Manasseh grunted in disgust.

"Cured, you say? Why, what's the matter with him?"

Manasseh looked at me in surprise. "You haven't noticed? His whole arm is crooked. His right arm. It hardly works. At least not for the shop work."

I thought a moment. And confessed, "I never noticed. He does all right tending the sheep."

"He covers it up. Clumsy kid. Maybe with training he could learn to handle the tools. But, no, not my son. He's always off fooling around, wasting his time. And I've got more work than I know what to do with."

I studied Manasseh carefully, trying to respect his confidence. Many words crossed my mind. Why, I wanted to ask, does Liske *have* to be a carpenter? And why does he have to be perfect?

I too am an outsider. I know how it feels to look upon the group from the outside.

Black skin. A crippled arm. Perhaps we all carry deformities. I had come to accept this. I no longer cared if I was the outsider. I could not escape it. But how would the boy feel?

I said nothing. Manasseh snapped the reins wearily.

* * *

While not a large village, Noke was as large as any around here. The main thoroughfare that ran from the capital city to the coast bisected the village, a dusty meridian dividing homes and shops that straddled its width. The largest structure was the inn that Tomit and Althea kept for their uncle, Zophar. It was to that very place Taletha and I had come years before, exhausted and so thin our bones almost knocked against each other. The desert was on our flesh and in our hearts, but under Tomit and Althea's care at that inn, we had begun to recuperate. Their stories about the Messiah, especially how he had healed their daughter, Sarah, had so fired Taletha's imagination that she had later insisted on traveling to the capital.

Beside the inn stood several small businesses, most of them dispensing replenishment for travelers. Busiest and most important among them, perhaps, was the office of the money-changer, Zophar. He kept his office in the inn that he owned, a natural convenience. This was a country in transition, most recently under Roman control, but enjoying a heavy commerce with many nations. Zophar knew how to take advantage of it. He had situated himself at the next convenient trading village over the coastal range of hills. He based his business on the calculation that travelers landing at the coast would try to exchange their currency further inland, to avoid exorbitant coastal rates of exchange. They would have been better off doing business at the coastal villages. The crusty old trader was probably the wealthiest man in the village.

But neither luck nor insight led Zophar to locate here in Noke. Despite his gruff attitude and a tongue as sharp as a legionnaire's saber, he was wholeheartedly devoted to his niece, Althea, whom he had raised from infancy, and especially to the little girl, Sarah. It was common knowledge that Zophar owned the inn, but Tomit and Althea had never permitted him to take advantage of that. Althea had inherited this, at least, from her uncle's upbringing—a tough and shrewd business sense.

When we had arrived, and Taletha and Althea had quickly established a friendship, Althea had marched to Zophar's office with us to ensure an accurate exchange of the valuables we had carried out of the desert. They had not looked like much to me then, slung in a little leather pouch at my waist: the remaining seven gold coins from the House of Kush that had been my birthright; a handful of jewels kept in their own velvet pouch; several small bars of gold carried all the way from Babylon. There were times in the desert when I would have gladly tossed them aside to relieve myself of their weight. But they were part of me—each represented a piece of my past—and I could never complete the act.

But here they represented a home, and I had handed them over gladly. Althea led the way.

"I know him too well!" she had said when Zophar set a time for the transaction. "I'm coming along."

I remember the gasp that escaped Zophar as he shook out the velvet pouch of jewels. When I laid several of the small gold bars on the table, Zophar leaned back, his eyes swimming in bewilderment. Behind him Althea chuckled in amusement.

I was confused. I was still far from fluent in this new language, even though languages came as easily as breathing to me. In rude speech I asked, "Isn't it enough?"

"Enough!" wheezed Zophar. "Enough for what?"

"For the bill," I said, pointing to Althea.

Zophar collapsed into his chair.

Under Althea's watchful eye, Zophar converted the gold bars into coinage. Later he arranged the purchase of the huge farm from an elderly couple. But he protested when it was all done that there was so much money left over he didn't know what to do with it.

"Then take care of it for me," I had said. "Taletha can take it however she needs it. I don't need it, and I don't want it."

"You surely don't need it," Zophar said. "The interest alone will keep you wealthy. But never say you don't want what others would kill for."

I shrugged. I kept only the strange gold coins. The intertwined serpents embossed on them, seal of the House of Komani in the Kingdom of Kush, held too many memories to let go.

* * *

When we passed Manasseh's home and carpentry shop at the western end of the village, I must have shown my surprise, for Manasseh chuckled softly.

"Not at my shop," he said. "Too obvious."

The weary ox balked at the reins but kept plodding down the main thoroughfare. We passed the shops—the metalsmith, the bakery, the basket shop. The closed vegetable stall still carried the scent of onions and garlic, sharp on the night air.

To my surprise, Manasseh wheeled the wagon into the courtyard of the small temple past the inn. Again he chuckled softly. "It is, after all, the Sabbath," he said. "Since sundown."

I nodded, determined to play the game out.

* * *

Oil lamps dimly lit the inside of the temple. One other wagon had wheeled in ahead of us. A fat man hunched over the reins of an ox, as if sitting there for a moment to gather strength for the dismount.

Again surprise stirred in me as I recognized the figure in the moonlight. "Not him too?" I asked.

"Who better?" Manasseh said.

* * *

Zophar labored out of the wagon, his breath heaving as though he had run a mile instead of having rocked slowly on the wagon seat from wher-ever he had been. Why did the very sight of him unsettle me?

Probably because as the self-professed skeptic Zophar too often mir-rored my own unbelief. Too often I found him raising *my* questions. For him it was just another kind of game, a battle of wits. For me it was a heart full of thorns. So I was surprised to see him joining this group of followers. Had he always been among them?

"I have a winch back at my shop," Manasseh called.

Zophar glared at him, his eyes fixed in a scowl beneath the shaggy white brows and the wrinkled mat of curly white hair that capped his round head.

* * *

Anyone who had seen the splendor of the temple in the capital city could not mistake this place for anything other than what it was—a rude little hovel catering to the religious needs of a humble people. Instead of tiled mosaics in the courtyard, this fronted a muddy sprawl of weed-infested land. Instead of polished marble gleaming like new money, this was of molded brick, mortared by riverbank clay. Yet the rudiments of tradition were here. It was, after all, a place for worship, a place where these people—my neighbors—believed God heard their cry.

The entry opened to a small room holding a soot-coated altar, the ceiling bearing a curved opening to emit the smoke of sacrifice. Tonight it simply leaked rain that collected in a dirty pool around the altar. Behind the altar hung a veil, separating a gathering room. It was there we met, standing or sitting in a cramped circle about a wooden table that bore years of abuse. A door to one side led to the ramshackle living quarters of the old priest, Napthali.

I had been in this place only once before. I looked around with be-mused interest. How common, how utterly plain and simple was this rude religious house. Save for the sanctuary and altar, it might have been any tumble-down dwelling in any peasant village. Always before, I had seen religion intertwined, like woven strands, with the power of the state. So I had grown to distrust all religion as an action of the powerful. But this? This was a place of the powerless, and it amused me with its dusty, earnest homeliness.

On that one occasion I had been here earlier, I had seen little, for it was on the day Taletha and I were to be married. *Were,* I say, for the ceremony had been interrupted by a lawgiver who accused me of being an infidel and an insult to their tradition. The ceremony actually took place that night in the privacy of Manasseh and Meridivel's home. I watched Taletha now, surprised by the ease with which she chatted with these neighbors, most of whom I recognized only by sight. I hardly knew them. I was the outsider. The black-skinned desert wanderer and one-time Magus. Believer in . . . what exactly?

I had all the facts—things I had seen and could not deny, the testimony of others. But they hung in suspension in my mind, like leaves upon the surface of a still pond. *What would it take,* I wondered, *to produce that sense of wholeness, of completion? And why do these others seem to believe so easily?*

The language flurried about me like a storm, far too rapidly for me to follow. While I could handle the language readily enough in individual conversations, I had been too much alone with my thoughts these past five years. Words careened here. Taletha was in the thick of it. I caught bits and pieces of a plan to travel to the capital city by wagon. By two wagons. I heard about prisoners there, about a plan to liberate them. Then the talk drifted into argument.

I leaned back against the wall, out of the way, and watched. Manasseh and Meridivel, Taletha, Zophar, several villagers I knew only by sight, the old priest, Napthali, silently bobbing his bald head at the head of the table. I caught phrases and words, not meanings.

I was nearly asleep when Taletha at last touched my arm. "We can sleep at the inn tonight," she said. I nodded and started to follow her out, hindered by the others who now took note of me and slapped my back or spoke polite, meaningless words to me. Taletha smiled over her shoulder and slipped outside.

When I stepped outside into the dense night air, I had to look around for Taletha. The rain had finally stopped, the clouds parting to show a vaporous sliver of moonlight. It took a moment to spot her, standing by herself across the courtyard, peering south to the river, toward the desert.

Suddenly, she grasped her stomach, bending over as if struck. She leaned forward, retching, and fell to her knees.

I ran to her and held her shoulders, while she knelt doubled over. I was going to call for one of the others for help when, as if sensing it, she held up a hand to stop me. She struggled to her feet, letting me lift her.

"Just something I ate," she said, wiping her mouth with her handkerchief.

I looked at her with concern, studying her eyes in the moonlight. "You're sure? I mean, shouldn't you get it checked?"

"By whom?" she chuckled, but her arms trembled slightly. "I'd have to go to the capital to see a physician. No, I'm all right."

"Has this happened before?"

"I was just sick, husband. I feel better now. Really. Much better. It just . . . came so suddenly."

"Okay. If you're certain. But tell me if it happens again. I'll go with you."

"To the capital?" She smiled at me.

I nodded. "Of course."

Taletha shook her head. "Sometimes I think . . . I'm . . . I'm . . ."

"You're what?"

"No. I'm talking like a madwoman. At my age. I'm only sick."

"Of course. Why else? Take it as a sign, Taletha. You have to rest. Let the others take care of this."

"No! I can't. It's just something I ate."

"All right."

I was confused. Sensing it, she said, "Just stay here with me a few minutes, Elhrain. Hold me."

* * *

Standing in the moonlight, wrapped in her linen robe, arms clasped in front of her, Taletha looked like a piece of intricately, lovingly sculpted statuary. Sometimes I forget how very beautiful she is, and when I saw her like this, the moonlight touching her upturned face, chiseling her features in perfect relief against all the surrounding darkness, I wondered how on earth I had ever been blessed to have her become my wife. My beloved.

I stood behind her, arms wrapped gently around her as she leaned back into me. Her willowy body felt as light as a breath against mine. The moonlight set the fiery points in her hair ablaze. She leaned more heavily into me, and I wrapped my arms about her, holding her like life itself.

"Do you remember the woman I talked to . . . when the Messiah was killed?"

Her voice was a murmur. I barely heard her. "Yes," I said. "I have often thought of her." The words sounded hollow in my own ears. Thought of her! Even now I remember the glint of golden light in the woman's eyes, and how it had ripped me to the core, carrying me back through the years to a young girl and her brother, Doval and Haggai. The memory had been so sharp, so painful in its proximity to joy, that I *had not dared* to think of her.

It is little wonder that Taletha's next words unnerved me completely.

"I have. And I have seen her often since then."

"What!"

I felt Taletha nod. "She is my sister, Elhrain. I am certain of it."

"Have you told her?"

For a long moment Taletha was silent, and I realized that she was trembling. She turned into my arms, weeping. We held each other, standing in the deep quiet of night. *Confusion.* I didn't know what was going on. These tears. These silences. These absences. I wanted answers. The desolate call of an owl was the only sound.

After a moment Taletha spoke. "What good would it do?" she asked. "It would be for my sake only."

"But she didn't have any family," I objected. "She was alone."

"That's where you're wrong, husband." She looked up at me. Her wet eyes glistened in the moonlight. "You see, before she met the Messiah she had nothing. She made her living . . . with her body. But when she met him . . . Elhrain, her past was not just forgotten. It was gone forever."

I think I understood. Her past. And with it Taletha's.

Taletha stabbed at her eyes with the back of her hands, wiping the tears away.

"Then, then she gained her family. Don't you understand? She has everything she ever wanted. In fact, she was one of the leaders in the cause. That's . . . that's why I've seen her. In the capital. The times I traveled there, I always met with her."

"I thought you were trading wool."

"Oh, I did, husband. Do not doubt me."

"Taletha. I could not, and will not, ever doubt you. But one thing."

"Yes?"

"You said she *was* one of the leaders. Is she no longer living?"

"She was one of those seized in the last raid. She is in prison."

Suddenly an old anger roared in me. I *knew* what prisons were like. And . . . if she were Doval, if she were my daughter, I would storm the gates of hell to get her back.

Taletha felt me trembling. She squeezed my arms. "I'm sorry, Elhrain," she said. "I had to tell you this. I just . . . didn't know how."

I shook my head. "I'm going with you."

"No! I don't want you to be hurt any more."

"You won't be able to stop me," I said. And I regretted the bitterness, but I could no more stay away than I could stop breathing. "So you had better figure out a way to include me."

Before turning to stalk off to the inn, I thought I saw that curious half-smile flicker knowingly across Taletha's lips.

Her words followed me. "You're welcome to come then, husband. Since you ask so prettily."

CHAPTER
FOUR

F or people accustomed to rising with the sun, it had grown very late at night indeed. Taletha fell asleep almost immediately.

Crickets whined in the brush outside, their song careening into the small, hot room of the inn. We were fortunate to have it to ourselves; sometimes people were doubled or tripled up in these little cubicles. I longed for the night breezes, floating down cool from the hills thick with the scent of grass and clover, that engulfed our farmhouse. The bedroom in the back of the house, shaded by the oaks and willows that held back the creek bank, was always cool and delightful. I stroked Taletha's shoulder. She murmured something in her sleep and sighed restlessly.

Often there were nights at the farm when I couldn't sleep. I would rise, light an oil lamp, and turn almost mechanically to my desk. It was good then, during the night sounds and in the vast darkness, to sit there, to remember, perhaps to write on the parchments.

Tonight I had nowhere to go. I rolled onto my back, hands behind my head, thinking. Far into the night I lay there pondering what I knew, and what I did not know, and the huge gaps in between. Somehow, during these years on the farm Taletha had become heavily involved in this religious cause. Well, I could tolerate that. It was her land, her religion. And her choice, I added. I had learned not to second-guess her choices. She referred to it as *the Cause*, or *the Way*—terms that struck me as being as ambiguous and uncertain as belief itself.

But worse, her activity had placed her in danger. Tomit and Althea's daughter had been kidnapped. Sarah. Little Sarah. The very worst thing that could happen to parents. The evil one's work. *That* I believed in. And, I thought, if I were to threaten any belief, it would be in precisely that way, by attacking the family. Now Tomit and Althea themselves were gone. Seized? Or were they on the trail of their daughter, pursuing with that blood-deep hope only a parent can know? The hound of love always bays at the heels of the children.

Now this. This talk of leaders in the Cause being imprisoned. And this madness of liberating them. What could these poor peasants hope to do? What did they know of power? Of imprisonment?

So I lay in bed tossing until late in the night.

When I awakened, the others were already gathered in the great room of the inn, arguing furiously.

* * *

"No!" Taletha was adamant. "We want to get them all. It won't do to remove one or two."

"And why, pray tell?" Zophar rapped his walking stick sharply on the floor. "Are all these people important?"

"That's just the point. Who is to say who is important? Do only the 'important' people deserve freedom, Zophar? Look, if the Messiah taught us anything, anything at all, it is that we are *all* important."

" 'If you do it not to the least of these my brethren . . .' " Manasseh murmured.

"Precisely. Even the least of these is 'important,' Zophar. We, each of us, have our tasks in the cause, and who is to say whose is more important? I loathe the very word. It should not be spoken among us. Man, woman, child—we are each *called*, not important.

"But this second thing. I don't think we will have another chance. Already security has tightened precisely against this threat."

"Remember the disciple?" asked Meridivel.

Others nodded. I didn't know what they were talking about. I said so.

Zophar interrupted. "They say that one of the twelve just *walked* out of prison."

"No," Meridivel said. "They *say*, those who were there, those who heard his own account, that angels broke his chains and opened the door."

Zophar snorted, rapping his walking stick. "Guards probably got drunk and fell asleep."

Angry voices broke out.

"That's not the point," said Taletha sharply. "The point is what we do now. And we must plan to strike swiftly, surely. To get them all. We won't have another chance."

"How many, then?" Manasseh asked. "Exactly how many is 'all'?"

"Three. Maybe four. That we know of. And they are, all of them, scheduled for execution on the first day of the month."

"Who are they?" someone asked.

"The physician, of course. He was just taken. And Mary and our Roman friend."

"Roman!" shouted Zophar. "The Romans are behind it all!"

"No. Not here. Not yet," said Taletha. "The same people who crucified the Messiah are behind it. They mean to destroy any dissent, kill any threat. Do anything to protect their power and position."

"But they have shipped some prisoners off to Rome," said Manasseh. "Where, it is said, they are burned in public view."

"Or fed to the lions," Zophar added.

"But we can trust *this* Roman," someone interjected. "He has proven himself. With Mary he has—"

"Two wagons, then," one man shouted. "We go for them all."

But my hearing had sharpened at the word. *Roman?* In the cause of these people, a Roman?

But the others were by then discussing plans, talking about the prisoners. I sat in the corner, wondering why I was there. I wanted nothing to do with prisons.

Zophar's reedy voice rose above the rest. "If you young folks are going to do something, do it right. Get them all, then. Do you know how many have been put to death already?"

"We're not sure."

"I've heard from the city," said the priest, Napthali, "that three were executed this past year. Two during the last month. With these scheduled for the beginning of next month . . . Well, as Taletha said earlier, it's obvious that the persecution is intensifying. I agree. We have to act quickly. These people have all—each of them—made great sacrifices for the cause. We cannot desert them now."

People nodded. Napthali's voice was old and thin, but it was also a voice of trusted reason that had encouraged the people many times before. Secretly, I was glad he was here. Some of the others were too reactionary for me.

"But," Zophar said into the silence, "how about my niece, Althea? And her husband, Tomit?"

"And the girl," someone muttered.

Zophar nodded.

Manasseh spoke with a sigh. "No news," he said. "We have a team of three young men searching."

"Then we should expand the search!" Zophar shouted. His face reddened.

"We can't," Manasseh said. "We have to do this now! Within a week, Zophar, they'll all be dead."

Suddenly the voices were babbling again, a confusion of anger and ideas.

* * *

I would not have seen him, but for the fact that the language once again started going too fast for me, and I lost track of the discussion altogether. Several people spoke at once, interrupting randomly, until it sounded like sheer noise to me rather than speech. I shook my head and stepped back.

I think only Zophar noticed. He lifted his red face—he had been making as much noise as anyone—smiled at me and gave a broad wink as if to say "Isn't this crazy? It's a good thing we know it."

Despite myself, I smiled back.

But my amusement fled when I saw a face peering in the corner of the window. I wanted to shout, but I froze on an intake of breath.

Wild hair overgrew the face like a tangle of grape vines. His eyes were wide, stricken in a look of absolute and perpetual terror, and crisscrossed with red veins that made the tiny blue irises look like bright pebbles. I was paralyzed by those eyes—eyes that had stared horror in the face and, unfortunately, survived. His skin was baked the color of old leather, seamed and dirty. Despite the cool weather, his shoulders were bare except for the straps of some filthy animal skin draped over him.

He saw me look at him, and he dropped below the window like a stone. Yet in that brief moment when his eyes touched mine I felt an incalculable chill of horror.

I was going to draw him to the attention of the others, but was struck by the ludicrousness of it all. What would I say? "There's a man at the window"? But he was not there anymore. And he seemed insane, a man-beast. Wasn't there supposed to be someone outside, to alert us if the lawgivers' henchmen happened by?

So I was reaching to tap Manasseh on the shoulder when the wild man appeared again, standing slightly hunched and arms akimbo, about twenty paces outside the window. Even at that distance, he seemed more animal than human, gaunt almost to the point of frailty, his body scabbed and filthy.

Somehow, through the window, his eyes found mine. They transfixed me. And they intensified like fires as he lifted one bony finger, pointing at the window, and he shouted in a voice as cracked and harsh as a desert wind, "Beware the skulls!"

His voice gave me a chill. I felt cold, as if I was touching something dead. Everyone in the room had fallen silent at his voice. They turned to peer out the window.

"It's only mad Philip," Zophar said.

"What's he doing here? Now?" Manasseh asked of no one in particular.

Again that weird voice rose and cracked on the air. "Beware the place of the skulls!"

Old Napthali quietly left the room. He walked outside, past a man I now saw standing by the cypress tree in the foreyard, the man who was supposed to alert us.

"Who is *mad* Philip?" I asked.

No one answered at first. They were watching Napthali, who walked toward the man. Napthali stood there a moment, his tiny, wizened figure like a speck before the man. Then Napthali gently took his arm and led him to the temple's back entrance. The man did not resist, but he glanced once more in our direction, and shouted, without conviction, more like a whimper of despair, "The skulls. Beware!"

Zophar shook his head mournfully. "Napthali will give him a bed," he said. "But he'll be gone in the morning."

"Back to the hills," someone said.

"Or the desert."

"No. Never the desert again."

"Who is he?" I insisted. I still felt the eerie chill of his presence.

"No one is sure," Meridivel said. "The story has it that he grew up by the coast, but was carried into the desert somehow. Perhaps he lived with one of the hermits."

"Hermits?" I interrupted. "In the desert? You mean people willingly live there?"

"I suppose you could call it willingly now," Zophar replied, stroking his white beard. "Not at first. It started already during the time of the exiles, oh, hundreds of years ago. They refused to leave. Went into the desert instead."

"Their women went with them?" Taletha asked.

"At the beginning, I suppose. Although I don't hear of women anymore. Except for Philip, who wanders around here and the capital, I don't know if there are any left. If there are, they have their secret places. The misfits, you know. I think they can't survive in civilization, so they run away. Can't be more then a handful of them left." Zophar enjoyed his speculations. He spoke, I thought, a bit too pompously about misfits.

"I think Philip just got lost there," Manasseh said. "He has lived around Noke for the better part of ten years now. Now and then a chicken disappears. 'Either a fox or Philip,' people say."

"Sometimes someone will find him sleeping in a hay mound. Some people leave food out for him," Meridivel added. From her tone I guessed she was one.

"But mainly," Manasseh said, "old Napthali cares for him. He keeps a cot for him at the back of his room when the weather turns cold."

"He likes the cold," another said.

"For a while," Zophar said, "the lawgiver was giving it out that he was Napthali's son. Tried to kick him out of the priesthood for it."

"Preposterous," Taletha said.

"Of course," said Zophar. "But since when has that stopped a lawgiver?"

"He has blue eyes," I said. I could not rip them from my mind.

Zophar nodded. "Probably the illegitimate son of some northern trader and one of the women of the docks. The coastal villages," he added, "do a good trade in prostitution."

He turned back to the table. "Too bad your Messiah isn't around," he said. "He could heal Philip, and we would know the truth." The sarcasm was thick in his voice.

"If he chose to," Meridivel said quietly.

"Yes, well," Zophar shrugged. "We seem to be just about done here. Agreed?"

A few people nodded. Some just stood silently. The call seemed to haunt the room. "Beware the skulls."

"Then, we'll leave in two teams," Zophar said. "A week from now. Taletha and Elhrain to start early. I will follow a bit later, depending upon what I hear from the capital. We will get further instructions when we arrive."

Manasseh objected to being left out. But it was Zophar who made it clear that he would not go. Someone had to stay behind to maintain order in Noke. Angrily, Manasseh agreed.

As the group filed out, I realized how little I had understood. Zophar's summary left nothing but gaping holes swimming with questions for me.

Taletha was quiet as we rode back to the farm. Both of us were eager for home. Especially, we wanted to check on Liske. We would spend the next days at the farm, then, while plans developed in Noke. Eventually we would return to hitch up Manasseh's large wagon for the trip to the capital.

It felt good to ride in the quiet afternoon, alone with Taletha. The sun had finally broken through the overcast, and, while the ox's hooves kicked up gouts of wet dirt, the sun fired the wet landscape with a golden sheen. Puddles of water shone in the pastures. The hills and trees shook their shoulders in the breeze as if coming awake again to the sunlight. Birds rippled overhead and sang lustily from brush along the road.

It felt good to ride in silence, Taletha leaning tiredly against me as the ox plodded along.

"What do you think he was talking about?" I asked after a while.

Taletha chuckled. "Who?" she asked.

"That stranger. Philip, or whatever his name was."

"I don't know, Elhrain. Just shouting, I think. Napthali will take care of him."

"Skulls," I mused. "Skulls? Isn't that where the man was crucified?"

She sat up straighter. "Skulls? No, that was the Place of the Skull. The hill looks like a skull from a distance. No, that wasn't it. But I wouldn't make too much of it."

"I'm not," I insisted. "But he bothered me."

While the ox plodded, I found it easier to talk than I had for days. Taletha nestled back against me.

"Do you think," I asked, "this Messiah could have healed him?"

"Certainly."

"Zophar seemed to mock the idea."

Taletha shrugged. "Zophar doesn't see things the way others do."

I laughed. "That's an understatement. But I like the old goat. He thinks for himself."

Taletha laughed too. It seemed ages since I had heard it. "See, he thinks of the Messiah in terms of a political leader. A ruler. A king. And since there has been no change in the kingdom, then this couldn't be the Messiah."

"Makes sense."

"Not entirely. It depends on your expectations. And whether you are willing to fit them to the reality."

"And just what is the reality?" I asked. I had spotted a hawk, flashing red-tipped wings, hovering over a distant field, and only half-listened.

"That the Messiah is not a political ruler, as the people said, but that he is what he said of himself."

"And what it that?"

"That he is God."

"Quite a claim."

"Indeed. That's just the point," Taletha said. "Either he is God himself, or a madman."

"Like Philip?"

"Oh, no. Much worse. For then he would be the prince of liars, leading people astray."

I didn't want to pursue the argument. It had always made me uneasy. I had heard of so many religions, of so many kingdoms, that want to make their kings gods. It was a custom everywhere. *But, I often wondered to myself, what if all these in fact pointed to some one truth? That there really was one God who was king?* But this Messiah seemed most unlikely. I myself had seen him die an all-too-human death, suffering the full horror of it. An unlikely God, indeed. It stood all our expectations on their heads.

Precisely because of that, I found it fascinating. I smiled to myself. I was beginning to think too much like Zophar. I shifted the subject.

"You think he could have healed the madman?" I asked.

"He healed others. Remember Althea and Tomit's daughter. She was sick with fever. For a long time she had been ill, unable to eat, unable to sleep. This was when the Messiah visited Noke . . ."

Taletha looked at me and I nodded. Manasseh had mentioned the visit.

Taletha continued. "He wandered around a great deal. People heard he was coming. They took their little girl, Sarah, and stood there in a crowd of people. They came in from everywhere, most of them just to get a glimpse of him. But, and this is what Althea said to me, nothing escaped his notice."

Taletha was remembering Althea's story. Althea had knelt by the oven at the inn while telling it, so long ago now, her eyes wondering as she spoke. "We had to wait and wait. We thought he would weary of the crowds, and we would never get a chance.

"Oh," Althea had said, "you may think, *Only a fever? Why are they so upset? First child, probably.*"

Taletha hadn't responded. Her task had been to listen. Not to give answers. Had Taletha been thinking, *First child? I have no child.* I sensed her loneliness as she told me the story.

"But," Althea had said, "the fever had gone on for days. Sarah could not talk. At the end she could not even cry. Or awaken. She was as thin as a twig, her skin cold and clammy. I kept wet cloths on her. Tomit tried poultices. Everything. We were up all night. Those thin little legs—they were crooked, you know. She was born with crooked bones in her legs. When she learned to walk, she would stumble all over. But she was all heart, was little Sarah. Oh, she walked. She learned to run on those crooked little twigs. But now she could not move.

"Tomit held her. Held her and she hardly had the strength to cry. Just a limp bundle in Tomit's arms. I could not bear to watch, thinking he would never get to us with all the people.

"Then he was standing before us. The strange thing was that he touched me—*me*—first. I felt his touch on my forehead and looked into his eyes, and . . . Taletha, it was like . . . I don't know. All the fear vanished when those eyes smiled on me. He said nothing. Rather, he said everything without saying a word.

"Then, he took Sarah from Tomit's arms." Althea had laughed. "Tomit didn't want to let go! He was so used to holding her. But he nodded at Tomit. He said nothing, Taletha. He just took Sarah, and he held her, and then it seemed everyone disappeared; there were just the four of us together in this whole, wide world, and he hugged little Sarah, her crooked legs dangling, then he gave her back to Tomit. And . . ."

"What?" Taletha had asked, her own heart hammering.

"Sarah cried. I mean, she howled. She was hungry. And we were laughing, and crying. The fever was gone and she was crying because she was hungry." Tears had streamed down Althea's face as she spoke.

Just then, at that time several years ago, the little girl had bounded into the kitchen from play. Her face was dirty, her little shift muddy from playing.

With some surprise, Taletha had noticed that the little girl's legs were indeed bent. It was as if the bone curved slightly from her knees to her ankles, twisting out of alignment.

Althea noticed her surprise. She laughed as she hugged her dirty little girl, handed her a piece of sweetcake and sent her back outside to play.

"Oh, yes," Althea said. "He gave us a well daughter, a loving daughter. Not a perfect one. I wondered about that, too, for a time. I understand now."

But Taletha wasn't at all sure she understood.

* * *

I too was remembering the story, as Taletha had told it to me that night long ago when she had returned from her friend's house. I think that was when she began to change. Oh, I know she had believed from the start. The start? I think she believed always, in the desert, in the Kingdom of Kush where she had been delivered from slavery. Always. Before she met me. Before we arrived here. And everything since had merely been proof to what she already believed. But that night there was a change in her.

We rode in silence now for a way, lost in memory, listening only to the sounds of the earth and the creaking of the wagon as it slid along the muddy road.

We approached the bend near the farm. The ox shifted its huge shoulders and tugged more steadily, sensing the proximity of feed and rest.

"I wonder what Zophar would say about it," I said.

Taletha was distracted, self-absorbed. She merely murmured, "Hmm? About what?"

"Miracles. See, if the Messiah could heal fever, it seems to me he could also raise the dead. There's only a quantitative difference, one of degree against impossibilities."

"Yes. I see what you mean."

"I mean, if you accept one, you have to accept the other, isn't that so?"

Taletha nodded. I saw a smile play over her lips.

"Because to heal a fever is contrary to nature's laws. To heal a lame leg . . . Do you see my point? They both require some magical—"

"But I call it divine," Taletha interrupted.

"Okay," I laughed. "Remember my past. A *divine* interruption of nature's laws. Then, to raise a dead man is precisely the same thing. Only a matter of degree. To admit the possibility of one is to admit the possibility of the other."

"Yes," she said.

"Or," I added, "to deny one is to deny the other. You can't govern the essence by quantification, by degrees. If he couldn't raise a dead man, he couldn't heal a lame leg."

"Yes, husband. The mystery, though, is why he would do either."

"I see. That's the mystery. Not what, but why."

"More than that. For who can change natural laws? No human, surely. Someone with authority. Only, husband, someone who had himself instituted those very laws."

The ox tugged into the foreyard and stopped. I got down slowly to unhitch it. I had much to think about.

To my surprise, Taletha worked with me, helping me wordlessly with the traces of the yoke, turning the ox into the yard where it moved with exaggerated weariness as if to say, "See how hard I have labored for you," and plodded to the hay mow. It cast one brown eye over its flank, hay splayed out of its mouth like whiskers, and bent to its feed.

Taletha chuckled. "Sly old creature," she said. "It will outlive us all." She took my hand.

It felt so small, so fragile, in my own. I let her lead me to the door of our house. She turned and leaned against the doorpost. She reached out and entwined those slim fingers behind my neck and a tremor ran through me. A light of bemused laughter danced in her eyes. She pulled me to her. "Husband," she said. "*We* need this time. Alone."

I nodded.

She whispered in my ear, "Carry me in, husband." Then her voice was more urgent. "Oh, please."

CHAPTER
FIVE

Tje road to the capital city passed slowly under the dull plodding of the ox's hooves. Motion seemed to lull my defenses, easing memory. Manasseh's wagon had been hitched and ready for us when we returned to Noke, after a week of solitude on the farm. I left my own light wagon with him for his use, and we immediately set out. We had a long way to go. Manasseh wished us well, but his broad face was pinched with worry.

Sunlight was all adazzle, dancing on leaves and leaning grasses.

It should have been hypnotic to me. Desert-born, I still often felt that I could never drink in enough of these verdant hills to satisfy my thirst for beauty.

This lonely picture kept intruding. Liske, bounding along a hillside, the dog a flurry of motion ahead of him, chasing a wayward lamb. Liske, standing patiently by the flock, leaning upon the shepherd's staff that was too long, too heavy for him, as the flocks watered by some pool in a meadow. And Liske as his father—Manasseh, my friend—described him. Clumsy. An arm and hand unfit for carpentry. Liske, the outsider, content to be apart, to be away, even while longing to belong. I had never noticed.

Not true. The boy begged for approval. I had noted the tender way Taletha directed him, one hand tousling the lad's hair, the other pointing out some task that he would pursue with abandon. But to me, he was merely the hired boy. I gave an order now and then, which he obeyed quickly enough. That's all. That's the whole of it. And I found my heart yearning with a nearly unbearable sadness for something I had now missed forever.

The wagon wheels clanked and groaned. The off-wheel needed greasing. I should strip it at evening and clean and grease it.

Creak, it went, a long groan and sigh with each revolution. It sounded to me like a heart breaking.

I found another boy's face emerging from the past, so much like the son I had never had. Or had been. In the Magi's palace in Babylon, where for those few years I had been a part of the most exclusive club in the world, my attendant had been the waif, the lost boy, Haggai. So faithful he was. In my room during those long summer evenings Haggai and I played the game bah-lah while the crickets chirped in the reeds outside. His sister Doval would be busy with . . . I can scarcely remember now. It was a lifetime ago, when I had a son and daughter, foundlings from the desert, not by birth, but son and daughter for all that.

Then, well into that mad quest to find a Messiah in this very same distant land, there was that terrible night: a desert attack by outlaws. Fighting side by side with Balthazzar. Stumbling over the body of Haggai lying by my tent—he died fighting for me! Then catching my last glimpse of Doval, an outlaw's hand clutching her raven hair, his knife at her throat, the horror frozen on her face.

In death, Haggai was lost to me. But Doval had lived, I learned later. Doval had lived, if being sold into slavery could be called living. Oh, I had pursued her path, but losing it, I set out in search of my own path, and in time believed her lost, or dead.

When grief overwhelms you like a river's flood, you either bow beneath it and hope to hold on long enough to survive, or you harden your heart against the pain. I realize now I had chosen the latter. The trouble is, the pain never leaves. You never fully surface from the river's tide. Oh, Doval. Haggai. Their memories were like fires in my heart.

Fighting to keep the fires to smoldering embers, I had hardened my heart. I learned to subdue my despair. Why couldn't I have opened my own heart to Liske?

He's *not* your son, something inside me said. It's Manasseh's problem.

Problem! This lonely little boy with the crippled arm a problem!

Taletha nudged me. "The off-wheel needs greasing," she said.

I grunted. "I'll do it tonight." And flicked the reins over the plodding ox.

It's none of my business, anyway.

The safe way out.

And don't confuse him—Manasseh's son—with Haggai.

Haggai's hair was a dusty brown. Like Doval's. With auburn lights when the wind tousled it. His eyes a deep brown. Doval's eyes were like the brown of rich wood, one iris oddly flecked by a spot of golden light. The skin of each was . . . like Taletha's, olive-colored, a golden-brown hue.

Liske had his father's reddish-tan hair, sprouting like a thicket of curls. His eyes . . . I have no idea.

He was just a boy. None of my concern.

I gritted my teeth against the squeal of the wagon wheel.

* * *

From the moment we entered the capital city I felt strangely disoriented. With each step I seemed to enter the past, feeling the press of memories.

Townspeople choked the streets. We had been waiting in line under a hot afternoon sun to pass through the city gate, and had now fallen to a complete stop. The weary ox lipped some dried grass by the road. I dozed. I was thinking of my past, and how I would like to undo some things I had done. But I will not try to relive the past. Someone behind us shouted that we were blocking the road. Taletha elbowed me in the ribs and grinned when I started.

I snapped the reins over the ox and shouted at it as if it were the ox's fault. Taletha chuckled and shook her head.

"What?" I said as we plodded ahead to the guards at the gate. One peered into the empty wagon and waved us on.

"I had to marry a dreamer," she said with a wry grin.

But then I was busy maneuvering the wagon through the narrow streets, trying desperately to remember the way to the lumber mill on the south edge of town. I figured if I kept making right-hand turns I would eventually get there.

I got lost. I vaguely remembered buildings here and there. I thought I saw the temple off to the north. Very well. It was where it should be, but where was I?

It had been, after all, five years, and then the city had been in tumult. Set me in a desert, with stars as clear as beacons overhead, and I'll find the way. Set me in a city of crooked streets, houses piled on top of each other like a child's maze, people careening about shouting and waving like they were possessed, and I would be, and was now, hopelessly lost.

Without my protest, Taletha snatched the reins from my hands. Her strong, thin wrists flicked the reins lightly, threading the hump-back ox one way, then another, guiding it deftly around and through groups of pedestrians, street-merchants, loading wagons. I sat next to her, admiring the strength in those tanned forearms. It was a joy to hear her chuckling softly, even at my expense. For a moment, the pure danger of our mission drifted away.

When the wagon emerged out of the melee into the quieter southern edge of the city, skirting inside the wall, within sight of the canal, I relaxed. I recognized the place and the route we were taking. But I let Taletha continue; she had no intention of relinquishing the reins.

"You do fine on a country road," she said reassuringly.

"As long as it has no turnoffs?" I asked.

"Right." But the mischievous smile had evaporated. Worry lines etched her forehead as she guided the wagon down the narrow alley, into the courtyard of the lumber mill. With light, snapping touches of the reins she wheeled the ox, backed the wagon to a shed. A young laborer ran from a saw in the courtyard to help with the ox. But he was too late. He looked with admiration at Taletha as she tossed him the reins and climbed down.

"Feed and water the ox," she said. "We're leaving at first light."

"No," a voice said.

She turned. All this I observed while still sitting in the wagon. The owner of the mill, a beefy man crowned by a furious swirl of red hair, grinned broadly. He had his hands fisted on his hips and stood like a post of thick cedar in the middle of the yard. I recognized him as readily as if I had seen him yesterday. It had been five years.

Taletha walked to him. "In his name," she said.

"And in his service," replied the man.

I recognized the terms, although I heard them seldom in our small village. Some sort of sign and countersign.

To my surprise Taletha idly picked up a long stick lying in the yard and etched a straight line in the dust at the mill-owner's feet.

He took the stick from her, made a bisecting line across the top of hers, then slowly rubbed it out with his foot. But the sign was clear to me. It was a cross.

"What do you mean, no?" said Taletha.

There was deference in the mill-owner's voice. "Please come with me," he said, "if you would be so kind. Perhaps we can have a drink of good wine while we discuss your . . . order."

Taletha nodded. The mill owner looked at me, still sitting in the wagon and watching the formalities with a bemused expression. I didn't think he recognized me.

"Does your helper join us?" he asked politely.

Taletha turned and grinned. "He may," she said loudly. "If he can follow us without getting lost."

"Very well," said the owner. He began walking toward the end of the courtyard. I gathered I was to follow.

When we entered the small office, sawdust tracked in and littered everywhere, the owner turned and waved us to a bench. His eyes widened slightly as he saw me up close.

"The mahogany man," he said, extending a hand.

I shook it. "So, you remember."

"It's not every day I get an order for fine mahogany. Was it good?"

"Excellent. Sorry we're not here for more."

His face immediately turned grim. "Yes. Yes," he said. "But I can get you more."

"My husband," Taletha said as if to remind us of the subject. "His name is Elhrain."

"Husband!" the man exclaimed. "Well, why didn't you say so? And I am called Elihu. Forgive me." He pumped my hand again. "Here I thought he was . . ."

"Hired help?" I filled in. "I suppose I am."

"No. To be sure, no. The husband of Betharden is . . . is to be honored. We are all in her debt."

Betharden? That's right. That was her given name. Betharden. Her lost name . . . daughter of a lost family. The name given by her people. Those she had sought so desperately in her longing for a home. And I? The husband of Betharden.

My head whirled. The past! Its scaly head kept intruding.

"What do you mean, no?" Taletha asked again. She refused to sit on the bench. It became evident to me that she was in control, not the mill owner.

CHAPTER SIX

Once more I was on the fringe of the conversation. My head whirled at the names and details flitting between Taletha and Elihu. It annoyed me that he kept referring to her as Betharden. I found myself studying this woman, my wife, as if seeing her for the first time.

She had cut her hair shorter, I noted with surprise. When? I hadn't even been aware of it. What kind of husband was I? But she hadn't even told me, my mind answered. But should she *have* to? it countered.

That gorgeous hair. How I had loved just to touch it, dark and lustrous, shot through with amber lights when the sun struck it. I remembered how angry she had been in the desert, as the sun attacked her hair, turning it thin, limp and tattered. When we first saw that pebbled stream as we came out of the desert, she had scrubbed and rinsed her hair, using the finely grained river sand to scrape the desert's grit from it.

It was shorter now and showing tinges of gray where once amber lights danced.

But her skin, despite the desert, was still as pure and unblemished as a young girl's. What beautiful skin. But look now, as she pursed her lips, concentrating on a point Elihu was making, how the tiny furrows tracked the contours of her mouth, the corners of her eyes. Her dark eyes glittered with concentration.

I wanted, very much, to reach out and hold her, to kiss those lips, to trace my fingertips over those cheeks and throat.

Yes, we had needed those days alone at the farm before coming. Now everything seemed to change.

Now, she didn't seem to realize I was there. I was the hired help.

No one noticed when I slipped out the door.

* * *

In the courtyard sheds the saws had been laid to rest, and an eerie quiet suffused the square. The young man who had assisted us swept sawdust in a long trail stitched with lengthening shadows. He didn't see me. Dust rose in golden clouds about his ankles, closing him in a separate world.

The ox banged noisily in a stall, shifting to get at its feed. In a stall next to it, an ox used for yard work stomped and groaned, unnerved perhaps by its new neighbor. Glancing at the wagon, I decided the wheel could wait.

The sawyer's courtyard was rimmed by buildings, warehouses, and stores that fronted the surrounding streets. The area was well protected. Save for the endless noise of saws and hammers and planes during the day, a passerby on the outside street would never notice it. One narrow alley threaded between two warehouses to the street. I understood the tactical value of the place.

The streets outside had also fallen quiet as the evening hour approached. A man hurried by with long loaves of bread tucked under each arm. He nodded vaguely, paused a moment as he noted the dark color of my skin, then continued. Apparently, people of other flesh tones were not uncommon anymore.

The streets turned golden under the evening sun, spiked by purple shadows on the paving bricks. Here and there people sat before their homes, drinking wine or chewing absently on pieces of bread, enjoying the peacefulness of the day's end. After riding in the wagon for the two-day trip, it felt good to walk.

Just as I was reminding myself to take note of places and directions—Taletha was right; in the city I had no sense of direction—I felt that same sense of reliving the past flicker over me. Strolling across one of those open squares that dotted the heart of the city, I realized that I did indeed remember this place.

I snapped a nervous glance off to the left. Yes. There it was. The huge and foreboding temple. Shadows crept up its thick face; the white marble above the line of darkness flashed golden in the setting sun. Rooted in darkness, fumbling toward light. It sent a shiver, like a cold wind, trembling over me.

I looked out over the square. It was dirty, ill-kempt. The pit with the scourging posts lay past the east wall. I walked past it, my knees weak and trembling. I could not stop my footsteps had I wanted to. I permitted the road to carry me.

It wound uphill in a curving trail like a serpent's back, slanting upward between leaning mud-brick buildings that choked the street with shadow.

Right about here he had stumbled. On that day over five years ago. I remember the fire in his touch as the beaten man, his body filthy and streaked with sweat and blood and dust, touched me. For only a moment. This . . . this ragged Messiah. This caricature, rude and earthly, of a god. But he *had* touched me, and the fire that broke in me then had—somehow beyond my knowing—changed the past forever into an awful present as I followed him up the hill. My feet seemed now to fall into those very steps.

I crossed the threshold of the hill, lipped its rude rise and . . . it was just a barren sweep of gray rock with dust eddying where the wind cut across its high barrenness. Had I expected, half-hoped, to see him hanging there yet? In my mind's eye I could see it just so. Right there, by the mounds of dirt, the crosses had etched their stark, grotesque forms against the darkening sky as the storm clouds gathered.

It was suddenly very cold. I hugged my cloak about me and peered back over the city.

The sun was a red sliver on the horizon. The spires of the city were a series of red-capped flecks rising above the shadows. A city sprinkled in blood.

Even the air here above the hill seemed filtered through scarlet.

The restless wind tossed sprays of dust up across the gray rock. I wondered whether, years hence, someone else would stand here, and standing so, in silence, feel his past. Feel it as something sacred, unutterable and awe-striking. This land was littered with such spots, and Taletha had a keen eye for them. "Here some ancient had built an altar," she would say, naming a name that meant nothing to me. It was just a pile of broken stone. "Here someone had been buried, or hidden in time of war." But it was just an empty cave. "Here someone had talked with God." But thistles grew underfoot, and sheep dung lay against the rock, and an ox cropped the grasses, and it seemed not at all sacred. To her, maybe. It was *her* land, her people's history calling to her.

But I who had no history—rather, who had found my own history twisted into knots by a southern kingdom and so had turned my back upon it—wondered if any others would find this spot of gray rock and eddying dust sacred. Or would they come looking for the tomb where the man lay? And from which, as Taletha and the others believed, he had burst free after three days. If they came looking, they would simply find a hole in the hillside. What is sacred is not the place but the event. If it happened at all. I don't know. I wasn't there.

Wrong, all wrong, I told myself in that dying light of day that had faded to violet feathers in the western sky. This place is important to me, perhaps only for what I had lost. I had seen, had heard, had *touched* this man the Messiah. I watched him die, and thereby lost the outrage and anger that had burned in my heart all those years. To be sure, I had much to be angry with now, especially the lawgivers, but I was no longer angry at myself. The realization dropped me to my knees.

But hard on the heels of the relief I relived came the remembered grief of a second loss. I recalled Lycurgus, the Roman legionnaire who had once saved my life, and who five years ago presided over the taking of the life of this Messiah. The last I had seen him, he had flung his Roman cape aside, its scarlet folds snapping in the wind, tossed to the dust. He had strode across the rim of the hill and disappeared from my sight forever.

How I longed to see him again.

Suddenly I bent. I could not help it. I was doing the one thing this place signified—doing something I could not remember ever having done in my lifetime of outrage and anger. The tears came at first like hot acid. They flowed without ceasing, washing the fire away. I bent on my knees weeping, pitifully, like a child. Longing for someone to cradle me. Face to the dust, I wept.

I wanted to open my eyes, suddenly snap them open, and see Taletha standing there. Or feel her hand on my shoulder and have her enfold me in her arms.

But only the wind keened across that barren rock. There was no one but myself, and the desolate ghosts of the past. I spent myself in tears.

The night grew colder. When I stood up the hill was in darkness and the wind whimpered. I would feel foolish walking back to the mill owner's house, and I was suddenly angry at myself for my own weakness. How could I walk in, red-eyed and windblown? Why had I stayed out, like a little boy? But I had not cried as a boy, had I? I was a Magus. A man set apart, even as a child. I had had no time to cry.

I rubbed my hands at my face, erasing the tracks of my tears, and walked down the hill back into the city.

It was just a hill. Just a city. Dark now under the quiet night sky, the whistle of the wind among turrets and balconies the only sound. Here and there oil lamps glowed behind shuttered windows. The smell of spiced food, the sweet aroma of fresh bread, drifted on the wind. From an upper room, its balcony door standing open to the cool air, someone plucked a lyre and sang in a reedy voice. Just a city.

Yet, even on this night, I knew the power of the place.

And I wondered. If some such places can be indisputably touched by the sacred, can there be regions of this earth as indisputably touched by evil? Would I ever shake the desert from me?

More by luck than knowledge, I found my way back to the house of Elihu, the mill owner.

When I slipped in the door, Elihu glanced at me as the wind shifted a piece of parchment laid out on the table. Just as quickly he shifted his attention back to the drawing. Taletha never moved, her head bent over the drawing, her lips pursed in absolute concentration. Next to them stood two men, one an older man, who looked more like a prosperous merchant, the other the young mill hand who had stabled our ox that afternoon.

I walked past them to the shelf, helping myself to wine from the reed-wrapped flagon standing at the ready. Aside from Elihu's momentary glance, none of them seemed mindful of my presence. In fact, they acted as if I were *not* there. A thread of anger stirred like something physical inside me.

I leaned over Taletha's bent back and peered at the drawing. The pattern of corridors and tiny cubicles meant nothing to me at first. Then, with a feeling like a knife twisting in me, I recognized it.

The drawing was the layout of a prison.

CHAPTER
SEVEN

T hat could be very, very dangerous," I couldn't help commenting. It was obviously a design sketched by some intimate of the prison system. The detail was amazing, and I noticed a careful bar scale drawn in the lower corner. It was also, obviously, a work not meant to be public.

Elihu nodded. "Very dangerous," he affirmed.

"But worth it," Taletha said. "With this . . . we can do it. I'm certain of it."

"If it's so dangerous," I observed, "perhaps you should be more careful. I just walked in here and," I couldn't help emphasizing, *"nobody noticed."*

Elihu barked a short laugh. "Our apologies, Elhrain. I'll admit we were absorbed."

Taletha turned and stretched, giving me a weary smile.

Elihu continued, "But you were indeed noticed. There are four guards outside."

"I didn't see any!"

"Of course not," Elihu said. "You weren't supposed to. Else they wouldn't be very effective guards, would they? We knew when you were within a block of us."

"Oh. I was . . . preoccupied."

The older merchant lifted his head for the first time. "You had much to think about, Elhrain. Apparently. Nor did you notice the woman following you through the city, into the hills."

"Woman!"

"She was there. We thought it necessary."

"But a woman? I mean . . ."

"*Just* a woman? Believe me, in our cause, they are our finest warriors. This woman would be more than a match for anyone who threatened you."

"Rachel?" asked the mill hand.

The merchant nodded.

The boy grinned.

"But no one did threaten me!" I exploded.

"True. But one can't be too careful. Again, I apologize. We thought, as I said, that it was necessary."

"But what about . . . what I think is necessary!" I felt Taletha's hand at my back, pressed lightly, like a warning. I shook it off.

I paced to the door, and suddenly the anger exploded. I kicked the open door so hard that it cracked against the frame, one hinge breaking loose.

"Answer me!" I stormed. "Guards? It was a spy."

"No," Taletha murmured.

A man stood in the doorway suddenly, another crouched behind him in the darkness. Elihu waved them away, and they disappeared into the darkness.

"Yes! Just like that," I said. "You would wave me away. Listen, you would-be warriors, you guard-guiders, you plotters." I flung out my arm, including them all. Taletha cringed. "Listen to me! I have seen war! Not through plots or intrigues. In all its bloody reality, people. I have seen those I loved die before me. I have walked the pit of darkness and survived, have gone where few others would dare go. You think me a simple farmer, a . . . a writer. I tell you people, before anything else, remember that I am a king. I am a Magus! By right and by gifts and by confirmation. I am the last Magus on earth!"

Her hands trembled on my cheeks. Holding me. Drawing me back to the present.

"I know, husband," Taletha breathed. "We all know. Because of that we wanted to spare you."

"Don't spare me. Include me."

* * *

The morning light was a misty gray, and my eyelids felt heavy.

The wagon creaked painfully. The worn hub of the inside wheel sounded like two stones dragged across each other, even after being greased this morning.

The lumber piled on the wagon bed had been carefully arranged. Elihu and two other men had worked far into the night in the lamp-lit shed, the guards alert to passersby, to arrange it just so. But no one intruded through the back alleys to this workplace, and the late sound of carpentry was apparently not unusual from his shop.

The rough lumber was carefully stacked over and around an empty housing, about seven feet long, three feet high, and four feet across. The structure left enough room in the wagon bed for a double layer of lumber all around, carefully arranged to look like a full load. The lumber was side-stacked and roped down and had the appearance of a unusually heavy load. It would be, too, when the hollow housing was filled with the prisoners we expected.

"More than enough room there for four," I observed to Elihu.

"Five," he said. "And we can't know what condition they'll be in."

"Five? I thought there were four of them."

"You haven't heard? No, that's right. You went back to your farm. The night after your meeting old Napthali disappeared. We have reason to believe that he was taken here. That he will stand a quick trial and be executed with the others."

"Napthali," I repeated. It seemed impossible. That harmless old man. No, not altogether harmless. He had dared defy the lawgivers.

Elihu had sawn out of the wagon bed a close-fitted trap door, pegged in place by a removable cross brace. With the bracing in place, no uninformed eye could tell that the trap door was there. It was expertly fitted.

Now in the first light of morning we were giving the wagon a trial run. Elihu had refashioned the harness for a double yoke and had teamed one of his own yard oxen with Manasseh's sturdy creature. "One could do it," he said, "but why take chances?"

Why, indeed. Manasseh's ox, balking and ornery, seemed to resent its neighbor at first. They didn't pull together as a team; one jerked at the yoke while the other lagged.

Elihu lightly snapped a whip from flank to flank, urging the animals to pull in tandem. Finally, after repeated stings to their backsides, they resolved themselves to work together.

Elihu grunted. "The lesson of the whip," he said. "They all learn it."

"Will they work together tonight?" I asked.

He handed me the whip. "Practice anytime you want."

I did, but there was little need. The team pulled smoothly now into the main thoroughfare. We had wanted to test them before the traffic got heavy, but already early drivers were wheeling into the street.

"Just as well," Elihu said. "You should get used to the rush." He nodded as I handled reins and whip to wheel around a parked wagon.

"Good," he said. "Turn here."

I angled for the side street, heading downhill toward a part of the city I had not been in before. "There's a world of difference handling two of them," I said. "I never had to use the whip on just one ox."

"Right. They're competing. It's instinct. The trick is to get them pointed in one direction. Right now they're trying to figure out which one will lead."

"Is that why you had me turn this way?" I asked. The crooked street wound and narrowed downhill. My muscles tensed and strained, heaving on the reins.

"Loosen your grip," Elihu said. "Let them figure it out. You guide, they work."

For a moment the two oxen stumbled together, banging their huge weights against the traces. Then they steadied. To my surprise it was Manasseh's steady old ox who dominated.

Elihu nodded his head approvingly. "Guessed as much," he said. "That's why I put him inside. Turn to the left here," he added.

And I saw the reason he had taken me on this route.

The prison was a long squat building. The brick, a yellow color at the top, darkened to mildewed and ulcerated gray at the bottom. The whole compound had a fetid air here at the bottom of the hill, like a cesspool—stagnant and confined. One might call it a tomb, rather than a prison. Technically, the city had no *prison*. Justice was strict and swift here, following the ancient code. But with the political turmoil of recent years, and the influx of partisans who respected *no* code, this decayed old hulk of a building, an old fortress really, had been converted to meet the need.

Involuntarily I pulled on the reins and slowed. The dismal walls leaned inward, as if pressing mournfully upon the lives within. Tiny little slit windows, like dead eyes turned to the light, broke the blank expanse. We passed a narrow door tucked into the brick.

"That's where we'll be going in," Elihu remarked.

I nodded, remembering the maze of corridors that lay past that door— a maze we had all committed to memory the night before. All would go well if the map was accurate. If not, we would be entering our own entombment in this most desolate of prisons.

The wagon creaked past, the inside wheel grinding like a plea.

"Better grease that again this afternoon," Elihu said.

I nodded.

We emerged around the prison to a run-down, vacant forecourt. Across from the prison stood a long warehouse constructed of mud brick and wood. It was near ruin, one wall partially collapsed. Two guards stood posted by the entrance of the prison, heads nodding as the morning sun sneaked tentative fingers into the square. Neither of them roused at our passing.

"Just a couple of old carpenters delivering our load," I said.

Elihu chuckled softly. "And we hope the guards are also drowsy tonight. If not, that will rouse them." He pointed at the warehouse as we plodded past it. A large rat darted into its shadow.

"The warehouse? How?"

"Because it will be burning. Quite wildly, we trust."

"A criminal act?"

"No less than jailbreaking," Elihu said. "As a matter of fact, the building used to belong to one of ours. He had a good business. But the authorities decided they wanted it. Thought they might need to enlarge the prison someday."

I glanced back at Elihu. His mouth was shut tightly. I knew then who the owner had been. But I merely asked, "And . . . what happened?"

He shrugged. "The authorities took it. Simple as that. Oh, they trumped up some charge about taxes, then condemned the building. The owner, after spending a few months there"—he jerked his head toward the prison—"gave up and signed over the warehouse. There are other ways of fighting back," he added, "than rotting in a cell."

I nodded. "Will it give you satisfaction?" I asked.

"What?"

"Burning your own warehouse?"

He chuckled softly. "You're perceptive, Elhrain. But, you see, it's no longer mine. Nonetheless, it will give me pleasure, and it will be done carefully. Oil fires started at six different spots. The warehouse still holds old lumber of mine. Including some mahogany. Don't worry about the fire, my friend. The pleasure will be all mine."

I nodded. I knew how precious mahogany was. "And the map? Your work?"

"Well, a good carpenter is also a good mathematician, true? The map, I assure you, is quite precise."

"Still . . . the fire is only a distraction."

"Yes. The final step is a sleeping potion, concocted from the supplies of our good friend the physician. We have someone, whose name will go unmentioned, on the inside. A simple matter to place it in the food and drink of the guards."

"Still, it's hit or miss. Some won't eat."

"True. That's the risk we take. And we won't be well armed. That's not our way." He paused, then added, "The physician, by the way, is among the prisoners."

I nodded.

We were silent as the oxen plodded back up the hill, in perfect unison now.

"It's the best we can do, Elhrain. And with plenty of risks."

I didn't look at him.

"Still plenty of time to get out."

Anger rushed over me like a wave. "See if you can keep up with me, carpenter," I snarled.

He laughed and squeezed my forearm. But I was not smiling. I was afraid.

* * *

What bothered me most was that no one, single, authoritative leader appeared to direct this strange group of conspirators. Much of my life had been lived among royalty and military powers. I had seen both the good and the dark sides of each. But I had learned this: someone has to seize, and wield, final authority for things to work. Someone has to give orders and be responsible for their execution. And those orders, either out of fear or respect, have to be obeyed instantly and without question.

This group was nothing like that. It worked together in an odd harmony unified by . . . what? By its desire to free the prisoners, surely. But also by something else. A mutual respect, perhaps. A sense of certain gifts or abilities in individual members that apparently went unspoken. *Each* person was needed; each had a task. But it was still something more than this: it was a shared sense that they could *not* fail, an unbending confidence in their basic rightness and purpose, a sense that something—or someone— larger than the group itself was ultimately responsible. They earnestly believed they would succeed. And against all human odds.

It was something of a surprise to me that the one who walked us through the afternoon practice, in Elihu's spacious woodworking mill which had been carefully cleared to an open space, was Taletha.

Saws and implements were stowed to one side. Lumber was piled in the yard before the open doors. The ventilation windows were shut. From the outside, the mill still looked simply like a busy mill. In fact, two young yard hands banged about noisily outside the whole time.

Inside, Taletha had carefully worked out positions by sticks and boards laid on the floor. It neatly duplicated the prison layout, much diminished in size. But even so, there was a painstaking exactitude. Every dimension, I noticed from a casual survey of the layout, was precisely downscaled, according to the map, from the actual dimensions. Each step, each action would be normal, but cut simply by about two-thirds. Seen in such a way, I easily picked out the outlined corridors, even the individual cells, of what we presumed the inside of the prison to be like.

Taletha placed us carefully about the mock prison, calling out instructions with the precision of a general. *Or*, I thought, *as if she had been trained by someone with military experience.* We follow the shortened paths. An imaginary fire blazes. We assault the doorway. Into the corridor. Down a flight of steps. Into the clammy dungeon. The first and fourth cells. Over the prostrate bodies of guards. Would they be sleeping?

The keys hang on the peg under a rush lamp. Seize them. Undo the doors to the cells. What next? The prisoners would be in chains. Would the keys fit? Yes, we were told. If the prisoners could not walk, carry them. How many? Five. Suppose there were more? Our information was spotty at best; at worst, all wrong. Up the corridor, the steps. Hide them in the wagon.

We were sweating by the time we finished. We took a break. Then did it all again, Taletha snapping out orders in that crisp voice.

"Okay," she said finally. "We're ready. Now we rest until evening."

I stepped over to her and smiled. "Very good, General."

She smiled broadly. "It will work, won't it?"

"With you giving orders, how can we fail?"

She snorted. "Someone had to do it. But I had a good teacher."

"Oh? Who?"

"Lycurgus."

"What!" I gasped at the name of my old friend.

"Yes. He's the Roman we spoke about. Didn't anyone tell you?"

"I . . . just never dreamed he was still alive."

She shook her head. "Believe me, he is with us."

"Maybe it will work after all."

Her face went tight, the lines around her eyes compressed. "It has to," she said. "They are scheduled for execution tomorrow noon."

CHAPTER
EIGHT

M y throat constricted as I swallowed nervously. A churning started in my stomach and fell in weak trembles to my legs. Even
my hands shook on the reins. I longed for the hard-eyed aggressiveness
of the others and wondered if they sensed the fear in me.

The purple haze of evening settled on the streets. We were just one last
wagon, laden with lumber and pulled by two oxen, following the snake's
spine of convoluted alleys. I sat slouched like a sleepy teamster heading
home.

Anything could go wrong! Everything could go wrong. This might be
my last night alive. And to spend it like this.

* * *

What was it Taletha had said as we parted?

We had briefly held hands in a circle, an act that made me slightly
uncomfortable. I waited for the slightest recoil at touching *me*. But there
was none. We stood silently around the table; the maps lay pinned down
on its surface, like a sacrifice upon an altar.

Maybe Taletha had thought that too. "If it is his will, and with his
help," she said, "we will succeed. If not, we have given the good sacrifice
and will be accounted worthy."

Others nodded and muttered agreement. This talk of "his will" and "his help" had made me slightly uneasy. I would rather provide for every contingency in this project that had more holes every time I looked at it.

* * *

Next to me rode the young yard hand. He would hold the oxen in place while we went in. Right now he could hardly hold still.

He was talking again, his youthful chatter unstoppable.

"What?" I asked. Did he smell my fear?

"I said, these must really be important people," he said. "I mean, to go in the prison! Do you think we can do it?"

"We'll know in a few hours."

"Sooner than that. We might all be dead!"

I looked at him obliquely. He was excited by it all, eyes shining. I noticed then that he fingered a short knife tucked in his belt.

I grunted. "Just make sure you stay with the wagon," I said. "You'll be safe there. They'll never know you are involved."

"But I am involved. I want to go in. I want to get those dirty—"

"No! You have a job to do. Do it right."

He sulked. The wagon creaked and groaned around a corner. "Are you scared?" he asked.

I waited a long time to answer. "Yes," I said.

"Do you know who they are?"

"What do you mean?"

"The prisoners?"

I was surprised to admit that I didn't. Not all of them. "Like you say, some important people, I guess."

"Worth our lives, anyway," he said.

"Be quiet now."

The young man grinned eagerly in the growing darkness.

* * *

Taletha and Elihu had gone on ahead to coordinate with others and now were waiting in the small house of a sympathizer across from the side door of the prison. Elihu promised that two others would be with them. That made only five of us to breach the prison.

"If all goes right," Elihu had said, "we won't need any more. We would just get in each other's way."

"And if it goes wrong?" I had asked.

"Then five times our number wouldn't help," Elihu answered.

There it was. Everything depended on the plan. But the plan held too many variables, too many *ifs*.

* * *

An hour before I rode out, two men left with heavy waterskins slung over their shoulders. Right about now, they would be working among the shadows of the old warehouse, the necks of the waterskins draining oil against the tinder-dry wood.

At the same time these men had left, the prison guards would have shifted. The oncoming guard would have eaten a communal meal, heavily laced by the cook with the powders from the physician's supply. By now the sedative would be taking effect. The men would be drowsy, disabled if not asleep. And, if such were the case, the prison cook would have left her post, slipped into the dungeon corridors, taken the keys from the wall peg at the head of the cell block, and unlocked the side door. With luck! Too many *ifs*.

The oxen lurched as they turned downhill. The streets were quiet. The sky dusked to darkness.

Soon. Soon we would reach the bottom of the hill and turn. If the timing was right, an orange glow would fill the night.

The prison map kept playing through my mind. It had to be accurate! I pulled on the reins. The oxen balked. Then turned.

The low squat shape of the prison lay before us, desolate and decayed. But where was the fire?

As suddenly as I thought the question, a flame licked up from behind the warehouse, cutting into the darkness like a bright knife. Others sprang up. Three, four plumes. The spitting crack of dry wood sounded as the fire fed itself. The tongues spread, covering the old warehouse, devouring it. Somewhere a bell began tolling.

I jerked sharply on the reins, halting the oxen, and thrust the reins at the yard hand. He slid over on the seat, wide eyes mirroring the plumes of fire. I jumped off, knelt beside the wagon and loosened the brace of the trap door, leaving it lying in the street.

"Whatever happens, don't move!" I ordered.

Then Taletha, Elihu and the two men surged past the wagon to the prison door. Elihu jerked at its handle and spat curses. It had not been unlocked. Already the plan was breaking down.

Elihu was about to slam a crowbar into the crack of the jamb when suddenly the door flew open and two prison guards leaped out into the street. The powerful carpenter and his two men handled the guards like rag dolls. Within seconds they were bound and gagged and dumped unceremoniously by the wall.

"They're supposed to be asleep," I hissed.

"We're going in anyway," Taletha said. "We can't stop now."

Far up the street we heard men shouting as they raced to the fire.

* * *

The air inside was hot and rank. A torch hung on the wall. Elihu plucked it off and waved it about, looking for the keys. A large peg stood empty beside the torch bracket.

"They're not here," he said. "Wait a minute. The guard used them to open the door. Search them."

Everything was going wrong! We needed to get out now.

I was ready to say as much when Taletha reentered with the keys in hand. "He dropped them. They were lying in the street where they fell."

We descended a flight of steps, taking us into the darkness below ground level. The sun-baked walls held the heat in here, cooking the air to a thick glue of humidity and foul odors. Our torch stabbed at the darkness like a child's candle, rebuffed at every turn.

I heard Elihu, in the lead, chanting off the number of steps we descended into the bowels of the dungeon.

One of the two men followed, and I saw now that he obviously had military training for he held a sword at the ready, easily and expertly, arm half-raised to parry or deliver a blow. Taletha and then I, carrying another torch, walked behind him. I glanced over my shoulder. The second man walked behind me now, also carrying a sword at the ready, his eyes probing the shadows left and right, avoiding the light to keep his night vision. He caught my glance and grinned at me.

Like a little boat, lit at bow and stern, we moved forward bobbing on a sea of darkness.

We reached the bottom of the stairs and paused. Somewhere water dripped into a puddle—a disconsolate sound, echoing in the black corridor.

A long silence masked the air as we stood getting our bearings. I could hear each one breathing, the sound harsh and raspy in the enclosed space. Behind me, the guard whispered, "Could the maps be wrong?"

Taletha shook her head. "No. We're in the cell block." She seized Elihu's torch and stepped forward.

And froze in her tracks.

A high-pitched wail, like that of a madman or of someone awakening from a nightmare, echoed down the corridor. The eerie notes reached high, higher, into a demented shriek. My skin turned cold, as if a bony hand ran long nails down my flesh.

The scream broke apart into silence, then was replaced by a dull mutter. "The bones. The bones. The bones." We stood still, listening to the voice of madness, muttering somewhere in the darkness ahead.

"Find the skull," the voice shrieked suddenly. "At the place of the skulls!"

In a flash, I saw again the face of mad Philip through the temple window. This wasn't, couldn't be, him. Yet it was the same voice of sheer terror.

Elihu stepped forward, holding the torch like a weapon. He paused at the first door. It was ajar.

Suddenly the door sprang open. Half naked and cursing, a prison guard stepped out bearing a sword. "I told you to leave me—" His eyes widened.

Our lead warrior darted past Elihu. His sword flashed in the torchlight. In blows too quick to follow he disarmed the guard and had him lying on the floor, the point of his sword pressed against the guard's throat.

Elihu leaned forward. "Where are they?" he hissed. He picked up the guard's fallen sword and held it above the man's eyes. I averted my glance as a wail of fear broke from the guard.

But as I turned I saw her—garments torn from her body and hanging in long strips to the ground, her hair hanging wildly in disheveled strands across a face beaten and bloody.

"Kill him," she hissed. "He was . . ."

Taletha brushed past me. Without hesitation she held the young woman, stroking her tangled hair.

"Taletha," I said urgently, "is she one of the prisoners?" Time! Even now guards could be finding the two tied up outside.

"Taletha," I hissed.

She shook her head. "The cook," she said.

The woman sobbed. "I tried. I tried so hard! Then, that one," and she pointed a finger at the man on the ground, "he grabbed me and—" she looked down at her nearly naked body and collapsed into tears against Taletha.

"Gag him and dump him in the cell," Elihu hissed.

The warrior looked at Elihu, hesitating, the point of his sword unwavering at the guard's throat. "No," Elihu said. "Even so, we don't want to kill him."

"Yes," screamed the woman. "Kill him. He tried to . . ." Her voice broke. "In the dark!" She said the last with a pitiful, forlorn wail. As if the forsakenness to darkness were the very worst of it.

The warrior bent over, cutting strips of cloth from the guard's own garments. He gagged the man, pulling at the knot until the prisoner grunted. He lifted him bodily and heaved him back into the cell, taking particular pleasure at the dull thud of the body colliding against solid rock. He slammed the door and savagely turned the lock.

"Are the prisoners here?" Elihu rasped at the cook.

She nodded as if awakening from a nightmare. She dabbed at the blood on her torn lips.

"You *have* helped us," Taletha quietly said to her. "We still need your help."

Slowly the woman regained control. "Yes, they're here."

The sigh of relief was clear in the cramped corridor.

"But the prisoners . . . also ate the food."

Of course. The leftover gruel of the sedated food, the garbage, would be fed to the prisoners.

Taletha took the woman's hand. The others were already moving down the corridor.

Elihu bent to the bolt of the next door, but stood up again in shock. He pulled the handle. The door opened easily. "It's not locked," he said.

As he said that, the door pushed slowly open. Standing befuddled in the doorway, one hand pressed against the wood, as if awakening from a long sleep, stood a figure I recognized at once. My heart leapt with excitement, but then I saw the thinness of his once powerful body, the bruises that stained his flesh.

Nonetheless, I pushed past the others. "Lycurgus!"

Only half-awake, he looked at me, a smile slowly moving across his face. He lifted his arms to me, and I embraced him eagerly. Feeling the bones beneath his filthy garment, I recoiled.

But he laughed. That old rich rumble. "Do I smell too?" He looked at us with a dazed expression. "But which of you was here earlier?"

"What?" Elihu said. "We just got here. And we must hurry."

Lycurgus shook his head slowly. "Did I dream it? I've been sleeping."

I laughed. "The food was sedated."

"Oh. But someone was here. At least, I thought so. He walked in that door. He touched my chains. Look!" He pointed behind him in the cell. The manacles lay on the floor. But they had not been unlocked; they were burst apart.

Lycurgus rubbed his eyes and swayed against the corridor wall. Gently I lowered him to the ground. One of our warriors stood over him protectively.

"Wait here," Elihu said. "We have to get the others."

A footfall sounded in the darkness of the corridor. The warrior leapt forward, sword ready.

A voice quavered, "Please. What's happening?"

Elihu thrust the torch forward. Standing outside the open door of the next cell stood the little gray-haired priest, Napthali. His eyes held that same sleepy, uncomprehending look.

Elihu stepped forward, a warrior at his heels. "Get these two up to the wagon," he barked.

The warriors looked at Taletha. "Go ahead," she said. "We'll be all right."

Bending to Lycurgus and Napthali, the powerful young men lifted each bodily, and walked soundlessly back down the corridor.

Suddenly I understood. The two warriors with us—these strong, capable young warriors—they were Lycurgus's men. Lycurgus, the renegade Roman general, this leader of men and follower of no one, was indeed part of the movement. Follower of no one? Lycurgus had chosen to follow the one they called *the Messiah*. He was a part of it all, turning his military skills to the liberation of refugees, working with Taletha, Doval and others on these mad schemes. And I understood also why Taletha had tried to keep it from me. She wanted only to protect me. One warrior returned silently in the darkness. The other, I had no doubt, waited with his leader.

"Two more," Elihu said. He shoved the next cell door open. It too was unlocked. The physician lay on the floor, snoring heavily. The manacles lay against the wall, the iron shattered as if struck by lightning.

"Quickly," Taletha said. "Time is running out." She bent to the physician, slapping his cheeks.

His eyes blinked and opened, the dilated pupils flickering slightly as they reacted to the torchlight. A smile swept his narrow, intelligent face.

"I should have known better," he whispered in a thick voice. "Nightshade?"

Taletha nodded.

"Yes. I thought I smelled it. Well . . ." He tried to get up and collapsed. "And I never had much of an appetite," he muttered.

Elihu handed me his torch and lifted the man as easily as if he were hoisting a piece of lumber. "The cook may have indulged too heavily, doctor."

"In my cell," he said in a drugged voice. "There's another man."

The physician's head lolled sideways as Elihu passed him to the warrior, who took him back up the corridor.

Waving Elihu's torchlight around the cramped cell, I made out a figure lying on a straw mat on a bench. The body was so emaciated that it looked like a corpse. Only the rasping rattle of his breath indicated life. I bent before him. His eyes were sunken to deep puddles in the sockets, as if turned inward so long by so much darkness they could no longer force the will to see. His grizzled cheeks were so fragile and slack over the jaw that his face looked like a mere skull. One hand lifted feebly and collapsed against his chest.

He was a man dying. Only the harsh gasping held death back, as if his lungs refused to do what his body insisted upon.

As I leaned near, his eyes opened to the light, two black coals barely burning in the thin slits. I don't know if he saw me; he saw the light and his eyes sucked at it greedily. One bony hand reached and fastened on my arm like a claw, drawing the torch closer.

His breath flagged. I thought for a moment he was dead, but the eyes burned again with a brittle intensity. The thin fingers dug into my arm. Then his breath heaved in a great gasp, a horrible rattling that chilled me to the core, and he rasped out, "Look to the skulls."

Again, those words. Involuntarily I jerked my arm. But the clawlike hand had already gone limp. The eyes were set, still catching the light, but they had glazed over. No breath came from the cracked lips. I pried his hand loose.

"He's dead," I whispered.

They were silent for a moment. "Leave him, then," said Elihu.

I didn't move.

Taletha pulled at my shoulder. "There's nothing we can do. We have to hurry."

I rose slowly, the words still burning in me. The place of the skulls.

Of this much I was certain: While this man had the same deranged appearance, the sunken frailty of a survivor of some physical or mental horror, and had spoken virtually the same words as mad Philip whom I had heard in Noke, he was certainly not the same man. It was more than coincidence.

The three of us, Taletha, Elihu and I, stood there a moment. The cook huddled uneasily behind us. Elihu assured her that we would take her along, but her fear was transparent.

"One more?" I asked.

Taletha grinned. "Yes," she said. "One more."

We rushed down the corridor, Elihu and I bearing the torches. Red light swam along the wet halls as we hurried by. We came to the last cell. Elihu banged on the door. It was locked.

Furiously he fumbled with the keys, twisting and pushing. At last came a loud click. He heaved open the door, fighting the grinding hinges. His light touched the slick stone within. The cell was vacant.

"Oh, no," Taletha moaned.

"Whom do you seek?" asked the cook. We turned in surprise at her voice, hardly aware of her presence with us.

Taletha took her by the shoulder, peered hard into her eyes. "The woman," Taletha said. "Do you know where she is?"

I could see the fear creep into the woman's eyes. "The woman," she whispered.

"Yes! Do you know anything. . . ?"

The cook nodded. "They took her to another place. They—"

"Speak up, woman," Elihu prodded.

Taletha raised a hand toward him. "They were going to use her?"

The cook nodded.

"Do you know where? It's very important we find her."

"Kill them," hissed the cook. "Kill them all."

"Please," Taletha said gently. "Please tell us where she is."

Raising a trembling hand, the cook pointed up.

"Upstairs? In another room?"

She nodded.

"But we don't know those floors," said Elihu. "And we have to get going. Get out of here!"

Taletha persisted, as if not hearing him. "Can you lead us there?" she said to the cook.

My heart was hammering. Time to get out!

In answer, the woman nodded and turned down the corridor, her feet scraping against the damp stone.

CHAPTER NINE

The cook walked rigidly past the cell that held her attacker. As we passed, we heard thrashing noises and stifled curses from inside.

Each step, each turning of the stairwell, brought fresher air. Only then, climbing out of that dank, oppressive air, was I aware of the sweat that bathed my body.

Each step up, still guided by the pale globes of light we held, delivered us from darkness. The light of the world above ground stretched tentative fingers *toward* us.

How many minutes had passed? Time was everything, and we had so little. By now, surely, the warehouse fire would be dying down. Guards would remember their posts and slink back guiltily from the excitement.

How long could the wagon wait by the side door before being noticed? It would have to move when the guards returned. Else all our work was lost. And what then of us, still in the maze of this prison?

We turned onto the landing by the side door, and I fought the temptation to peer out.

The cook continued up a short flight, approaching a doorway to the main passage. She set her face rigidly, like one condemned. We had ascended above the level of last resort, those scheduled for execution. Here the prisoners were of another sort, those awaiting trial, misfits of society held for a time before being sent on their way to another part of the country. Thieves, vagabonds. Rapists.

The irony did not escape me. Those condemned for their beliefs had lain in the pit. They were more dangerous in the eyes of the lawgivers.

Elihu, walking beside the cook, shoved the door open. The corridor was brightly lit.

"Here?" Taletha asked.

"Yes, in the guard room. At the front."

The worst place. Where the guards would be returning.

Elihu took a deep breath and walked quickly down the corridor. The cells here were simply open cubicles, the prisoners shackled by chains to posts in the rock. Two or three prisoners to a cell. They were sleeping. Of course. They would have eaten the food also. Good!

Save for one man, halfway down the corridor. Seeing us coming he banged on the walls with a metal cup. I held up the keys. "On the way out," I said, "I'll release you. Wait."

Taletha looked at me in anger. "You can't," she said. "They're criminals."

"Aren't we all?"

But I was thinking of that time, years ago, when I was held in a dungeon like this, and my own escape had been effected by freeing everyone. Creating a mad confusion. Perhaps . . .

The end of the corridor opened into an administrative space. Off to one side, in a little room vented only by a chimney, stood the ovens, still hot from the evening meal. The main space was littered with benches and a few stools placed randomly about a large table. Smoke from the warehouse fire drifted in, burning in eyes and lungs. Through the open front door, the night sky was still streaked with orange tongues of the dying fire. Across the square the fire silhouetted dark figures. They would be returning soon. All this we caught in a glance.

Two offices were spaced at opposite ends of the room, doors shut.

"Which one?" Elihu asked.

The cook shook her head. Impatient, I shoved Elihu toward the closest one and ran to the far door.

I leaned against the door. It was barred from the inside. I slammed my shoulder against it, and a shock of pain jarred my body. Someone coughed and cursed inside. He called familiarly, thinking I was one of his comrades come back.

Fury raged over me. I wanted him! Put an end to it. But how . . . the bench.

Elihu and Taletha were out of the other room now. I grabbed the center of a bench. Fashioned from a piece of raw oak, the wood was unfinished and heavy. Elihu and Taletha held the back, keeping their weight behind it.

The makeshift battering ram shattered the door, ripping hinges and scattering wood.

She hunched on her knees on the floor, folding herself in like a package sealed against pain. The guard gripped her head by a handful of hair wrapped in his thick paw.

Once before a young girl crouched in my tent in the desert. The bandit with a blade at her throat. Taunting me.

Only this brute had no knife. Seeing me, he lurched upright, twisting her head painfully to one side as he rose. Her eyes widened and fixed on me through the tears.

"Doval," I said.

Her voice, a child's voice, pleaded, "Father. Help me."

* * *

Hands pulled at my shoulders.

Through a blur, I kept hitting him.

Hands seized my own. A woman's sharp cry.

I kept pummeling. My daughter! Nothing would stop me. Never. Not ever.

Then someone grabbed my hair and pulled my head back. My mouth flew open in a shout of pain. The haze before me became drops of blood from the blow the guard had landed, and the woman holding my wrists was Taletha. Almost immediately, I felt Elihu's grip on my hair relax.

"Get ahold of yourself, man," he snapped in my ear. "We've got to leave."

Dazed, I looked around again. The guard lay in a heap. Doval and Taletha were already gone. I raised one hand to my face. The pain. Suddenly it was like a hive of bees had flown up my nose. Blood smeared under my hand.

The club the guard had used lay next to his inert body.

The cook grabbed a rag and thrust it over my nose. "Squeeze," she ordered. "Right at the bridge." At the same time she shoved me out the door.

Elihu glanced out the front door. Urgently he hissed, "They're coming back."

I tossed him the key ring that I had kept on my belt. "Give that to one of the prisoners."

"We can't let them go!"

I grimaced at this same high-minded morality. "Do it," I said, and I was running unsteadily down the corridor behind the cook. Behind me I heard a whoop of glee from one of the prisoners, and I smiled.

We barred the door at the end of the corridor, making sure the prisoners would head for the front exit. Down the steps. The side door stood ajar. We leaped through it and slammed it tight. And stood there.

The wagon was gone.

We soon saw why. The fire was nearly out. Far ahead guards and bystanders were returning across the square. Suddenly a cry went up. The escaped prisoners bolted from the front door into a melee of guards. *Well, I thought, maybe their morality will be satisfied after all.*

We pressed to the shadows of the wall, moving down the street.

Out of the darkness a darker figure rose. I struck out at it. Powerful fingers seized my wrist in midblow, stopping it as if I had hit a brick.

"Shh." The shadow metamorphosed into the shape of a man. One of Lycurgus's warriors. "Quietly," he said. "This way." Without waiting for reply, he darted across the street, into a narrow passage between buildings. We followed, the darkness a friend now, hiding us.

The warrior moved deliberately, as if he knew no haste. He paused often to check on us as we labored uphill, following a labyrinth of alley. "We'll rest a minute," he said at one point. And we slumped gratefully against a fence.

In the darkness a cat mewed. There were no other sounds. Only our ragged breathing stabbed the night.

Then Elihu began to chuckle. It sounded like weeping at first, starting deep in his throat, making a choking sound as he tried to control it.

"What's so funny?" I asked.

But the silent laughter possessed him. I could feel his thick body trembling with it. With surprise, I found it floating through the air and infecting me. A smile first, just at the seizure of uncontrollable laughter affecting the man. Then it spread. I chuckled. It was like an itch that spread with scratching. Taletha giggled. She made strange little snorting noises high in her nose that told me she was on the verge of collapse into laughter.

"Shh!" our guide hissed in a loud whisper. The cat meowed loudly in response, and for some reason it struck us as the funniest thing in the world. Elihu rolled on his side, desperately trying to stop the laughter that flooded over him. He was being attacked by laughter. "We . . . we did it," he whispered between gasps. "We really did it!"

All of us were shaking with silent laughter as the bewildered guard hissed and the cat mewed fetchingly in the darkness. Even the cook wrapped her tattered rags around her and shook her head with a disbelieving smile.

A patch of silver light crept over that small place as the moon poked one of its twin horns out of a cloud. A narrow ribbon of moon followed, ending in the duplicate horn of the perfect quarter moon. Tremulous silver light floated over us, and we stopped laughing, looking at each other.

"Yes," said Elihu, unbelievingly now, "we really did it."

For the first time I could see Taletha and the woman side by side. They were both dabbing at their eyes. Whether from relief of the tension, for joy, for laughter, I knew not. Like the twin horns of the moon rising above them, the two women were perfect mirrors, albeit ragged and filthy mirrors this night. I studied their faces—sweaty, drawn, smudged. Hair tousled like blown birds' nests. The one—Taletha—five or six years older. But mirrors, nonetheless.

"Doval," I whispered.

Her eyes turned to me. She smiled, a tentative smile, but the moonlight radiated around her like a blessing.

"We have to get going," the warrior said. "They will sweep the city soon enough. Get the soldiers out."

"Are you one of Lycurgus's men, then?" I asked. I recognized him in the moonlight as one of the guards who had been at Elihu's shop, one of those men capable of melting into or materializing out of utter darkness.

He grinned. "No. Lycurgus would say we are the Master's men. But, yes. He is our leader. If you ask me when he is not around."

I grinned back. Of course. For as long as I have known him, since that day decades ago when our paths improbably crossed in a desert wasteland,

Lycurgus had never compelled the men who served—no, *followed*—him. He was the renegade, the one who followed principles and ideals rather than kings or princes. Because of that very independence, and these unwavering ideals, Lycurgus—one-time Roman general, one-time leader in the Emperor's wars, blood relative to the Emperor himself—never had to pick his men. They chose him. They followed his authority rather than obeyed his orders. And now, it seemed, Lycurgus had found his last ideal to follow. I was anxious to see him again. We had much to talk about.

I stood up. "Let's get going, then." The others rose also, wearily. Elihu shook himself, as if awakening from a dream. "We really did do it," he muttered unbelievingly.

As if agreeing, the cat beyond the fence gave one loud squawk and rustled off into the alley.

"The wagon will be at the lumberyard," the warrior said. "We can walk there in an hour or so. Then a short nap. You have to be ready to go before first light."

"We can't all fit in the wagon," I said.

The man shook his head. "Arrangements have been made."

He turned and began threading his way through the narrow passages that wound among houses and shops, taking us safely away from the main streets. The wind threaded a wisp of cloud over the moon. The cloud thickened, and the light faded out. We moved in darkness, trusting the warrior's instincts as he moved silently through the darkness.

* * *

I had gone into this out of desperation. Too long I had shut myself off—since others thought me odd, I simply agreed and made a habit of it. Avoid others.

I shut myself off on our farm, kept to my chores and my chronicles, and fought the visceral loneliness. Fought against belief.

It was like putting a viper on a leash and pretending I had tamed it.

I have been outside too long.

But it has been necessary. Finding oneself on the outside, for whatever reason—beliefs or unbelief, habits or tradition, looks or skin color; all of which fit my own case—either one can capitulate to beliefs, traditions and appearance, trying to be like everyone else, or one can recognize the difference and cling to that. It is a cry of assertion, sometimes as weak as a whisper—the everlasting *I am*. I have been mouthing it all my life. But it is also the habitude of pride. The cry of "I am" can become the monstrous bellow: I alone.

So too I have walked, wavering, on the edge of these people's beliefs. Truly they have offered me a home; yet I have not entered and taken up dwelling space. My walls, so long in the making—a lifetime's work—have been slow to crumble. But I had begun to understand that even those dearest to me, Taletha first among them, stood on the other side of the wall. We held hands of brick.

It had never been so much that I had been shut out, as that I had not stepped out.

So my insistence on joining this madness—I could be safe on my farm, apart from them—was a stepping over the wall.

But I had not fully crossed. I still had many questions. Who shattered the manacles? Melted the locks? My fear grew from the fact that no one—not one of these comrades—questioned it. They *accepted* it. But such things don't happen! There's the madness. But the real insanity is that I myself saw the shattered manacles. To this I make testimony, even as I try to understand the *why*, the *how*.

Truly, on the other side of the wall that I was crossing lay mystery. On my side lay the safety of routine, albeit with the viper on a leash. On that side mystery, walking in the everlasting unknown. But that walk, at least, was not alone. Here's the paradox. I began, then, to sense—not understand, to be sure—what Taletha meant when she spoke of *faith*. Perhaps it is not to be understood at all. Mystery and madness seemed, as I straddled this invisible crossing line I kept calling the wall, the twin torments of the other side. I stood here with others, who accepted with utter simplicity the mystery of shattered manacles and the madness of hope.

Perhaps the wall was only an invisible line after all.

* * *

The alley passages seemed interminable as we wound through their maze. Save for the occasional glow of lamps in a house, the streets were darkened. We moved past the backside of houses, dodging piles of trash, floating across smooth stretches as if walking in a dream. Then warehouses and shops known only by their blank darkness. I had no sense of direction, yet the guard plunged ahead unfalteringly, stopping only once more to let us catch our breath. We did so in silence, the rush of excitement now dissipated to weariness. When we made one last turn, and threaded our way through the narrow passage that led to the enclosed square of the millyard, we were stumbling like exhausted laborers, half-asleep.

The wagon with its fake load of lumber stood in the yard. The oxen were quartered in the shed, their hooves stomping against the dirt floor.

Another wagon, heavily loaded, stood alongside ours.

The yard hand who had driven the wagon met us, melting out of the shadows.

"Quickly," he said, pointing to the workshed.

"Everyone safe?" Elihu asked.

"Safe and sleeping," murmured the hand. "The fat man is in your house."

"Very well," Elihu said. He turned to us. "You'll sleep in the loft. He'll show you." He waved at the yard hand. "You get in through the mill shed, but it leads to the hayloft of the cattle shed. That way, you have a way out."

"Will they come searching?" asked Taletha.

"It's likely. But probably they won't get this far tonight. Still," he looked around, "we have precautions." The warrior, I noticed, had disappeared. "There will be food and water in the shed."

"You're leaving us?" I asked, even as I realized the question was a foolish one. The risk was far from over.

"They would expect me in my own bed, wouldn't they? Besides, I have an important guest tonight. A major buyer." He pointed to the second wagon.

"Good night," Elihu said. His massive shoulders were bowed and utterly weary as he walked away.

* * *

Taletha, the cook, Doval and I threaded our way through the mill shop, past the long razor-sharp saws, the ungainly vises and braces, and climbed a rickety ladder to a storage loft. A small door opened to the hayloft.

I heard snoring and followed the sound to bodies sprawled in the hay, lying as if clubbed. The prisoners were still sleeping off the effects of the sedative. Napthali lay curled in a fetal ball. The physician snored grandly.

Lycurgus, sitting up, leaned against the wall. He rose at our entrance, embracing each of us, and with a lingering tenderness, I noticed, for Doval. "It's like sleeping in the middle of a beehive," he said with a laugh. "And besides, I couldn't sleep until I knew you all were safe."

I wanted to talk. My mind was still snapping with excitement. Lycurgus sensed it. "We'll have plenty of time to talk later," he said. "It would be best for all of us if we tried to sleep now."

But I couldn't. I lay awake for a long time. And when she rustled in the hay, then got up, and slipped silently toward the doorway, I rose and followed.

* * *

She stood in the foreyard, leaning against the wall of the work shed. Her arms were folded across her breasts, and her head tilted back, looking up at the myriad pinpricks of light that danced now in a black sky. The quarter moon had wearied, broken free of a thin gauze of cloud, and floated low in the southern sky like a lonely boat.

"You called me *Doval*," she said, still looking into the sky. Her face was framed there, silver-hued against night.

"You called me *father*."

She nodded. "It is true, isn't it?"

"Yes, Doval."

"So long ago. You may call me Mary, if you wish. Others do now."

"I will. Forgive me if I slip."

She laughed. "I have nothing to forgive, Elhrain. Only it has been so long, and so much has happened."

"Can you tell me about it?"

She shook her head and smiled at me. "It's not important anymore. I wish you wouldn't ask."

"Okay." Still, I longed for answers. So many years. I still saw her as the young girl. Frolicking by my side with her brother. Happy. Carefree. And I saw her with the bandit's sword at her throat. So many years.

"Understand," she said, "that it was all a darkness. Oh, I would sense certain things, look at something, and I would remember. Hear a voice and fill with longing. I was so lonely." Her voice broke with a choking sound.

I waited, not trusting my own voice.

"But it's gone," she said. Her voice grew stronger. "That's all I want you to understand, Elhrain. It's not only gone, buried, but it's replaced. When I met . . . the Master. It was like a white light . . ."

"Yes?"

She looked up again. "I was the sky. Like the darkness. Only tiny dots of pure light pierced the darkness from time to time. But they hurt. It hurt so much to remember. Like the sky. But then . . . he touched me. And it was like the sun rising in that sky."

I looked into the black vault above. The stars were so cold, so distant, so lonely.

"It grew larger until there was only the purity of the light. The sun, Elhrain. That's what it was like. Like the sun was in me. Like I had swallowed the sun. But it was warm and sweet, and it flooded me. And the loneliness . . . the bad times, they fled. They can't touch me now."

"You're Taletha's friend."

"And sister. We knew. Oh, we knew, Elhrain, from the first moment we set eyes on each other."

"Then you must have known—"

"About you? Of course. Taletha never stops talking about you. How she loves you." Doval shook her head in mock bewilderment.

"Then why didn't you tell—"

"I don't know," she interrupted. "We knew you would find me. It's better this way."

"And you and Taletha? You've been involved in this thing?"

"Yes. From the start. From the very start, Elhrain. There are no secrets between sisters. It has always been part of the Master's plan. That is why I am able to forget the past, because it has been made new. In me."

"I don't understand."

She smiled. "In your own way, I think you do. Or will. You are what he made you, for the purpose he made you. Know that at least. You don't have to be anything other than what you are."

I shook my head.

"Elhrain. I am Mary. But I am still Doval."

She turned to me. Tears that lay in her eyes now fell streaming down her cheeks. "Always Doval," she whispered and met my embrace. "Please hold me, Father. Just please hold me."

My own tears fell on that dark hair enfolded in my arms. Raw, heaving sobs choked me as I clung to her.

Oh, my daughter. I saw the tint of red light in her hair and looked past her to see the sun devouring the darkness in a red line to the east.

Someone stirred behind us. Taletha.

For one moment she wrapped her arms around the two of us. Then she said, "We have to get going."

"Yes," said Lycurgus behind her. "Now for the dangerous part."

CHAPTER TEN

H e was a thick, fuzzy man, waist as round as a waterflask filled, white beard fluffed around a red face. Zophar popped out of the alley leading to Elihu's office/residence, glaring like a slave driver.

"How come the wagons aren't ready?" he thundered. But in his hand he carried a large basket crammed with bread, cheeses and wine.

Of course. The "fat buyer" Elihu mentioned last night. I greeted him with a laugh, which infuriated him.

From the shed, Taletha called, "Good morning, Uncle," her customary greeting for her friend Althea's uncle. Zophar greeted her and permitted himself a chuckle.

"Why am I not surprised?" I asked him.

"Did you think I would be left out? I said I would come, and here I am. Just in time. A second wagon will make the pilgrimage look better. Besides, they can't ride all the way in that blasted cave you made under your lumber."

"Shh, Zophar," Taletha said.

He walked to the ox shed and began ordering the yard hands into action. He blustered about like a short, fat storm brewing.

"He's Napthali's best friend," Taletha offered while we ate a hurried breakfast. "He wouldn't be left out for anything."

The eastern horizon had flared red with false dawn, then darkened.

Now the first sheen of true daylight rose with the sun. Birds began crying noisily overhead.

"Right," I agreed. "Who else can stand to argue theology with the man but Napthali?"

"And he really did pay for the lumber," Taletha said. "Although I have no idea what he intends to do with it. Zophar is known here. He has credentials. Official status. We need him."

"And he has a fat purse," I mused.

* * *

By the sun's rising, the two wagons were moving into the narrow street. In the lead, I drove the wagon with the precious hidden cargo, Taletha next to me on the wagon seat. Secreted within the wooden vault rode Lycurgus, Napthali and the physician. The cook, it turned out, preferred to stay in the city where she had friends to protect her. As we turned onto the street the wagon wheel screeched loudly. I shook my head. We had rubbed grease on the axle, but the hub was far out of true, and the noise started almost immediately. I wish we had had time to fix it properly. But we wanted to pass the gate with the first rush of travelers—just one more wagon setting out on a long journey, getting an early start on the day.

Behind us, Zophar drove the other wagon. Doval rode next to him, wrapped in a well-decorated cloak and an elaborate scarf that both veiled her appearance and also marked her as the wife of a well-to-do merchant.

Zophar held bills-of-lading for both wagons. I was to be his hired hand.

I had told him what I thought of that. Zophar looked at me and bellowed, "And I'm not paying you a penny, Elhrain. Exactly what you're worth as a working man.

"Besides that," he continued, his broad face flaming, "your accent is still as thick as river mud. Five years here and you still can't speak properly."

I told him what I thought of it all in the language of the Beshali, the jungle people south of Kush.

"See," Zophar said. "Still can't talk right."

* * *

Bit by bit, more wagons and pedestrians filled the road. As we neared the western gate, a small line had formed. The guards were checking carefully this morning. We pulled into line and tried to relax. The two oxen stomped impatiently.

We drew nearer. They were checking very carefully. Rifling through loads. Checking loading receipts. The guard had been doubled. Four men posted by the gates, four more walking from wagon to wagon.

We creaked forward. I let my body go limp, breathing deeply. Relax. Be polite, servile. Don't talk.

Just three wagons and a peasant leading two mules ahead of us. A shout behind us.

"Make way." A horse-drawn chariot wound around the line and stopped at the gate. A captain of some sort, dressed in a uniform flashing with shiny metal. Two more guards ran in the wake of the chariot. The guards at the gate seemed to double their intensity under the gaze of the captain, who stood to one side now, watching like a hawk.

Then we were next. Zophar climbed off the wagon behind us and strode puffing like a little potentate to the guard.

"They're both mine," he said, handing over the bills.

For some reason the captain walked over, taking the bills from the nervous guard. The captain studied the documents carefully, silently. Time slowed; minutes clanked like chains.

He looked up. "Ah, yes. Zophar, is it? From Noke."

"Indeed," said Zophar. But the captain looked past him, as if dismissing him.

I willed Zophar to relax. The last thing we needed was him losing his temper. I kept my head down. The hired hand.

"You doing a lot of building in Noke?" asked the captain.

Zophar shrugged compliantly, spreading his hands. "An innkeeper, sir," he said. "Yes, we're busy. Have to add two rooms."

"I see. Yes, I've heard of Noke. You have a lot of traffic there for a small town." His bleak gaze riveted Zophar. I had seen that look before, the glance of absolute disdain. From the lawgivers. "Yes, a lot of traffic," he mused. "Some of it clandestine."

Zophar grew effusive. "About that, sir, I wouldn't know. Innkeeping is an honorable profession, sir."

I glanced away, hoping that Zophar wouldn't overdo it. In that instant I caught sight of an official-looking man on a horse as black as ebony, its muscles quivering with pent energy as it stood perfectly still. The rider held the animal at rein a short distance behind the guards, off to one side. He sat tall and erect in the saddle, his hair and beard as black as the animal he sat upon. Though young, he possessed an imperious air, like the law-givers, but it was different, altogether different. Clearly a person of status, likely some high government official, he immediately impressed me with his quiet authority.

His gaze met mine, and I blinked away, startled and slightly embarrassed at being caught scrutinizing him. Yet, before I turned away, did I see the smallest acknowledgment, a slight smile, an almost imperceptible nod of the head?

"And the woman?" asked the captain. Like the others, he was still unaware of the watching rider.

"Oh, my wife's sister. They were shopping, of course. You know how women are."

Taletha turned her most dazzling smile on the captain. It could melt lead. I gritted my teeth.

The captain hesitated. Then shoved the papers at Zophar and turned his back on us.

The oxen strained at the yokes. The heavy wagons trundled forward. Through the gate. Past it. Freedom!

Then the off-hub screeched horribly as the wheel hit a rut in the road. I sucked in my breath. Not now!

Out of the rut. Another groaning creak of strained wood. Out of the corner of my eye I saw the captain stand in the middle of the road, frowning, hands on hips.

A bit further. Zophar's wagon through the gate. His off wheel hit the same rut. I was hoping for a similar squealing noise. He rode it through soundlessly. At the same moment that the axle of my wagon again emitted a piercing screech.

The captain shouted and motioned. Four guards sprinted from the gate, hauled on the reins of the oxen, bringing us to a stop. When the captain strode toward us, he had a smile on his face. A smile of triumph.

Zophar was climbing down, his face volcanic, suffused with outrage. Or was it all bluster, covering his fear? I felt my stomach drop, creating a whirling sensation inside. Taletha laid one hand on my arm, removed it, remembering. The hired hand.

"Stay right here," the captain commanded Zophar. His words were knife points.

"What is the meaning—" Zophar sputtered.

"The meaning, fat innkeeper, is that last night there was a prison break."

I hunched forward, bracing myself. Yes, I would . . . I could . . . fight them. Maybe Taletha could get away.

"A wagon, it seems, pulled up to the side door. Two of our guards were beaten. But they remember that the wagon had lumber on it. And one wheel squeaked, as the guard said, like the devil singing." The captain laughed.

I noticed movement out of the corner of my eye. The man on the black horse. Lazily he rode forward.

"I wonder," said the captain, looking at our wagon. "I just wonder . . ."

"Captain!"

The officer whirled, looking up angrily at the interruption. Immediately his posture changed when he saw the horseman, who sat poised and calm astride the animal. With one hand the rider idly held the reins, the other cocked at his waist, drawing his silver cloak back over a powerful chest, the fist resting on the hilt of the sword.

"Your Excellency," said the captain. "I was just—"

"Yes. But you have already checked these people through, Captain."

"But the wagon, sir. It squeaks."

"It squeaks, Captain?" And suddenly it seemed the most foolish thing in the world, that a wagon should squeak. "Captain, many wagons squeak." He paused. "And there are many, many wagons in line." He looked down the road. Traffic had backed up into the city. The sun was full and hot now, the people restless.

"But, Your Excellency—"

"I would like you, Captain—if you don't mind—to let people whom you've already checked to get on their way. I would like you, furthermore, to get on with moving this line."

The captain scowled malevolently. When his face turned toward me, it was whiplashed with rage.

"Right now, Captain."

"Yes, Your Excellency." He spat the words out. Snapping a command at the guards, he wheeled on his heel and stalked back to the gate.

The horseman caught my astonished gaze. Again, that slight smile, the dip of his head, and casually, as if it were just one more beautiful morning with birdcalls floating across a sky as blue and pure as if just minted, he rode off.

* * *

We had ridden perhaps an hour when I heard a strange sound winding upward through the stacked lumber on the wagon. Muffled and faint at first. Laughter. They were laughing there in their vault. Louder and free it broke, and it was the most beautiful sound I had heard in days. It infected us. Taletha giggled. I laughed with her. Then threw back my head and pounded laughter at the sky. I laughed until it hurt, echoing the banging inside the vault. I hauled back on the reins at the first opportunity, turning the team into a small copse of trees.

Quickly I jumped down and undid the brace. They tumbled out, covered with road dirt and sawdust, looking like children who had played too long in some field. And laughing. Arms about each other's shoulders.

"We made it," the priest gasped.

We decided to risk it. They rode topside the rest of the day.

Oh, the health of laughter! Foolish, and for no reason save relief and the simple freedom to laugh.

It would be the last I would hear for a long while.

PART TWO
THE PLACE
OF THE SKULLS

CHAPTER ELEVEN

L ike the eagle flying too long in the face of a gale, we needed a
sheltered place to rest out of the wind.

The prison break, the dangers at the gate, the flight from the capital—
now the reunion with old friends and a time to rest.

But that was how things should be. Not how they went.

That first day we traveled late into the night, hoping to put as much
distance between us and the city as possible. The oxen were weary from
a long day's plodding, especially when, by midday, the road began to wind
among the hills. The off-wheel still creaked angrily as we rode. Our pas-
sengers dozed under the hot sun. A cloud of flies hovered over the sweating backs of the oxen.

Toward evening we began looking for a good place to make camp.

The hill country west of the capital was stitched with little side paths
winding off the highway. Perhaps they led to a farmer's house tucked into
a valley among the hills. Often we caught glimpses of vineyards on the
protected slopes of the hills. Perhaps a path led to some northern village.
Or perhaps a trail led to some outlaw camp; for the hills also hid those
who preyed upon travelers. It would not be unusual along this outlying,
wilderness stretch of road to find a body dragged into the weeds along
the ruts worn by wagon wheels. Or to find someone staggering dazed along
the road, stripped of clothing and possessions. Travelers tended to band

together on the road for their own protection, and to seek the confines of a village as nightfall approached.

With the size of our group and our two large wagons, we felt we had little to fear from outlaws. Yet we couldn't tell how far word of the prison break would spread, and we wanted to avoid suspicion. It would be the normal thing for a group our size to stop at a village, stabling the animals and wagons protectively, staying ourselves at some inn.

We couldn't risk it. In the late afternoon hours we searched for some road that would take our wagons off the highway and into the hills. At length we found it, a path turning among rocks, through a stand of trees. We followed it and found a place to camp with a small stream and grass for the animals. Wearily we climbed down, went numbly through the motions of unhitching the oxen, led them to the stream and picketed them in the grass. We dared not risk a fire. We leaned back among the trees, listening to night sounds rise about us. We sat huddled together, unable to sleep, pondering questions that rose like waves while the oxen pulled noisily at clumps of grass.

With the questions, solutions seemed farther out of reach.

For myself, I was restless to get back to the farm and to find again some familiar routines. The longing in itself became a clue to me. I was beginning to understand just how remote anything like routine had become. There comes a moment in nearly any life where one longs for nothing quite so much as the commonplace; such moments arrive when the commonplace seems irrecoverable.

So I gave in. I let the questions come. If no answers appeared, at least I would know where I stood.

*   *   *

The first question was this: Would they pursue us to Noke?

By the end of the day, the prison guards would have completed a sweep of the city. They would be ruthless in their search. Their jobs, if not their lives, depended on it.

Finding nothing in the capital city, where would the lawgivers' men turn? Out of all the little towns that dotted this country, why on earth should they turn to Noke? Could we still find sanctuary at home?

From that first question, others quickly grew. Would home be safe or under attack? Napthali, the village priest, had been taken, cast in prison, scheduled for execution with the others. And what were his crimes? Blasphemy? There was no one more righteous than Napthali. The man had a heart as pure as starlight and as courageous as starlight in utter darkness. Napthali's heart lay with the people, not the law. That was *his* crime.

But how did they know about Napthali? What was the importance of this village priest to the lawgivers from the capital?

Five years prior he had defied the lawgivers by secretly marrying Taletha and me. Of course the lawgivers would have heard. But from whom? Whose tongue could they pry loose for a few coins? Was that the start of Napthali's crimes, disobeying the lawgiver and responding to the needs of the human heart?

A curious thing how these people killed their prophets, their priests, their Messiah—for the crime of loving humanity instead of human rules. Napthali seemed to me, at that moment, precisely like the Messiah. I believe it was then that I began to understand.

For Napthali, religion had become a way of living—caring for the madman, Philip, accepting gift offerings for those people who could not afford them, denying self-interest for the needs of others.

As I thought of the little priest, I began to sense a pattern in events that had all been random to me before. Perhaps Napthali's quiet defiance became known too easily. But by whom? Just to the lawgivers? Or was there an informant in this village—our home—itself? And if so, if there was such a spy keeping watch, how much did this person know? How much did he or she pass along?

I had also begun to wonder, early on the way back, what would be best for Doval. I thought I could not bear to part with her, nor could Taletha. A return to the capital was out of the question. But would she be safe in Noke? Or even out at our farm? Was it fair to have her live forever fearful, thinking that at any moment some captor might turn up around the next corner?

Doval had been a leader in the cause in the capital city, nurturing, directing, working underground in dozens of ways that helped establish the fellowship. In these last months her work had become increasingly subversive. As the persecution had intensified, it had been Doval working with Taletha to set up the escape network. All this time—and I had scarcely been aware of it. But Doval was known, had been arrested and literally had a price on her head.

And what of Taletha, then? I understood now. The lawgiver and his thugs who had come out to *my* farm. Had they come to give warning? Or to arrest Taletha?

I could not bear the thought of running again. Nor of risking Taletha. Then, must we too flee?

Clearly the authorities suspected Noke. Why else would the lawgivers mark this insignificant village for their attention? Their spies, trading information for coins or favors, were everywhere, even in Noke. Whom could we trust? But, I reminded myself, Noke was *not* insignificant, nor innocent. The defiance had been festering in many ways. Noke also bore strategic significance as the first trading town inland from the coast. I was surprised to find myself thinking in terms of warfare. That was what this was—warfare for hearts and minds. Too many questions. And questions bred fear. This rejoicing little band of escapees seemed nervous and insecure that night in the hills. It was very late when we finally gave in to exhaustion and dozed off.

* * *

When we arrived at Noke late the following night, we left the wagon loaded with lumber at Manasseh's shop. The big carpenter came out to greet us, but I sensed something wrong with him. He was subdued, unusually quiet, as he helped us unhitch the oxen. Too weary to unload the wagon, we simply left it in the yard before the carpentry shop, stabled the oxen and went into Meridivel's kitchen, where a bright fire glowed on the hearth.

Perhaps it was our weariness also—we had not slept soundly for days now and moved like drugged people into the kitchen—that made us unaware of the slightest trembling in all of Meridivel's gestures, and of her own silence. Manasseh sat apart while she served us. I remember those things now and regret I had not perceived their own affliction as we sat wearily at the table.

But then when our meal was interrupted, we ignored everything else.

We had not been seated long, crowded into the narrow kitchen while Meridivel passed fresh loaves of bread and platters of cheese about the table. Manasseh stood up and poured wine from a flagon into our cups, and I remember making some forced joke about it not being my wine and asking why he was serving us his second-best. "All out," he said abruptly and sat again by himself beside the fire. But I was hungry then and attacked the food with the others. At a timid knock on the door, we all looked up.

Tomit and Althea entered. Our gladness at seeing them turned swiftly to surprise, then dismay, when they told us what had happened.

During that first night of hiding in the cave above our farm, Tomit had been unable to sleep. He knew the shepherds were watching; still, an unease crept upon him and during the night he slipped outside the cave. Yes, there was a guard—a shepherd—watching. Still he watched. And he had seen three men slinking through a passage in the hills far below. Moonlight that had broken through the clouds that night had revealed them, and they were making their way slowly toward the cave where they hid. Tomit had run back to the cave, aroused Althea and fled with her into the hills.

Liske, we learned, had discovered the shepherd's body after we left for the capital. It had been buried under rocks in the hills.

Tomit and Althea hadn't stopped. No longer trusting the escape route, they had circled back behind Noke and plunged into the desert to find their daughter. It was an act of desperation, by people who thought they had no alternative.

Two young men from the village had tried earlier to track the kidnappers into the desert. The trail had disappeared. The whole thing could have been a random act of violence. Noke was no more immune to banditry and threat than any other village in these unsettled times. And the kidnapping and selling of young women to foreign traders, the exchange taking place along the desert caravan route that ran south of Noke, was still a profitable enterprise. That was the likely story. A story close to us, I reflected, thinking of Doval and Taletha, who had themselves endured such a fate.

But it could also be a part of the pattern of persecution, striking at the very heart of village unity. Destroy the family, and you destroy the town. Capture the children, and you capture a people's hope.

The earlier trackers had found nothing. Nor had Tomit and Althea.

Thoroughly lost in the desert, falling prey to a maze of barrenness, wandering from place to place in widening circles, finally Tomit and Althea had huddled in the shelter of some rocks, out of food, out of water.

They awakened, staring into the blinding glare of the morning sun. And there stood mad Philip—disheveled, frightening, like some desert apparition before them, wild hair flowing about his face, his body burned to the color of old leather where the animal hide failed to cover him. He stood there barefoot, on those burning sands, holding a waterskin in his outstretched hand. Wordlessly, Philip beckoned and led them back. When they arrived at the river bordering Noke he had slipped away into the foliage.

They had been back in Noke for only a day. Now Tomit and Althea were already once more preparing for hiding. It seemed they had no will of their own left, mutely bowing to whatever decision the others made about them, or for them. Worn and gaunt, too weak to pursue their daughter, too distraught to flee.

* * *

Tomit and Althea sat among us that next morning after our arrival back at Noke as we gathered again at the inn to make decisions. They were among us but apart from us. Their faces were haggard, not with the weariness of labor alone, but with that deathlike pallor of hopelessness. The muscles around the mouth were drawn and constricted downward; their eyes focused on little, likely seeing the desert and their daughter more clearly than anything else. Even without tears, they seemed to be weeping, as if they had wept themselves dry.

At the inn we learned a second bit of information no less devastating.

I had suspected something was wrong when I had seen Manasseh and Meridivel upon our return. They had stared hollowly at us, as if seeing strangers. They seemed in shock. But, greeting us upon the successful return of our own adventure, they had not wanted to burden us.

I see this now, looking back, wondering why I didn't have the perception to ask my friend what was troubling him. I regret it. Not until after we related our story that next morning did we hear fully about events in Noke while we were gone.

Liske had felt responsible for the betrayal of Althea and Tomit's hiding place. This much I had sensed already before we had left. How much can any adult assure a child that it is *not* his responsibility?

Some children take upon themselves greater challenges than any adult should have to manage. I don't know why this is, what explains it. Where comes this strange heroism among children in the face of all that's unholy? Why this compulsion to redeem the errors of others? Liske had felt it so.

He and Sarah had been closest of friends. Perhaps this was not surprising, for they both bore some infirmity that marked them as outsiders among the village children—Sarah with her twisted legs, Liske with his crippled arm. Despite the age difference of several years—had Liske always seen himself as her protector?—a kinship as tough as iron had grown between them.

Liske's absence had gone undetected for several days. That was not unusual; he would often be out with the sheep for days at a time. But a fellow shepherd had found his—our—flock wandering untended except for Liske's faithful dog. The shepherd investigated back at our farm, thinking perhaps that Liske had fallen ill. Instead, he found the place vacant. By the time the shepherd got word to the village, Liske had been missing for some days.

Either alternative was bad. Either he too had been kidnapped, or of his own will he had sought to redeem himself by going in search of Sarah.

Manasseh sat morosely, wringing his massive hands, looking lost in confusion while Meridivel huddled helplessly by his side.

When we met that morning after our return, then, it was not a time for rejoicing. It was a time for urgency. A time for decisions and actions.

And all the decisions seemed bad ones, for there were no alternatives. This much was clear. We had to act, and act quickly. We could not afford to keep the escaped prisoners in Noke. To get them out, we would have to rely upon the dangers of the hills. Their safety was our first responsibility.

CHAPTER
TWELVE

W hile we met that morning in Zophar's inn, we took precautions. Trusted young men of the village kept watch. We had an escape route planned toward the river. But we also needed answers to that storm of questions. We needed plans that would give direction instead of just a way out.

None so far was satisfactory.

We agreed that some of the fugitives would leave that night for the coast. Just who would leave, we had not yet determined. Althea and Tomit? Old Napthali, surely. There was no suspicion turned on Manasseh and Meridivel. Not yet. What of the physician? And what of Taletha, Doval, Lycurgus and me?

We would attempt the escape through the hills by the old route. If the hills were not being watched, we could get to the coast and safety within days. Arrangements could be made by sympathizers there—a new life.

While we were discussing the hill route, I noticed the odd silence Zophar kept. He seemed to be struggling with something, his white head bent intently. When he stood up abruptly, it took us all by surprise. His face was redder than usual, but not with anger or anticipation.

He opened his mouth as if to speak, but no words came. His face reddened further. *He is ashamed,* I thought. His gaze grew bleak. Embarrassment stood like a stranger in those eyes.

We were awkwardly silent at the spectacle. "No," Zophar said. He fought the word out as if dredging it from somewhere deep within him. A harsh, guttural croak of denial. Then, "No. You can't go that way."

The blustery, proud man stood weeping, his shoulders shaking uncontrollably. For a long moment no words came. Then, "It's my fault," he croaked. "I'm responsible. It's all my fault."

Althea moved to her uncle's side. She reached out a hand tentatively. He was, after all, Zophar, denier of emotion, his tears notwithstanding. "Whatever on earth do you mean, Uncle?"

Zophar sank to a bench. His tears were streaming now, as if some dam had burst. The dam was himself. He bent his head, kneading his temples with his fists. He wiped his nose on the sleeve of his garment, the way a child would.

"Always," he muttered, "always I talk too much."

He fought for words. The room was uncomfortably silent.

"There was a stranger here. At the inn. This was weeks ago. He asked questions. He *knew* so much; I thought he was one of us. I . . ."

"You told him about the smuggling route?" Manasseh asked. He didn't hide the outrage in his voice.

Zophar nodded. "I didn't mean to. It's just . . . he asked these questions. I don't know what I answered. I talked, talked too much."

Manasseh stood, dumbstruck. "It wasn't Liske, then."

"What do you mean?" I asked.

"It was obvious," Manasseh said. "They *knew!* They knew, you see. It was clear. And I thought Liske had—"

"That Liske had told them?"

"Yes. I . . . I even accused him."

I could well imagine. I fought to control myself, the words I wanted to say.

"All my fault," muttered Zophar. "Just a big windbag. Oh, Liske . . . I let him take the blame."

"What do we do?" pleaded Meridivel. Her voice was plaintive, a thin wail.

"Find him," Manasseh hissed. And we stood there silently, wondering *how.*

* * *

Lycurgus had been silent throughout the morning, perhaps sensing that these were private decisions, personal revelations. Like me, he was the outsider.

I had known Lycurgus longer and far better than anyone here. But when I looked at him, I no longer saw the Lycurgus of the past. I saw a man grown much older for one thing. His body was gaunt from imprisonment and bore the deep purple marks of countless beatings. I comprehended, then, the torture that this one-time elite legionnaire must have suffered from the common rabble of guards who loathed any authority. My heart sickened with the understanding.

He saw me watching him, and his eyes twinkled. No, Lycurgus may have been beaten, but never broken. And he wouldn't be until the spirit that shone now in those predatory eyes was altogether quenched. What I saw when I looked at him was a lion caged.

"And you, Lycurgus?" I asked. "What do you think?"

Suddenly every head swiveled to him. He sat on the floor, leaning against the wall, knees drawn up and arms resting easily upon them. Those forearms were still thickly corded with muscle. Streaks of gray tinged his beard, and a bruise rose across his cheekbone, ending in a puddle of mottled, multicolored flesh that darkened his left eye.

He smiled slowly. A *lion caged*, I thought again.

"I think," he said slowly, "that we *should* find them."

"*Them?* Who?" Manasseh said. Every eye riveted on the man. I think we all felt it—a sense of possibility. We needed to believe in the possible again, then to act upon it.

Lycurgus stood up, favoring one leg. He looked at Tomit and Althea. "Your daughter," he said.

"But we've tried! We've been there. In the *desert!*" Tomit's voice was a wail. Althea laid a hand on his arm.

"And your son," Lycurgus said to Manasseh and Meridivel. They nodded eagerly, not even certain to what they assented. Possibility alone.

Lycurgus spoke slowly, as if remembering something from a dream. "We must act quickly," he said. "But I don't think they're lost. Not yet."

"Why?" Tomit insisted. Hope flickered across his face, muscles quivering.

"Something the man in the prison was saying," Lycurgus said. "It's starting to make sense to me. You see, I thought they were just the words

112

of a lunatic, but . . . no, I think he was referring to a place. A terrible place. One that drove him . . . well, to the state he was in."

"The Place of the Skulls," I said. The words thundered in my mind. "The prisoner. The one who died. He was saying something about—"

"Yes, a skull. Or skulls," said Lycurgus.

"Listen," I turned to Taletha. "Do you remember? Before we left Noke. I can see it now. That man in the street? Philip? He was screaming at us. 'Beware,' he said—"

" 'The Place of the Skulls,' " finished Taletha carefully.

"I think it really is a place," said Lycurgus. "And I think it is a sign, not an accident."

"Wait a minute," said the physician. "What is this? The Place of the Skulls?" His features were intense, focusing keenly on Lycurgus.

"In the prison, Doctor. Just before he died, one of the prisoners kept screaming that. It was a nightmare, I thought. But then, I remembered I had heard of it. Or some echo of it."

"Well you might," said the physician evenly. "I shared a cell with this man. He was ill, perhaps mad. I did my best to care for him but could do little. He spoke incoherently, mostly of this place."

He turned restlessly, one thin hand pressed against his forehead. "But," he said, "I too have heard of it before." He spoke slowly, as if examining his own thoughts. "Listen to me. The task of science is to apply knowledge. I am a scientist, a doctor, so I apply knowledge to heal. The enemy of science is not ignorance, people. Rather, it is knowledge of a contrary sort—knowledge applied in darkness, not to heal but to destroy.

"There are rumors," he continued, "that to the south of the capital, through a land more bitter and desolate than you have ever dared dream—"

"I have lived in the desert, Doctor," I reminded him.

He shook his head. "This is not the same. This is a land afflicted by darkness. It lies beyond a lake that burns in its own bed, emitting poisons into the air that have killed the ground for miles around. There the rocks are eroded by wind and weather to grotesque shapes. They have eyes, some say, that watch the traveler. Mouths that devour them."

"Skulls," whispered Taletha.

"Yes. No one willingly travels there," the physician said. "Caravan routes skirt it for miles. Yet some have been *brought* there. Few have survived it. Oh, the stories . . ." He shook his head.

"It is said," he continued, "that what we fight in the lawgivers is not their persons, their flesh." He paused as if unwilling to say what followed. I felt a shiver leap down my spine on cold feet. "It is a spirit of darkness that lives in them. And," he added, "there are places on this earth given to that darkness. Where the darkness lies caged, you might say. But it is a power that breaks free in dozens of tendrils, reaching out to afflict humanity.

"They say," he finished, "that one such place is the Place of the Skulls. There dwell wizards who keep the darkness alive. There are the demons of darkness." He shook his head.

"But why," Althea's voice was a whimper, "do you think Sarah is there? And Liske?"

"I'm not sure," Lycurgus said. "I have traveled in many lands. As has Elhrain. And it has always struck me that some places—it's hard to describe—are especially touched by the sacred. It may be a garden. It may be a waterfall, or a forest, or even a stretch of desert. And it seems hallowed ground. But in some places the very earth breathes desecration, and such ground seems held in bondage to evil."

"But what has that to do with—"

Lycurgus lifted a hand wearily. "In such places I have also noted that there's a rage for power. I can't explain it more than that. But the powerless suffer. The children, Althea, suffer. I don't like saying this; it's simply what I have seen. The children are pawns to the powerful, bartered like objects. Children are a commodity, to be kept in bondage, to be sold into slavery, to be used. I know I paint a grim picture. But even here one hears rumors of the slave-trading of children."

Doval shivered.

"No one," Lycurgus continued, "has ever been sure just where they're taken. Someone disappears. 'Into the desert,' people say. But I have long wondered—"

"We have to find this place," Tomit interrupted. "We have to know."

"That is what I have been thinking," Lycurgus said, "and if we find it, we have to rip it out by the roots. To restore the land."

"We?" Meridivel asked.

"There are two ways," Lycurgus said, "to do this thing. One is to march in with an army. But they would know, wouldn't they? And they would fade into their maze of darkness like shadows themselves. The other way is to come with but a few—a handful who know the desert." He looked meaningfully about the circle.

"Count me in," said the little priest forcefully.

"No," Lycurgus chuckled. "You'll be leaving, Napthali. We can't rely on the hills anymore. We know that; I suspected it before. Nor you, Althea. Nor you, Tomit. The desert is a brutal place."

"I owe it to you," Zophar said. "It is my fault."

"We need you here, Zophar. You have to hold things together. And let's have no more talk of *fault*. That is settled."

I looked around the small group, sensing the stillness, the uncertainty. "We are not so young anymore, are we, Lycurgus?" I said.

He chuckled. "I think we have one more adventure in us yet, old friend."

"And I," said Taletha.

"And I," said Doval quickly.

Lycurgus nodded.

Manasseh stood up. "I must come. I owe it."

"That is a dangerous thing, Manasseh. Owe it?"

"To Liske. To myself. I'm coming."

Lycurgus shook his head ruefully. "I understand your desires, Manasseh. We will do our best to fulfill them. But, no. You're not coming with us."

A flame of anger seared Manasseh's face. The room was suddenly hot with tension. "Who are you to tell me what to do, soldier? He's my son!" The carpenter's huge fists were balled. Even Meridivel stood back from him.

Lycurgus smiled wearily. "Because we need you elsewhere, Manasseh." He shook his head. "You know the hills are jeopardized. We can't trust them. We—this cause, Manasseh, needs you. The only hope is to get the fugitives out quickly. That means by the highway, using the wagon with the load of wood. You'll be yourself, Manasseh, a carpenter trading to the coast. You've done it many times."

Manasseh's face struggled. His fist clenched and unclenched.

"He's right, Manasseh," I said. "We need *you* for that. And each of us— Doval, Taletha, Lycurgus and I—knows the desert. We need you here. And . . . we may never return."

Angrily Manasseh shook his huge shoulders. Then he nodded agreement. "Find him," he murmured.

"The Lord willing, we will," Lycurgus said. He laid a hand on the carpenter's shoulders and smiled comfortingly into his uncertainty.

"Then it is decided," Lycurgus said. "What of you, Physician?"

We all looked at him, who now seemed to have been a part of this circle forever. He looked accustomed to listening more than speaking, his narrow, intelligent face soaking up information, reflecting on it. Yet he had proven himself a man of courage on more than one occasion, one disdainful of the proud and arrogant, and more than ready to side against them.

He stood now, leaning against the wall, a musing smile on his lips.

Manasseh turned to him. "Yes. And you, Physician? What happens to you?"

The doctor's smile widened as he looked at us, catching each person's eye, as if weighing that person and finding him or her a worthy friend. One had the idea that not much in this life could startle him, but also that he was always looking for something that might. He shook his head slightly. "I'm afraid," he said, "that I can follow neither alternative. Neither flight to the coast nor this venture into the desert. Although it intrigues me. Indeed it does. I wish you well."

"You can't go back, surely?"

"Oh, I could. My being in the dungeon was as much my design as anyone's."

Taletha nodded. "It was the doctor's mad scheme. With our people being cast into prison and facing death, the doctor wondered what it was like."

"What kinds of stresses on mind and body, actually," the physician finished. "So I put myself in the wrong place at the right time, taunted certain people and got the expected result. It was the captain who said to me, 'Well, if you defy us for putting people in the dungeon, then you'll have a taste of it yourself.' It went exactly as I planned."

"You could have been left there to rot," Manasseh said.

"Well, I did have safeguards." He chuckled.

"What do you mean?" I asked, thinking that he looked considerably more stable than his so-called plan. I couldn't imagine anyone *wanting* to go to prison.

"Do you remember that young man who met you at the gate? As you were leaving the city?"

"Yes." We all remembered. I could see him on the black horse—authoritative, decisive. What would have happened had he *not* come?

"I didn't see him, of course, since I was squashed up in that torture chamber you designed. Napthali falling asleep and lying all over me. Lycurgus hunched up like a caged animal. Anyway, I was nearly certain he would come. And had none of this worked out, he would have been my safeguard."

"Yes, and who is he?" I asked.

"Well, he is effective behind the scenes," the physician said, waving a hand. "And I shouldn't say too much about him. But it is enough to know that he too is at one with the heart of the Master. Called, to be sure. In this case to a position of power. He is in a position of very high authority."

"Indeed," Zophar said. "That captain nearly licked his boots."

The physician laughed. "He had good reason. Let it suffice to call him Theophilus, one of my dearest friends."

"Theophilus," mused Zophar. "The name means something."

"Yes, of course. That's why I said let it suffice. Theophilus means 'friend of God.' "

We sat a moment, reflecting. Then Zophar stood. "So you're going your own way now, Physician?"

"The Master's way. Not my own."

"Distrust it. You're not the first scholar to wake up one morning and think something has been missed. All of a sudden you have an urge for adventure, an excitement addiction."

"It's not that. Although that may be part of it."

"Sure. You've had one taste of danger and developed an appetite."

The physician laughed. His lean, ascetic face, so forceful and scholarly, wrinkled up in delight. "You have quite the gift for diagnosis, Zophar."

"You'll grow out of it, young man. It happens to everyone. One morning they think they've missed something, so they go out and do something very foolish. All you've missed is being a fool."

"I confess there's something to it—this adventure wish. And I confess I have missed something by searching for it in books and science."

"Good," snorted Zophar triumphantly. I smiled, glad to see Zophar restored to his old, needling, cantankerous self.

"*But* that's only part of it," the physician added. "The larger part of it is this sense—odd term for a physician—of being *called* to do something."

Zophar rolled his eyes magnificently.

"Yes. I'll even admit to being a fool, you see. For what I want to do has no place in logic. I'm going with the apostle. We're going to spread the word of the Master's way. Here's what I have come to understand, Zophar. There's a hunger for health among people. All people. But there's also a hunger for healing. It's a raw need that science doesn't touch. Do you understand the difference? A soul—yes, I use that profane word— a soul is dying. A soul requires healing. I understand now. I have been called not just to be a physician, but a healer. So I'll be going soon."

"I've heard about this man," Manasseh said. "This man you call the apostle. He made quite a noise, for evil and for good, among our people. Then he went away."

"Yes," the physician said. "For three years. Into Arabia. It was necessary, you see. He had to nurture, to learn and understand, this call in him."

"The apostle." Zophar grunted. He made the word sound like a curse. "I've heard of him also. You don't want to go with that criminal. Calls himself an apostle now, as if . . . humph!"

"*Was* a criminal," the physician said. "Even so, he thought he was doing the right thing."

"Oh, and he did the right thing, didn't he?" Zophar said. "How many people suffered by his hand? Now he wants to ally himself with those he persecuted? Shameful, that's what it is."

The physician grinned. One gathered that he had heard this argument before. "The way I heard it," he said, "the Master called *him* to an alliance."

"Yes, yes. I've heard the story," Zophar snorted. "Sounds like some Roman claptrap with visions and blindness and whatever. It's a good thing he left these parts, I tell you, or there would be some hard questions to answer."

I couldn't believe this was the same man who only moments before had been admitting his own misdeeds. But that was Zophar—the man thrived on contention.

"Uncle," Althea murmured gently, "don't get so upset. What do you care, as long as he works *for* the Master now?"

"It's not fair!" Zophar thundered. He smacked his fist against the table, sending small bits of parchment flying, and winced at the pain. "It's not fair. Besides, he doesn't like anybody. Someone like that . . . he should like people."

Manasseh shook his large head in bewilderment. "Doesn't like anyone? I'm not a profound man, Zophar, but—and don't be so quick to agree with that—maybe 'liking' isn't what this is about. All of us have had to do things we haven't 'liked' to do. Especially the Master himself. And as for fair? Well," he spread his hands as if to explain, "fair? How does one begin?" Instead he shrugged his large shoulders and said, "As I say, I'm a simple man. But I think it is proof of everything the Master taught that the criminal is now the apostle." He looked straight at the physician. "If you go, go with the grace of God."

"The only way," acknowledged the physician.

"Do you trust him? I mean, a person who changes like that?" Zophar snapped his fingers.

"Trust? Maybe so, probably *because* he changed like that. Fearful? Yes, I'm a bit afraid of him. Always have been. You see, we are natives of the same town. Didn't you know that? I've known him—*of* him—for years. Talk about a compulsion for adventure. He always went to the extremes. And now he will be in the cause, also. And I'll go with him."

Doval stood up. She walked to the physician, looking small and willowy before his long frame. He smiled down on her. She reached out her arms and embraced him.

"I'll miss you," she said. "Of course, go. But I'll miss you. You believed in me. Even when . . ."

"Hush." He placed a finger on her lips. "It was *you* who guided *me*. Always."

* * *

"Then it is settled," Lycurgus said. "Agreed?"

He looked about, catching each person's gaze. Taletha. Doval. Me. He came to Manasseh and shook his head. "I wish you well," he said. "It's a dangerous voyage to the coast." His gaze continued. "Zophar, you will stay."

"I know. I am not fit for the desert."

"It may be that none of us are. But we will have need of someone in authority here. They *will* come looking, you know. And the rest of us—we will begin preparing immediately. The sooner we leave, the better."

Instantly, we began dividing responsibilities—supplies, contacts, transportation.

The physician drifted toward the door. He caught my glance and smiled at me. It seemed to me a smile of pity, for one going to his doom.

CHAPTER THIRTEEN

Lycurgus's shoulders were still broad and powerful, his muscles ridging the loose desert cloak. His hair was flecked with gray, with two small silver patches arching back from the temples over his ears. He looked like one of his old gods, face bleak but defiant, turned already by the sun to deep brown. His eyes probed the valley before us and the ridge of purple rock in the distance like a predator.

I stood several paces behind him. The early dawn touched the distant rocks with a faint golden sheen. The darkness in the valley seemed momentarily to deepen. We were on the seventh day of our journey and had covered roughly the distance of the two-day trip to the capital by ox and wagon. But we had kept well off the main thoroughfare, skirting the northern fringe of the desert to avoid people, moving carefully during the early morning and the evening hours. Now we were about to cross over. There would be no need for secrecy. Our enemy henceforth was the desert.

Lycurgus did not turn when he spoke; he stood looking out over the valley.

"Soon we'll be in its belly," he said. "Are you ready, Elhrain?"

I shrugged, even if he couldn't see me standing behind him. "It has to be done," I said.

Glancing over his shoulder, Lycurgus chuckled softly. "Does it?" he asked. "We could ignore everything, you know. Pretend it isn't there. We could be safe."

"I suppose. But we're into it now, aren't we? Whatever *it* is."

"The adversary, Elhrain. That's what it is. Darkness to light. Desiccation to growth. The desert to farmland. It's the adversary. The only reason we go to meet it is because it thinks it is safe out there. Untouchable. Ignored, it will spread its dark wing over this land, over all lands. It will slide its dry claws into the heart of the land. And squeeze."

"You sound like a poet, Lycurgus. Or a philosopher."

His laugh was a harsh bark. "And you know better." He turned around. His face was dark against the rising sun, but I thought he was smiling.

"Yes," I said. "I know better."

Lycurgus nodded. "Tonight we will sleep in beds," he said. "But they will be our last. We have people in the cause who will protect us tonight."

"Where?"

"A town called Bethlehem. Just south of the capital. Oddly enough, it is the town of the Messiah's birth."

"I thought he was born in the capital. That's what the records said."

Lycurgus shook his head. "No. I too have learned to read the records. But it appeared in a later prophecy than you probably had. The least of the villages. How fitting."

"You jest."

"Not at all. God ungodded himself—right there, in a cattle stall. Only your Magi acknowledged him as king then, you know. They were the only ones . . . on earth."

"And you? How do you see him?"

"Oh, as much more than king. For the ungodded was, for all that, God."

"It doesn't make sense."

"No. It doesn't. But it's true, nonetheless. And that's why I believe, Elhrain. Because it's mystery that compels my faith, rather than my fear."

I snorted. "You afraid?"

"Oh, yes. Right now I'm afraid of the desert. What we might find there. I'm glad you're along."

I thought about it. I'm not sure I was glad I was along. Yet—here's the mystery for me—I had freely chosen, and there is no other place I would rather be. Even if it were to be the end of us all. How different, I thought, from the way I had set out from Babylon all those years before, pursuing a Messiah who only lived in prophecies. No wonder the lawgivers were so opposed. If the prophecies had in fact been fulfilled, how terribly dangerous that Messiah was to them. So they believed the prophecies, but not that they could indeed be fulfilled.

"Then," I said, after a moment of reflection, "that's why you didn't want Manasseh along, right? You didn't, did you?"

Lycurgus chuckled. "So now you can read my mind? You're right, though. The last thing we needed was someone with a personal vendetta. I have learned that, at least, in my military life."

"I think there's more to it than that."

"Yes?"

"I think it was for Meridivel. Look at us. You, me. Doval and Taletha. Beyond each other, what ties do we have? Only each other. You don't think we're coming back, do you?"

The affectionate look on Lycurgus's face changed to one of sadness. His voice was soft. "You read my mind too well, Elhrain. But I am *not* ready to say that yet. Let's say only that I recognize the risk."

We walked back to our sheltered campsite. Our blanket rolls lay scattered under a large tree. "Tonight, Elhrain. A soft bed."

"Just where, though? In the cattle stall?"

He laughed. "Oh, we'll do much better. Someone named Benjamin. And his wife. And some children, I hear."

"How do we know where to find it?"

"I have no idea."

"Then . . ."

He winked at me. "Then they'll find us. At least that's what I'm told. Have faith, Elhrain."

* * *

Children! Children everywhere. And if it was not quite a cattle stall, it was not altogether a great deal larger.

Our guide had not met us, but in fact had slipped up from behind as we neared Bethlehem. He had been trailing us for some time without our notice. Suddenly he walked by our side. It was Taletha whom he approached as our leader. Again those phrases, sign and countersign. But there really was little need. We had been traveling well off the highway and had seen no one but farmers, and those from a distance.

He was a lanky, grinning young man, who couldn't even stop smiling through the password process. Life seemed enormously funny to him.

"Then you will take us into the city?" Taletha had asked.

"No room," he said with a grin. He tried to bow, but stumbled slightly and thought it was enormously funny. "Never could do that!" he said. "Bowing! Have to learn how."

"Then don't do it now," Taletha said.

"But for you! You . . . I practiced it for you." And he burst into a fit of laughter. Then as quickly, he began walking ahead of us, shaking his head, chuckling to himself. Taletha caught my glance of surprise, shrugged and followed.

"Oh," he called over his shoulder. "Outside Bethlehem. No, no, no . . . not in the city itself. Benjamin's house!"

"Whatever you say," I muttered.

*　*　*

Benjamin's house was on the outskirts of this little dot of a town no larger than Noke. The house was a true home, packed to the walls with adults and children—a hubbub of people. The oven, cut into the brick wall of the kitchen, glowed like a furnace around a huge kettle that flooded the hot room with the scent of lamb stew. Children dotted the floor like litter, playing games, laughing, fighting.

We were hardly inside the door when one man wrung my hand in welcome and with the other handed me a diaper-swaddled baby. I recoiled in embarrassment, but in an eyeblink he was into the crowd. He grinned over his shoulder and shouted, "I have some chores to do. Back soon. See Naomi if you have trouble with the little rascal."

Trouble! I still held the tyke at arm's length. He was heavy. Close to a year old. I cradled him awkwardly. One pudgy hand reached up and slapped my nose. No, he grabbed my nose in a chubby little hand and hung on for dear life. Who was Naomi? Four, six women in this jammed, laughing madhouse.

Heavy indeed. His diaper was heavy. I felt the gooey wetness against my arm. The child—this infant—pulled my nose painfully as if to remind me. I brushed the little hand aside. The boy giggled, flung out a little fist and grabbed hold again. He drove his little finger up one nostril a get a better grip.

Diapers! Where was Naomi? The mother, I trust.

I tapped a woman on the shoulder. "Naomi?"

"Outside. Getting Tabitha."

"And who is Tabitha?"

"Her daughter. Her baby. Suanna is showing her the goats."

"I thought this was her baby."

The girl leaned forward, looking closely. "He is. This is Aaron." She looked at me, red-faced and grinning. "He likes your nose," she said.

I brushed the little hand away again. "He needs a diaper."

She wrinkled her nose. "Yes, he does." She pointed to a corner of the room where a stack of folded cloths lay piled.

"But . . ." Her back was to me.

Taletha! Ah, there she was, bent over the kettle, helping one of the children with a bowl of stew. The noise here! The cacophony of children's voices. How could anyone think!

"Taletha," I growled.

"Yes, husband." Her eyes danced. I knew that tone. Dangerous. She giggled like a little girl.

"It . . . *he* needs a diaper," I pleaded. I held the baby toward her. Suddenly it bellowed, a huge throaty wail! This . . . this baby had lungs like a bull calf. The unholy noise shattered my ears. Its face grew purple. Out of desperation I held him to my chest, whereupon the little fist clamped over my nose again. The crying ceased like stopped water. How can it do that? The diaper felt heavy and sodden against my chest.

Taletha pointed at the stack of diapers and ladled stew for another waiting child. "Clean ones are over there," she said.

I had to do it myself?

I wandered to the pile, laid the infant down in a couple of feet of clear floor space. The little hand flailed around, desperately seeking my nose. I saw a little carved wooden cow, some child's toy, lying on the floor and pried it into the baby's fist. He studied the cow, made a few tentative bites at its head, then, as I bent to the squishy mess in the baby's diaper, began cracking it against my head.

"This kid belongs in a barn," I muttered as I dabbed at the mess with a rag. The baby kicked, sending a clot of mess sprinkling up my forearm.

"He likes it when you sing," someone said.

I swiveled desperately. Naomi? No, it was a little girl, about four, studiously watching my work. I had gotten the sodden diaper off, and was trying to clean the glop from between my fingers before putting the clean one on.

"Sing?" I said.

"Yes. Daddy sings."

I gritted my teeth. Where was daddy *now?* "I don't know how to sing," I admitted through clenched teeth.

"Oh. Then I'll sing for you."

And she did, voice croaking loudly about some sheep on the hillside with their little lambs.

I worked furiously while the baby smiled benevolently to the song. The wooden cow stopped beating on my head. Almost done.

Someone placed a bowl of water by my side.

Taletha smiled at me. "Nice job, husband. Don't forget to wash up." She wrinkled her nose at the mess on my forearm.

"Here," I said. Too late; she was back with the children.

I thanked the little girl. "You want him?" I asked.

She shook her head. "Now you walk him," she said. "His name is Aaron."

Yes, of course. I lifted the little child and nestled him in what I thought would be a comfortable position, holding him like delicate pottery. Then closer to my chest, his head on my shoulder. I walked him. A little hand reached up, brushed my nose, latched onto my beard. The fingers caught there, held on, little fingers brushing it like silk.

Softly, tremendously embarrassed, I tried to sing. Only harsh croaking sounds came out. I coughed. The baby started, then laid his head on my shoulder.

I walked in small circles, threading my way among little bodies. The baby breathed softly in my ear, his breath a warm, loving sigh.

When a woman, holding a very young infant, stood smiling before me, I did not want to give the baby up.

"Naomi?" I said.

"Yes," she said. "Thank you. I needed extra arms tonight."

Her husband came beside her, holding the hand of a little girl. He nodded politely. "Sorry, I've been getting the mules together for you."

I thanked him, although I had no idea for what. Reluctantly I handed his sleeping son to him and watched them leave.

Others left, group by group. They did not seem so many now. The house felt quiet, peaceful, as if in a sort of afterglow left by an explosion of noise. The adults ate quietly while Benjamin and Ruth's two children cleaned up toys.

It was not a bed exactly that Benjamin led us to. Doval slept in a spare bed in their house, one of the children's it turned out. Lycurgus left with another couple to spend the night with them. Benjamin led Taletha and me to the barn, and I groaned. Another night in a hay mound. I would prefer the open spaces.

But in the hayloft they had made a little room, divided by a linen curtain. Nestled in the hay lay a boat of pillows, as if neighbors had contributed them. So many there were. Covered in silk and linen. It was very much like sleeping quarters in Babylon, where silk pillows lay fluffed up everywhere. I wondered if they knew; I was profoundly touched by it. Across the pillows lay blankets, handsewn, warm and comfortable.

We nestled there among the pillows, held in each other's arms.

"When we come back," Taletha murmured, "I would like to stay here."

I smiled and nodded. Her hair lay against my cheek, her small body curved to mine. I stayed awake a long time, enjoying the warm scent of the barn and the touch of my beloved beside me.

* * *

"Aren't you afraid for the children?" Taletha was asking. We sat in the predawn hush of the kitchen, before the children awakened. Before us lay fresh bread and goat's cheese. A small fire crackled in the hearth.

"We have people watching all the time," Benjamin said. "And, of course, with the capital this close we keep pretty well informed. Eyes and ears are everywhere. Out here, everyone knows each other. We are used to watching out for one another. Each child belongs to everyone. It has always been that way." He handed the bread to Lycurgus, who broke off another enormous piece with a grin.

"Still," I said, "we could say much the same about Noke. But there we are under attack. They have taken a child. Another . . . well, we think he went to find her. They were friends."

Benjamin nodded. "So we have heard. We are very careful. Maybe the darkness will fall upon us too. But until then, you see, we refuse to submit. We will rejoice."

"No," said Ruth. "I think the Lord has placed a net about us. He has kept evil at a distance. For that we are grateful. Because of that we rejoice."

"May it be ever so," Taletha murmured.

"True," agreed Ruth. "That is our prayer. Let all who take refuge rejoice."

"Let them ever sing for joy," Doval added.

With a smile, Benjamin said, " 'Though the hosts of my enemy encamp against me.' "

I said nothing, wondering at it all. Through the east window I saw pink light fuzz the horizon. Toward the desert. Toward the enemy.

We ate quietly. After a time Ruth said, almost casually, "But it is not only because of the two children that you are going."

Lycurgus nodded. "The darkness there has a heart. I want to find it—and rip it out. Then I will rejoice." He stood. "Do you have the weapons?"

Benjamin stood also. "They'll be here in a minute. Adoniram has kept them. No one would suspect Adoniram. They'll be coming with the mules."

"Weapons?" I asked. "Mules?"

"Yes," Lycurgus said. "Weapons. You may take them if you choose. But remember, Elhrain, I am a soldier. I am not called to go into this empty-handed."

I nodded. I would do without them. Whatever my calling, it was not to arms. I had seen too much of dying. "And the mules?"

"Someone will guide us into the desert. Then we go afoot."

"Why not keep the mules?"

Lycurgus shook his head. "It would be easier, true. Also sloppier. For one thing, you look at the land differently afoot. You live in it then, learning to read signs. We don't know where they are. Riding on mules, one tends to ride past the signs. But also, if we have to rely on anything in *our* power, it will be stealth. Remember, I'll be the only one armed, and I am no longer a young man."

"Wrong," said Doval. "I also will be armed."

Lycurgus grinned. "I thought so," he said.

* * *

The lanky, laughing boy appeared at the door. He was still wound up like a child's wooden top—dizzy with excitement. "The mules are on the way," he announced. "Samuel's bringing them from Adoniram's farm." I took it that we were all supposed to know Samuel. The lad was an announcer, the village news magnet, who knew everyone and their business.

"And," he added, "did you know there's a man at the gate? Really big man? Red hair? I said hello to him, and he didn't say anything. Just stood there." Then, "A really strange man," he murmured.

"A big man?" Benjamin said.

"So much for security," I muttered. Taletha elbowed me.

Benjamin heard me. "Oh, he would be safe, whoever he is."

"Your guards would have screened him?" Lycurgus asked.

"That, yes." Benjamin shrugged. "And the Lord."

I stifled a snort. "Well, let's see who—"

Manasseh stood in the doorway. A strange man indeed. "I want to come along," he said.

"Why don't you come in, first?" Lycurgus said.

Manasseh came to the table, sitting nervously. Instantly, bread and milk and cheese appeared before him. He hesitated, head down, then began eating. He ate like he was feeding a fire inside.

Lycurgus chuckled. "They are safe, then?"

Manasseh nodded, swallowing a mouthful. "We made it to the coast without difficulty, driving straight through. Yes, they're safe."

"Hmm. Meridivel agrees with this?"

Manasseh stared blankly for a moment. Again, he nodded and finished the last of the warm milk. "Yes," he said. "She agrees."

"Well," Lycurgus said, looking at us, "we may have need of the carpenter's strength."

Manasseh answered eagerly. "I may come? I have to do this, do you understand? Atone. Liske is my son."

"Yes. But not for atonement, Manasseh. To aid us. As we say. As *I* say."

He nodded, but his hands knotted dangerously.

"So, tell me. How on earth did you get here on time?"

"I was prepared to follow. Once Meridivel agreed. She knew, you see, she understood that I had to . . . I have to try. So I drove straight back from the coast, arriving the following night. Then—I knew you would be taking a route off the highway, that it would be slow and careful. So . . . I ran."

"You ran!"

"Yes, during the night. Along the highway. No one saw me."

"How did you know where to go?"

"Zophar told me. Then, on the outskirts of the city, one of the watchers spotted me. He stopped me, and two others came. At first I thought they were, you know, the others. But they quizzed me and at last led me here. I slept in the pasture last night."

"And now we have to go."

"I'm ready," Manasseh said.

"Yes, Manasseh," Lycurgus answered. "I believe you are. So are we all. And," he added, "we may be grateful for this carpenter's strength in the end. So, thank you, Manasseh."

CHAPTER
FOURTEEN

B ethlehem lay on a demarcation between fertility and aridity, between life and death. To the west, fertile hills tumbled in gentle
rolls of plotted and pieced landscape. To the east, towering like savage
brown lumps, rose the wilderness mountains, a land of drought braved
only by nomadic shepherds who somehow knew where small pools of
water lay hidden in shadowy hollows. Beyond those eastern hills lay a sea
that boiled in its own poisonous bed—a sea of utter sterility, thick with
salt brine and surrounded by vapors. It was a place of death, a place to
avoid.

This was the hidden backside of Taletha's "promised" land. It made me
wonder if the term was a cruel joke.

In an instant the green hills latticed with grape vines and the rolling
plains divided into farmland and pasture seemed to disappear. One moment, cresting a string of hills, all of that lay behind us. Ahead lay a world
of parched sand and broken rock. It made me wonder if I had ever left
the desert.

On the eastern side of the hill, stubborn shrubs raised crooked arms,
groping for the last bits of moisture from an unclouded sky. The slope
fell away to wasteland.

* * *

Six donkeys plodded wearily along. Dull, hard-working beasts, they ignored the violence of the sun, stopping every so often to shake large, blue-bellied flies away from ears or eyes. We rode on thin blankets, and every jolt of the animal felt like hammer blows. By noon, when we stopped in the shade of an overhang of rock, deep in a gulch, the beasts still seemed unperturbed by the heat. They looked at us with scorn as we lifted aching bodies off their backs.

Samuel, the lad who brought the mules to us, chuckled as we groaned on our feet. He still sat astride his donkey, legs splayed out, body slouched comfortably. When he swung down, he flexed his muscles easily, as lithe as a young sapling.

"Mercy," Manasseh groaned, rubbing his back, "I think I would rather run."

"You'll walk soon enough," Taletha said. But she too rubbed at stiff muscles.

This was punishment, but it covered the ground, nonetheless.

The young man busied himself off-loading the donkeys. With infinite care he unstrapped a large pottery bowl, miraculously unbroken in the bone-jarring trip through the rugged hills, and emptied a large waterskin into it. The donkeys crowded around, shouldering each other roughly out of the way to get at the water. One beast lifted wet rubbery lips at the sky, showed a mouthful of yellowed teeth and brayed happily. The lad laughed as loud as the beast.

He spread grain and a thick bundle of hay on a shadowed rock. After watering, the donkeys wandered over to the bundle, tearing great mouthfuls and slobbering happily with spears of dried clover hanging from their lips. One by one, while we rested among the rocks, the donkeys ate their fill, pawed at chosen places on the ground, out of the sun, and lowered themselves to rest.

"They should be happy," Lycurgus said. "They're turning back here."

Manasseh looked at him in surprise. "What?" He gaze swung out at the wind-sculpted wasteland as if sizing up a new, unknown opponent, and his eyes narrowed.

"Right, carpenter. From here on we walk."

Samuel surveyed his animals, which now lay in the shade, long ears twitching at flies, eyes shut. He sat slightly apart from us.

"Well, when do we go?" Manasseh asked.

"First, we rest."

"But—"

"We leave at nightfall," Lycurgus said. "From now on we find our way by the stars."

"The stars!" Manasseh snorted.

"They don't lie," Taletha said. "Trust them. We know your urgency, Manasseh. But urgency is the way to certain death. From now on, the stars lead us; the earth directs us."

Manasseh stared at her in incomprehension. This world was foreign to him. Nonetheless, he nodded. He shut his eyes, leaning against a couch of gritty rock. "Yes," he muttered. "Yes."

We watched the shadows lengthen across the gorge, climbing up the opposite rock like water filling a bowl. The boy stood suddenly. Without a word he roped the reluctant donkeys together. He climbed aboard the lead beast, then looked to us.

"In his peace," he said.

"And in his service," Taletha responded.

He nodded, unsmiling, switched the donkey's withers with a small lash and kneed it up the gorge. Little spirals of dust followed the animals. They rounded a corner of rock and were gone.

Still we did not move.

I looked at Taletha. She smiled, but her face was like iron.

"Back again," I said.

She nodded.

Lycurgus chuckled at the remark.

"What are *you* thinking?" I asked.

"I am wondering," he said, "if we aren't just a bit old for all this."

"And that's funny?"

"Indeed, friend. But . . . who else? If, as Taletha said, the stars and the earth lead us, then perhaps we are the right ones."

"Perhaps the appointed ones," Doval offered.

Lycurgus nodded. "I have wondered that too. I was wondering also . . ."

"Go on," Doval urged.

Lycurgus sighed, shook his head. "All my life I felt a call, and I wonder if it was all to this. The funny thing . . . I believe it is."

"Tell me," Doval said. "Tell me about yourself."

"Am I a mystery to you?" He looked at Doval with a smile. But I saw something else in his eyes as he looked at her. My glance shifted quickly from Lycurgus to Doval and back. Yes.

Doval shook her head. "No," she said. "I just want to know."

I knew that Lycurgus did not like to talk about his past. He took a deep breath. Sighed.

"How do we measure things?" he asked himself. "Sometimes we think that our own way is the only way, just as the lawgivers in the capital believe theirs is the only way. Yet neither way is entirely true. You know, dozens of men have claimed in these last years to be the Messiah. Why is this? And the religion of the people—it is not one belief. Not at all. That's why the lawgivers have such a time of it. Belief is always shaped by custom and traditions by which people make belief their own."

I agreed. "They home their faith in their own houses of tradition." I had seen this yearning for belief in my travels.

"Exactly. Even so," Lycurgus continued, "there has always also been antibelief, not just a rejection, mind you. People have *contrary* beliefs. See, the people here have always lived surrounded by witchcraft, wizardry, sorcery. That darkness has always riddled the people's belief, luring them by the riddle itself away from the light.

"Two things," he observed. "First, I came to belief in the Way because I saw all these other beliefs, including those of my native land, pointing *toward* the truth."

"And the truth is in the Messiah. *The* Messiah?" I asked.

"Yes. Fulfilled in him, I would say. But this second thing. As all those customs of belief shade by degree toward the true light, I find shadings of unbelief toward the heart of darkness. It begins in threats to people's beliefs, legalities."

"The lawgivers," I said.

He nodded. "You begin to see it? Instead of shaping the longings, the practices, toward the true light, they block and check and confine. The threat grows. It has a heart, a source. A power."

"And you are saying that we go to that . . . heart?"

"Ah, Elhrain, I wish I could be certain. I think we go to a manifestation of it, a particular source where all fealty goes to the power of darkness, the power to seize, grasp and destroy. I think it is but one place, but it is the important one for us now."

"If *it* has power," Manasseh said suddenly, "then what do *we* have?" I saw fear in his eyes, as if he was just beginning to understand that strength itself was not enough.

"Our might and knowledge are nothing before power," Lycurgus said evenly. "If we have anything, anything at all, it is authority. Not power."

Manasseh scowled and wrapped his massive arms around himself.

"I thought you were going to talk about yourself," Doval said. Her voice was teasing. "Finally."

Lycurgus chuckled. "Yes. I sort of got off track, didn't I? But are not one's beliefs oneself?"

"Yes. But don't avoid me."

Taletha leaned against me. "Go ahead, Lycurgus," she said. "Tell us a story." I wrapped my arm around her, feeling the soft tickle of her hair against my neck. The afternoon sun painted the upper ledges of the rock a soft gold. Shadows tiptoed up after the light.

Lycurgus reflected. "Maybe I am already talking about my past," he mused. "You see, the Emperor's rule was not unlike the religious conflict here. He was a strange man, my father. He did us much good, yet . . . he did it blindly. I scarcely remember him now.

"He did not look like an emperor. Nor did he desire to be one. He was a common little man, smallish. He looked peevish, almost timid. Yet he was heir to Caesar at eighteen. At thirty-one he was master of the world. Somehow he unified the politicians, who spoke only for themselves, into one voice that spoke for the state. The people needed this.

"Yes. They needed him so much they gave him the title *Augustus*. And so, Octavian became a god, worshiped by the people.

"And as a god, Octavian did a fair job. I wonder if he sometimes believed it himself. Probably not. But if the people insisted, well, then . . . He lived for the people, for the state. He had the courage to do that. He wanted them free, and I can't forget that he permitted—encouraged—the freedom of this little province here also.

"He loathed tyranny. He lived quite simply for that very reason, though he could have tapped, at any time, into the greatest wealth the world has seen. Do you know that he was given a mountain of gold at his coronation? He gave it all back to the people. He would rather have them free.

"But, then—this is curious—he got the idea that freedom was an ethical thing. Strange? Yes. Freedom was moral, a state of mind before anything else. So he enacted his great campaign of reform, and that was his downfall. Wanting the people not just to be happy, but good. It is the curse of the legislator—for one cannot legislate goodness."

Lycurgus leaned forward and looked around, as if studying to see whether anyone but us was listening. Then I understood. He was studying the light; the shadows were deepening and it would soon be time to go.

"What did he do?" Doval asked.

"He passed laws. Remember, as *Augustus* he could do as he pleased. Laws guarding morals—in marriage, relationships, the family. In effect, he put fidelity under the protection of the state. Particularly among Romans, for he wanted to protect 'pure blood'—Roman and Roman together, for life, and in order to have Roman children.

"There, you see, lies the great irony."

"Yourself?" I asked. For I had knowledge of this.

Lycurgus nodded. "My father was happily married. Several times. But he had only one child by his three wives—a daughter. And despite all his acclamation as a god, and all his insistence upon morality, he was fond of his concubines. Oh, in secret of course. And by one of them, he had at least one son."

His eyes widened humorously as he looked at each of us.

"A son without rights. So I became a warrior, where, I like to believe, I served well. At a distance from Rome.

"I suppose I could view the final years with dispassion. Gratefully so. Octavian lived too long—an old, worn-out, senile man who at the end had nothing to cling to but the people's one-time presumptions of godhood and his own fanatical moral code. Did you know that he caught one of his retainers in the act of adultery and forced him to kill himself? How's that for morality? An emperor's prerogative, I suppose. Even more dangerous than a good man setting laws too strict for people to follow is a man who doesn't follow his own laws. So while the tyrants clawed each other for power, the old man made sure his rules were followed. And now there is nothing *but* power; the new tyrants sit in the seat of a god. And they care nothing for morality.

"Still," he said wistfully, "I like to think there was something good in his rule. For many years, anyway, the world was at peace."

"Something very good came out of it all," Doval said.

Lycurgus looked at her and smiled. Then his face stiffened. I followed his gaze, where a twin-horned sliver of moon rose in the evening sky.

One by one we gathered our packs, hoisting them heavily to our shoulders, and stepped into the gulch.

* * *

I have been given three gifts in my lifetime that have enriched me beyond all mortals. I have been given three friends who are closer than a heartbeat. First among them is Taletha; for before I became her husband she became my friend. In marriage our friendship is no less.

Two others. The first was the son of the King of Kush, Eldrad, whose long homely face knew no guile, who bared his soul and opened his home for me, and who was willing at the end to lay down his life for me. Perhaps I played the worst of tricks on him; the last time I ever saw him I made him a king—curse beyond compare.

The third was the one who walks beside me now. Who for the third time I thought I was seeing for the last time—Lycurgus. He had found me in a desert, my rescuer. Weeks later, our lives took separate paths, and as I left Babylon to search for my real home I thought I was seeing him for the last time. Years later, I saw him again in that fateful place—the Skull—in the capital during the mad days when the Messiah was slain. It was under Lycurgus's authority, a centurion then in the capital, that he was slain. When my friend walked off the hill of the skull that day, flinging aside the scarlet cape that the desolate wind blew in the dust, I thought again I was seeing him for the last time.

Yet I walked beside him here in the dark, encroaching the greater darkness. Its jaws were agape. It breathed fire and death. It was the desert. And I wondered, again, if I was with him for the last time. There was no other I would rather be with for the plunge into those cavernous jaws.

I have sometimes wondered, back in that alcove of our house on the farm, when I sat at my desk watching the evening sun cast violet light across the hills in a world that also now seemed forever lost, what would happen if Eldrad, Lycurgus and I sat down together in the same room. Would the two of them feel for each other what I felt for each? Would friendship embrace, surround, us all?

Gifts. How else does one explain it?

We walked now on the rocky horizon at the edge of the world where all our seeing was uncertain. Maybe in another world such a thing as friendship that never ends might be possible. But not here where the demons dance in delight at our coming. It seemed that I could watch them flitting gleefully in the heat waves that rolled from the rocks into the gathering darkness.

CHAPTER
FIFTEEN

I n all normal patterns of life, it is light that clarifies and defines. But the desert receives definition under darkness.

During the day, the sun lacerates the landscape with a blinding white glare. Rocks and earth lose color like bleached rags. They all blend to pale. The air itself hangs in a bright haze, thickening to something almost tangible, as if you move through air bearing the density of water. This thickness, the illusion of weight, arises from its very brilliance; even with the hood of the desert cloak drawn far over the face, the eyes recede like those of some religious mendicant exercising humility. The wanderer finds the harsh brilliance a kind of carapace over the land, too solid to penetrate, too weighty to breathe. But it is only air.

Since the desert in daylight is a world without apparent color, directions or life, we huddled then in the shadows thrown by random rocks or rested in the recesses of a gulch carved from the desert floor by wind or by some primeval upheaval of the earth's crust or by some impossibly distant torrent of rain.

Sleep came simply with exhaustion. During the first day or two, sleep was nearly impossible. The intense heat and brightness careening off nearby surfaces afflicted us. Each of us, save for Manasseh, was a veteran of the desert, but even so we had forgotten this worst of all the desert's tricks—the deprivation of sleep. When you lose sleep, you are vulnerable but too weary to be aware of it.

After a few days, it was impossible for us not to sleep. Our bodies grew so exhausted that we collapsed into its relief even before the morning rays approached the horizon. We stumbled through the nights in a walking dream.

I wonder how Manasseh did it. Perhaps only by the power of his will, for his physical energy melted away like water. I could almost watch his body thin.

Even *knowing* that this stage of acclimation—this sort of drugged submission—was necessary and that it would pass, we could not prepare thoroughly for the *reality*. Somehow, the body is loath to remember pain. Yet when the pain recurs, it is all the more frightening for the memories that it dredges up.

We knew we had to become one with the desert, once more at home with its horror, in order to find and confront this evil we sought. We had to think like those who made the desert their home.

Attack the desert—think to beat it on our own terms—and we would lose. Instead, we had to live at the heart of the desert, learning its rules first. The danger is clear. By doing so, we would be exposed to the desert. It holds too many tricks. It can suck a person up like a drop of rain.

* * *

After three or four days we realized we were adapting once again to the desert.

We knew it, first of all, by awareness of subtle colors again. Gradually we became aware of the infinite variation of light, shadow and color. It appeared first in the small things, like a few fine grains of sand the wind layered just so, leaning golden upon each other, casting their tiny shadows down a miniature slope. I saw it in the sudden flash of pink and gold from a gecko's belly as it twisted into its hole ahead of the tremor of my footstep. I noticed the way the evening sun layered bands of tawny gold across the wall of a cliff and how the lower bands deepened to lavender as the shadows rose.

We could feel the subtle, building tension of an inner adaptation to the desert as well. At first, the will hardens, as if attacking the desert. When the will turns inward, it burns like a white sun. Brightening. Intensifying.

Knowing this, we veterans traveled those first nights in virtual silence, each struggling with the demon of self-control.

Not knowing this, Manasseh suffered the worst. His pain collided with his anger. He became moody and fretful. We never moved fast enough to suit him. When we returned his urgings with silence, and maintained a steady course to the south and east at the stars' directions, his impatience seethed.

During one long night Taletha heard him muttering angrily, and she held his hand for a way. I did not hear their words. I don't know if any were spoken; they walked far behind us. Perhaps her touch alone sufficed. At morning light we located our resting place. After chewing down his ration of unleavened bread and dried meat, Manasseh rolled himself into a tight ball facing the rock and slept.

But even in his sleep he tossed and muttered.

* * *

It was morning on the fifth day when we noticed a change in the desert air. Doval sensed it before anyone—the faint, acrid burning scent in the air. She paused, noting the disturbance.

As we walked through a defile of rock that rose about us in jagged layers, we began to sense the sharpening odor. Moving out of the defile and topping a small rise, we paused. Lycurgus pointed into the distance where moonlight shifted uncertainly in a dim haze. The moon itself now wore a veil across its brightness.

"So. We're getting near it," he said.

"The lake?" Taletha asked.

Lycurgus nodded. "The Lake of Death," he muttered. "It will soon be day. We should look for a place to camp."

It was several hours until daylight, well before our usual stopping time, but we understood. We were now at the boundary, where order stood behind us. Crossing that boundary, we moved at the heart of a violated land.

* * *

We awakened in the afternoon, stirred out of sleep by a heat more harsh than before. The heat seemed intensified with the strange odor in the air.

All of us automatically reached for waterskins to wash throats clogged with a gritty film.

141

This desert was different from any I had known. Twice, without really searching, we had found rock formations that hid a small pool of water. We knew there would be water in this strange land, but were surprised by the ease with which we had found it. It was simply and suddenly there before us, a small pool cupped by hard rock, tucked in the deep shadows of a gulch. Even where there was water, however, there was little plant life. Some moss clung to the edge of a rock; a few scrub plants grew where the stream dove back underground, roots digging into the rocky soil like ropes. There were no tree-shaded oases, no reedy grasses, like the desert oases of my native land.

We believed also that people lived in this inhospitable region. If Lycurgus's reports were true, somehow they learned to live with the land, enduring its violence. Small groups of radical believers fleeing persecution had made their way to this place where none other dared penetrate. They were safe here in a land of death. A few mystics, we had heard, came here willingly to flog their bodies and spirits into some impossible holiness. A horror of holiness.

This we had heard. If it were true, we had not seen them. Nor had we expected to. If someone wanted to hide here, the hiding would be thorough, the seclusion and secrecy nearly perfect. The land was a maze of distortions. All the rock looked carved by some mad sculptor. One could see any of a dozen shapes at any one time. There was little choice anymore but simply to keep moving, and to trust we would know the place when we found it.

* * *

Manasseh's anger and strength combined at first to drive him like a whirlwind. He attacked the night stretches, unwilling to stop, restless when we forced him. The raw nervous energy continued into the day. When the rest of us sought shadowed spaces to sleep, he tossed and turned, got up, walked around in the sun like a caged animal.

We expected the collapse, and on the seventh day, he broke.

Toward daylight, when the stars had disappeared in a purple wash of sky and we began scouting for shade to rest, we found ourselves on a harsh, undulating plain of stony ground. To the north, spires of rock twisted to the sky. The rising sun singed their flanks like torches. The wind picked up, sending low waves of sand across the rocky marl, stinging our ankles.

We had to keep going since there was no shelter in this stony ground. The sun flashed waves of white light over the rock. The surface of the earth seemed to slide with the wind and the sun.

Manasseh started, suddenly and mindlessly, running ahead of us. I was going to chase him, but Lycurgus restrained me.

Manasseh stumbled, then disappeared into a wave of heat far ahead.

When we caught up, we found him on hands and knees, clawing at the hot rock. "Water," he gasped.

Lycurgus locked his arms around the carpenter, who fought back for a moment, then went limp. Carefully, Doval held the nipple of the waterskin to his lips, drawing it away when he grabbed at the bag. His eyes were red-streaked and wild. He looked at us as if we were enemies. He broke loose from Lycurgus's grip and lunged ahead, only to collapse a short distance further.

I studied the horizon, looking for some break in its flatness, some bulge or twist that signaled shade. As I squinted, shielding my eyes by holding out the hood of my cloak, I thought I saw a stubby, brown shape that glided through the white heat waves. It looked like an upthrust of rock, and I distrusted my own eyes when I saw it move in the distance.

"An animal?" I asked Taletha. She too was peering hard into the eye of the sun.

"I thought it was a rock. We need shade."

Leaning in Lycurgus's arms, Manasseh moaned. His body was limp now. I doubted he could walk at all.

"It is drawing nearer," Taletha said.

I studied the distant shape. The figure neared, a crooked brown bundle, moving slowly. Two legs detached from the shape, then a third, a staff. The hooded head took definition. A man.

Lycurgus murmured softly, as if unsure how far his voice would carry. "I have seen one before," he said.

"What?"

"A desert hermit. One from the old people."

I could question him no further, for the figure had stopped about ten paces away and appeared to be studying us. His cloak, unlike our whitened, close-woven linen, was a dusty brown, the color of desert rock. The hood was pulled so far forward that the man's face was lost in shadow. His cloak fell only slightly below the knees, and his sandals, instead of the pounded leather we wore, were made from rough strips of animal hide with the hair surface worn against his own flesh. The effect was like seeing a man's body propped above thin goats' legs. He held his long staff loosely, just below its curved neck.

One hand lifted from the folds of his cloak. He beckoned to us to follow and turned his back on us, walking slowly back into the white eye of the sun.

I looked at Lycurgus. He shrugged and nodded. Between the two of us, we held Manasseh upright, steadying his arms over our shoulders, and half-dragged, half-carried him in the direction of the little hermit while Doval and Taletha shouldered our extra packs.

* * *

I twisted on the bristly fur of an animal hide and sleepily sat upright. The embers of the fire glowed like red snake eyes in the pit, and the meat spat and hissed.

Doval sat by the fire, her figure outlined at the mouth of the cave against the moonlight. She twisted a stick that held the meat, propped between two short supports, spitting the meat over the fire. She stared into the red light eagerly but turned and smiled when she heard me move.

Manasseh snored powerfully against the far wall, his chest a dark mound rising and falling, his arms flung out in a gesture of utter collapse.

"They're looking for more wood," Doval said.

"How's Manasseh?" I asked.

Doval chuckled. "Andrew gave him something to drink. He won't be awake for a while yet."

Taletha knelt across the fire from her. Glancing back and forth over the fire, I studied the two of them. They looked like mirrors of each other in the glow of the embers. When Doval met my eyes I saw the tiny fleck of gold in the iris of her right eye twinkle.

"Smells good," I said.

"Almost ready," she said. "They will be back soon."

Even as she spoke, I heard the sound of feet outside the cave. I remembered now, coming here at late morning, our bodies at the point of collapse. The ravine was a gash in the unyielding rocky plain. While we stood staring, the hermit had simply climbed over the lip of rock and disappeared, as though the earth had swallowed him. We approached the edge of the ravine carefully, half afraid something would rise out of it and suck us in. But below, balanced easily on a narrow trail, stood the little hermit beckoning us to follow. Again he turned his back and went on.

About ten feet up from the rocky bottom, the trail twisted into the hermit's cave. It was a cool, clean cave, not the dark spidery blackness I usually thought of with caves. Somewhere nearby there had to be a spring, for the hermit—he called himself Andrew—had full animal-skin bladders in the cave.

But we had already been well on our way to sleep by then.

Lycurgus walked in with his arms full of thin twigs. Andrew followed, his face still hidden in the fold of the hood. He rummaged in a stockpile against the far side of the cave, found a candle and lit it by holding up a twig from the fire. He set it carefully on the floor, sensing its orange light rise and dance over the rocky walls, then sat back cross-legged to one side. When Doval offered him the choicest meat, he waved it aside.

"That's for you," he said. "I have no need."

While we ate he studied us. When at last his high, querulous voice spoke, it cracked unevenly, like one unaccustomed to speaking. He chuckled and snorted each time his voice cracked.

"Well, well," he said, then was silent. We finished eating, feeling his eyes studying us out of the darkness under his hood.

"You want to ask me questions, but you're too polite," he wheezed. "Isn't it terrible?"

We laughed.

"But the only manners of the desert are survival. Perhaps I should begin."

We kept silent, smiling at each other.

"An interesting group, now. A strange group that came seeking me."

"Seeking you?" Taletha asked. Her voice wore a smile.

"Well, and you found me, didn't you? You just didn't know you were seeking me."

"I think you found us," I said. "And at the right time too."

"Carpenters are strong men as a rule. But this one is troubled inside."

"How did you know he was a carpenter?" Taletha asked.

"The way the calluses are arranged on his hands. And he is often too rash, or too clumsy. The scars on his hands are from saw bites. He probably does good work, but he always wants it done yesterday."

We chuckled. He knew Manasseh well enough.

"But the rest of you," Andrew said. "Here a Roman." The hood turned toward Lycurgus. "Well, that's not so strange. They rule this land now."

"The people are their own governors," Lycurgus reminded him.

"But it is not the same thing. The Romans are hungry, still, for land and power. But their power is passing, isn't it?"

Lycurgus nodded. "That it is," he agreed.

"And then," he said, looking at me, "this man. He knows all about power."

He kept looking at me for a long time, and I had the feeling he was reading my mind, my life, and there was nothing I could do to stop him. But I felt no threat in his doing so. I had no fear of him. I wouldn't have minded, right then, telling him every fear that ever threatened me.

"And power costs a great deal," the hermit said gently. He left it there.

The hooded face turned at last to Doval and Taletha, still seated across the fire from each other. They returned his gaze without hesitation. "But most puzzling of all," Andrew said, "are you two sisters."

I saw Taletha's lips tremble. Her hand went to her cheek, and suddenly her tears came.

"Oh, yes. You know. Of course. And of course you don't want to talk about it because it would bring back memories that hurt. But all your pain is past. A prophet is supposed to tell signs and portents. This one gives a blessing instead. I will not say your suffering has ended. But your pain has ended. For you," he nodded at Taletha, "carry in you the sign of a promise."

He studied Taletha intently. "Oh, daughter. Tears are good, aren't they? This is a safe place. Weep and be happy, daughter. But your sister perplexes me."

Doval bent, and it seemed as if she bent under a torment of a remembered past. But quickly the hermit spoke. "She perplexes me because among all the humanity I have now left behind, I have never found one with a heart so pure, a soul so full of light. The glory of the Lord shines in you, daughter, and it is a precious light you bear."

Doval turned. "Thank you," she whispered.

"And now," he said, "before I get tired, what do you seek? Perhaps I can help. Perhaps not."

Among the four of us we sputtered out the pieces of our story. Strangely, we felt no unease telling the hermit the most intimate details. With the telling, with his intent listening, the story itself began to take some sort of pattern in my mind. In this cave, before this comical hooded figure—shadowed confessor—it all made an odd sort of sense. Defiant of rationality, it made sense, nonetheless.

While he listened—signaled only by the twist of his hood, the bob of his head—Andrew made only comical clucking sounds of agreement or encouragement. When we finished, awaiting his response, there was only silence.

"I have seen the boy," he said at last.

The normal immediate response would be "Where?" We were too stunned to say anything. Finally it was I who breathed the word.

Andrew shook his head. Apparently he was not ready for that telling yet. Instead, in his crooked, thin voice, he said, "I am not a hermit. I am a prophet."

He knew what we had been thinking then, that he was one of the lost ones, the wild ones, like crazed Philip back in Noke, shouting about the skulls. But even that had been authenticated by the man in prison. Andrew was proceeding in the old way, establishing credentials for what he wanted to say.

"A prophet?" said Lycurgus. "With no one to prophesy to?"

Andrew chuckled. "No one listens. So I speak to the wind as a sign against the age—that they and their offspring shall be as wind against the Lord's great anger."

"There's plenty to be angry about," muttered Lycurgus. "But all people?"

"The wind winds among the rocks. God's children shall be like the rocks. They will endure."

"The wind erodes the rocks," I observed.

"The wind reveals the rock," he corrected. "It strips away surfaces and shows the heart."

"Where did you see the boy?"

"Walking on the earth."

"Where on the earth?"

"Above the ground. But he goes underground. You're headed the right way."

"Which way?"

"The way you're going! You too will go underground. Fear the emptiness of the earth. But you shall fill it with light."

"You must be a prophet," Lycurgus said. "You speak in riddles."

Andrew nodded. He pushed back his hood slowly. The fire and candlelight wavered over skin the texture and color of old sandal leather. A few white whiskers dotted his chin. His eyes were blank white orbs, as incapable of vision as polished stones.

"Riddles," he said, "because no one listens to the truth. So it becomes habit, a means to disclose the truth by making others seek it. For, in the end, that's all any of us can do."

"You say you're not a hermit," Taletha observed, "yet you live alone. In this wild land."

"I have not always been alone," Andrew said. "There was my brother. He had ties to a group of . . . what you would call hermits . . . to the north. They camp on a mountain called Masada. I call them hermits because they have given up speaking to the people and seek to live wholly unto themselves."

"Do they succeed?"

"They do for a time. But not long now. Their days are numbered. They will be hunted out. They would rather die than be taken. So it shall be."

"Your brother? Is he with them now?"

"He was arrested. He went to purchase supplies for them. I do not know where he is, but I think he is with God. He should have returned weeks ago, and I can feel nothing of his presence on earth anymore.

"And there was another. A younger disciple who wanted to tell the truth. He felt the Lord calling him to go back to the people. He left a long time ago. I have not heard from him since either. But I believe you have.

"Either way, I am alone."

Lycurgus began, "The younger one—"

"Philip. He went often to the villages. And returned defeated. The burden grew too heavy for him. I told him to give it to the desert, to the grasshoppers. To let them carry the load. But Philip had seen the heart of evil, and the urgency of warning consumed him."

"The Place of the Skulls," Taletha said.

Andrew merely nodded.

There was so much we wanted to ask him. Specifics. Details. These we needed. But suddenly he said, "And now, we have talked enough. Join our brother here." He nodded at the slumbering Manasseh. "Rest."

He got to his feet, walked to an animal hide against the wall, curled up and fell instantly asleep.

CHAPTER
SIXTEEN

I n the darkness I smell him coming. It is a smoky, grimy scent stronger than the wet stench of my rotting cell.

Water dribbles through the walls of the underground dungeon and stands in stagnant, mossy pools on the rocky floor. A rat steps into the corridor and stops at my cell door. I can almost feel its broom-straw whiskers brush the air. It feeds on things dead and dying in the dungeons, where the stench of rot is a living presence.

But I can smell him above the sickly odor of rot and decay. No, he is the odor. Kurdash! He carries the smell of smoke from the palace throne room, the stench of power in his nauseatingly obese body as he steps toward me.

The rat stands for a moment, then darts off.

Kurdash chuckles.

I lie bent over, huddled away from the wetness in a dry corner of the cell. I am folded in on myself, muscles as tight as strung wire, and I am hiding from his coming.

I hear a sound and know it is the footfall of Kurdash, the despot ruler of Kush, and I lie there forsaken by his brother—my friend—Eldrad. Forsaken and alone in this prison cell where only the rats survive. Kurdash is coming to kill me.

His step sounds again on the rocky floor, and the sound hurts my ears. I twist away. His face is like fire before me, eyes red as coals against the blue-black *embers of his skin. When he speaks, I feel a hot wind in my face and I can hardly breathe.*

"I have come to kill you." His words are tongues of fire.

I protest, and my denial is a groan.

He reaches out a hand. He is grinning, his flesh quivering obscenely. A ball of fire falls from his hand and sears my body. I jolt backward at its touch. Another falls, and I can feel it near me, like a whip of hot flame lacerating every nerve. My voice is gone, but I try to shout, "No, no, no." And no sound will come. His hands seize me, and the pain and fire crash over every inch of my flesh as I huddle weeping in a frightened ball.

* * *

Her hands are on my shoulders, rubbing, stroking away the knots of tension.

She whispers in my ear, leaning over me so that her short hair brushes my cheek with cool tips. "Shh," she says. "It's okay."

I feel my breathing quiet as her strong, thin fingers knead my muscles. She works the clots of tension from them, bit by bit.

"Is it a bad one?" Taletha asks.

I nod, and she feels it in the darkness, drawing my head to her breast. I let her hold me. I feel her heart beating like a strong bird against my cheek.

"Kurdash," I whisper. And she strokes my shoulders. "I dreamed I was in the dungeon, that—"

"I know. It is all right now."

"Kurdash is dead," I said. "I saw him die. Why can't I forget?"

I was thinking of a time long ago, a time my mind couldn't let go. Sentenced to death and imprisoned, I was freed by my friend Eldrad—Kurdash's brother. Others did not survive Kurdash's purge that night when Taletha and I fled forever from Kush.

It was a new beginning for us, but never quite an ending. Yes, I saw Kurdash die, struck down by the sword of Arabia, Taletha's brother-in-law. Yes, I saw Eldrad receive a necklace I had inherited from my own father, one of the last of the Magi. I had worn it without understanding it; I understood it when I gave it away. Power! I *gave it away*, when Kurdash had lived every moment to achieve it.

I was a fool if I mistook the emblem for the deed. Oh, yes, Kurdash lived. In the arrogant, in the power-obsessed, his spirit still lived. The spirit of Kurdash would not die as long as there were such things as pride and power and persecution.

"This is the first time you've awakened. Or cried out," she said.

"There have been others?"

"For weeks, husband. Off and on. You would lie trembling in bed, and in the morning you seemed to remember nothing."

"I'm sorry."

"I'm sorry I haven't been able to help you."

"He won't leave me alone. Kurdash keeps coming back. He wants me."

"It's only a dream, Elhrain."

"I don't think so. I'm . . . I'm scared, Taletha."

"So am I. That's why I want to end it."

"What does it mean, then?"

"Dearest, if I knew that, I would be a prophet."

Taletha rocked me gently, holding my head against her. The motion washed away the dream. But to be held so—like a child. I gave in to it, loving this woman who loved me. And, held now against her, I heard a tiny tick-tick-tick, faint but quick, pulsing in the small bulge beneath her breasts.

She felt me sense it, and her stroking hand pressed my head close to her abdomen, ear pressed against the firm flesh.

I heard her heartbeat. Its steady, firm pulse beat between her breasts. There was silence below, then I heard it again, the high, faint, fast tick-tick-tick like a melody playing to her rhythm. It was a heartbeat within her heartbeat, her heart directing, supporting another. I lifted my head and looked into her eyes and saw the smile there.

"How long have you known?" I whispered.

"Shh. I have felt the heartbeat only a few days."

"But . . . but . . ."

She choked a laugh. "That's what I've been saying." She mimicked me, "But . . . but . . ."

I started chuckling. "I'm too old!"

"Oh? Are you? But . . . but . . ."

"When? Before the prison break?"

"Silly man. It hasn't been that long."

"That isn't what I meant. I know that! But what I mean is, when?"

"It must be two or more months along, husband."

"It? What do you think? A boy?"

"How should I know? I think it is a daughter. *Our* daughter. My daughter."

"Oh, my."

Our voices had risen. This time the chuckling was not my own. I turned my head. Sat up. The fire had brightened, and I saw him, bent like a wizened monkey over the fire, feeding sticks to the warm flame.

Andrew grinned like a blank-eyed imp. Firelight glittered in the white orbs that were his eyes.

"You don't have to live in a cave to be a prophet," he said in a low voice. "But it isn't so bad when you get used to it."

"You heard?" I asked as I sat up. Taletha leaned against me.

"I wasn't sleeping," Andrew replied. "I don't have much need of sleep." His sightless eyes bored into us, but it was not a fearful thing. His eyes on us felt like arms, reaching out and holding us. For that moment, despite the sleeping shapes of our comrades, it seemed we were the only three people left on the face of the world.

"He will be your consolation," Andrew said.

"*He?*" Taletha said.

Old Andrew nodded, his face a wrinkle of smiling.

"Well, okay, then," Taletha said.

"And the consolation of many others. For you will know the hope, but he will know the deed of the Lord's vindication. He will be great in the name of the Lord and in his kingdom."

"Now you're scaring me," I said. "One step at a time for me."

Andrew chuckled. "You're right. Rejoice in what the Lord has done. Let it suffice."

I thought a moment, searching for the right words. "Perhaps," I said, avoiding Taletha's gaze, "perhaps . . . ah . . . you should . . ."

"Go back?" Andrew finished. He shook his head. "She cannot, for she is chosen. But, my daughter," and he looked with his sightless eyes deep into Taletha's wondering eyes, "it is the sign of a promise for you. Even when your world seems ended, know this: You shall not fail. The Lord himself is with you. You will not go in peace, but you shall be held in his peace."

I wondered at the words, then as now. *How does he know?* I remember thinking. Neither of us asked.

As sleep overtook me again, I was vaguely aware of Taletha, still awake, looking into Andrew's eyes and talking in excited, low whispers with him.

* * *

I awakened the next morning to feel his staff poking my ribs. Manasseh sat awake, smiling pleasantly, as if he were facing a day's work in his shop. Lycurgus was getting water from the tiny spring that puddled into the sand just past the cave. He had to scoop out a narrow, deep hole, then laboriously fill the waterskins bit by bit. Taletha was baking some unleavened cakes over the diminishing embers. Doval sat thoughtfully watching.

It almost seemed we were a relaxed, happy group on a picnic. I smiled, wondering if I would ever see us so again.

I knelt by Taletha. "How do you feel?" I asked.

"Better this morning," she said. "No nausea, thank goodness."

"Are you sure it's . . ."

She scowled at me. "Didn't you hear him?" She glanced at Andrew.

"Yes. Yes, only—"

"I know. I'm too old."

"I didn't say that."

"Maybe it's just you who is too old."

"What?"

But she was smiling as she knifed the bread off the fire stones.

After we finished eating, we began bundling our packs.

"I think I will go with you a ways," said Andrew.

Doval objected. "But—"

"But my eyes? Oh, daughter. That is no matter. Like our friend here," he nodded in my direction, "I have a gift of earth-knowledge. The Lord speaks through the earth, doesn't he? After all, he made it."

"But evil has twisted it," Doval said.

"Ah. Then the trick is learning to hear the voices, and which to listen to. I will be all right, and I won't go far with you. This is your task. I'll just point the way, if you'll permit me."

* * *

We stayed in the cave through the heat of the day, and with the first shadows of evening climbed up the trail, out of the cool depths of the

154

ravine, back into the heat of the desert.

Only when we stepped from the cave did we fully appreciate the protection of rock. Scooped out of the rock by some long-ago erosion of water, the cool recesses of the cave also protected from the cutting wind. In the cave, one heard every whisper; outside the wind whined noisily among the rocks.

We stood blinking at the threshold, eyes sore and squinting, as a lowering sun flung its brightness—bouncing and breaking like waves over the landscape.

Andrew set out in his unhurried, steady gait, expertly threading his way up the narrow trail along the face of the cliff. I remember thinking, *Of course the light doesn't bother him—he's blind.* Then I marveled at the practiced ease of his climb as he stepped unfalteringly along the trail. My old fear of heights came back as we neared the top, and I almost felt envious of Andrew.

I don't know why we trusted a blind man. No one asked.

He climbed out of the gorge and turned southeast without hesitating. *Right now,* I thought, *we walk on the roof of his cave.* It was probably the last safe place we would see.

That strange burning odor we had noticed in the air before, and which had been strangely absent in the cave, now intensified. Perhaps it was from the heat of evening, when colors deepen and the wind dies and the landscape holds its breath.

As we walked on, little Andrew always a step or two ahead, his staff clicking against the rock, his rounded shoulders giving him the appearance of some small desert animal, I began to sense the difference in the air as a violation, a perception of wrongness.

All the colors collided in the lavender light as the westering sun lowered. When I glanced back, it was a huge red disk burning through some nearly impenetrable haze.

The air smelled. It held the ordure of death and burning.

We walked on into the night.

The moon rose, an orange ball rimmed with fiery tears that dripped on the desert as it tore itself loose from rock and sand. In the distance, strange spires of rock resembling living shapes stood against the rising moon like dark fists. In the uncertain light the rock piles seemed to move, to sway, to walk toward us, their edges sharp as claws.

Andrew veered south, skirting the rock formation.

As night deepened, he led us across a long, flat plain, occasionally changing our course as if some unseen snare lay before us, but otherwise bisecting the plain like an arrow. To our left the rocky spires rose and tumbled, as if watching, as if following.

At times the air was so thick and potent it stung the eyes and we had to hold the edges of our cloaks over our mouths and noses.

We were well rested by our stay at Andrew's cave. I wonder if we could have made that journey without it. Wordlessly we plodded along, hour after hour. Andrew in the lead, Taletha close behind him, then I, and Doval, Lycurgus and Manasseh. We moved in silence.

The moon grew like a great orange flower blooming above the desert plain. As it rose higher, it silvered, and the whole desert landscape was washed in an eerie white glow. It was deceptive—the opposite of noonday sun when light drove shadows into hiding. Now shadows flitted through the silver wash like living presences.

The stars glowed like distant blue candles.

During the night an odor like sulphur, as though something in the earth were burning, grew steadily. Still the land was flat and empty, our footsteps muffled by the dust.

In the deep night, when the moon stood overhead, its white face still trailing mists that obscured its hue, muddying its color, we halted. Quietly we circled together and ate and drank. Somewhere in the night a jackal yipped. Another answered. Far overhead we heard the brush of dark wings, and Andrew stiffened. But no one saw what it was.

Then, as we traveled again, the moon tumbled to the west and the night deepened. We walked through the thick, cold blackness of utter night, and it lasted forever. Still Andrew's staff clicked on. The file closed. Taletha was a ghostly shadow before me. I could hear Doval's breathing behind, and several times I felt her reach out to touch my cloak. Lycurgus murmured to her now and then in reassurance. I don't know how one could bear to be alone out here in this place. I wondered if Andrew had ever traveled it alone.

Truly, he had earth-knowledge. This land was impenetrable to my senses. I told myself I had been for too long a farmer—the ease had dulled my knowledge.

I moved closer to Taletha, half fearful of being left behind. She may have turned to look at me, sensing me in the night; it was too dark to tell. Her white cloak floated like a ghost before me.

Then the haze of dawn filtered through the east, and I could make out the twisted shapes of rock all around. They had grown huge and leaned about us. Andrew paused, and we nearly collided behind him. He muttered almost to himself, "Careful now. This is the dangerous time," and he stood quietly a moment. No one thought of his blindness. I heard our breathing hoarse and ragged behind the masks we held to our mouths to filter the air.

"You'll get used to it," Andrew said, sensing our labored breathing. "Careful now. We're very near."

More slowly he walked on.

Dawn rose like a line of blood over the rocks. I had sailed the seas once, many years before. The sailors had a slogan about a red dawn—it presaged a storm. Meaningless here. There would be no storms in this desert. Yet each of us sensed threat as tangible as a blow. The red light leaked down through the rocky spires, and the land lay thick with their crawling shadows.

Andrew paused. "Wait here," he said.

He moved on slowly. His body dwindled to a little crooked shape rimmed by the red light of the rising sun. He stopped, then waved us forward.

* * *

The flat trail winding among the rocks was riven by a chasm practically unnoticeable until one stepped to its very edge. Traveling by darkness one could easily step over from the flatness of the plain into an abyss.

Lycurgus stood by its edge—too close for my comfort. Vertigo attacked me as I stared into the abyss, and I had to sit down, away from its edge. That old dizziness, the sense that the world was spinning violently and I was about to be thrown off, surged through me. Nausea. The abyss.

I had always feared high places, and I reached out a hand now to hold the level earth. Red sunlight rooted through shadows in the abyss. I saw the rock formations scattered over the other side, this place where the world dropped. Rock spires, eerie with salt-sided shapes, lunged upward. Many others were rounded, gouged with crevices and stippled with holes that gave them the shape of horribly distorted human faces.

The Place of the Skulls.

The others stood transfixed at the edge of the abyss. Unsteadily, I heaved myself to my feet.

Andrew approached and stopped before me.

He leaned forward, the glazed eyes as blank and pitiless as the moon. He was close enough that I could smell the wilderness odor of him—the scent of sun-bronzed skin, dried animal hides, the peculiar odor of gravelly sand and scrub brush. All the time his blank eyes held me. "You don't believe me either," he said. "Do you?"

I shrugged, remembered he couldn't see it. "I no longer do not believe."

"Not very artfully put," he said. "But it will do." He smiled, straightened and moved around me.

When I heard the tapping of his staff, I realized that he was leaving us. For an instant I wanted to turn and shout, "Come back."

Andrew looked very small and alone against the plain, in the wind, in the harsh play of shadow and light. I wondered how the blind man would find his way back. But he had found us; surely he would find his way home.

Earth Master. So Andrew named himself. And named me.

Earth Master. It had been my calling as a Magus, all those years ago. One who has not just *knowledge* of earth—one who shares understanding and percipience. But it was so long ago, the sense felt numb and lifeless now.

I had made a good farmer. That was all it had amounted to.

I wish I had had more time to inquire of Andrew. I am no longer a young man, to be sure; yet I seem ever seeking the master to tutor me. I wonder if this is so for others, or whether I bear it alone.

There was so much to ask Andrew about! So much he hadn't told. We had relaxed around the fire when we could have been getting answers.

This Philip, whom we had thought a madman. What had he seen, what experienced, so that the only shred of sanity left was to scream out his "Beware"?

What about the man in the prison cell, echoing Philip's cry, in a dying croak, "Beware the Place of the Skulls"?

They were twin signs from out of the desert, messages from a blind prophet, and the signs themselves blind in their ambiguity. But they had been enough to bring us *here*.

And Andrew said he had seen the boy. Well, and he must have meant figuratively, or in a dream, for his white-veiled eyes saw nothing. Here too we should have questioned more closely. Saw the boy, but saw him underground?

Not for the first time I wondered how Manasseh would handle it when we did find Liske. For if we did, I was convinced, it would be his corpse.

* * *

The others had walked ahead of me along the rim of the chasm, searching for a way down. I heard the dusty swish of their cloaks, their shapes ghostly and dim in the morning haze. Then I nearly walked into Doval. They stood silently in a spaced line, like a series of statues, and I saw why.

Lycurgus was in the lead, and he stood at the rim of the chasm. The ground simply dropped away, a foot ahead of him, as sheer and steep as if the land had been cut away with a knife. Ahead, as far as one could see in the darkness, the air was alive with swirling shapes. The air stank, biting at nose and lungs. A wind keened in the darkness and sang of desolation.

Lycurgus was rigid. A step further and he would have plunged to his death. But it was the preternatural weirdness of the swirling, acrid mists, the wind whimpering in torment among unseen rocks below, that froze him.

This was a valley where shadows hung like death.

CHAPTER SEVENTEEN

"I f we stand here any longer," Lycurgus said, "we'll cook like a bunch of eggs."

Taletha chuckled. It wouldn't take much to get us moving toward some shade; the heat on the salt-washed plain was insufferable. As the sun rose, it refracted upon tiny quartzlike granules, intensifying with each grain, and the grains were innumerable—a gray-white carpet.

"Right," I said to Lycurgus. "We jump?"

"Ropes might do it," Manasseh observed.

"Want to run back and get some?"

Manasseh shook his head angrily. "It's insane. Why did we follow that madman? Now he's deserted us. If we had left right away instead of hanging around that blasted cave—"

"Manasseh," I said, feeling the acid on my tongue, "you weren't fit to walk another step."

"Stop it." Taletha whipped the words at us. "Stop it. He wouldn't have brought us here without a reason . . . a way."

"You're pretty confident," Manasseh said with a growl.

"Watch your tongue, friend," I cautioned softly.

"Or?" he hissed. His shoulders rolled dangerously.

"Enough!" Taletha said.

"She's right," Lycurgus said softly. "Don't give in to it."

Manasseh breathed hard. His features calmed. "I'm sorry," he said.

I shook my head. The sun was pulsating behind my eyes. "We have to find shade."

"Shade is down there," Lycurgus said. He stood by the lip of the rock, studying the escarpment that grew now out of the shadow. "I think," he said slowly, "old Andrew knew precisely where he was leading us." He pointed down.

I forced myself to his side, sinking to my knees to steady myself. Like a thin string, a nearly invisible path, really just a crease of rock, undulated downward along the cliff. It was as if some untold eons ago the rock itself had shifted in two parts, leaving that narrow hairpin trail. It disappeared into the darkness of the shadow-held chasm. Across from us the leering faces of rock mocked us. Far beyond them, now in the morning light, I could discern the thick haze of the Lake of Death.

"The rock shifted," I muttered. "It slid on plates during some earth upheaval."

Lycurgus grunted. "Then the earth gave us a way."

"I can't do it," I said flatly.

Manasseh kneaded his eyes with a meaty palm. The air stung us. "I don't know," he muttered. "Suppose the old man is tricking us? Sending us to our deaths. It's a maze down there."

The thought turned me cold. Was it possible?

"You don't mean to say—" Doval began.

"That the old man is a traitor?" finished Manasseh. "Think about it, woman. Who else is there out here? How did he know? And if there is evil here, as we believe, why did he take us here so willingly?"

"Because I don't think he did," Doval snapped. "And don't call me 'woman' again." Her eyes glinted.

"Think about it," Manasseh said, undeterred. "We're lured to our deaths. Sarah isn't here. Liske isn't here. How could they be? Nothing can survive here."

" 'I tell the truth,' " Taletha murmured softly, " 'and there is no one who believes me.' "

Recalling Andrew's words broke the spell.

"He doesn't deceive us," Taletha said adamantly. "He told us—how did he put it? 'I will point the way'? Well, it's our turn now. We didn't come all this way to turn back. Think of Liske, Manasseh. If we fail, I at least want to say I gave it everything I had."

I couldn't help smiling at her. This mystery. This woman tested in the desert's flames by my side: my beloved.

"Well, wife," I said, "if you lead, even down there," I pointed, "I'll follow."

"Of course," she said smoothly. Then she grinned. "Of course."

But I peered hard into the depths. *Can I do it with my eyes closed?* I wondered. Maybe Andrew had the advantage.

As I studied the winding trail, light filtered into the chasm, and I saw something—a splash of cloth coiled behind a boulder—and I shouted.

* * *

Manasseh dropped down the trail like a rock exploding. One instant he stood by our side, the next he was pummeling his way downward. He shoved space, height and depth aside as of no account. Only the angular turns, where the trail twisted outward precipitously, winding around a thrust of uneven rock, slowed him. Several times he waved his arms for balance. Meaty hands clawed at rock. Feet slipped on the salt-lined path.

Then he hit a smooth section near the bottom, and his huge body flew over it. He paused, ten feet from the floor, and leaped. His body floated out, and we heard the impact. Running back to the boulder, he bent to the coil of cloth, and his voice howled as he held something in his arms.

We were all moving then. Carefully. Step by step. Taletha was before me, and even as she went I recalled her own fear of heights. I remembered that when I *had had* to climb that mountain in Kush long ago, she *could not*. My eyes on her back, I followed her brave shoulders.

Lycurgus was behind us. Then Doval. Often I felt Lycurgus's hand on my back or my shoulder steadying me, as if to say, "It's okay. I'm here. We're going to make it."

We rounded the promontory where Manasseh had nearly lost his balance, the trail a sliver around the jutting rock. I leaned into the rock, hugging it, and my steps slowed to a shuffle. Pebbles broke loose, cascading down, and I froze, heart hammering, hands sweating against the boulder.

"Don't lean in," urged Lycurgus. "Try to stand up straight."

"But I—"

"Do it. You'll keep your balance standing upright."

I clung tighter. Taletha had made it around the promontory. She waited, watching me, her eyes steady as starlight. "Elhrain," she said softly, "think of a line on the desert floor. On the floor of your own house."

My home. Impossibly distant. No home any longer.

"Yes," she breathed. "You are in your study. You don't think about walking across. You just do it. You don't lean," she said softly. "You just walk. Walk on that line, Elhrain."

I pictured the room and straightened. My feet shuffled as if half-asleep. With a sigh I reached the other side. The trail widened. Lycurgus and Doval followed, and we moved down. I heard Manasseh's wails above the blood thundering in my ears. We passed the point where he had leapt. Then we were on the floor, standing at the base of rocks that towered above us like ancient idols. Manasseh's wail was louder, and we ran to where he bent over the small, tousled shape.

* * *

Seen from above, the harshly eroded rock formations had appeared as grotesque distortions of any natural order. One eerie rock leered like an empty-eyed skull. Above it stood a huge figure of rock that looked like some macabre giant of death, wielding a club over one shoulder as though to smash the skull. Some upthrust jags were as sharp as daggers, as if some huge mythic warriors had waged battle here and littered the field with remnants of death. The earth was gouged and pocked with caverns and sinkholes, some dropping away into black depths as if sucked down by Hades itself.

Seen from the floor of the chasm, the rocks looked an impossible, bewildering maze. Points of light flashed from salt-encrusted ridges. Shadow and light danced drunkenly back and forth.

But there was no mistake about what we saw in Manasseh's arms. Liske looked like a shrunken doll in those powerful arms.

* * *

Lycurgus scanned the formations about us. "Over here," he said. He led us to a gully that wound down into a protective pool of shade. Quickly we followed. Manasseh sat, rocking Liske in his arms.

Taletha and Doval bent over him. His flesh was burned and crusted, his face a blistered pool of suppurating sores, his skin clammy with dried sweat. Taletha pried the nipple of the water flask between his swollen lips and squirted a thin stream. The water lay for a moment in his mouth. Then his tongue moved, and he swallowed, coughing.

Forgetting our own need for water, Taletha wet strips of cloth torn from the hem of her cloak and laid them on Liske's face. Carefully she sprinkled water over his body, moistening the entire cloak.

Lycurgus located a small hollow of rock in the shaded gully. Working with a sharp piece of stone, he scraped it clean of salt deposits. When he was finished, he had a smooth, cradlelike hollow. Quickly he emptied half a waterskin into it. Then he took Liske from Manasseh's arms and laid him in. Taletha and Doval dipped their fingers in the water, letting the drops fall in a constant, gentle flow over Liske's body.

Manasseh shivered as he watched. "Will he . . . ?" He stopped, fearful of the answer. Taletha tried to smile at him, but her face was tight with worry.

"In the bottom of my pack," she said, "there's a leather sack. The physician gave it to me before we left."

Frantically, I found the pack where she had tossed it aside, and dug through it. Several small pouches lay in the bottom. I took one out and handed it to her. She shook some powder out into her hand, then wet it, forming a green-colored poultice. She carefully dabbed it on Liske's sores, soothing the sun-blistered flesh.

She leaned back as Doval continued laving the body, her fingers dripping the water over his torso. Against the wet cloth one could see Liske's ribs protruding, but also the steady rise and fall of his chest. He still lived; just how was a miracle.

* * *

When darkness entered the chasm, we looked for wood to start a fire. There was none here, and we were hesitant to go looking far into this maze of rock. The air was thick and oppressive. For the moment, we seemed safe in the protected gully. We waited in darkness.

During the night we took turns keeping watch over Liske, one person constantly laving the body. One time his breathing suddenly accelerated, the thin chest rising and falling like that of a terrified hare. He thrashed in the cradle of rock and cried out.

The cry chilled us to the bone. It was a wail of overwhelming fear and horror. We held him in the cradle until the thrashing stopped.

"His body is cooler," Lycurgus remarked. Doval, who had been tending him, nodded.

* * *

It was morning. Lycurgus and Doval had gone in search of fresh water, carefully marking their trail. "There has to be water here," Lycurgus had said. "The sea is fed somehow, by underground springs probably. If we hit the right one, that has gone deep enough, the water ought to be pure."

But they found nothing, not even a trace of water.

"We have enough," Taletha said.

"For now," Manasseh argued. "But to get us back? We have to have enough to make it back to the hermit. *If* we can even find him."

"Our task hasn't even started," Lycurgus reminded him.

"What! We found Liske," Manasseh said. "We ought to get out while we can. Each moment we stay here, man, is a moment closer to death."

"Liske is in no condition to travel," Taletha said.

"I'll carry him!" Manasseh exploded.

"And what of Sarah?" Lycurgus asked quietly. "And what of the task we came here for?"

"I don't give a goat's hide about that," Manasseh said. "I've got my son."

"I tell you he can't travel!" Taletha said. Her face was adamant. She stood protectively between Liske and Manasseh, who stood huge and fuming before her.

I rose instinctively. Taletha motioned me away.

"Manasseh," she said gently. "I know how you feel—"

"You don't have a son!" he exploded. "Don't take mine."

Taletha winced. "Manasseh. We have to stop it. For Liske's own sake. Can't you understand? We have to stop what caused this!"

At that moment, Liske bolted upright. His body trembled violently, mouth gaping as if to vomit. His eyes shot open, and the pupils were as large as pennies. He was choking, as if hands were at his throat, throttling him. His small arms battled back.

A scream erupted from his constricted throat, so fierce, so terrified, we all stood as if struck. The horror in that sound was complete and undiluted.

Manasseh darted forward and hugged his son.

Liske's huge, unseeing eyes whirled wildly. He batted at his father, trying to strike him away.

Manasseh wept as he held him, looking into those dark, bottomless eyes that held no recognition. Then the small body went limp, the wounded eyes closed, the constricted jaw closed with a sigh.

Manasseh cradled him for a long time. When he at last laid his son back into the laving pool of water, he stood, looked at each of us in turn, and nodded.

"We can take him out of the water," Taletha said. She leaned over and stroked his body. "The fever is gone."

CHAPTER
EIGHTEEN

A h, Liske. You foolish, brave-hearted boy. The desert is a grown man's work. Would you be old so soon? For the desert can age you, beyond your years, beyond your spirit.

Where does such courage come from? And how does it come to the heart of a child who should frolic in the green-clad hills among his sheep, dreaming all the things a boy dreams? Not living in a nightmare from which there seems no awakening. You don't belong here. In the desert one dies many deaths. The loss of innocence is only one of them.

The second death is the time—and it comes to everyone who sets foot in the desert—you first think of dying, for death is all around you. The desert is the home for the unliving, and contrary to living. Inevitably there comes that moment when you think, I might die. The thought comes with increasing urgency as you sojourn in the desert, then turns to, I will die. The fearful certainty arrives— I will die.

I who have died many deaths in the desert am alive today. But the desert lives in me. This I have come to understand, even accept. It is only a matter of time until it overcomes me, and each moment is an act of grace.

But it should never be so for you. You would be old so soon. To face the questions at your age, brave-hearted boy, that is the tragedy. You will spend the rest of your days, no matter how long or brief they be, trying to find the answers.

* * *

When Liske opened his eyes again, they held the stunned look of a desert hare that has just escaped the jaws of the hyena. Liske tried to heave his body upright, and fell back exhausted. Lycurgus scooped him out of the bath and handed him gently to his father. Manasseh held him delicately, like something about to break.

Liske's eyes opened again. "I'm all wet," he murmured.

Manasseh hugged him, laughter rippling in his massive chest. The laughter took hold, a release from fear.

"He's all . . . wet," Manasseh gasped. He shook with laughter, cradling the wiggling shape in his arms. "My boy is alive. And he's all wet."

Tentatively, Liske reached exploring fingers to the poultice-caked scabs on his face. He withdrew his hand and shivered.

"Are you hungry?" Taletha asked. Liske nodded. Manasseh's laughter turned to groans as he smothered his face in Liske's sun-scorched hair and wept. "I have my son back," he whispered.

*   *   *

Too quickly we tried to ask Liske questions. The fear crept back into his eyes. His jaws locked. He drew his arms around himself and shivered. When his crippled arm dropped away from his body, he held it by the wrist with his other hand, protecting himself.

Finally it was Doval who led him. Something transferred between them, a living current between their eyes. They had an understanding bound in a shared suffering.

They sat across from each other in the last light of that interminable day. The heat in the chasm was suffocating, yet each of us shivered as we heard the tale that broke from Liske's lips in bits and pieces as Doval quietly encouraged him.

He had, as we surmised, left the hills of Noke, leaving with little more than a pack of supplies and a waterskin taken from the house. Looking up apologetically, he told how he had at the last moment taken one of Taletha's old cloaks, cut the hem, and draped it over his shoulders.

"It fits you well," Taletha said with a smile. "I recognized it, but it's yours now."

"I'm sorry," Liske said. "I didn't mean to steal it."

"You've earned it," she said.

And so, armed only with his small shepherd's staff, he had entered the desert hoping to find his friend Sarah when all else had failed.

Liske had traveled south into the desert, then east, not bothering to understand just why or where. He had seen the trackers set off in that direction. That was enough.

He understood enough about the desert to know that he must travel at night, so he had done so. Clutching his staff fearfully, he listened to the hoot of hyenas and the strange, harsh barking of jackals. At times, that first night, he had been so terrified that he just stood there, waiting for an attack. When morning came, the desert looked precisely the same as it had the night before. He found shelter under the shade of some scrubby brush near a rock pile, thinking that he would turn back that night. It was hopeless. A boy could not do this thing. The desert was too big, and held too many terrors.

But during the day the wind arose, and when he looked for his tracks under moonlight he couldn't find them. He grew afraid and began running, calling. When he could run no farther, he sank to his knees in the dust.

It was then he heard the voices. They sounded a great distance away, but they carried clearly over the desert air. He ran shouting, and then he saw firelight among some rocks and smelled meat roasting. Certain it was the trackers, he ran calling for them. By the time he recognized them for what they were, it was too late.

One of the two men, the shorter one, stood up and seized him by the neck.

"Right into our own filthy hands," he said with glee. His breath in Liske's face was hot, stinking of garlic and wine. The man wore a ragged cloak and had a bracelet on his left wrist. Liske remembered that he had only one eye, the other a scarred wound. "The gods smile upon us, Moab." He flung Liske to the other man.

Liske tried to run, but the man put out a foot and sent him sprawling face down in the sand beside two restless mules.

"Worthless," muttered Moab. "Did you see his arm? A blooming cripple."

"Let's see," said the first. He staggered drunkenly toward Liske and kicked him. "Stand up, boy." He seized a handful of Liske's cloak and hauled him upright. He muttered a curse and flung Liske aside.

"Blooming no-good cripple. You're right, Moab. Still?"

Moab shrugged. "Tie him up," he said. "We'll see later."

After being trussed, Liske waited for the two to sleep. When he heard their heavy breathing, he rubbed at the bonds that chafed his ankles and wrists. He could not move them. Finally, exhausted, he fell asleep. When he awakened, he heard the two men arguing.

"Turn him loose, I say. He's worthless."

"Turn him loose to tell tales."

"He'll be dead in a day out here."

"Unless someone finds him. The same ones looking for us."

"Right. And whose fault is that?"

"I swear I couldn't help it. She didn't have to come along right then."

"You didn't have to hit her, either. Think sometime. Or is that too hard?"

"Leave me alone."

"You're nothing but a curse to me. If you'd listened we'd be heading for the coast with some money in our pockets."

"I forgot when I hit her. I tell you—"

A blow snapped through the air. Liske burrowed his head into the dust, pretending sleep.

The voices lowered for a moment.

"Listen," the first man was saying, "kill him and bury him under some rocks. Let's get going."

"What for? Leave him out here and he'll die anyway."

"So? It's a mercy-killing then." He chuckled. "Besides," he added, "if someone finds him, he tells."

"No, listen. We can get something for him."

"Traders won't take a cripple. He's worthless, I say."

"Not to some I know of."

"You don't . . . No. I don't want to go there."

"Scared?"

A long silence. "How much do you think they'll give?"

"Who knows? More than we have now."

"That's your fault."

"Will you forget that! Listen, we don't have to go in there."

"How do you know?"

"I know, I tell you. See, we just get close. They know we're there. We leave the kid there; they leave something for us. It's the way it works."

Another silence. "He rides behind you. This animal's dead on its feet."

"Ride? Let the little bugger walk."

"Yeah, and what will they give for a corpse?"

"Sooner or later he will be anyway." They laughed, and Liske wondered what they meant.

"Still," the one called Moab said, "they want their meat fresh. He can ride."

In the end they all walked. The mules were no match for the desert, and the thieves didn't water them sufficiently. Nor did they give Liske much.

* * *

As if remembering that thirst with every tissue in his body, Liske paused to drink. Once again we were grateful for replenishing the waterskins at Andrew's cave, a place we now increasingly thought of as the last place we felt at home. After he drank, Liske was hesitant to continue. The terror slipped back into his eyes like a curtain.

When he finally spoke, the words were half-strangled in his throat. "They have her," he shouted suddenly. "They do. And—"

"Who?" Lycurgus interrupted. "Who? Sarah?"

Liske nodded violently.

"Who are they?"

Liske trembled. "The old ones. The . . . ghosts."

"Listen, Liske. We want to help Sarah. We have to know how. We have to know about the old ones! How to get there. Are there guards?"

"No guards," Liske said. "They don't need guards. They have . . . they have the stones."

"Stones?" I asked. Earth is earth. Rock is rock. Then I remembered the physician's words, "There are places on this earth given to darkness . . . where evil lies caged . . . kept alive by the wizards of darkness." And with the memory I felt Liske's fear as my own. But stones? No, they would only be objects of manipulation. The manipulators themselves were those we needed to confront.

Lycurgus must have been thinking the same. "We can't approach them head on," he mused. "They'll know long before we get there."

"Maybe they know already," Manasseh said, and his voice was as tight as a rope stretched to breaking.

We turned back to Liske. "How did you get out?" Taletha asked.

"There's another way," Liske said. "They live in the cave. There are three of them, and they seem so old . . . they seem dead."

"What? Men? Women? What are they?"

"I don't know. They sit by the fire, three of them. Around the stones."

"What does this cave look like?" Lycurgus asked. He was the general, the military man. He wanted facts.

"It's big," Liske said. "When you go in the front, there's a door."

"A door! In the desert?"

"Yes. Inside a ways. You go in the cave, and it gets . . . sort of skinny, and there's a door."

"Is it heavy? Barred?"

"I don't know." Liske looked frustrated, near tears.

"Go on," Taletha prodded. "Just tell us what you know, what you can remember."

Liske nodded. He scratched at a blister on his forehead, studied the bit of skin that peeled loose. When he spoke, his voice was a monotone, and all the while he looked at the blistered piece of skin. It was as if he was back *there*, seeing rather than remembering.

"The two men stood by the mouth of the cave," he said. "They made me walk in. I stood by the door, and it opened.

"The light inside was red, I remember. It is a scary light. They didn't look at me, the three old ones. They sat on the floor. But I couldn't run. I thought I would run when the men let me go, but I couldn't. It was like . . . like I had ropes on my feet. And the door shut behind me.

"One of the old ones got up and took my arm. Her hand . . . I think it was a woman . . . was cold on my arm. She steered me around the outside of the cave, along the wall, past the . . ." His voice broke.

"What did you see?" Lycurgus asked. "We have to know everything, Liske."

He nodded. "There were heads on the wall. On shelves."

"Heads? Animal heads?"

"Not heads. They were people, though. Just the skulls. They looked red in the firelight. And they were very small."

Lycurgus looked sharply at us. Taletha sucked in her breath.

I had learned much about this religion of her homeland, had even come, against my own will, to believe in this Messiah of hers. But I had also learned the darker passages of the history of that religion—when the people had turned from their God and followed a twisted religion in the land. A religion of a perverse god, opposed to the true God in every way. One gave life; the other took life.

The taker-god was a despot, never content with what the people gave, not even when they offered their first-born in the sacrifice of flames. That god—sometimes called *Baal* or *Melqart* or *Beelzebub*—had many names, many faces. Suddenly he was not just a myth; he was a presence. And we stood at the edge of his sucking flames. By all that was unholy, I wanted to turn and run. But I thought of Sarah, and of this brave-hearted boy, Liske.

"There was another door," he was saying, "at the back of the room. They just put me there. That was where I found Sarah. And another."

"Another!" said Lycurgus.

"Yes. But when I awakened, she was not there anymore. I don't know where she went."

Oh, Lord. The anger rose like bile in me.

"They fed us something, but Sarah could hardly eat. She slept almost all the time. But she knew me, I think. She held my hand."

"How did you get out?" Manasseh asked, his voice tense.

"At the back of this room, where they kept us, there was a little hole. I think air came through there. When I sat by it, I could feel air moving on my skin. I started digging at it, but soon I hit rocks. I could just squeeze through them. I tried to take Sarah with me. But she was so tired. She just wanted to sleep. And I couldn't . . . I wasn't strong enough to get her, to carry her.

"When I got out, I wanted to get help. But I didn't know where to go . . ." Liske's voice was telling the strain. Every word broke now. His eyes were closing.

"Liske," I said urgently. "Tell me. Can we get in that way?"

He nodded. In a whisper, he said, "It's dark inside. I crawled a long way. And there were . . . things in there."

We looked at each other.

Liske looked up into Manasseh's face. "I tried, Father. I tried to be brave, but I don't think I can go back."

Manasseh's head was bent as he choked on his weeping and said, "You won't have to, my son. You've already done the bravest thing a boy can do."

"Good," Liske whispered, and his eyes closed. He slept quietly against his father's chest.

CHAPTER
NINETEEN

B ehind me, Doval's breath heaved against the thick air. As trespassers upon evil land, we felt as weak as the torchlight in this
darkness, as if we too could at an instant be pinched out. I had felt the
threat the moment we entered the dried watercourse, following it to the
crooked little hole in the rock, its edges sharp as teeth, opening like jaws
to the underworld. I fought against the voice howling inside me, "I don't
want to go in there!" But I thought of Liske and went on.

When I lit the torch and bent to the hole to squeeze through, I had
looked into Doval's eyes. They were as cold and resolute as stone. I knew
there would be no going back, even if we died in the bowels of this earth.

We crawled on hands and knees. The natural light from the jagged
entrance shone only a short distance, faded to an oblique point behind
us, and winked out as the tunnel turned inward.

Then came subterranean darkness, not night. The night, even darkest
night, holds variations of intensity, striations of shadow. And it has space.
Night goes outward, into the infinite reaches of the heavens.

Everything here compressed inward, as if the air had been sucked out
and only a thickness, too heavy to be air, remained. Torch in hand, I
bruised my knuckles against rocks as I lunged and thrust it before me. The
flame spat insignificantly.

I tried not to think of the tons of rock pressing around me, growing
tighter by the inch.

We felt we were being engorged, eaten alive. Worse, we crawled under our own power into those constricting bowels.

Liske is but a boy, I was thinking. *Narrow and thin. How did I ever think I could do this?* Regardless, he *had* done it. Now we had to finish it. I wondered if I could ever get back out, if I could do this again, and I knew in my heart I could not.

Sweat poured from my body. I felt Doval's hand bump into my ankles from time to time, and her hands were slippery too. Her breath seemed like a pounding rasp, then I realized it was my own breathing I heard. Slithering to my stomach under the low-ceilinged tunnel, I felt my heart hammer against my chest, against the rock. I pushed the torch ahead of me, but the smoke fouled my eyes and caught in my lungs. A thin passage of air, slipping by our bodies, carried the smoke past us.

Soon we would have to extinguish the torch. It took up space and air. And there could be no scent of oil, no trace of smoke, to give us away. Yet I clung to its light, could not bear the moment when I would have to shut it out.

Liske had told us there was a small cavern, a place where you could sit up, before the final plunge down. We would leave the torch there.

How much further? I wondered.

* * *

We had decided Taletha would stay with Liske, apart from whatever happened.

"I am not helpless because I'm carrying a child!" she protested angrily.

It was Doval who convinced her. I'm not sure what passed between them, but Taletha finally nodded and hugged her sister. She kissed me, took Liske's hand and walked back to our shelter.

Manasseh and Lycurgus were to circle the front of the cavern and wait among the rocks until I gave them a signal; I had no idea what that would be yet.

We thought of some prearranged moment when they would rush the front door and we the back. A surprise attack made good military sense, but here it was nonsense. We had no ability to measure time. Already time seemed suspended. An hour in here? Minutes? Impossible to tell. We measured time by the space we moved—mere inches with each spasmodic jerking forward.

What then? We would breach the back entrance. Somehow I would rush through and open the front door, while Doval fled back through the tunnel with Sarah. But could she? Sarah had been unable to leave with Liske. Drugged or exhausted or stripped of volition by her captivity, she had been unable to move.

Could Doval herself endure the tunnel again?

In the end, we left it that Manasseh and Lycurgus would wait as long as they thought necessary. When they could wait no longer, they would storm the door. And pray that we were out of the tunnel, that Sarah was safe.

* * *

Abruptly the tunnel widened. The light touched the walls. We had made the cavern. I wrenched into the opening, reaching behind to half-drag, half-help Doval out into it.

I propped the torch against the wall and sank back, leaning against it. Everything felt strange to my senses. The air should be cool this far underground. Instead it burned, as though from subterranean fires. Sweat dripped from my face, ran down my body. Whatever earth sense I had once had during my years of training as a Magus seemed obliterated. Rather, this place perverted and distorted nearly every pattern of earth lore I had ever known.

Doval's face was a mask. Dirt clotted in the sweat and dripped down her cheeks. Blood trickled from cuts on her hands, forearms, legs. I looked at my own hands and found them ribboned with abrasions.

I leaned back and tried to control my breathing. The longer we waited, the less certain I was I could go on. But I could not go back.

Across from us in the tiny cavern the tunnel reentered the mountain. It was a pathetically narrow hole, and in the weak light I could see it twist down.

I began to understand the early pattern of this place. At one time, impossibly remote, when rains or floods ravaged this land that was now everywhere desert, the water had cut the gully that we had walked down. This would have been long after the storms of earthquake that heaved the land around like building blocks, creating the chasm itself, the ridged wall and the sea of salt beyond us. That was the first thing.

But the rains had come, eroding the earth's crust with the mighty force of water. It is indeed the most potent force this world knows. And as it surged through countless watercourses to form the sea that now lay trapped in its own salt bed, the water had pounded against the rock formations left by earthquakes. It found a weakness in the rock, a striation in its resilience. It pushed and washed against it, carving out a hollow. It found the weakness and tore at it, diving in its relentless trek to the sea ever downward, eating out a vein in the rock like some monster.

Then it found a soft space, the tiny cavern where we now sat, and the waters pooled and eddied until it formed another tiny passage, and whirled against it, diving down, rampaging against the rock, until it hit bottom. And there it exploded outward, forming the lower cavern, tearing out to meet the waters that coursed around the monolith of rock outside.

And the water flowed freely and chiseled against the rock within and the rock without, depositing sediment, carving the surfaces.

Then the time of the floods ended. The sun beat down, leaving this seared and desolate landscape.

Animals of prey would have crept in for shelter at first. But as the land grew arid, prey left, and the beasts moved north, vacating their burrows. Save for the strange creatures who adapted to this weird and primeval land, little had remained.

Until darker creatures came. Those who had no home. And they held the land and its dark places.

All this I knew, I understood. It was earth knowledge. What I did not know was the shape of this present darkness that held sway over the land. Somehow it fed upon its worst energies, magnifying the distortion itself.

* * *

Doval nudged me. "Do you want me to go first?" she asked.

I shook my head. The tunnel was too narrow. Impossible.

I stood up and stripped off my cloak, naked save for my loincloth. Already the fabric of the cloak had begun to catch and tear against rock on the way in. In the torchlight, my dark flesh was bathed in sweat.

I looked at Doval. She shook her head. "I can make it," she said.

In her look was something that made my heart weep, my soul bleed.

Once, impossibly long ago, I had been her protector. Now she was stronger than I. But the love was still there, and I couldn't help smiling at her. Even at this grim moment. Before putting out the torch, I told her that—"I love you, Doval"—and she hugged me, my daughter, enfolding this gaunt, repulsive body in her arms.

Then I rammed the torch into sediment dust, extinguishing its precious glow, and bent to the dark hole into the greater darkness.

* * *

I slithered forward, jerking my body spasmodically like a snake, Doval behind me. The harsh sound of our breathing was overpowering; it thundered. I pulled and wrenched downward, desperate to get out, growing ever more certain I could not, ever, go back this way.

How did Liske do it! He would have had to grope blindly *uphill*.

The walls constricted. The ceiling now pressed on my shoulders, my back.

I was caught! I could not move. Blind panic hit me. I had fought it so hard. So very hard. It didn't seem fair. I thrashed against the rock, pummeled it with clawing fingers, heaving legs.

Doval's voice was a plea, then a shout.

"Elhrain! Elhrain!"

I thrashed the harder. My feet struck something behind me. Heard the whimper. Then I fell limp, heart pounding wildly, sweat scouring my eyes.

"Elhrain," Doval whispered. "Don't."

I fought for breath. For control. "Sorry," I whispered.

"Relax. Just relax," she pleaded.

"I . . . can't." I fought for control. "I'm stuck."

"No. You can do it. We'll do it together. Elhrain, listen to me." Her voice was surprisingly firm. She commanded me. No. She met me in my fear and bathed me with her spirit.

"Listen to me," she said. "First, just breathe. Relax." She counted breaths—in and out—several times. My bunched muscles relaxed a little.

"Imagine, Elhrain," she said, "you're not where you think you are. You're . . . swimming."

I saw her then. The girl-child who had come to my home in Babylon. How she loved to walk with me from the palace to the river. She was always the athlete; her brother the student. Doval would slip into the river with scarcely a splash, darting through the water with the slippery ease of one born to it.

"Yes," I breathed.

"Can you picture it, Elhrain?"

"Yes, at Babylon. Swimming."

She was silent a moment. I felt her tremble. "Yes. Now slowly. Don't fight the rock. Glide. Glide through the passage."

I let my body relax, felt the knotted muscles uncoil.

I budged, only a few inches at first. Then we slowly curved around bulging edges, then more rapidly slid down a straight passage.

"Doval," I whispered. "I think I see light."

"I can't tell," she said.

The tunnel broadened slightly. Its path leveled.

The light was a sick red glare leaking between boards. My head entered the cavern. I reached forward and pulled myself out. I sat on hands and knees, trembling over every inch of my body. I couldn't stop shaking.

Doval crawled past. She leaned over a small bench, cut into rock. A little body lay there under a thin blanket. Doval groaned, deep in her throat.

"Is she alive?" I asked, and my voice felt like ashes in my throat.

"Her heart is beating. She's breathing."

I crouched in the low-ceilinged cavern and crawled to them.

Sanguine light touched Sarah's tousled hair. Despite the oppressive heat of the confined space, no sweat lay on her skin. She shivered. When I touched her arm, her eyes squeezed tight, then relaxed when I removed my hand.

"We have to get her out of here," Doval whispered.

"Any minute," I said, "Lycurgus and Manasseh—"

Doval shook her head violently. "No, you don't understand. We have to *free* her."

I did understand, and the fear I felt then was like none other I have ever known.

I turned to the door, a span of ribbed boards about four feet high, framed over the entrance to the larger cavern. I bent and peered through a crack where the red light glowed.

A harsh cackle, like hot wind over dried ground, rose from the other side. The voice was a dry croaking sound, more a primitive force than a voice.

"Come in, Elhrain. We have awaited you."

CHAPTER
TWENTY

The three creatures leaned toward the flame, as if taking energy from its crimson depths. The flame itself wavered in a whorled mass, too red and too thick to nurture. It sucked inward, feeding on the dense air of this funeral chamber; it was light perverted.

The creatures sat like withered husks, wrapped in brown cloaks with their hoods pulled so far forward that their faces were absorbed by darkness. One of them reached out an arm, the cloak falling over the outstretched hand, and scattered some powders on the flame. The fire writhed in the shallow bowl that held it.

I could not rip my gaze from the fire. It thickened to impossible density, and though the saucer was empty of wood, it coiled like a serpent. The flames were hypnotic. It took great effort to tear my eyes away, to probe the vault for a way out.

The three figures sat cross-legged before the flaming saucer, backs bent and hunched. They looked—although I could discern no features—impossibly old. I don't know how, but I had the sense of years upon years. They seemed, even then, somehow beyond time.

About the bowl lay a ring of stones; another surrounded the figures on the outside. The walls were a deep crimson. And as Liske had described, the entire chamber—a hollow cell, like a inverted bowl—was ringed by a shelf, about chest high, upon which stood human skulls. They were of infinitely varied sizes, arranged in an order, starting with tiny bone cups, in which the hollowed eyes and sinuses were barely discernible, and progressing to full-size human skulls, gleaming with the crimson light. Several were lacking the lower jaw, the teeth clinging to the rock shelf as if in an outburst of pain.

My stomach twisted suddenly, but when I turned to gag, the air seemed to close in my throat. I stood panting, sweat dripping into my eyes. The figures slid before me, and for a moment I thought I was going to pass out. I heard whimpering behind me. Doval.

And another sound. Like the grating of desert sands. The hunched and shriveled figures were laughing in silent mirth.

"At last." When the voice came, it was impossible to tell the source. It was just from somewhere in the circle, as if there was but one voice for the three. "Step forward, Elhrain. You have come a long way."

A second voice cackled gleefully. Still I was not certain it was not the same figure. The voice seemed feminine, either that or aged to a dry, high whine. "But we have never been far from you, wanderer. At last you have found us. All your seeking is finally requited."

"Who are you?"

"Was it hard, Elhrain? Traveling here? We could have helped, you know, but for her."

An empty sleeve waved to the room behind me. The dried voices chuckled obscenely.

"Caught now," said one voice.

"Trapped," echoed another.

A cascade of dry laughter.

Madness. Old crones. I could walk right past them.

The laughter rose with my thoughts, beating in my ears. "The door, Elhrain? It doesn't go out. It only goes in. No one leaves by this door."

Madness. "Who are you! Tell me."

"We are Golem."

Their voices echoed in a weird chant, sound interlacing, impossible to tell the source.

"We are Golem.

"We are Hartm, Mistress of Stars," said the voice.

"We are Habr, Mistress of Signs and Oracles," said the voice.

The *same* voice, dry, lifeless, rising in a mad chorus.

"We are Gulda, Mistress of Histories and Tongues," said the voice.

Nausea attacked me like grief. Howls of dry laughter rolled through the vault.

"Master of . . ." I muttered.

The mad laughter ended. "Oh, you remember, Elhrain." The voice was like ice on my flesh. "The gifts of the Magi. The Wise Ones. The Old Ones. But they are *our* gifts. So you come to our Table. Welcome, Elhrain, to your true calling."

"No!"

"Yes. You are called to be one of us. To take your place among us. To *be* us. To be our power. Master of Earth, Elhrain; we are complete."

The door. I had to reach it. The one thing I was certain of was that I could not stand here debating them. And for one weird moment I seemed to be standing, young and bewildered, at the Table of the Brotherhood in the Palace of the Magi. Before me were Gaspar, Master of the Stars; Balthazzar, Master of Dreams and Signs; Melchior, Master of Histories and Languages. And they awaited me. Balthazzar, my father, waved his hand and motioned to my seat. Elhrain, Master of Earth. And, as then, I stood confused. Of Earth? The ways of the desert, the interplay of sun and moon, the rhythm of planting and harvest.

But it had never been just that! Never.

"No," I croaked. "That isn't it."

The Table shifted redly.

Balthazzar spoke, but it was not his voice speaking. "We have waited for you a long time."

"You knew we were coming?" I asked.

"Since you crossed the divide."

"The chasm.

"The rocks.

"The dry place.

"You came down to us. From that moment you were ours."

The shapes were Melchior, Gaspar, Balthazzar. The voices were the crackling of the flames.

"Earth Master, join us."

No! Knowledge of the Earth—I had put it behind me. But never behind me. The earth was law and pattern. The knowledge was how pattern was distorted or how it held in harmony.

"Come, Elhrain."

The figures vibrated violently. I looked into dark faces under brown hoods where eyes burned like red coals.

I wanted to wail out, *I don't understand! Leave me alone!*

Incarnadine light flickered along the walls, tongues of fire licking the hollow skulls. Their blank eyes probed me, empty jaws howled silent laughter at me.

The Table seemed to float bodily, as if I had to take but one step and enter irreversibly into its madness.

"Take your seat, my son." The voice was deep, profound. The tones urgent and pleading. Gaspar and Melchior sat smiling at me. Balthazzar beckoned, arm outstretched. "We will be one."

"It's a lie," I hissed.

His smile was like a weary scar. It cut along his broad, handsome face like a wound. "I am waiting for you."

"What do you want?"

"For you to join me. Then we will be complete. Father and son. It's what you always wanted."

"No! Balthazzar found *him*."

The shape that looked like Balthazzar gasped as if in sudden pain.

The cackling dry voice rose shrilly. "Don't deceive yourself, hypocrite. Here lies power."

"Here lies distortion. *That* isn't my father."

"You're confused, Elhrain. You said it yourself. Join us, and you shall be complete."

"This is *complete!* Lying in the bowels of the earth?" Suddenly I understood the deceit. The Table of the Brotherhood shimmered and disappeared. "Be at peace, Father," I said.

Waves of red light attacked me. I was aware of a hammering sound at the door. Then, like rocks smashing, its sound reverberated in the vault.

"Whatever power I have," I said, "it will never be given to deceit."

"Elhrain," the voice cackled. "You have *no* power. Don't you know this yet? Earth-power? Don't you see? It is nothing. By itself it does nothing. You yourself have said the earth has its own laws. You don't even understand, much less work power."

"Then why . . ."

The cackling sound was a thunder. Or was it the blows on the door?

"Your child, Elhrain! Bargain now. Your time grows short."

As the withered crone spoke, a tongue of flame licked over the edge of the bowl. She flung powder at it, hissing in some inarticulate tongue. The flame twisted, crawling along the rock, rearing, a living thing. It coiled toward my ankles. I could not move a step, while everything in me fought to crush it. Slowly, it twisted past me, turning malevolently at the threshold where Doval knelt by Sarah's side.

"No!" I shouted.

"Elhrain," Doval whispered, "they cannot touch me. Believe me. Free yourself. I am safe."

"Free myself . . ."

"Yes, Elhrain," hissed the crone. "Bargain and you shall go free."

"What do you want?"

"Not you. You are nothing."

I know, I wailed inwardly. *I know. I am nothing.* "What?" I spat. "Tell me!"

"Your child."

"My—"

"Yes. This one for that one."

"My child is unborn."

"All the easier then."

"Never."

"Remember, Elhrain. You are nothing. We give you length of days to remember it. If only—"

"Then I would never be free."

"Yes," the voice was urgent. "Free. With power. You will stand at the head of our hosts, and your child shall carry on. The gifted one."

I wrenched a step forward. "I know you, Adversary," I muttered. "I've seen your face a thousand times."

Something powerful shook the door.

"Stand and show your face," I said and took another step. The serpentine flame spat and hissed at my ankles. Doval murmured something; I could not understand the words.

"You would tempt me, would you, Adversary? You, who hide in darkness, buried in this earth?"

"We rule! We rule the earth."

"But cannot break its laws, can you? Yet you would tempt me, for my

184

own child. Don't you see? It is the one thing needful to me, the one thing beyond price. There is nothing in heaven or earth that can tempt me. Fools. Utter fools!" I spat the words at them, hardly understanding what I was myself saying. The serpent of fire coiled about my feet, yet I wrenched another step toward them.

"Threaten me! Make me afraid! Show me your magic! But don't you dare tempt me."

A dry moaning scraped the vaulted walls. The crooked figures huddled over their flame. Powders smoked the air.

"I will tell you why, Golem. I will tell you, Earth Creature. There is a word you don't know. A word you cannot speak."

A sudden crack rent the air. My eyes were fixed on the bent figures, but I knew the door was splintering.

"The word I have learned, Golem, the word you cannot speak, is the only one that holds the pattern of the earth together." I swung an arm back at Doval. "I know why your power cannot touch her!" I screamed. "It is because of the word that cannot cross your tongue."

The red air split and whined. Flames coiled and reared.

"Love," I whispered. "It is not in your vocabulary. Yet it stands behind me in the shape of this woman."

"She is a whore!" whined the voice.

"Love stands outside your door, Golem."

"No!"

I heard Doval's weeping. "Yes," she called. "Yes."

"Dry and desolate your days; for you have chosen *against*. You can never more choose *for*."

I kicked at the flame. It spat back like a serpent rearing.

"You would ask me to choose . . . my own son. Fools!" I thundered. "It has already been done! Never again."

The figures hunched and cried out. Their withered shapes shriveled inward.

I saw a rough, calloused hand reach through the rent in the door. It slipped the bar, and the door pushed open.

"Stand aside," I shouted.

Beyond the door, harsh desert sunlight cascaded into the mouth of the cavern. Its cruel radiance filtered right though the dark-robed figures.

Lycurgus twisted back, a hand covering his face, as the flames shot and spat from the saucer.

Manasseh crouched, his massive shoulders bunched, sweat rolling over his torso.

"No, Manasseh," I called. "It's not necessary."

With a growl of rage, he launched himself into the flame. Kicking, he fought his way to the altar of fire. The serpents of fire surged up his legs, cascaded over his torso. For a moment he rocked back.

Lycurgus spun inward, his sword slicing through the tongues of flame. They gathered on the blade, weighing it, and crawled up his arm. He coughed with pain.

Then Manasseh lurched forward, flames wrapped around his body like a sheath. He bent and grasped the edges of the shallow bowl. The hooded figures fell back, gibbering in the shadows. One tried to fling powders at the flame and I kicked out. My foot met the furled cloth and passed through it with a crackling sound. A sudden scorching pain shot up my leg, as if I had kicked a burning rock. But the figure tumbled back, its loose robe writhing.

Manasseh held the altar in both hands. It had seemed so light, nearly floating on the rock. But as his shoulders bunched, muscles quivering like ropes, he seemed to be pulling at the roots of the rock itself.

A cracking sound knived the air. Still the flames singed and blistered about him. His entire body seemed afire. His eyes squeezed shut. His teeth clenched so hard his jaw trembled.

He heaved, thigh muscles working like an ox. His powerful forearms pulled. Inch by inch the bowl rose. He staggered under the weight of the shallow dish, as if holding the weight of the mountain in his hands. Slowly it rose, higher, a bit higher. He staggered under the weight. Then, in one fierce wrench, with a cry that thundered through the chasm, he raised the bowl over his head, standing a moment with the flame hissing and snapping the length of his body, and flung the bowl crashing and splintering into the wall.

The very rocks shook and trembled. I reached out for Doval. She was already on her feet, Sarah in her arms. The little girl clung fiercely to Doval's neck, her eyes wide with terror.

"Lycurgus," I ordered. But he was already bent to lift Manasseh, helping him toward the mouth of the cave.

The ground trembled. "Quickly now."

Ahead of us the three creatures crawled on hands and knees to the entrance. As they went, the tattered cloaks peeled off them. I stopped, even as the rock shifted, appalled at the sight. Doval placed her hand protectively over Sarah's eyes.

As the first creature crawled toward the entrance, the harsh sunlight seemed to attack the cloak. A sleeve peeled away, revealing a brown, furred limb, crooked and angular, long twisted nails scrabbling desperately at the rock. The cloak shredded, revealing a humped spine, blotchy patches of hair tangled on the dark skin. It crawled like an animal now, some hideous freak with claws scraping the rock. When it neared the light, the angular head twisted backward, skewed on the neck. Brilliant yellow eyes flickered at us; the jaws gaped on yellowed fangs. A red tongue spat incoherent words.

A large rock whistled past my ear and thudded near the creature. I turned and saw Manasseh, his hair and beard burned away to single strands and his eyes starting savagely from a blackened face, bend to reach for another rock.

The creatures howled and scuttled out into the chasm, where the sunlight fired their bodies into a livid glow.

Tremors attacked the rock. We lunged to the entrance.

I saw Taletha standing boldly among the rocks, her hands on Liske's shoulders. They stood watching. For a moment I thought the creatures were going to veer and attack them, and I began to run. "Hide," I shouted. But the two stood unmoving, bold and defiant.

From above, high on the rim of the chasm came a shrill whistle. The creatures gibbered desperately as they surged past Taletha, and I saw her look up.

High on the rim of the chasm stood a crooked little shape. He leaned for a moment on the staff, his blind eyes staring into space.

Howling, the creatures attacked the cliff, scattering rocks as they climbed. They flailed at boulders, slipping and turning, but always climbing. One of them beat at a rock, and a bilious green stain, like bubbling acid, trailed it upward. Even as they climbed, I heard jaws snapping hollowly.

As they neared the rim of the cliff, Andrew slowly spread his arms. His crooked body straightened, and he looked as though he had grown larger, the staff a mighty weapon in his outstretched hand. But then the rock was trembling, and the sun seemed to spin in the sky as the earth shook. Running behind Taletha and Liske through the rocks to the path, I just barely saw the creatures surge over the cliff and fling themselves upon Andrew. A brilliant flash of pure silver light erupted above the cliff.

When we stopped, gasping for breath near the foot of the trail, I scanned the rim of the chasm. A pure argent gleam hovered over the rock. Andrew was nowhere to be seen.

We felt the earth crumple as we climbed. Behind us the Place of the Skulls began to collapse upon itself. But we were very high on the trail then, and I didn't dare look down.

*　*　*

We walked without once looking back. If I looked, just once, I believed, something terrible would happen. This was past. It was finished. I refused to look back.

The afternoon sun boiled in the sky and the desert held its breath. The heat was withering.

Manasseh lurched in broken steps, his eyes sunken and fixed directly before his feet, as if willing each step. Liske clung to his hand, half-leading his father. We staggered along in a ragged band, Lycurgus and I taking turns carrying Sarah on our backs. No one spoke.

At midafternoon the sun wore a veil, its light obscured by haze.

The great plain was unbroken by rock, as flat as a line stretched to the endless horizon.

Only once Taletha spoke. "Are we heading the right way?" The way was toward Andrew's cave. Toward protection. Toward recovery. There was not a chance if we missed it. I glanced at the sun and nodded.

But the sun hung obscured, and we felt the lessening of its power. Far in the west I noticed a gray pall on the shimmering horizon. I studied it for a moment, my heart sinking. *What more can we handle?* I thought. For the shimmering pall was growing. I remembered the violent sandstorms that ravaged my native land, the terrible stillness and the sudden fury, and my heart quailed. *It's not fair.*

I transferred Sarah to Lycurgus and leaned, hands on thighs, panting for a moment. The others trudged on wordlessly. My legs were spent, quivering as I stood.

I stumbled to keep up. Taletha turned. "Are you okay?" she asked. Her

188

eyes were clouded with concern.

I could not help saying it, though I knew I should not. The words wouldn't stop. "They wanted . . . our child," I said.

She recoiled slightly. Then she said, simply, "I know."

"You know?"

"Somehow . . . I heard every word."

I stared at her standing there in the graying sky.

"It is over, husband. You prevailed." And she smiled at me and wrapped me in her arms. I looked over her shoulder at the darkening sky and started to chuckle.

She felt me, and thought that I was weeping, and held me harder. But I took her shoulders and forced her to turn and look.

The gray cloud had risen to the rim of the sun, now cutting into its fierce glare. It rose, huge and monolithic, like a swelling from the earth. Pillars of cloud, gray and trembling, towered toward a tremendous balloon of black storm that covered all the southern and western sky.

Suddenly lightning ripped through the pillars. The earth reverberated to a long peal of thunder that rolled on and on.

The others stopped, transfixed. The lightning cracked again, whiplashes of white fire, again and again.

"We need shelter," Lycurgus called. Desperately he scanned the empty plain.

I chuckled and shook my head. "No," I called. "Look. It will pass behind us. But who," I said, "ever heard of a storm in this desert?"

"I think it was called here," Doval said. For some odd reason, I found that totally plausible.

Even as the storm rose, blotting out the sun entirely, turning the entire heavens a frenzy of gray and green exploding with lightning bolts, I felt no fear, for the storm was on a leash, as though governed, guided. We watched awestruck, feeling completely safe even as the earth trembled under our feet.

Only then did we look back, sinking to our knees as the incredible fury of storm swept the desert. A softly blowing drizzle draped us in moisture, but only a short distance away the rain pounded the earth. Rivulets scoured the desert's crust. We tilted heads back, opening mouths to the moisture that saturated us.

On and on the monster ravaged the earth, passing through the desert to the south. In my mind's eye I saw those rivulets cascading together, to a wall of water pushed by lightning and wind, blasting over the chasm, plunging in waterfalls upon the violated earth below.

The storm lasted for a long time, and we knelt on a puddled desert bathed by water. When the last rumble washed away, we looked around at a new and different land. We ourselves seemed strangely different, as if cleansed and rendered whole again. When the first stars blinked through the clouds we picked up our way, following the unchanging chart in the heavens, to Andrew's cave.

* * *

He wasn't there. Nor did we really expect him to be.

We crossed into the gentle canyon. The far fringes of the storm had touched even here. Pools of fresh water still lay among the rocks. In the morning light they winked boldly at us. The earth was littered with tiny green shoots from seeds that had lain dormant for many months.

We threaded our way among the rocks to the narrow ledge of his cave. The coals of a fire still burned softly in the fire pit, casting a warm, friendly glow over the cavern. Lycurgus collected an armful of branches piled by the entrance and laid them on the coals. As they licked into the flame, he murmured softly, "A good place."

"What did he call it?" asked Doval. "The last safe place?"

"Not any more," Lycurgus said. "For now, it's just a place to rest before we return."

Doval leaned against him as he sat down. Sarah placed her head in Doval's lap and was asleep almost instantly.

As firelight filled the warm walls with its glow, Liske stood up and said in a wondering voice, "Look!"

At the entrance, propped against the wall where we couldn't see it at first, was Andrew's staff. Liske walked to it, lifted it and touched it gently.

"Mahogany," Manasseh said. "Best in the world."

"Why did he leave it?" Liske asked.

"I think he left it for you," I said.

"Really?" The boy's eyes shone.

"Really," I said, and Manasseh nodded, chuckling gently as he leaned against the wall.

"Bring it here, son," he said, "and let's keep it safe."

190

Timidly, Liske sat next to his father. He held the staff with wonder. Then, as morning light filtered into the cave, he laid his head against his father's chest. I noticed that the rain had washed away every trace of soot from Manasseh's body. But at that point he wouldn't have cared. He too was sound asleep.

Taletha curled against me. My hand brushed her abdomen, and I was surprised at the distended bulge. Gently I placed my hand there. I felt the faintest flutter. I pressed slightly. Yes, there it was, like little drums beating against my palm. I looked down at Taletha, and there was a smile on her sleeping face.

PART THREE
THE CAPITAL CITY

CHAPTER
TWENTY-ONE

G reen hills rolled beyond the river, rising past the village of Noke.
I relived the awe I had felt years before, when I had first let my
eyes rove over this lush landscape. Except now I could identify those mist-
shrouded rises far in the distance, where the valley ran up against the hills,
and knew that there truly lay home.

As she had years before, Taletha squeezed my hand with her eagerness.

* * *

We had stayed at the house of Benjamin upon our return. We tarried
there long enough for Taletha to share the news of her pregnancy. I
watched her, as she searched shyly for the right words, then simply burst
out with the news—"We're going to have a baby." And what a sweet
clamor met that declaration. The men thumped me joyfully on the back.
The women cooed over Taletha as if she were a young married woman.

Stories of sore backs, of cramps, of foods and indigestion mingled with
smiles and tender words.

This warrior, this woman of the desert, loved every minute of it. She
might have been a young married woman, expecting her first child. I
shook my head in wonder, feeling a million years old. I stared at the
millrace of children perpetually about Benjamin's house and wondered
how I would survive.

* * *

Then we followed our winding trail west, avoiding the highway, camping in the brush between desert and fertile land. We felt like skirmishers, forever in between. But we also felt we were heading home.

At last we stood at the embankment from which we could see, far ahead, the crooked little buildings of Noke and, rising in the distance, the blue-green hills over which cloud shadows tumbled like great, gray butterflies.

Manasseh hurried ahead to the narrow ribbon of the river that wound around the southern edge of Noke. Sarah clung to one massive hand, her bent legs thin as twigs. She seemed a mere wisp, hurrying to keep up. On the other side, Liske, his curly red hair like spongy wool in the light, also hurried.

Finally Manasseh simply picked one child up in each arm and ran down the long embankment. The river water cascaded up as if struck by a boulder. It scarcely slowed him. He whooped with the spray of water and plunged on to Noke.

But not us.

Noke was no longer a haven, at least not for Lycurgus and Doval, both of whom had a price on their heads as escaped prisoners. They simply stood there, watching, with smiles on their faces.

I turned and looked at them after Manasseh disappeared into the village streets.

The sun was well up in the east. Lycurgus's powerful features, his hawklike nose and piercing eyes, were aglow in its light.

"Can you stay with us, at least tonight?" I asked.

Lycurgus looked at Doval, as if asking.

"I think we can," she said.

"Very well," he agreed. "We must leave during the night." He gazed at me. "They'll be looking, you know."

"Yes," I said. "But you also need supplies. We can help. I have more than enough."

He chuckled. I had no idea if this illegitimate son of an emperor of all Rome had any need for my help or not. But then I remembered that that was so impossibly distant in Lycurgus's past as to be irrecoverable.

"Where do you think you'll go?" Taletha asked.

Lycurgus shrugged. "To the coast first, of course. We have sympathiz-

196

ers willing to help. From there . . . I'm not sure."

* * *

We passed north around Noke, keeping to the river. During the heat of the day we rested among some willows by the river's edge. The day was warm for this climate; one is still ever mindful of the desert's proximity. But a breeze worked down from the hills and, as always, carried the fragrance of the sea and grass and hill flowers with it.

Taletha was ready for a rest. I had noticed how she paced herself on the way out of the desert, a trek which took us almost twice as long as going in. She tired more readily and was able to eat less. I could see, very perceptibly now, the swelling of her womb as she lay back in the grass.

I had been standing at the water's edge, letting its cool flow wash my dry skin. I could have stood there, just so, for hours. I stepped out and leaned down by her side, stroking her strong thin arm with my fingers. I palmed some cold water from the hem of my cloak, and let it drip from my fingers upon her forehead. She shivered and smiled at me.

"Do you think we'll be safe here?" she asked.

I knew the question would be on her mind, as it was on mine. Only I didn't want to ask it; I simply wanted to go on and pretend the danger didn't exist.

I shook my head. "I don't think they'll leave us alone," I said. "Maybe they can't connect us with the prison break, but, remember, they were aware of your work long before. They were watching even then."

"Why? Why can't they leave us alone?"

"They can't tolerate it. No dissent can be permitted. It's always the way."

"Funny, isn't it," she mused. "How often haven't we, you and I, Elhrain, felt different. Like outsiders. Yet the greatest thing in the world is to be free to be different. To believe the way you want, do what you feel is right."

"Speak out against what you feel is wrong," I added.

She nodded sleepily, musing. "And they can't tolerate that difference, so we get singled out."

"Because you're dangerous, woman."

"No I'm not!" She chuckled.

I watched her lying there. On the bank behind us I heard Lycurgus and

Doval talking quietly. Making plans? Where would they go? I reached out and touched Taletha's gently mounded womb, and I felt that little flutter of life. She laid her hand on mine, holding it there.

"I don't want to run anymore," she said. Her eyes looked bottomless; to look into them was like drifting into warm water, like being bathed in some unnamable safety. Taletha looked back into my eyes. "I want to stay here," she said.

I nodded, and breathed a sigh of relief.

"This is my home," she said. "I want to have our baby here."

"Yes," I breathed.

I heard footsteps. "You understand the danger, though," Lycurgus said. "You could come with us. We've just been talking about it."

I couldn't help myself. I quoted his own words back to him, "If it is the Lord's will."

He smiled then. "In his peace," he said.

Peace.

*　*　*

It is quiet in the countryside now. The days saunter by.

Standing in the pasture with the dew wetting my legs to the knees, I watch the sun poke its first interested rays over the land. It glints off the walls of our farmhouse. A grove of trees at the edge of the pasture bends to a breath of wind and the leaves tremble with light. They are so beautiful, so tender.

In shadows the leaves are deep and green, hanging like heavy weights from the branches. But in the sunlight they brighten to gold. Gold is nature's color of rejoicing. Spring arrives with gold; after the deep, green summer it takes on its autumn hue as if recollecting a spent youth.

It is so quiet standing here I can hear a cricket in the underbrush, creating a solitary brave song.

I have become at home in this land. Its rhythms are the rhythms of my life now.

I hear the dog barking, and I turn to watch. Curving over the bend of the hill the tiny flock of sheep moves like a puffy cloud. The dog herds a baffled lamb, yipping at its heels. Liske sees me, and he raises the staff, Andrew's staff, and waves.

Then he and his sheep are gone, and the dog's barking fades under the song of the cricket. There are only a handful of sheep now, those rescued from their wandering, those not lost to predators during our time in the desert.

They are starting over.

* * *

We have heard nothing from Lycurgus and Doval.

When they left, I tried to give him the handful of golden coins, embossed with the seal of the House of Komani—the intertwined serpents. I had kept them all these days.

Lycurgus grimaced when he saw the image of the serpents. I don't know what meaning he read into the figure. He returned the coins. "I am provided for, Elhrain," he said.

But I wanted him to have them, for I had nothing else to give. Then he understood, and took two: one for Doval, one for himself.

They were to head for the coast, taking the mountain trail. That was weeks ago, and we have heard nothing. Yet I am certain of their safety. I only wish I knew where. Rome? As I understood it, Lycurgus had kept, all these years, a villa in some northern province of that land. Or had they gone elsewhere, still working in the cause they now cherished more than life itself?

* * *

The little priest, Napthali, died at the coast. His passing was altogether peaceful. He was an old man, who carried all his battles behind a bemused smile and eyes full of laughter.

He simply grew old.

The night before his ship was to leave for a northern port, he had shook his head.

"I'm not going," he said. "I'm going home."

During the night, his breathing slowed, spaced finally to gasps between interminable stillnesses. Then, near dawn, he relaxed, and his body went limp.

This we heard weeks later, as news filtered along the underground route to Noke and eventually to us.

* * *

We do not go often to Noke. We stay here waiting.

But I am nervous about Taletha. Maybe this business of having babies is for younger women. I don't know. I have no experience. But her energy wanes daily. Certainly she makes every effort to appear normal. But I see the effort it takes, and that unnerves me.

I see the food untouched on her plate, or the tiny portions merely nibbled at. Then I hear her, when she excuses herself for a walk, retching dryly by the creek. She returns with a smile and busies herself in the kitchen. And I see her stiffen suddenly with some pain.

"Babies are never born easily," she says wryly. But I catch a tremor in her voice.

"But it's not ready to be born yet," I say. "How long now?"

"Weeks. Three months maybe."

So I stand in the field, watching the sun tremble in the grove of trees, and I grow worried. I no longer hear the cricket song; I hear the sudden gasp of pain she made this morning as she brought in the bucket of water from the well. I ran to her side and said, "Let me do that. Don't do any more."

There were tears in her eyes. She said, "But I always do it!"

* * *

That afternoon I hitched up the old wagon.

Taletha came out. I tried to keep my voice casual. "Just some supplies. We need vegetables. I want to get some fresh bread. Then you won't have to worry about it."

Her eyes were fearful. "Will you be long?"

"Back by sundown," I said with a forced smile.

Her voice choked. "I . . . don't want to be alone."

My hands shook on the harness traces. This was not Taletha. She had never been afraid. Now she's afraid to be alone at her own home for a few hours. I almost stopped altogether, but my own fears forced me to go on.

"I'll be back soon," I said, and gave her a hug before leaving.

* * *

Driving into Noke, I felt a peculiar intimacy with the dusty little town, a sense of safety. That in itself was troubling. Home should mean safety.

I threaded the wagon onto the east-west road. Some acquaintances waved, and I smiled back. The streets were not busy. Travelers sat in the foreyard of Zophar's inn, wearily surveying the town. Several stalls were lined up along the road, the dealers hawking their wares.

I passed the square little house of worship, and I thought I saw a man in a dark robe standing in the doorway. Of course. There would be a new priest.

As I passed, I saw the priest talking with someone and noted that the priest was younger than I would have expected. I chuckled. Maybe I associated all these village priests with old Napthali. The priest talked earnestly with a short, broad-shouldered man in a worn red tunic over a dirty set of clothes. They both turned and watched me. The man in the red tunic had a scar arching over one cheekbone, distorting his mouth into a perpetual sneer.

I wondered what he had to bring for his propitiation. A few doves maybe, a coin or two. How utterly wearisome, this buying of forgiveness. Sins according to what one could afford.

I averted my gaze to the street ahead but felt the weight of the priest's eyes upon my back.

I pulled into a vacant space where some children played near a few ox carts and tethered mules. A young man hurried over, offering to water and feed my ox while I shopped. I slipped him a coin and told him I would be back in a couple of hours.

It felt good to walk. I passed the vegetable stalls, thinking I could pick up something on the way back, and made directly for Manasseh and Meridivel's house near the edge of the village.

* * *

Why I bypassed the carpentry shop, where Manasseh labored noisily, to go directly to their house, I'm not sure. I even caught sight of Manasseh's shoulders bent over the work bench, curls of wood sheathing off a plane as his powerful arms tracked it back and forth. Sometimes I loved to just sit and watch him work, smelling the rich odor of the different woods flooding the shop.

But I hurried past, keeping to the trees.

Meridivel sat in a small alcove adjoining the kitchen. The window was flung wide open, flooding the room with light. A large loom took up almost all the space. Strands of wool dangled from a half-dozen different pegs on the wall. The loom was the common upright form, the weft threads hanging tautly by weighted balls of clay. As I peered over Meridivel's shoulder at the work, however, I noticed subtle improvisations she had made.

Above the weight balls, for example, she had had Manasseh fashion a wooden space bar that put extra tension on the threads. The bar, with its myriad grooves hooked on the threads, could be used as a pin to tighten the weft threads. Far more fascinating, though, was the delicacy of color in the thread. Unerringly, Meridivel's fingers danced through the threads, stranding in lightly dyed colors to form a kind of painting, some scarcely begun design, in the fabric. Instead of finishing the garment and plunging it in a dye or a bleach, she was creating a work in the process.

She must have sensed me standing there behind her. She tugged the pin through the thread, jiggled the roller with her knee, and slipped it up to tie the weft. The weighted balls, I noticed, held the fabric absolutely firm, although the design as a whole shimmered slightly in the light.

"It's beautiful," I said. "Really beautiful."

"You like it?" Meridivel leaned against the wall, rubbing her forearms. "It takes a bit longer, but I can do more with it."

She stood up. "Here," she said. "I just finished something. It's for Taletha." She bustled about in a large reed basket in the corner of the room, sending flecks of wool dust flying. "Or for both of you," she said absently. "For the baby, I guess."

She pulled out the carefully folded blanket and shook it out, holding it so that the light struck it from behind.

"And this is more than beautiful," I said. "It's . . . art." Light colors of the fields and flowers playfully ran through each other. The pale yellows looked like sprinkles of flowers against a light green pasture. Fleecy splotches of white cloud bounced gaily in a blue border. Beautiful, indeed.

Meridivel waved a hand. "I tried spinning flax," she said off-handedly. "You can do more with dying on linen. But it's so boring. I wanted to work with the color itself. Do you really like it? Do you think Taletha will like it? It's from her wool, you know."

"I'm sure she'll like it," I smiled.

"Let me get Manasseh. It's almost dinner time. You'll stay, of course? It's been so long."

I laid a hand on her forearm, restraining her. "Meridivel." I took a deep breath. *How do I say this?* "I'm not sure Taletha's well. I mean, the baby and all."

"Oh, nonsense," she said dismissively. "It's just part of it. What? Vomiting?"

I nodded.

"Cramps? Tired?"

"Yes."

"Don't you worry. When the time comes, we'll come and help. I've helped with a dozen babies, Elhrain. It hurts, but it's no mystery."

"I know. I know, Meridivel. It's just . . ."

"Yes?"

"Tired is one thing. But she hardly eats. I mean . . . I wish she could see a doctor. I'm afraid, Meridivel."

For a moment, a shining amusement rose in her eyes. I was ready for it—the scorn for the worried husband who had to do nothing. This was the women's work, where men were proved weak. But beyond that first look, it never surfaced.

"I'll get Manasseh to take me out to see her," Meridivel promised. "It has been so long. We've missed you, both of you, so much."

"I know. We've missed you too. It seems, I don't know. Safer," I said.

Meridivel understood. "I know. As for a doctor, Elhrain. What can I say? All the way to the capital?" She shook her head. "It's too far, of course, to ride in her condition."

"Isn't there anyone closer?"

"Well, yes. By the coast. And there's one at—" She named some small village a distance away, but I wasn't listening.

"I don't want some village medicine man," I said too shortly. "I want someone with training. Do you know where—"

She raised a hand. "He's gone, Elhrain. We're not sure just where. We think with the apostle to spread the word. But it's not even safe to speak the name here anymore."

"That's why you haven't visited?"

She nodded.

"They're watching all the time. But we will come, Elhrain. I promise. And if I can think of a physician, not just a 'medicine man,' " she winked at me, "I'll let you know. I'll talk with Zophar. Maybe he has contacts."

I nodded agreement. "Maybe I'm worried about nothing."

"Probably," she agreed blithely. "But now let me get you something to eat."

I shook my head. "I promised I would be back before nightfall. I'll say hello to Manasseh on the way out."

* * *

It was nearly impossible to wrest myself away from Manasseh. He wanted to tell me about every one of his projects, to know about Liske, to wonder when we could talk. I left him with promises that I wondered if I could fulfill and turned down through the trees to the main road. I still had to buy some vegetables and bread.

I purchased some melons at a fruit stall and cradled them in one arm. When I stopped at the vegetable stand, I saw far more that I wanted than I had expected. And inevitably, I had arrived without a basket. I needed some beans, and I glanced across the street at the wagon to see if there might be a basket left in the bed, or whether I should just walk over there and deposit the melons.

The man in the red tunic was standing directly across the street. He looked away, as if caught in some wrongdoing, which in itself caught my attention.

"Why don't you buy a basket?" the stall-keeper was saying.

"What? Oh, yes. That will be fine." I turned back to him. Why had the man unnerved me? He was just another traveler.

Of course. It was my skin. The townspeople no longer paid me any heed, but how many out here in the country were dark-skinned as I? It would catch a stranger's eye.

"That's fine," I said to the keeper. "Beans, then. And olives. Do you have olives?"

"Back at one of the fruit stalls," he said. "We don't sell them here."

I nodded. I could get olives another time. Honey too. Honey would be good. I placed the melons on top of the beans in the basket, and crossed the street to the bakery.

Baking bread was no particularly hard chore. In fact, I often enjoyed it, shooing Taletha out of the kitchen while I pounded the dough, the air sweet with flour and yeast. I chuckled to myself then. It was one of the pleasures of living in the country. If one of the townsmen would see me laboring in the kitchen, I would be soundly ridiculed. I would guess they wondered often enough what I did anyway. I never confessed my writing to anyone but our closest friends. To others I was just a farmer, one who somehow had acquired enough money not to have to work very hard.

But fresh rolls baked with honey for sweetening would be a treat. I left the shop with my arms full, grateful to get out of the terrific heat the ovens produced, and nearly bumped into the man who had been watching me. He stood, arms loose at his side, feet spread, blocking my path. This close to him, I could smell his odor, see the scar like a purple snake cutting across his cheek, pulling his mouth into a snarl. The beady eyes stared at me. He said nothing.

I moved to walk around him. He stepped into my path and grinned evilly.

"What do you want?" I asked.

He shrugged his shoulders.

My arms were full. I grew angry. "Then get out of my way, please," I said.

He stood there, and I began to smell my own fear. People circled around us. Still the man said nothing. I knew it was provocation. Why, I didn't know.

Suddenly I heard a bellow from behind me. My name called. "Elhrain, you forgot this!" I turned. Manasseh ran down the street, waving the woven blanket. He ran up sweating with the effort.

"Glad I caught you," he said.

I turned back to face the red-tunicked man, taking strength from the brawny carpenter. The man was gone.

"What's the matter?" Manasseh said. "You look like—"

"Nothing. Nothing's the matter. Thank you, friend. We'll get together soon."

"Perhaps next week," Manasseh said. "Give my regards to Taletha."

"Yes. I will."

I turned the wagon out of the yard. On impulse, I peered at the small religious house as I went by.

No one was there.

Still, as I rode out of town, I felt someone watching.

CHAPTER
TWENTY-TWO

When Taletha began eating more regularly some days later, enjoying her food and able to hold it down, I wondered why I had ever worried.

"See," she said to me, "this is just the way it is with pregnancy. I told you not to worry."

Her color appeared better. She tended some routine chores on the farm with new energy and resumed her daily walks out across the pasture. Day by day the walks grew longer; as I watched, she diminished to a small shape against the hills before returning. I secretly rejoiced. Taletha had never been able to sit quietly. She needed motion.

Sometimes Liske would spot her from the hills and run down to greet her.

And I told myself, *Everything is all right. Everything will be all right.* It was silly to worry.

Sometimes I joined her in these walks, yet I sensed as I did so that she really preferred to be alone. At first I resented it, even as she laughingly passed some comment. "Really, I'm all right, Elhrain." Or, "You don't have to worry about me, husband." This is not a subtle woman. So I let her go.

I puttered with chores, realizing that I was counting days. I was restless. A new supply of parchment arrived from the capital, but when I tried to write I felt I was wrenching the words out. In frustration one day I tore up an entire sheet. Then I stared at the expensive parchment, thinking, *What a waste,* and nearly wept with frustration.

I turned back to the land, working a full, hard day in the neglected vineyard, tying vines, stretching the awkward trellises. The weeds were shameful, choking the ground, and I hacked at them with the hoe until I thought my arms couldn't lift another stroke.

When Meridivel and Althea rode up to the farm, then, I was delighted to see them. They had packages with them, and within minutes they were chattering with Taletha in the kitchen as if I weren't there.

"I think I'll ride into town," I said.

I wasn't even sure Taletha heard me. Then she glanced up. "Good," she said. "And goodby," she called.

* * *

When I got to town, I wondered what I was doing there. Just something to do.

I rode past Manasseh's shop, but decided not to stop. Instead I pulled in by the inn.

Tomit was inside, working on the building addition he had started after the prison break. The two extra rooms had been closed in, and I marveled at the tight structure and workmanship, especially where he had cut into the main structure of the inn, which was made of the common mud-clay brick. The work was seamless, and at present he was enclosing a shuttered window in one of the rooms.

We passed meaningless chitchat. I was restless, without knowing why. I left soon, following Tomit's directions to where Zophar was working at a desk in his anteroom to the inn.

Zophar was cordial enough, but I could tell he was harried with work. He pushed back on his stool, pot-belly sagging, his chubby fingers twiddling the quill he had been writing with. Even while he asked polite questions about the farm and about Taletha, he let his eyes stray to the desk. I had the feeling I could have told him the farm burned and Taletha was running around naked in the hills and he wouldn't have heard.

"Listen, Zophar," I sharpened my voice. "I asked before about a physician. That is, I talked to Meridivel. She said she would see what she could do. Did she talk to you?"

He sighed, laid the quill on the desk, scowling at the blotch it made, and folded his arms.

"She did, Elhrain. I have letters out. I haven't heard anything."

"I'm concerned," I apologized.

He waved a hand. "It's woman's work. Don't think of it."

"Woman's work? I have some part in it."

"I said I sent out messages, okay?"

"Yes. Well, yes indeed." I rose to leave.

"I'm sorry, Elhrain. I can't keep up with the work here anymore."

"Zophar. Quit."

"Quit! Impossible. Nobody else—"

"Tomit is perfectly capable." I excused myself. When I glanced back through the door, Zophar was hunched angrily over the desk.

* * *

I stood outside the inn watching the street. A big dog rolled in the dust, then ambled to the shade of a tree where it sat scratching. Very well, I would say hello to Manasseh. Maybe stop at the bakery for fresh bread, and leave.

As I crossed the street, I again had the restless feeling that someone was watching me. I slowed, and turned suddenly, whipping my gaze along the street. Nothing. I heard the rap-rap of Tomit's hammer. People moved about in customary ways.

Nothing.

Manasseh, at least, welcomed me. In fact, he bellowed with delight. "Didn't even stop to see me last time," he roared. Then he locked that bearlike paw upon my arm and steered me to the bench. "Just a minute," he said, "and I'll get some wine from the stream."

Manasseh had a habit of leaving a flagon of wine in the brush of the stream to keep it cold. In a minute he returned with the dripping flagon. "It's the last I have from your vines," he said. "Time for harvest soon."

That's right. I hadn't been looking forward to it. Maybe I could get Liske to help.

We chatted in the dusty workroom until the sun began lowering. I looked up the road and was startled to see Althea and Meridivel approaching in their wagon. Remembering that I wanted to buy some bread, I left and cut back across the street.

I saw a flash of red ducking into an alley between two shops. I stopped, then began walking toward it.

No, I thought. *Force him out.*

I continued leisurely down the road. I paused by the blacksmith, a stout, rugged man I scarcely knew, and watched him laboring at the forge. He looked up and grinned. I nodded to him and casually walked on.

I passed a vegetable stall and bought a thick clove of garlic, its odor so intense it made my head spin. I still hadn't gotten used to all the spices in this land. As I paid, I glanced sideways and thought I caught a glimpse of him, standing behind the blacksmith's water barrel.

I was going to cross to the bakery but at the last moment made a desperate, stupid move. I passed the bakery and entered the forecourt of the village temple. It was dark inside the vaulted door. Napthali had fashioned his own living quarters off the altar room, through a little low door. If I remembered right, the alcove opened to the back. I was counting on it. I needed a back door.

As I entered, the priest rose from prayer and looked at me. His face went pale. His breath a hiss.

"You! Infidel."

"What?" I said with a smile. "You want me to get out of here? Very well."

From the shadows I saw the man in red coming, a look of confusion on his face. He crossed the road, walking quickly. Then he broke into a little run.

I slipped through the curtained entrance to the priest's quarters.

"Hey!" The priest shouted at me. "You can't go in there. Those are my rooms." He was a young man, strong and broad-shouldered. He took a step toward me.

I saw the other man hurrying across the forecourt.

"I thought this was the house of God, priest," I said. "Excuse me."

I slipped through the room, noticing as I did so, in the soft light of an oil lamp, how extravagantly the priest had redecorated Napthali's spartan quarters. But I didn't stop. I ducked out the door and immediately turned back to the front of the temple.

I heard their voices as I circled back.

"Why did you let him go?" demanded a voice.

"I let him go! You're supposed to—"

"And not touch him. Yet. Watch only, he said."

"Then I had to let him go. He walked right in—"

I shouldered back through the front door, grabbed the man in the tunic by the shoulders and flung him against the wall. He was younger, stronger, but I had surprise. I levered my forearm against his throat, pressing back into the wall, leaning my weight on him, lifting my knee up into his groin to brace him. His eyes whirled dangerously, his breath a hot steam in my face. The scar turned a vivid purple. As I increased the pressure on his windpipe, he struggled against me.

"Watching me? Why?" I hissed into his face, my own only inches from his.

I jerked my elbow into his throat. "Why!"

He shook his head, gasping.

I was losing control. A rage seared behind my eyes. All the anxiety over Taletha and the waiting boiled up in one hot flame, and I wanted to hurt him.

I felt the priest grab my shoulder, and I kicked out viciously, blindly. He tumbled back, tripping over the altar, a shower of dust and ashes cascading over him.

The man before me squeezed his eyes shut.

There could be others, I realized. I had to get out.

I meant to order him. When the words came they were a scream, and the man turned sideways as my spittle and words stung his face. "Tell them," I shouted, "to leave us alone!"

Relaxing my arm across his throat, I felt his body collapse toward me, and I grabbed his arm and twisted, heaving his body across the small room. He collided head-on with the priest. Both sprawled in a mess of ashes.

I pointed my finger at them. "You stay away from me."

And I strode out the front door, past a couple of villagers who stood with mouths gaping at this violation of their religious house. They moved back in fear as I walked past.

* * *

I have had enough, I found myself thinking. *You have had your way with me, now deliver me.*

Rather, it was praying. Alone in my wagon as the trustworthy ox threaded his way, unbidden and undirected, through the dust on the way home, I was praying to something, someone. I couldn't remember ever having done this. Not like this.

Enough. I had thought the desert was the end of it, I, who have had too much of the desert. I wanted to lie down in peace.

Someone? The picture in my mind—as vivid as life—was of the man I had seen on the cross. Was I this desperate? Sending prayers to a dying man? His face imprinted on my mind now like a lightning bolt that blazed behind the eyes—the afterimage somehow more real, more powerful, more fully alive than what the eye itself perceives.

I thought the desert was the end of it. What peace we felt on those days hiking back. It was the last time we were all together. Lycurgus. Doval. Taletha and I. And the baby that grew now in Taletha's womb. I chuckled with the pain of longing, and it broke the dam of tears. Enough. I long for the commonplace, Lord. Yes, Lord.

I confess.

The ox's footfalls were as steady as heartbeats. The cricket's song rose from the underbrush. I rode weeping like a lost child.

Enough. Make them let me alone.

* * *

A man rode up to the farm on a horse. This in itself was unusual. Riding by wagon was most likely, a donkey, possibly. But when I looked down the path from the window of our house and saw the horseman, I had the sense of some military person arriving. For a fleeting moment I thought it was Lycurgus. I had had a long day of working in the grapevines. The fruit was heavy now and had been poorly tended. Much of it had been lost to slugs and insects. I worked desperately to salvage what I had so sorely neglected.

He was a horseman. Well, then, perhaps he was an aristocrat, if not a warrior. Expensive, these animals were. And as he rode closer, I saw that his robe too was expensive, a piece of white linen with embroidered scarlet trimmings. A black cape was flung over his shoulders.

I went out to help him with his horse, leading it around to the sheep stable where I kept some grain while he introduced himself.

"Zophat sent for me," he said as I led him into the house. He carried a small black medical purse.

211

"Zophar, you mean?"

"Yes. Of course. Zophar."

"And where do you come from?"

He named a village to the west, just over the hills. I wondered that such a small village should have a physician of such apparent eminence when we in Noke had none at all. He introduced himself as Eupolemus.

I saw Taletha wandering in from the pasture. Even at this distance I could see her stepping carefully, as if balancing her bulging womb while she walked. I willed her to haste. A physician was just what we needed. This was no time for folk remedies and village midwives. Secretly I thanked Zophar for getting through. Everything would be all right now.

Why then that look of sudden distrust on Taletha's face as she walked into the house?

The physician was friendly. He stood courteously and half-bowed as I introduced him to Taletha.

She looked nervous, putting the handful of primroses she had picked carelessly on the shelf. I poured water into a small vase and put the flowers in while she talked in polite, formal tones with the physician. Yet I noticed the catch in her voice as she spoke with him.

"Really, I've felt quite good now," she was saying. "I had cramps at first, but Meridivel—"

"Meridivel?" asked the physician.

"My friend."

"Ah, yes. One of the village women, probably. I know how it goes. The old wives' tales. What did she tell you? Every woman has them? Every woman has to suffer?"

"She's not an 'old wife,' " Taletha said. "And she doesn't tell tales."

"Of course. I apologize," he said smoothly. "No offense meant."

I poured wine into small goblets, setting one before the physician and one before Taletha, pulling up a stool for her at the table. She sat down unwillingly.

"Excellent wine," said the physician with a broad smile. He licked his lips. "Really excellent."

I nodded. "My own," I confessed.

"Really? I noticed the vines up on the hill. A good place. 'The land makes the wine.' " He quoted an old proverb.

"Well, I think the rain and sunlight are important too. Too much of one or the other, or too little, and the crop suffers."

"Exactly," he pronounced enthusiastically. He was a handsome man, and he knew it. His curly black hair was expertly trimmed, his beard was oiled, a custom I had seen among some of the wealthy aristocrats. When he moved, I caught the glitter of a golden necklace, discreetly tucked under his tunic. His teeth were flawless, flashing white when he smiled, as he did now.

"Exactly so," he repeated. "And so it is too with medicine, and this business of having babies. We have grown out of the age of ignorance now, don't you think? We know when there is too little or too much. It's best for the mother, you know."

"Yes," I said. Exactly. But I was also wondering, too much or too little of what?

"Tell me," Eupolemus said, leaning confidentially toward Taletha. "With the cramps. Did you have any bleeding?"

"Yes," Taletha murmured warily.

"Hmm." He frowned. "Very much?"

"I don't know. Some spotting."

He shook his head slightly, the frown deepening. His dark eyes were liquid. "Just spotting?"

"Well. At first, in the early days, some flow," she admitted.

"When? Two months? Three months?"

"Three or four. I'm not sure," Taletha said. "I'm about seven now."

"Yes, I can tell that. It's not too late though."

"Too late? For what?"

He shook his head, as if to say, We'll get to that. "And the cramps? Did you have much nausea?"

"Of course. All pregnant women do."

"Oh, oh," he said.

And I was thinking, *Old wives' tales.*

"Well, some do," he admitted. "Not all. Not always a good sign. Appetite? How's your appetite?"

"I'm eating okay now," Taletha said.

"But not before?"

"She hardly ate anything at all for a while," I interjected, and Taletha shot me a look of anger. "But it's true, wife," I said. "Tell him."

"I . . . I had some problems eating. It's not unusual though. If you

remember, husband, it's not the first time I've gone with little food."
Anger was in her voice.

"The first time you've been pregnant, though," I shot back. And regretted it instantly.

The physician nodded his handsome head in concern. "Perhaps I could examine you?" he asked.

Taletha stared at him uncertainly. "Who sent you?" she asked suddenly. "I didn't ask for anyone."

The physician looked at me.

"I'm afraid I did," I admitted. "I was concerned. I asked Zophar if he could get someone. I was hoping he could contact our friend . . ."

"Oh?" said the physician. "Trust me. I'm your friend too. And," he said as if dismissing his very credentials, "I assure you I am properly trained. In Rome."

"Rome!"

"Yes. The latest science, you see. Of course, if you'd rather wait for your . . . friend, I'll certainly understand. No problem there. I only wish to help." He turned to Taletha. "And, my dear, your husband's concern is well founded. I'm concerned too. A problem pregnancy. And at your age. You see, there are certain risks. But, as I said, I won't impose."

He half-stood, as if to leave.

"What can it hurt, Taletha?" I asked.

She shook her head in exasperation. "Oh, very well," she said.

The physician nodded. He looked at me. "You may leave, if you wish."

"He stays," Taletha said firmly.

"I'll stay," I said.

* * *

The physician's hands were nimble, agilely feeling the contours of Taletha's womb. She had reclined on the floor, leaning against the wall. The physician stroked her bulging womb. He pressed. Taletha winced.

"Sorry," he said. Then, "Hmm, yes. I'm afraid so." He shook his head. He pressed his ear to her womb, listening intently. It seemed I heard it too—the fast, fluttering heartbeat. Flick-flick-flick, pulsing within her. I half-smiled, imagining it.

But he rose with a deepening frown. He leaned down and helped Taletha stand. She straightened her skirt, looking at him warily. He pressed one hand to his forehead and walked slowly around the room, deep in studied reflection, as if drawing upon all his vast medical knowledge. He stopped and sighed deeply.

"I don't know if there's any way to put this gently," he said. He clasped his hands before him in a gesture of supplication.

To whom does the man of science pray? I remember thinking. And then I thought of our friend, the physician. How I wished he were here.

Taletha slipped her hand in mine. I felt it trembling. Perhaps it was my own. "Is there a problem?" I asked.

He straightened, his handsome face composed, full of grace and compassion. "Several things," he began. "Individually, perhaps not so serious. Taken together, I'm afraid," he shrugged slightly, as if shivering, "I'm afraid we have an emergency."

He caught our gaze. "Oh, yes. You see, the health of the mother, Taletha, is my primary concern. And the history of cramps, of bleeding—especially the bleeding—and of the nausea. All these are warnings, you see, that the body gives us. The body does indeed send signals. We—scientists, medical people—just have to learn to listen and interpret. I'm afraid," he sighed deeply, "too often people mask them with poultices and superstitions. But they give me grave concern. Frankly, I don't know if you can survive the delivery.

"And, then, there's the position of the baby."

"What position?" Taletha asked. Her voice was iron. "The baby's turning all the time."

He nodded. "Yes, that intensifies the problem. You see, it's twisting further, lower into the birth canal. Quite prematurely, I'm afraid. It will almost certainly be a breech birth."

I saw Taletha wince. Once before, one of her ewes had delivered a breech lamb. The ewe suffered horribly, its canal ripping, tearing, its bleats horrifying. The mother died two days after the birth.

The physician noticed also; not much escaped his scrutiny. "Moreover," he added, "I'm sure you've felt the heartbeat. High. Fast. Irregular."

"All babies have that," Taletha interjected. But her face had gone very pale.

"True," he admitted. "But not to this degree. The baby is in jeopardy. One or the other of you," he said in a flat, unemotional voice, "will not survive. Perhaps neither."

He walked slowly to the black purse. I had forgotten about it. Suddenly it looked very ominous lying on the shelf by the oven. "Our only hope," he said, "to save the mother is to induce the birth now. While the baby is still small enough to pass through."

"What!" Taletha and I spoke almost on the same breath.

"Yes," he nodded. "I hate to say it. And if I knew any other course, I would recommend it."

"The baby wouldn't live. Not now," Taletha said woodenly.

"I know. Probably not. But would you want it to go through life maimed? Born in pain? Probably terribly disfigured? But it's you I'm thinking of, Taletha. I'm concerned about whether you will survive at all." He opened the bag, withdrawing two small vials that he twirled casually in his fingers.

"But that's . . . that's killing the baby," I said, and another part of me wailed, *Taletha!* How could I live without her?

"No. Not at all," the physician said. "Every part of our law—for I am of your people even though I was educated in Rome—can be construed to approve. I assure you, you will not be held accountable."

"To whom?" I muttered.

He ignored me. "Take these, the contents of these two vials," he said to Taletha, "three times during the course of the day. Divide them in equal measures. If you take them with wine, you will scarcely notice them." He stared into her wooden features, his voice bland and objective, the equable man of science. "Within twenty-four hours it should be effected."

Taletha made no effort to take the vials. When she spoke her voice was hoarse. "Get out," she said. "Get out of my house."

The physician cautiously laid the two vials on the table. "Certainly," he said. "I'd advise you to take them soon. Tomorrow. Time is urgent."

"Get out," she hissed. "Take them with you."

He smiled, packing his purse, leaving the two vials where they lay.

I took a step forward. "You heard her," I said threateningly. "Get out."

He looked at me. The rage in his eyes now was transparent. Yet his voice was smooth as silk. "Certainly," he said.

I took another step and he walked out the door. Taletha took the two vials off the table, squeezing them with white fists. She whirled and flung them into the fire in the hearth. The vials made a popping sound, the contents erupting into a plume of green smoke. She fell against me, weeping.

Outside, I heard the thunder of horse hooves on the road.

CHAPTER
TWENTY-THREE

W here are you going?"

Beyond the doorway, the light of dawn streaked the east. I had been awake all night.

"I thought you were sleeping," I said.

Taletha shook her head. "No. I heard you get up. Where are you going now?"

"To see Zophar. That big, fat—"

"You don't know, Elhrain."

"I'll find out."

"Please don't leave me here alone."

"Leave you! I'm just riding to Noke."

"I don't want to be alone." Tears pooled in her eyes. Her mouth tightened, fighting it back.

"I want to know, Taletha. I want to find out what's going on. He said Zophar sent for him."

"And that you had asked for it."

"All right. I'm sorry. I'm worried about you."

She walked to me, standing between me and the door. "Do you believe him?"

"What? What he said about the baby? No. I don't know what to believe."

Chapter Twenty-Three

"It's not true. The baby isn't deformed. And even if he was . . ."

"Why would he say *that?*"

"I don't know. I'm coming with you. I'm afraid to be here."

* * *

Zophar's eyes were burning with anger, also with fear. "I swear, Elhrain," he said for about the tenth time, "by all that's holy, I do not know the man. I did not send for the man. I had nothing to do with it."

I paced the room. With Manasseh at my side, after I had left Taletha with Meridivel, I had barged in on Zophar's office. He was already at his desk in the small anteroom. Within moments the sound of my voice brought Tomit in also. He stood near his uncle, as if to protect him, but his face deepened in worry lines as I told my story.

Zophar was adamant. He had never heard of a physician named Eupolemus, had never contacted anyone like him, and was absolutely certain that the village Eupolemus had named had no physician. I think that I have never fully trusted Zophar. At once expansive and generous, he could also be tight-fisted and selfish. Although he numbered himself in and acted with the Cause, he was also always something of the skeptic, more in love with questions than answers. And, most tellingly, he had already admitted to betraying the secrets of the Cause by talking too much to a stranger. Yet it was the very fact that he had admitted an earlier betrayal that made me believe him now. Whatever else worked against Zophar, he was a very successful businessman, and not prone to make the same mistake twice. He was as shrewd as a serpent. His very faults, perhaps because they mirrored some of my own, made me believe him.

"Let's think this through," he was saying. "When you asked me to find the physician, or any physician of reputation among us, I take it . . ." He paused and looked at me for approval. I nodded. "Well, at first," he continued, "I didn't take you seriously. Understand, Elhrain, I've never had children of my own. Although Althea has become like a daughter to me, and Tomit, my son.

"So, I was disinclined. All fathers, especially first-time fathers, even if they are grizzled old men, get nervous.

"But I did so anyway. Simply because you asked. You have to know something about the network here. We have certain safeguards, and it was a long time developing. Each person in it knows only the persons from whom and to whom he receives or gives messages. That has always been the way. And we are sworn to secrecy about those two persons. Even now I can't tell you from whom I get word, except to say it's someone in the capital. Nor can I say to whom I relay news, except to say it's someone you would never guess.

"Oh," he said, "I have a rough idea of destinations. We all know, for example, that Joppa is our most important city on the coast, that it assists in the safe passage of refugees. But the network is like a vast spider's web now. And it is ever growing. It spreads to different lands, different regions. Corinth. Rome. Even, some say, north into the barbarian lands.

"So I took you at your word. At your need, rather. I passed the message along. It's possible it was interrupted. I don't think so. It's possible it is still en route somewhere, that someone is working on it. This is an unusual request after all, when most of our business is saving refugees or planting cells of believers in new places. It may even be that someone, some physician, is now on the way, although I doubt it. What I do know is that that person would have to come through me."

"Unless," I interjected, "he knew me personally."

Zophar shook his head. "I know what you're thinking, Elhrain. But our friend the physician is probably abroad right now. His plan was to accompany the apostle."

"I know that. Still—"

"You're missing the point, Elhrain. A stranger would be required to come to me first. I would take him to see you."

"But he said he came from Zophar. No. Wait a minute. He said Zophat first."

Zophar smiled. "Oh, yes. I am under suspicion and have been for a long time. But it tells us something, doesn't it? Zophar is a coastal name, a peasant name; Zophat is a variation found among the wealthy in the capital city. It is not an unusual mistake among the uninitiated."

"He said he was schooled in Rome."

"Very likely so. The elite have gone to Rome for schooling since the time of Judas Maccabee, when he enacted the alliance with the Romans against the Greeks."

"I don't know anything about that," I said.

Zophar looked at me with some surprise. "This happened only two hundred years ago. Its effects are still felt today." But he said it with a chuckle. Then added, "But you are not Master of Histories, are you?"

I looked into his cunning old face.

"It was a long time ago, Zophar," I said.

"Yet some things endure," he replied. He spoke slowly, as if musing to himself. "Even knowledge of earth. Your mastery has served you well, Elhrain."

I felt suddenly disarmed. "You've known all along?"

"No." He shook his head. "Only some things Lycurgus told me. But I respect your confidence. If a king wishes to live as a farmer, it is well with us. We all respect that."

I looked at Tomit and Manasseh, the latter grinning with embarrassment for me.

"But," Zophar said, "you are the last Magus. Never wonder that there will be others who wish to destroy you. What they cannot understand, or cannot live with, they want to destroy. Your past is safe with us, Elhrain."

"I just want to be left alone," I said. My voice broke on the words. "To have my baby, and be left alone."

"That is exactly what we want also," Zophar said. "We will do everything in our power to make it so."

He stood. "If someone comes, I'll let you know. But I think Taletha and your baby will be kept well by the women of the village. They have their own experience, and it is not to be discounted."

"Thank you, Zophar."

"Yes, well. I have work to do now. Oh, if you wish, we can place a guard on your house. Or, there is a place available here in town. We have been keeping it open for you."

"What?"

"Exactly what I said. Just ask."

My mind was spinning with questions when I left. I felt the need to get my hands dirty, to work in the soil, to nurture the grapevines. Still, as we rode back to the farm I raised the questions with Taletha. She was adamant. She wanted to stay at her home. As for the physician, this Eupolemus, she dismissed him like a vapor.

"It didn't work, did it?" she said casually. She was in better spirits than I had seen in weeks.

And I was thinking, *It didn't work because of you, my beloved.*

* * *

The grape crop was better than I expected. I borrowed Liske for a few days, leaving the few sheep in the care of a fellow shepherd. Those few days stretched into several weeks as we worked the vineyard until suddenly the harvest was upon us. At first Liske was shy and tentative working with me. He would smile and say hello when his head popped up around a row of grapes. The lad had an incurably good humor. Sometimes I wanted to say, "Don't you understand? This is hard work!" But then his mop of reddish hair, curls akimbo, would pop up and that grin break wide. I found myself simply enjoying him, especially since he did all the bending, the hard work low to the ground, sparing my back a myriad of aches.

On the first day the mangy shepherd dog rambled among the vines. Once he spotted a squirrel and blasted after it, knocking over a trellis in his mad gallop to herd the squirrel to the nearest tree. The next day we left the dog with Taletha.

She was glad for the company. She seldom ventured far from the house now. Her womb bulged magnificently. I told her once that she looked like the prow of a ship sailing through the pasture. She needed, I said, a lantern to signal her coming so that others could get out of the way.

She was not amused.

"Here," she said, placing my arms around the swell of her abdomen. "Lift it." I felt the baby squirming in my hands, a flutter of hard urgent shapes kicking under my hands.

"Prow of a ship, indeed," she said as I let go.

"Pretty full cargo, too," I couldn't help saying.

She playfully slapped at me. "This is *your* baby," she said. "He acts like you—restless and ornery. I've carried him nearly nine months now. Then it's your turn. I'll be sitting out by the grapevines thinking up stupid jokes."

* * *

It took us a week to harvest the grapes. I began to enjoy Liske's presence. Even favoring the crippled arm, he did more than his share. I began to think he could run the farm quite well by himself.

Once the process started, it was a never-ending series of steps.

Like the vineyard, the pressing cistern had been terribly neglected. We

222

had used an old, hollowed rock that had come with the farm. It was about five feet across, its cavity carefully chipped out, with two small holes drilled out of its sloped bottom. But the stone was overgrown with moss and weeds. As I scoured at the surface, using chipping tools and blades first, then polishing the surface smooth with pumice and fire-sand buffed by old rags, I promised myself to rebuild the oak cover.

While I worked at cleaning the cistern, Liske carried load upon load of grapes to the press. The scent of them filled the air with a tangy sweetness. Manasseh was supposed to deliver a set of wooden barrels, their staves wrapped tight with iron by the blacksmith, and while we waited for the delivery I set aside a large quantity of grapes for making raisins. They were a favorite of Taletha's, and terribly expensive. Each of these grapes had to be individually picked, laid out on a net, then covered by another net in the sunny foreyard. Each morning I had to douse them with olive oil, and painstakingly turn them with a small rake.

When at last the barrels arrived the grapes were swollen full to sweetness.

Pressing is supposed to be a holiday time in this land. A time when neighbors gather, singing and dancing as they stamp around in the cistern. For us, it was just hard work. Liske and I kept at it. Taletha even joined us for a while, her skirt tucked up under her belt, her bare feet splashing. She laughed like a little girl, but when she nearly slipped, and stood there holding her swollen belly, I helped her out. She obliged, satisfying herself with moving the casks to the spigot holes. The sweet juice flowed freely. By the end of the long day the pile of grapes was far down.

Still we kept at it, until I thought that I couldn't stand the sight of another grape. Feet moved mechanically. Taletha brought out a couple of rush lanterns as darkness settled.

By now my legs pumped mechanically, dissociated from the creeping exhaustion that slowly infected my body. Up, down.

"That's the last cask," Taletha called.

"Any more grapes?" I asked.

"Some. We'll save them. Use them for juice. Or bring some into town."

"All right." I crawled down out of the cistern and washed my trembling legs. Liske had gotten out earlier to eat some cheese and bread. He lay asleep in the grass, sprawled out in exhaustion. I picked him up and staggered into the house. He didn't stir, snoring deeply as I laid him on a blanket on the floor.

"A good harvest," Taletha said.

"Yes," I agreed. "I still have to clean the jars." I was thinking of the clay jars we used to store some of the wine after it cured in the casks and was poured off from the lees that settled to the bottom.

"I'll help," she said.

I smiled at her, but I was already on my way to sleep standing up. She led me to the bed, and I collapsed, seeing in my dreams all night bunches of grapes tumbling about my legs.

* * *

The grapes were finished. I let Liske sleep long the next morning, then dismissed him back to the hills and to his sheep.

Day by day Taletha grew to readiness.

We had made the arrangements. It would be easier for us to ride into Noke than to have the women come out to the farm. Meridivel had a room prepared. All was ready.

* * *

And yet, never ready.

Taletha awakened me from a dead sleep. "It's time," she said.

"Time to get up? Already?"

"Time for the baby."

I jumped up, unraveling myself from the damp bedding. I staggered outside and hitched up the reluctant ox. When I finished, Taletha was waiting by the door, holding a small bundle.

The night was cold, the sky crystal clear with stars glittering. My hands shook on the reins, and Taletha laid her small hand on mine.

About halfway she said, "Do you think you can hurry?" I felt her body tense next to me. She held tightly to the wagon seat while her body stiffened. She gasped in pain.

I snapped the reins over the sleepy ox, but barely raised it to a slow walk.

Again she stiffened. "I mean *really* hurry," she gasped.

In the starlight her face was rigid with pain. She gripped the wagon seat with clenched fists, her body trembling in the spasm of a contraction.

224

I cracked the reins like a madman, goading the ox into a quicker pace. Still, even while the wagon bumped along, it seemed we were standing still. The ox snorted over its shoulder at me. I responded with a new thrashing.

I counted off landmarks that passed with nearly interminable slowness. Past the willow grove. Again I slashed with the reins.

Taletha gasped and cried out.

Past the mound of the rocks by the stream, then over the narrow bridge.

Then I wheeled into Noke, to Manasseh and Meridivel's house, shouting out their names from the foreyard, hauling on the reins. A light winked on in the house. Taletha fell into my arms, and I carried her into the house.

Meridivel sent Manasseh scurrying out for Althea and the village midwife. She ordered me to stoke up the fire in the hearth, to set on a kettle of water, then pulled shut the curtain of the birthing room in my face.

* * *

Dawn fired the eastern horizon. It would be a warm day. The leaves of the trees hung limp, dew embroidered like lace around their edges.

The hours crept by on lame feet.

Several times I heard piercing cries from the room. Each time I leapt to my feet. Each time Manasseh laid a hand on my shoulder, and we sat again. Our clothes were damp with dew.

* * *

Meridivel came out late in the morning. She stood wiping her hands on a piece of cloth. She looked very tired.

I stood up quickly. "What happened?" I asked. "Isn't it time?"

"It's a breech birth," she said. "That means that instead of the head coming first, the bottom—"

"I know what it means," I snapped. My head whirled. He was right! How did he know? "Sorry," I said.

She waved her hand. "It will be okay. Taletha's exhausted. The midwife will be delivering him soon. I just needed a breath of fresh air before she starts."

I slumped to the ground. "Listen," I said, "if anything happens . . . Taletha. She comes first."

"It's not that easy, Elhrain." Meridivel shook her head. "We'll know soon." She drew a deep breath and walked back inside.

* * *

The sun stood overhead. The street down at the end of Manasseh's spacious forecourt had emptied at noon. People would be eating. Or napping. Going through their routine. Measuring off the days of their lives.

Time stood still for me.

How long?

Then came a long, heart-rending wail that froze me to the marrow, followed by a terrible silence. I trembled, waiting. A squall that seemed to rock the ground rolled out to the trees, setting all their leaves atremble. It rose up and finally broke apart in the high blue sky. And I ran into the house, ripping the curtain aside. Althea dabbed a cloth at a shaking, livid, angry baby, who was just opening his mouth to emit another piercing howl when she tucked the cloth around him, bundling him, and handed him to me. I stood stunned, hardly seeing the midwife still working, doing something with Taletha. I asked Meridivel what was happening, and she smiled. I knew everything was all right.

I turned, holding my son. Manasseh stood in the kitchen. His broad, red face was split by a grin as wide as a road, and I said, "Look."

"A boy?" he asked.

I nodded. Tears splashed down my face, falling on the little blanket. He opened one eye, then the other, waved a chubby little fist, opened his mouth and squalled, and I could no longer tell if my tears were from my laughter or my relief.

* * *

I slept at Zophar's inn that night.

Taletha was exhausted. She would open her eyes groggily and smile at me, then doze off. Even when she nursed the baby, she leaned against the wall, eyes half-asleep. Recovery would take several days, Meridivel told me. At minimum. There was no discussion.

I grew restless by noon. I decided to return to the farm for the night. After all, there was work to be done. I left at evening, when the air began to cool.

226

The ox plodded along. Occasionally he turned his large, liquid eyes upon me as if to say, "How could you mistreat me so the other night?" I let the ox have its desultory way; I was thinking of the baby.

He was a bit early, but one wouldn't know it from the size of him. A fine, husky baby, a mop of curly black hair ringleted his scalp. And he had an astonishing roar. This was not a baby that whimpered. From his first thunderous greeting of the world, to his sudden insistence upon nursing, this baby bellowed. All that time he was growing so big within Taletha, this baby was growing lungs. His thick chest would swell as he sucked in air, and it erupted in noise.

How he nursed then, greedy for nourishment. Mercy. This would be an aggressive child; I pitied his playmates. But then, after nursing, he would doze off against Taletha's breast, chubby hands still fisted, mouth open, and he nearly broke my heart with love.

Very well, I would stay the night, do the chores early in the morning, and come back. I could do it as often as necessary. After all, I had to prepare a place for the baby. I had gotten so busy with the grape harvest I never attended to it.

What preparations would he need? Nothing I could think of. The old house was spacious enough. I glanced back over my shoulder into the wagon bed. The cradle was carefully nestled in the bed. It was Manasseh and Meridivel's gift, and I imagined Manasseh laboring over its fine craftsmanship in his shop. Yes, Manasseh, you are an artist. Each pegged slot was perfectly balanced, and Manasseh had figured out some system of weights so that the cradle rocked gently back and forth. It was a beautiful piece of work.

Had I not been lost in this world of wonder, reflecting on the miracle of this child, I might have seen them earlier.

Had I not been looking over my shoulder at the cradle, I might not have seen them at all.

There were three. On foot and heading back toward Noke. They had seen me coming, no doubt. They had drifted off the road and were moving down to the brush by the stream. While two scrambled for hiding places, one watched me, boldly, now that he had been discovered. He looked for all the world like the man in the red tunic. He wasn't wearing it, but even in the dusky light of evening I could distinguish the scar on his mouth. His back to the setting sun, he stared at me defiantly while the wagon turned a bend in the road, and I could no longer see him.

I felt a chill crawl across me and snapped the reins over the startled ox.

It was nearly dark when I arrived. I could see the ruins of the coops. A flock of doves sat in the elm tree, mewling uncertainly. The storage shed was still smoking, its embers a red glow. Liske stood before the house, his back to me. Several of the heavy wine casks lay smashed at his feet.

When he heard the wagon, he looked startled, ready to run. He recognized me and walked slowly out to the wagon.

"I couldn't save the shed," were his first words.

"I was coming down for some supplies when I saw them. My dog . . ." He pointed to the mound of fur lying in the yard.

I walked over to the large animal. The head sagged limply under my hand, its neck snapped by a blow from a club of some kind.

"Your dog attacked them?"

Liske nodded. "They were trying to burn the house. When they killed my dog, they ran away. I used the barrels—"

"They're heavy, Liske. How did you . . . ?"

He shrugged. Walking to the door, I saw where the flame had worked up its surface. The house was mud brick, but the fire had eaten into the framing and was headed for the rafters and roof. Another few minutes and the house would have been lost.

I kicked at one of the two empty barrels.

Liske took it as a rebuke. "I didn't know what else to use," he cried. "The stream was too far, and the well would take too long."

"Oh, Liske, Liske." I hugged him, felt his thin, muscular body sobbing against me. "You did the right thing. You're so brave. I'm just sorry . . . that you had to do it."

"It's okay? That I used the wine?"

I smiled at him. Stroked his bushy hair. "Let's bury your dog," I said. "We can't leave him. He's a brave dog too."

I got a lantern from the house. Liske held it while I carried the dog. I let him find the place he wanted, a spot under the willows near the stream. I didn't tell him the roots were too many there. I walked back in the darkness and found an ax and a shovel that had not been destroyed in the storage shed. I noticed then that many of the wine casks had been smashed. Well, I thought, that explains why the ax wasn't burned in the shed.

When I retraced my path to the lantern light, I saw Liske on his knees, cradling the huge old dog's head in his arms.

It took a long time to dig the grave. I cut through many roots. I wanted it deep. And safe. When we hit damp soil, I lined the grave with stones from the stream, then laid the body of the dog in it.

Liske covered the body, slowly, scooping the heavy dirt on it.

I had him sleep with me in the house that night. But I slept little. Even my home was no longer safe.

CHAPTER
TWENTY-FOUR

The house smelled of smoke, and it was hard to sleep. Somewhere during the interminable night, during which I imagined a thousand horrors, exhaustion overcame me and I slept.

Still, I awakened before sunrise with the first outline of a plan.

When I returned to Noke, I took Liske with me. I was anxious to get him back to safety. He would stay with his parents for now. The sheep could be scattered among the other shepherds.

I spent most of the morning with Zophar. I had many arrangements to work out and many contingencies to account for. Dutifully, Zophar drafted my plans in his ledger. Once he looked up and protested, "But I am not a lawyer!"

"You're better," I said.

He was. He thought of items I had missed. Carefully, he raised each point with me, suggesting alternatives, then letting me have final approval. It was as if he sensed what needed to be done, and, more important, thoroughly understood the need to do it.

"I'll still have to get it officially sealed," he said as we finished.

I nodded. "Read it back to me," I said. "From the beginning."

And so he did. "In the event of my death . . ."

Zophar protested when I left payment with him, but I insisted. "If I know the lawyers," I said, "you'll need it. I want it done right. Beyond question. Beyond reproach."

He agreed. He would know what to do when the time came.

* * *

I spent the afternoon with Taletha and the baby. He had looked so belligerent and bulky when he was born. When he slept in my arms as I walked him about Manasseh and Meridivel's yard, he felt like a fragile doll. He nestled his curly head against my neck, a thumb thrust in his mouth.

Often he would jerk awake, arms and legs kicking wildly. He had so much energy. It was as if he had things to do, and awakened from sleep at a dead run to do them. But then I stroked his back and murmured promises in his ear, and he nestled back against my shoulder.

Taletha slept. She was utterly depleted. Still, she greeted me with an eager smile when I laid the baby in her arms at evening.

"Are you going back?" she asked.

"It's best," I murmured. "There's no good place to stay here."

"I understand." She knew too well my own restlessness, my need for a place to be myself. I nearly choked with tears when I left her. This, I realized more powerfully than ever, was *my* home. How dare they violate it!

* * *

In such a way an odd sort of routine began.

At the farm I refastened the burned door with tools borrowed from Manasseh. During the long restless evenings, I sat at the table writing by the light of the oil lamp. I felt an urgency now. When weariness overcame me and I was ready to sleep, I carefully wrapped the parchments in oilskin and hid them in a space I had fashioned out of the bricks by the hearth. When I inserted the facing brick, only a careful eye could tell it had been disturbed. And the bricks would withstand fire.

I feel a compulsion to get these words down while there is still time, yet I wonder if they have any worth or place. I do it now because I am compelled.

There are things I would add. About finding a home. About the mysteries of belief that are stronger than unbelief. How I have lived both sides of that forked dilemma and for too long tried to straddle it, wavering toward the adamancy of unbelief even while clinging to belief. I could enumerate the reasons. I could add how even now I have hope, not because of the plans I have made with Zophar, but in spite of any planning I have done.

I could add how all the past struggles have diminished in my memory. They have no hold upon me. That is precisely why I have written what I have. They have no hold upon me because I now have hold of a higher hope.

All this would take so long to explain, and I have no time. I have no *way* to explain it. I am not, have never been, one given to explanation. That has not been my story.

Well, what has been then?

To arrive somewhere, I think. That is the end of all my traveling, all my searching. To arrive somewhere and know it as the end which is also a beginning.

I know now I have arrived. Maybe I shall be given time to reflect further on it. I don't know. But I am content.

* * *

I knew what was coming, what *is* coming. What might be the end of my long scratching at this table.

I awoke from troubled sleep, my heart pounding, my body sheathed in sweat, a warning hammering in my mind: something is wrong. Panic. Dissociation of time and place.

Lying perfectly still, I felt again all the childhood monsters that flooded my nightmares so long ago. But this was not a nightmare.

Something *is* out there.

My legs trembled getting up. Back pressed to the wall, standing in darkness, I wished to melt into it. Across the dark corners of the room moonlight seeps in. The window. It stands open. Why had I not shuttered it?

They are all around. I know it now. I will not wait like a dog, cringing, afraid. So I do what I can and must do.

Light the oil lamp. Take out the parchment. Sit here at the table and write. This is who I am. So let it—

CHAPTER
TWENTY-FIVE

Though years have passed, I remember Elhrain vividly.

I hold his parchments now, and they tremble slightly in my hands. They tell me his story, as if he were here beside me again. Or as if I am at his side as he wrote those words, the thoughts of his last safe moments, there at the small table, where he always sat writing in the night hours by the light of a lamp.

As I recall him, I see how powerful his influence has been upon me, and why his parchments make my hands shake—even now, eleven years since he ceased writing his account.

Elhrain himself would never have guessed at this influence. He was a man who suffered much, who endured much, yet somehow met life with an equanimity of mind and spirit that tempered all he met. Somehow, he remained unaware of how deeply he affected the lives about him. Perhaps his own suffering drew a carapace about him, turning him inward, as if he were unable to recognize the many ties he had with others even as others welcomed and worked at those ties.

Yet that is not entirely true. Elhrain was a man set apart by the nature of the person he was.

Elhrain sought peace. He was, nonetheless, a man of volcanic feelings, of ragged anger and relentless tenacity. He was also a man of deep love and unbelievable compassion. He was, insofar as I can determine, of royal birth, although much of that is shrouded in mystery. He was also, in fact, a member of the Magi, those strangely gifted kings from the East. Yet he wished nothing more than to live as a commoner with his wife and child on their farm. Elhrain was a puzzle. Belief always seemed to elude him, yet he was adamant as granite in the beliefs he acted upon.

His character is impossible to understand fully; it is the enigma itself that so compels me, even as I sense the difficulty of my undertaking.

He wished to be a farmer, I thought, but now I discover that that was as much Betharden's wish as his. What he wished for was to be at peace, and it happened in the place Betharden selected. Had she known? He wanted peace so that—and here is the surprise for me—so that he could write. Perhaps Betharden was the only one who fully understood the man.

* * *

When Liske and Sarah delivered these manuscripts into my hands, I could not put them down. I read them at times with tears in my eyes, at times with laughter in my heart. I understand why Liske and Sarah brought them to me. They could not read the manuscripts, for they were all in the language of the Romans. They delivered them to me because they sensed, even looking at words they could not understand, that here was a history—something that had shaped a bit of their own lives.

It is a task to be finished. So they delivered it to a historian, one who witnessed the events of those tumultuous days. While I cannot hope to capture the drama of the heart, I will attempt at least to set forth an orderly account.

I have said I cannot fully understand the character of Elhrain, but that his very enigma of person and personality compel me. Yet everything I add to the account, I suppose, will be directed precisely to that end—to understanding not just the life of the person, but the nature of the person who lives that life.

Even so, certain lacunae in the eleven years between his manuscript and this addendum should be explained at the outset. These details help describe the person; for I understand now that many events of the past years were set in motion during those last feverish days before his arrest.

First of all, the matter of Liske and Sarah, for that is where my recent involvement began.

Days before his arrest, Elhrain drafted legal papers regarding the ownership of his and Betharden's property. The papers were impeccable, and providentially so, for certain parties gladly would have seized farmland as rich and productive as theirs. The papers had been filed with Zophar, countersigned by legal authorities in the capital, and endorsed by none other than my friend Theophilus himself. It was at considerable risk, but the plan and execution were, as I say, impeccable.

He must have known, even then, the course events would take because the property in its entirety was placed in trust to be delivered in full ownership to Liske upon his twenty-first birthday.

Nearly a year after moving there, Liske and Sarah noticed the loose brickwork in the hearth. Rain inside the chimney had weakened the mortar, and Liske had asked Manasseh to help rebuild it. So it was they found the parchments, this remarkable testimony of one man's life. They had been carefully wrapped in oilskin, safe from moisture and from heat. Only the last few pages, hastily written and hastily secured, suffered damage. In a few more years, they might well have been lost.

I had but recently returned to the capital from my voyages with the apostle, and had begun to order my own notes to record them, when Liske and Sarah sought me out. Manasseh was by that point an old man and unable to travel to the city. He died this past spring. Meridivel still lives, having moved to the farm with her son and daughter-in-law to help with the baby. At least, that was the reason she gave. She is an elderly woman, with stories of her own to tell. In Liske and Sarah, she has willing ears.

All this brings me back to the life—or some would say "the curse"— of the historian. I cannot claim that title, having been schooled in other things. I only claim the calling, mine by default.

But I was there, at the trial, and I remember it clearly. Zophar's messages to me, delayed through the innumerable stages of the movement, had in fact been delivered, but I was too late for the birth of Betharden's child. I arrived for the horror that followed. In that way, perhaps, I find my kinship with Elhrain. Once before, he had missed a birth, but attended the horror of a death.

While I was given the opportunity to speak with him only once during those days, I was there. He knew it also. Even though he was wrapped in an inexplicable calm—unlike any stoicism I have seen but rather a calm of fulfillment—he did at one point spot me among the spectators. He nodded and smiled at me.

It was enough. After that one time he fixed his gaze unwaveringly upon the court.

I see him in my mind's eye even now, seated on the bench of the condemned, the trial more a ritual than a real process of adjudication. It was a sham. We all knew this.

His shoulders are gaunt but erect, even defiant. His white tunic, embroidered with scarlet, stands in stark contrast to his ebony skin. His skin is so dark the purple bruises are barely distinguishable. His hair is lightly tinged with gray at the temples, and, unlike my countrymen, he has shaven his beard. It must have been a deliberate act, for I had always seen him with a beard previously. The settled calm upon him might be mistaken for resignation, and well it could. But it is not resignation. In fact, in his calmness, his innate force seems to multiply. He evinces such a subtle but real power that the court of the Sanhedrin is wary and uncertain how to react to him.

I began to realize, from the moment I saw him on the stand, that what we were seeing was royalty, one possessing power not by might of arms or wealth, but by his mere presence and the ineluctable force of authority born within him. Accustomed to seeing miscreants beg or bargain and seeing neither in him, the court was taken off guard.

So I record this now not just because I was eyewitness to these final days, nor because I happened to stumble over the manuscripts and sensed the need to complete them. I write it to record a kingship and to try to understand one who fought against belief, but having found it was prosecuted for that very discovery. That is the sum of it, then. For while Elhrain took that stand as an offense against the kingdom, he stood there as the last Magus. But more than that—he stood there as believer. All his life he longed for a home. When he discovered it, he found it was a place in the heart. But he also discovered that while usurpers could uproot him and his family from a place, they could not touch that place in his heart. It was inviolable.

* * *

I saw him a full ten days after his arrest. Even though I had finally received Zophar's message only weeks before, and although I felt completely free to move at will in my native land, travel was still difficult from the northern territory where we were. Already much had transpired in those ten days, and it set the tone for the events, and surprises, that were to follow.

As Theophilus told it to me, the difficulty lay first in Elhrain's citizenship. Technically, the lawgivers had no legal jurisdiction over him, a point Theophilus made clear at the outset. So he was remanded first to the Roman procurator, the appointed ruler, Agrippa II. He was a man who, although young for his position, had a wisdom and a background beyond his years.

The lawgivers, according to Theophilus, had no recourse. They would have liked to have tried Elhrain quickly and quietly, thereby disposing of the problem. Little they expected Theophilus to intervene. It unnerved them all, I believe, that one so high in their circles, and so thoroughly from within their class, should outmaneuver them on a technicality of law. For this tiny homeland was still a principality under Roman governance.

The relationship between Agrippa and the Sanhedrin was at best a delicate one, always riddled by suspicion and distrust. The complication was that Agrippa was so very young, so young, in fact, that the Roman emperor had at first refused him the rule when his father died, forcing Agrippa to an apprenticeship elsewhere. But in addition to his youth, he was also very new to his position here. He was thoroughly Roman, and had spent nearly his entire life in Rome. To the Sanhedrin, the court of the lawgivers, Agrippa would be either an easy mark or an unknown entity that could eventually be molded to their point of view. What he proved to be was a fiercely independent thinker. Worse, he seemed sympathetic to many of the beliefs Elhrain held.

* * *

"So why," Agrippa had said, "is the man a threat? What crime has he committed?"

"That is precisely why he does not belong in your court," declared the Accuser, a priest named Baruch. Baruch realized it was the wrong tactic when he saw Agrippa's frown deepen. He tried to correct himself.

"His offense, Your Eminence, is against traditions of our people. Long traditions."

"But he is *not* one of your people," Agrippa said. "Any *fool* can see that. Do you take me for one?"

"He is married to one of ours, Your Eminence."

"And what does that have to do with it?"

"The marriage is therefore illegal, Your Eminence. Our law clearly stipulates that—"

"Wait a minute. If the marriage itself is illegal, then, pray tell, what right do you claim to try him?"

"He is a heretic."

"Heretic? Interesting word. With a lot of latitude in interpretation. One who goes contrary to beliefs and laws? One who *denounces* beliefs and laws? One who observes no beliefs or laws? Which one do you think fits, Baruch?"

"The latter. The prisoner rebukes our laws by refusing to believe they are just and proper."

"By what actions? What has he done?"

"Our law will stipulate—"

"Baruch, my good Accuser, of course you shall have your say about your laws. But I remain interested in this case. Here I have a man who is guilty of marriage with one of your people, but the marriage is illegal, so is there a marriage at all?"

"He has fathered a child through this marriage, Your Eminence."

"A child! Imagine that. Now there's a crime. Where is the woman, by the way, this illegally married woman?"

"No one knows, Your Eminence. We have reason to believe—"

"Yes, yes, I'm sure you have all sorts of reasons. But no woman." Suddenly he turned to Elhrain, who had yet to speak a word. The hearing, after all, was to determine who would pass verdict. "And you, sir," the young Agrippa said. "Are you married to a woman, or a figment of your imagination?"

The slightest smile touched Elhrain's lips. Agrippa went on. "I know people who marry figments of imagination, you know. They are common in Rome. They are rich and idle, so they marry verses. They call themselves poets. Or writers. Or artists. Now, is that the kind of man you are? Is this the kind of woman you married? An imaginary one?"

"She is a real woman," Elhrain said evenly.

"And where is she?"

"God knows. I don't."

"Hmm. Indeed. But you yourself are not of this land. What did you do? Come here and pluck this woman, unwillingly, from the midst of good protectors? Protectors like our esteemed Accuser, Baruch, here?"

238

Chapter Twenty-Five

"She came to me."

"When?"

"Years ago. I have lost count."

"Yes. You're getting to that point. Not young anymore, are you? Well, so. This woman came to you, years ago. You didn't attack some place here and carry her off."

Elhrain shook his head.

Agrippa smiled. He was enjoying this. "My, my. Did you know she was not to marry you?"

"Neither she nor I was aware of the laws of this land," Elhrain said. "We were living in a southern kingdom."

"Your Eminence," Baruch said, his voice raised in exasperation. "They were married by a village priest by the name of Napthali in the village of Noke."

"What! Twice married? Same woman?"

"Yes," Elhrain said. "She wanted to satisfy the law of her people. Thus we were married by a priest."

"Most interesting. A woman so intent on observing the law she marries the same man twice. Once should be enough. Or never in most cases I know of. Is there fault with this, Accuser?"

"All the more reason, Your Eminence. She should have known the law."

"Is ignorance a crime? If so, half the people I see here should be beheaded."

Agrippa seemed to realize that he was only trading words with a wordmonger, that he was slinging barbs at a target unable to trade back in kind. It seemed finally to disgust him. He leaned back in his chair, fingertips together, steepled before his chin, and stared out at the people assembled before him. Black eyes peered from his lean, ascetic face, his intelligence almost tangible, slightly predatory.

"Very well," he said after reflection. "You shall have your hearing on your laws," he said to Baruch. "I hope your people can make more sense of it than I can."

"Thank you, Your—"

Agrippa waved his hand. "But I shall have an observer. Tell me, Baruch, did you know my father?"

"Yes, indeed, Your Eminence. A most esteemed man. A delight to all who served him."

"And you, Theophilus?"

The magistrate looked slightly startled. "Sir?"

"Did you know my father?"

"Yes, Your Eminence. I did."

"And was he a 'most esteemed' man, as Baruch says?"

Theophilus paused. "King Agrippa made some errors in judgment," he said.

"Indeed."

"It was not necessary to kill the disciple. It was what the lawgivers wanted. I don't think he should have acceded."

"And was he a 'great' king?"

"No, Your Eminence."

"For the record, my father was mad for approval. He knew the curse of poverty, having lost nearly everything until Caligula restored his fortunes. My father was so insecure he would have agreed to anything the authorities here asked. My father's grandfather, the 'Great King' as he styled himself, was simply mad. Insane. He was victimized by women, by nearly everyone. But he was himself a monster.

"I say this, gentlemen, to keep the record straight. I give you the right to try this man, Baruch. But please remember: I am neither my father nor my great-grandfather. I neither beg nor decree. I don't need your approval, nor am I, insofar as I know, mad. I say this to remind you that I will be keeping an eye on this case. I will permit no nonsense. To ensure that, Theophilus here will be my witness, as well as advocate for the accused. Is that understood?"

"Your Eminence." Baruch bowed so low he nearly bent double. When he straightened, Agrippa was already talking to the next plaintiff, and Elhrain was being shackled for removal to a cell.

As Elhrain stood, the chains clanging, Agrippa suddenly turned. "Oh, one more thing," he added. "I want the guard doubled on the prisoner's cell. I want all precautions taken for his protection. And," he added, "against any attempt to liberate him."

For the second time that morning, Elhrain's lips flickered in a small smile.

Was he thinking that all the charges might go back to the prison break? It was time, at any event, to discover the real issues.

CHAPTER
TWENTY-SIX

E lhrain's trial before the Sanhedrin began six days later, on the first
day of the week, probably in defiance of the cause with which
Elhrain was now associated.

I arrived during the interim, having traveled first by ship, then overland
to Noke, and thence to the capital. I went first to my brother-in-law,
Theophilus, from whom I received the foregoing account. Even though
I was weary from travel, and happy to be in the company of my younger
sister, Judith, and her husband at their spacious home at the edge of the
city, I was eager for information.

The home of Theophilus and Judith was always a sanctuary to me.
From the moment we passed through the gate, the outer world, with all
its connivery and conflict, ceased to exist. Beds of flowers bloomed with
all the profuse abandon of the countryside, belying the essentially arid
climate of the capital. There were lilies, bordered with rows of rue. Roses
sprawled out, holding long branches of dazzling flowers.

A servant opened the door, but Judith brushed by him in her hurry to
greet me. The hall opened to various rooms, paneled in wood. The tiled
floor was swept spotlessly, and carpets were laid here and there in random
patterns. It was a luxurious house, but a warm and comforting one. It bore
none of that cold order I had seen in the homes of others of Theophilus's
rank and wealth.

Not until after dinner and after exchanging family stories did Theophilus begin to inform me of these events. He was patient and exact in his telling.

Years ago, I had met Theophilus in Rome, when I was studying medicine and he was studying the law. From our first meeting I was powerfully struck by rare qualities in him—the obvious intelligence was only part of it. A certain moderation, a decorum or order, guided that intelligence. And it was Theophilus, in fact, who first nurtured and guided my belief. Several years younger than I, he, nonetheless, had a security of conviction that surpassed my own. That he had fallen in love with and eventually married my younger sister, who was living with me at the time, was only a bonus of our friendship.

What was remarkable, moreover, was the complete respect he now enjoyed from all quarters in the capital city. His position was a high one, and even though he was now a political legate, he still held a military rank of captain. At a time when the political ties with Rome were impossibly complicated, Theophilus carefully unraveled their complexities; he was a native of the region and he had, as well, complete access to and understanding of the Roman occupiers. As such, he was invaluable to both sides. The current situation would test both capacities because that relationship, strained throughout its history, grew ever more tense day by day.

We walked out into the garden after dinner. Some energetic vine that I didn't recognize perfumed the air from a trellis; its large orange flowers were open like trumpets.

"Listen," I said. "This Agrippa. What do you know about him?"

"Yes," Theophilus said. "He's the key to it all. And almost unpredictable at this point."

"How much power does he have here?"

"Technically, very little. His rule, in fact, is *not* over this territory. That's still under the prefect. But Agrippa has a reputation already for knowing the people. And so, as he did with Agrippa's father, the prefect called him in on this case."

"That's what scares me."

Theophilus chuckled. "Yes. Agrippa, the former Agrippa, was no friend to our people. He was a weak and spineless creature. The man craved approval, so when the Sanhedrin called him in, and they had to

242

of course since they have no power to execute their own verdicts, he did whatever they wanted. It was a bloodbath.

"But," he added, "it also backfired. The people began to wonder, 'Who next?' Basically, the Sanhedrin was out of control. The people wanted blood; the lawgivers decreed it. Herod Agrippa enacted it. Whatever the lawgivers asked, he approved. While swimming in blood, the people were drowning in fear. Even when a mob mentality reigns, someone is going to start thinking that this is no mentality at all. It's insane."

"What of the present Agrippa? The son?"

"An interesting case," Theophilus mused. "Much different from his father, that's for sure. He has had to fight for everything he has. He is Roman to the core, but he knows our law and customs as well as any priest. He made it a point. It's hard to tell where his allegiance lies. I think it lies to himself—not his own survival, but to his own will."

"Can we trust him?"

"Trust? No. I don't think so. I can't crack that skull of his because he reveals so little. Yet I think his very independence may be in our favor."

"He appointed you as his representative. That should be encouraging."

Theophilus gave a harsh laugh. "That was a masterstroke too. If he rules against the Sanhedrin, he has me to take their heat. If he rules for them, then he can toss me to the people as the villain. I wouldn't be surprised if old Lemuel from the Sanhedrin set it up. He has to protect himself these days." Theophilus reflected. "I think," he said, "that Agrippa wants to carry this thing through. Albeit to his own ends, whatever they are. The last thing he could afford, for example, would be a prison break."

"He knows about Elhrain's involvement in the earlier break."

"That was some time ago, but yes, I'm sure he suspects it. And there have been other attempts since that have failed. But you're quite right, I think he fears the effort."

"Will it come?"

Theophilus shook his head. "I doubt it. I doubt it very much. I don't think Elhrain believes it will come either."

I paused. That prison break was quite a while ago now. Would the lawgivers try to bring that up? Make a case of that? What proof had they? But I had other concerns.

As if reading my mind, Theophilus chuckled. "If you're thinking of your part, brother, set your mind at rest. I hate to disappoint you, but no one noticed your absence that night."

"They didn't? I've wondered."

"Officially you were never there."

I don't know how he took care of it. I'm sure he had it done in a way that was beyond question.

"So you're free to come and go as you wish," Theophilus said. "As a matter of fact, knowing your interest in these matters, I've arranged for your presence at the trial."

"How?"

"As my assistant, of course." He chuckled again.

"Some assistant. I'm a physician. I have no idea how these things proceed."

"That's just it," Theophilus said. "There's no set rule. Elhrain is at the mercy of the seventy men on the Sanhedrin, which now has its collective back against the wall. They don't have to *prove* anything. They just show a transgression of law, which they themselves determine, pass a judgment, and recommend an action to Agrippa."

"And the action in this case?"

"Oh, execution. Believe me, it will be execution."

"But Agrippa doesn't have to comply."

"No. But at tremendous risk."

"Tell me," I asked, "this Sanhedrin—I've been out of touch—how do you assess them?"

Theophilus had walked under the trellised vine. He lifted one of the flowers, cupped it in his hand and breathed its fragrance. He looked at me. "What can I say? They appear like this flower—God-ordained, orderly, purified by the very sanctity of their position." His voice turned bitter. "But every time I see one of them I sense the odor of corruption. Their law is their end, and any law that becomes an end in itself bears the danger of corruption."

"All of them? I remember some village priests."

"Don't mistake someone like Napthali with these. Napthali wouldn't have a ghost of a chance of sitting with this body. They appoint their own in order to perpetuate their own."

"Who are the leaders?"

"Old Lemuel is Court Father, of course. Has been for thirty years. A conniver. A militant. The Chief is Baruch. He presented the case to Agrippa and no doubt will be there. And the Sage is a young man. His name is Asa. Too young for a position of such importance, some would say. But he is a rabid scholar of the law; he can recite any point from memory, complete with commentary. Those are the officers. The others? The usual temple priests and some wealthy landowners."

"So, there's little hope for mercy?"

"There is no hope for mercy with them."

"And our only hope for Elhrain lies with Agrippa?"

"Our only hope."

"And not much of one."

"True, brother. Not much at all."

CHAPTER
TWENTY-SEVEN

I confess—from the start I was more interested in the person than the proceedings.

The depravity of imprisonment could not diminish his stature. I saw no arrogance in this man, nor any fawning humility. Elhrain seemed to me a man at perfect peace.

This was odd, given the circumstances. His world looked to be falling apart.

At times I was so absorbed by him that I lost track of the nearly interminable wrangling over fine points of law. In his thin, reedy voice, the Sage, Asa, recited points of law that pertained, as well as a dozen points that did not pertain at all. Knowledge was a weapon here, and it was used liberally if not judiciously.

Through it all, even when the arguments erupted violently, Elhrain sat erect, shoulders squared, body slightly tense. His only nervous mannerism was to turn, over and over in his nimble fingers, a flat piece of glittering metal. From where I sat it looked like a gold coin of some sort, and I wondered about its significance to him.

All of Asa's recitation seemed pointless. He would babble a point with a kind of doglike eagerness on his pinched face. Seventy heads inclined to him, smiled and leaned forward. Then one of the seventy would query a point, and Asa again recited. Lemuel nodded often. Occasionally Baruch would stand, providing summary or requesting definition.

Theophilus and I sat to one side, deliberately set on the fringes in the spacious temple hall. In the center of the semicircle of the seventy sat Elhrain.

This babble of recitation went on for over an hour. I was growing restless. I leaned over and whispered to Theophilus, "What are they doing? This is a trial?"

He grinned tightly and whispered back. "Preliminaries, brother. They're showing what they know. Establishing credentials. It's a strut of law, where knowledge parades like a peacock. It's designed to intimidate the prisoner."

I looked at Elhrain, idly slipping the coin through his fingers. "Doesn't look like it's working," I said.

"Intimidate *him?* It's precisely what he wanted, brother."

"I don't understand."

"Wait and see."

But there was nothing to see. As suddenly as it started, the babble of voices ended. Lemuel smiled and nodded. As one body, the judges stood and filed out. Some wore black robes of the priestly castes—the lawgivers. Others were garbed in expensive tunics. Two guards strode over to Elhrain and ushered him through a doorway into an anteroom.

"What now?" I asked.

"A break," Theophilus said. "All that hard work strained their throats. They'll be back in a few hours."

* * *

When they returned, I sensed a new eagerness in the court. They sat in their long semicircle, in three rows of chairs; Lemuel, the Father of the Court, was at the center on a raised platform. The men leaned forward slightly, eager, waiting.

After Elhrain was brought in and seated, Baruch arose. As Chief of the Court, he would lead the interrogation. From the start I was impressed by his tactics.

He stared a moment at Elhrain, letting the silence in the court thicken. "You are a stranger in our land," he observed. "Do you understand the language?"

Elhrain looked at him in surprise. "I'm not clever with words," he said.

"This language has always been difficult for me."

"But you do understand me?"

"I understand the words you speak."

Baruch smiled thinly. "We only wish to assure your comfort and well-being. If you did not understand, we would offer a translator. We understand that you know the Roman tongue well."

"I will be all right."

Baruch arched his eyebrows. "Indeed. That is the question, is it not?" He paused meaningfully. "If," he said slowly, "you understand the language, then you have had opportunity to understand the law?"

Now I saw the point. The basis of his culpability as transgressor lay in his knowledge of transgression.

"And if you had the opportunity to understand the law, especially during the many years you have lived here, then surely you would know that it is a violation of that law for a foreigner, a heathen, to wed with one of our own? You would know that it is a repudiation of our law not to meet the most basic, fundamental requirements of that law? To observe the feast days? To worship on the Sabbath? To abstain from labor on the Sabbath? Then you would know that it is a denigration of that law not to support it with your heart and soul and mind and strength? And that part of that strength is to pay your just dues to the proper authorities? You would know all these things, wouldn't you, prisoner?"

Elhrain paused. "I pay my taxes," he said finally.

"Oh? Do you, prisoner? You pay taxes. Do you pay the sufficient amount?" Baruch turned to the small desk fronting the assembly, unrolled a record and read a long list of figures. "You see," he said, "you have only paid a part of your just share. Now, why is that, I wonder?"

"I paid everything I was asked," Elhrain said. "More, in fact, than any of my neighbors."

Theophilus stood. His deep voice was even, emotionless, entirely formal. "Your Highness," he said, addressing Lemuel. "The matter of taxation is a civil matter, not a concern of this court. The proper authorities will research and resolve that issue."

Lemuel nodded. Baruch took it as a signal.

"The esteemed Advocate is entirely correct. Nor does this court wish to intrude upon civil matters." He paused, gazing thoughtfully at the faces of the seventy. Several nodded their heads in agreement.

"The point," he added, "is, nonetheless, important. As a matter of analogy. Civil law states that it is the responsibility of all citizens to consult the tax rolls to determine their proper taxes. Yet, for the last two years, the prisoner has *underpaid* his just requirement. He knew the requirement; he lives in this land; he *profits* from this land; he ignored the requirement.

"So, too, the prisoner has a responsibility to the moral authorities of this land. To *the Law!*" Heads bobbed behind him, agreeing vigorously.

"Understanding the language, living in this land, the prisoner willfully ignored that law, choosing his own way over the *right* way. He illegally married a woman of this land, jeopardizing her eternal soul, and produced of that union a bastard son."

I shot a glance at Elhrain. His jaws tightened slightly, muscles flickering. His gaze did not flinch. "Where is she?" I whispered to Theophilus.

"Later," he hissed.

"Moreover," Baruch intoned, "knowing the sacredness of our offerings, he deliberately subverted that sacredness by providing offerings for others to give. Asa . . . " he said, but he didn't need to finish. Asa rattled off the applicable law and commentary. Baruch finally stopped him with a wave of his hand.

"Failure to observe is one thing," Baruch said. "For such, a man places his soul in jeopardy. But to lead others not to observe, to subvert, pervert, deny—for this, the prisoner sits before you with the weight of every one of those precious souls upon him."

Baruch paused significantly. This was a court of scholarship, where knowledge was foremost, yet Baruch was also canny enough to ply the court with emotional emphases. He was a showman. He was, I thought, enjoying this. And I sensed him working to trigger a response from Elhrain, something that would immediately prove the point he was making.

"So," Baruch said. He appeared to lose himself in thought. "So there are many things this man could be charged with." He shrugged. "Some of them are, as our excellent advocate points out, civil matters, not of concern to this body. There is, for example, the matter of taxes. There is, moreover, the knowledge that the prisoner is subversive to the state, that he in fact once fomented an assault upon the very prison where he is now incarcerated. The fact that the loyal guards of the state were brutally assaulted. There is, for further example, the arson of a valuable property on that night in question."

Baruch shrugged. "All these are civil matters, of only peripheral concern to this court. Except," he paused, "one wonders why it has taken so long for the state to act." Baruch stared at the ceiling a long time, letting the court draw its own conclusions. "Such matters are important to us only as an indication of this prisoner's *character*. For they all point to the same thing. They point to a man madly defiant of authority. They point to a subversive. They point to a dangerous revolutionary. They point to this question—" he whirled on Elhrain. "Who do you think you are!"

Baruch was breathing heavily.

Elhrain had a slight smile on his face. "You know my name," he said.

"Oh," said Baruch, "one name. But a name is not a person. In fact, prisoner"—for such was the only name he used here—"is one of the names you go by that of *king?*"

The court sucked in its collective breath.

"If anyone," Elhrain said, "has used that title, that person is mistaken. A king, after all, must have a kingdom to be such."

Baruch positively gloated. "Ah, yes. Precisely. And where might this kingdom be? A king seeking a kingdom. We see how it fits. The subversion, the trespass, a foreign king." He turned to Theophilus. "So you see, I submit to you, esteemed Advocate, that this *is* as much a civil threat as a religious transgression. Surely you know the wave of subversion that has swept this country in recent years?"

"I know," Theophilus said as he stood, "a number of people in this country have been put to death by this court on that charge." He sat back down quietly.

"And now," Baruch said, "we're getting to the core. Subversion, you see, is like an illness. It eats inward. Sooner or later, after attacking the symptoms of the illness, one has to eradicate the core of it altogether. Gentlemen," he looked over the court, "that core sits before you today." He pointed at Elhrain.

Lemuel nodded. "The prisoner will be given the chance to defend himself," he intoned. "And that will take place tomorrow. We have had enough for today. Well done, Baruch."

As one, the body of the court rose to leave. They filed out and, as if by crossing a magic line of decorum at the door, began babbling like excited children over the threshold.

250

Chapter Twenty-Seven

The guards led Elhrain away.

* * *

Theophilus was required to consult with Agrippa following the proceedings. I awaited him anxiously at his house.

When he came his normally impassive features were tense.

"What did he say?" I demanded.

Theophilus shook his head. "Agrippa wasn't available," he said. "Occupied with other business."

"That doesn't sound good."

Theophilus shrugged. "I learned long ago not to judge by appearances. It wouldn't do any good in this case anyway. Agrippa is not well known here. It's hard to tell how he will act."

"He only has two choices," I reminded him.

"True. To approve the court's decision and execute the prisoner, or to deny the court and let him go. Or a host of options in between."

"Such as?"

"Remand him to civil authorities for trial. Banish him."

"The easiest thing would be to agree with the court," I observed.

"Indeed. Especially for a young man trying to establish his place. But Agrippa is unpredictable. Also, unlike his father, he is sensitive to the people of this region. He has studied them, knows their customs."

"More support for the lawgivers, then," I said.

"Not necessarily. The people were thirsty for blood for a period. Those were unsettled times. But now they're growing afraid. Starting to wonder, 'Who next?' It has gotten out of control. Agrippa may see this as a chance to exercise power *over* the court."

"The court," I scoffed. "It was a babble. What exactly is Elhrain's crime? Half of that didn't make any sense at all to me."

Theophilus chuckled. "It's not intended to make sense," he said. "In fact, just the opposite. It's intended to confuse."

"We have knowledge; you're ignorant?"

"Precisely. We have knowledge; we're correct. But their aim is more subtle yet than that."

"Tell me," I said.

"They aim to defile him. To make Elhrain look like a fool. It was the same with the Messiah. And now with all his followers. Defile and discredit. They're not just trying Elhrain, my brother. Never make that mistake. They're trying the entire movement. They will make it look foolish; they will make people afraid."

"Will it work? Can the movement be stopped?"

Theophilus smiled. "When you look at Elhrain, brother, see there every believer. He will be vilified, denigrated, mocked. But see there also the Messiah, who went before him. Then ask the question. I'm not sure of the answer."

I paused before asking the one question I had wanted to ask. "So much depends, then, on Agrippa," I said. "How do you think he will decide?"

Theophilus stared darkly across the room. "I think," he said evenly, "Agrippa will give the court everything it wants."

"So Elhrain is a condemned man?"

"The moment he was taken. And I think he knows it."

CHAPTER
TWENTY-EIGHT

I awakened early the next morning. In the garden outside the house a mourning dove called plaintively. It was such a little lonely sound. Dew hung heavily on the leaves of flowers and trees, untouched by any breath of wind.

I dressed and walked to where the garden fell away to a rocky hill. I peered past the brown boulders to the city that lay wrapped in bleak fog. The tops of buildings emerged as obscure clots in the haze.

At the heart of it all lay the temple. Although hidden by fog this morning, its thick, stalwart flanks were clear in my mind. Down the hill from the temple, lost in a valley of fog this morning, was the prison. The building, its warrens dug out of rock like funeral vaults, had been bolstered by gates and guards making it impregnable. Yet one prisoner in there now had once participated in a mad plan to breach its warrens of desolation and despair and liberate a handful of prisoners. It had been a grim design of hope and daring. Now he sat within those very walls.

I wondered what he thought when he looked out this morning. Of course, I reminded myself, he would see nothing but the darkness of the cell block, the guttering oil lamps only accentuating the deprivation of light. How he hated confinement of any sort. It was like trying to trap the wind, so restless was he. Yet it made all the more striking the perfect composure he evidenced in the courtroom. I expected an eruption of outrage; I would have condoned it. What I saw, however, was not anger or even resignation. What I saw was absolute calm, as if in these last days the desert wanderer had indeed found his home. *Someday*, I thought, *the minds of men will probe the stars themselves. How many will find what Elhrain has?*

How much did the court know about his past? Would it have mattered? For their own reasons, they perceived Elhrain simply as a threat they must destroy. Then the people could sleep easily.

As if the absence of suffering or threat equals true peace. I know how Elhrain longed for the commonplace, how he sought quiet seclusion, the mere routine of his life on the farm. But he had been willing to leave that routine for his beliefs. Some people made of routine a god, never daring to challenge the predictability of their lives. That to me is a hideous waste.

Elhrain, precisely for the threat he brought to the routine of the religious order, was considered evil. It was so apparent. In Theophilus's words, they would "defile and discredit" him. To protect the routine, the lawgivers would not bother to defend the routine; it was an accepted fact. Custom was right because custom had endured. Elhrain was a scapegoat because he was different.

These protectors of routine did not want alternatives to be known. Elhrain was the alternative incarnate: a stranger, a foreigner, a man who *looked* different, *acted* differently, a *believer*. Thus they would attack, vilify and impugn him. With such abuse and shame, they sought to make alternatives to the routine appear dangerous.

And Elhrain, I believed with absolute certainty, *knew* this. It was, after all, the way of the Adversary to make the good thing look spurious.

As Elhrain would no doubt testify, the opposite of routine was not mere randomness of belief. Nor was it the troubled, ceaseless questioning. Nor even comfort, since faith, at nearly every turn, questions our comfort. The opposite of routine is inward peace. That was his discovery.

Theophilus tapped me on the shoulder, and I jumped, so lost in thought had I been. "It's time to go," he said.

"I want to see him," I said.

"Who?"

"Elhrain. I want to talk to him."

"Impossible. He's under guard. Double guard. Even I am prevented from talking with him through the course of this trial."

"You're his advocate!"

Theophilus shook his head. "Only his witness," he said. "I have no voice in this trial before the Sanhedrin. Elhrain knows that. Only before Agrippa may I speak in his defense."

"But by then the verdict will be in hand."

He looked at me. "It already is," he said. "It has been from the start."

"Still, I want to see him. Arrange it. Use whatever tricks you can."

He smiled at me. "I'll try," he said.

"Not good enough. Do it."

*　*　*

Baruch was eager to begin. He paced restlessly before the court until the prisoner was led in, then turned his back on him to speak to the Sanhedrin.

From the start, he surprised me with his tactics.

Speaking first to the court, Baruch summarized. "Yesterday," he intoned in his large, round voice, "we established certain things. First among them is this fact. While this court makes no pretense to adjudication in civil matters, and while it esteems all such matters and indicates its deep respect for them, and while we are privileged to have this esteemed advocate"—a nod toward Theophilus—"among us as representative of such matters and defer entirely to his wisdom and counsel in all such matters, nonetheless, we observe certain analogies. It is proven by civil tax records that, with the complete opportunity of knowledge of that law that protects his interests in this land, the accused did willfully avoid his just and due obligations of proper taxation under that law."

Baruch took a breath, sliding into his transition as effortlessly as an athlete. Still, I wondered what had been proven in the matter.

"In the same way, the accused has lived under the protection and privilege of the religious law of this land, a law antedating that of the civil structures we enjoy and uphold: the law of our fathers. The law revealed by God himself to our forefathers. He has transgressed that eternal law. In what ways?

"The law requires an offering according to stipulation. The accused not only ignores his own responsibilities in this regard but supplies the offering for others, thus rendering them of no account. Now, our law is one of mercy. If one has little to offer, one is required to offer but little.

255

Yet, by giving to the needy that little, Elhrain has robbed them of the opportunity to give of their own free will. He has robbed them of their immortal souls, has denied them the opportunity of absolution, has led them on the road not of mercy and grace but of condemnation.

"He stands accused of murder. Of killing the opportunity for grace for many people, of guaranteeing their guilt under the law.

"Second," he continued without pause, his voice calm, assured, "we established the accused's personal culpability. That while having the opportunity to know the stipulations of the law governing marriage, he did take to be his wife one of our daughters under the law and by so doing cast *her* under the threat of eternal punishment. This is no marriage; this is fornication. And, as if the devil himself bargained it, they have produced by this unlawful union a bastard child.

"It is obvious to the court that the accused who sits before you has deliberately, systematically perverted all that we esteem holy. He has wrought disorder in our land. He has led others astray. He bears all the arrogance of one," his voice rose, "who pretends to play God!

"Now," Baruch said. "There are criminal charges that have been associated with this conniver, this agent of the Adversary who sits before you. There has been talk of his complicity in a prison break that freed people condemned for their crimes." Quickly, even as he saw Theophilus half-rise to object, Baruch insisted, "But that is not our interest at the moment. Although it should be," his voice softened, "the interest of the civil authorities.

"What we are interested in today is merely this. Who is this man? Defiler? Deceiver? How can such a force be unleashed in our homeland? How, indeed, can anyone permit this threat to continue?

"So. Where do we start? Seducer of one of our daughters? A woman, Betharden, whose name is entered on our books? Whose father—the esteemed merchant, Samuel—and mother were so brutally murdered years ago? One wonders if the accused was not part of it all."

Baruch finally turned to Elhrain. The scorn in his voice was like an acid. Yet he remained some distance from Elhrain, as if his very presence were a disease.

"What would you say, prisoner, if I told you I had Betharden in our custody even as we speak?"

Elhrain blinked. It was the first time I noticed visible tension in him.

256

Then he relaxed. The question was hypothetical, a taunt.

"Then," Elhrain said, "I would say you transgress your own law."

"How is that?"

"You have based *my* villainy on her uprightness. You imply I seduced her, I perverted her, I may even have stolen her. The crime is mine. She is, sir, one of your people. And above reproach."

Elhrain's voice was slightly halting, as if he struggled now and then for the precise word. Yet his voice, with its deep resonance, carried force.

"Indeed?" said Baruch. "Free from trespass?"

"One cannot have someone seduced without an agent of seduction. Nor can one have a seduction unless the person who is seduced is guiltless. Else there is complicity and no seduction. By your own argument, she is guiltless."

"She bore a bastard child. Out of wedlock."

"We are married."

"A child you have not even bothered to name."

"The child has a name."

"Oh? I don't find it on the temple rolls, nor on the civil rolls. I don't find it recorded. I have no notice of a temple offering for the child. Plenty of trespasses, prisoner. No wonder you have not named the child. He too lives under condemnation according to the law."

"He lives under freedom according to grace."

"Then why doesn't he have a name? And what is it?"

"He is named after his grandfather."

"Yes?"

"Balthazzar."

"Ah."

I nudged Theophilus. "Do they have Taletha?"

"Impossible," he said. "And Elhrain knows it. He also knows they don't *want* the child here. It would complicate things immeasurably."

"Call it a lie then," I hissed.

"Not technically. Remember the way he phrased the question. He's just trying to break Elhrain."

"Balthazzar," Baruch murmured. "Balthazzar. Haven't I heard that name before?"

Elhrain said nothing.

"I seem to recall," Baruch pressed his long white fingers to his temples.

257

His black robe trembled. I had no doubt that he knew exactly what he would recall.

"A pagan king," Baruch said with a touch of wonder. "Yes. A pagan, when that troublemaker was born." His eyes seemed to brighten. He turned his back on Elhrain, facing the court. "Yes. You recall, no doubt, the pagans who came when the child was born. This one, the people thought he was a king, a Babylonian—those ancient enemies from whom our friends the Romans delivered us."

He whirled back to Elhrain, his face livid. "And you called him . . . what? Grandfather! Your father!"

"My father," Elhrain whispered.

Baruch snorted. "Then . . . then you claim to be king also!" His voice was full of mocking disbelief.

Elhrain said nothing.

"Let me see what I remember of these . . . kings," Baruch said. "Wise men, yes, they were called wise men. Sort of like priests. Priests and kings."

"They were not priests," Elhrain said.

"Then what do they mean, 'wise men'?"

"Gifted. Called. Each had special gifts granted to him."

"Were you one of them, then? Of course. I forget. The son of a king."

"No! I mean, yes. I was one of them."

"Your calling then?"

"Earth Master."

A small rippling sound disturbed the courtroom, like the slightest breeze on a summer day. The ripple grew to a chuckle that rose higher than the rest.

Elhrain, the fool, was himself laughing. Laughing in the face of his executioners.

Lemuel looked up, his narrow face furrowing into a frown that gave him the look of a predatory fox. Elhrain saw the look, and his laughter deepened.

"Do you mind," snarled the justice, "if we proceed in an orderly manner? Or do you find your trial amusing? Or are you laughing at *us?*"

"No," Elhrain said. He sat suddenly composed. "I am not laughing at you."

"Explain or cease!"

"Yes, well . . ." Elhrain sighed deeply, but the glint of humor did not leave his eyes. "All my life, you see, I have struggled against belief. Testing, doubting, never wholly accepting."

"An infidel, you mean," sneered Baruch.

Elhrain ignored the barb. "Against belief." Again that chuckle erupted in the court. "And now, I am being convicted for the very belief I fought against."

He burst into laughter. "Don't you see?" he roared. "Belief is *not* a birthright! That's where you're wrong. I truly must believe. This is the proof of it. I will die for my belief. It is final proof."

"Are you insane?" hissed Lemuel. His teeth clenched in a spasm of anger. "You are being tried. If it is the judgment of this court, you will be executed. I have qualms," he said self-righteously. "But I *will* have an orderly courtroom."

Elhrain nodded. "Earth Master," he mused. "As such I took my place at the Table of the Brotherhood, never fully understanding what it meant. For no one ever 'masters' the earth. Knowledge. Knowledge, man. Understanding that on this earth, one is not master of, but mastered by. Except that one chooses one's master. You have chosen mastery of the law; you have been mastered by the law. You are," and he looked steadily at Lemuel, "a slave of the law, unable to see life beyond it. Being mastered, you are impoverished, and your greatest poverty is not to know how impoverished you are. For the law is your idol, and you are its slaves."

Appalled, the court was murmuring loudly now.

"Earth Master," he repeated. "It is the lesson of freedom. No one can tame the earth. One learns to live in its rhythms. Only as one gives oneself to it does one learn freedom to know it. Each is great only in proportion to the degree to which one serves. Yes, I believe. I have given myself to the Master and have learned the freedom to know him as such."

"Take him away," screamed Lemuel. He stood, body shaking. "I said take him away."

But the two guards were already grasping Elhrain's arms, dragging him from the court.

* * *

I don't know how Theophilus arranged it. Perhaps it was testimony to the esteemed and flexible position he held. He was one of the people, yet

259

an intermediary with the authorities. He was as independent as a magistrate and wealthy landowner, yet somehow a daring ambassador, respected by all sides. Even so, it surely took all the power at his disposal, all his finesse. Perhaps it was simply that the verdict was so stunningly clear and that the religious court felt, in their confidence, that it wouldn't hurt, in fact that it might help, to have the physician examine the condemned on the evening before his execution.

I met with Elhrain that night in his cell.

Theophilus arranged for a Roman officer to accompany me. In addition to all his other duties, Theophilus did in fact hold a position of rank in the military. Apparently, through his ties with Rome, that position also held some authority. I certainly welcomed this no-nonsense officer. He walked close behind us as a surly guard led me to the cell block.

It was the same subterranean dungeon with the same suffocating stench, stupefying heat and humidity. I had come once before, but then I had failed to take it seriously since I had safeguards. I never had that sense of utter abandonment.

A guard sat at the end of the cell block, half-asleep. Another sat before Elhrain's cell. He stepped aside as the guard opened the door. When I suggested he take a break, he looked at me quizzically. When the Roman officer called him, he left quickly.

Elhrain was sleeping. I shook him gently. His pupils narrowed before the light of the torch as his eyes opened. He raised an arm to shield his eyes; then, recognizing me, he slowly sat up. His lean body sagged wearily. He had stripped off the white tunic, and sat only in his undergarments. Sweat dotted his body in little pools. He leaned back against the wall and smiled.

"We meet again," he said.

"You look pretty sleepy," I said. "Perhaps . . ."

He waved my concern aside. "For the last day of my life?" he said. But he still smiled.

"Perhaps not." I replied. "There is still the chance—"

"Doctor," he said. "Don't play with me. We both know the outcome."

I nodded. "Is there anything I can do to help?" I asked.

Again, Elhrain let that weary smile slide over his face. "Not unless you can work a miracle," he said.

"I can't. That doesn't mean a miracle can't happen."

"I know, Doctor. I also know better. This is what it all comes to, but I am at peace with it. And it is good to see you in the courtroom, to know . . . I am not forgotten. So, I appreciate your visit, but there's nothing you can do."

"I meant on the outside."

He looked at me sharply. "I don't know. I think everything is taken care of."

"Taletha? And your son? Did you really name him Balthazzar?"

Elhrain chuckled. "Yes. Really. I am sworn to tell the truth, after all. But I would guess they will call him something else where they have gone."

"Do you know where Taletha is?"

Elhrain nodded. He leaned toward me. "I trust you, Doctor. I tried to contact you through Zophar. Taletha had a hard birth."

"I know. I did come. Too late, I'm afraid."

"At least Zophar made good on his word," Elhrain muttered.

"Do you trust him?" I asked.

"I really have no reason not to. I *needed* him. I took precautions."

I didn't ask what they were. I had heard things about Zophar from settlers and refugees as I had traveled through coastal cities. What I had heard disturbed me deeply. Always there was money involved, and I sensed Zophar's weakness.

"I took precautions," Elhrain was saying. "There were certain things that had to be above legal reproach. Papers, that sort of thing. But Taletha and my son, well, suffice it to say that Zophar only supplied the contacts."

"They are out of the country, then?"

Elhrain nodded.

"Good." My sigh of relief was audible.

"Yes," Elhrain chuckled. "And in good hands. You remember when Lycurgus and Doval had to flee?"

"How can I forget?"

"Lycurgus was more than he appeared. More than a mere soldier in the Roman army."

"I could have guessed that."

"My information is safe with you, Doctor. Long ago, Lycurgus divulged to me that he was also the son of the Emperor."

"But . . ."

Elhrain nodded. "Yes. The Emperor has died, of course. And the fact is that Lycurgus was an illegitimate son. But he had proven himself to Rome long before, and the Romans are far more tolerant of such matters than the people of this land. You see, Lycurgus had a place to go. Even in the long years of his absence, he had maintained an estate along the coast, north of Rome. Secluded, as befits the man. I knew this. It is where he and Doval would have gone. And where, I believe, Taletha and my son are now. It was not easy. Her sacrifice was greater than mine. One of us, you see, had to remain so that the other could escape.

"That, Doctor, was the hardest thing I have ever done." His shoulders slumped, his head bent. It was a moment before he could speak. When he did his voice seemed strangled. "That woman . . . walked through the desert by my side. *She* made my home. She salvaged what was left of me. And she gave me a son." Elhrain's voice broke. The gaunt shoulders shook. I placed my hands upon them, and Elhrain sagged against me.

It was some moments before he regained control. "She was still weak. The birth was hard. Bitterly hard."

"A breech, I heard," I said.

He looked up at me in surprise, eyes reddened by his weeping. "Yes. We had to lay her in the wagon to escape afterward. Manasseh's wagon. You remember how it's done?"

I smiled.

"I had to say goodby as they—Manasseh, Meridivel, Tomit—stacked the wood around her, our son lying at her breast. Her eyes . . . She has the most beautiful eyes in the world. The soul of her speaks through those eyes. I seem to see her now. She watches me . . ." His voice trailed off. He jerked himself, as if coming awake. "Am I talking like a madman?"

"No. You're no madman. Just a man in love, fortunate enough to be blessed with love."

"If ever you see them, Doctor, will you tell them? Both of them?"

"I will tell them both. How a wife never had a husband who loved her more. How a son never had a braver father."

"Thank you," he breathed. By an effort of sheer will he recovered his poise. "I received word that they had sailed from Joppa the night before I was arrested. The plan was that once they had landed, I too would flee. I had taken necessary steps for the farm in the papers I filed with Zophar."

"So Zophar still has a responsibility."

"Zophar," Elhrain said, "has a disease. It's called greed. Only he can cure himself, but he can't even do that unless someone trusts him to. Besides, as safeguard, I had Tomit and Althea witness the papers."

"Well, we're clear on that score at least. Zophar would never harm his niece."

"He would harm no one willingly."

"So all we can do is wait?"

Elhrain looked at me. He raised his hands. "Look, I am unshackled. Perhaps I could walk right out of here with you."

He chuckled deeply and lay back on the cot. "Good night, Doctor. I am very tired."

* * *

The sound of the doors slamming behind us sent chills down my spine.

I had seen many condemned men, had officiated at more than one execution. Never had I seen someone so convinced of its inevitability as Elhrain. And yet so at peace with the inevitable.

CHAPTER
TWENTY-NINE

H earts beat faster when Agrippa entered the room. He was a tall,
rather thin man, and when he strode into the hearing room reserved for him, followed by a retinue of assistants, he brought with him
also a commanding authority. People assembled there knew that by his
word alone fortunes could be held or lost, lives saved or lost. His red cape,
flung casually over glistening white garments, boldly pronounced: the
authority of Rome itself.

The anticipation slowly waned as the morning passed, one case after
another brought before him. Soon returning to his palace at Chalcis, he
would not be in the capital long, and local officials were determined to
make the most of every moment. One after another, officials or merchants
were summoned by an assistant to Agrippa's presence. Some cases were
dispatched in moments, the supplicant leaving the court with a smile of
pleasure or a dejected frown. Other cases took longer as Agrippa consult-
ed with advisors or questioned the petitioner sharply.

The room grew hot. Even as the number of petitioners decreased, the
smell of nervous perspiration grew more intense. The hours wore on.

Throughout, Elhrain stood between two guards. Baruch waited in an
anteroom until summoned. Theophilus and I sat on a bench waiting. It
was clear that Agrippa was saving us for last. Why? Did he want the room
cleared to enact this final bit of business, to keep it tidy and neat? Would

it be rushed through at the end of a busy day?

Resenting the petitioners, I groaned inwardly as individual cases dragged on. *They are talking about trade agreements, about a bit of gold or silver,* I thought, *while a man's life hangs in the balance.* But then I thought, *What balance? The case is set, discussions are pointless. At least Elhrain will acquire a few more hours of life, however wearisome.*

At times I studied him. At first he stood stiffly. As the hours wore on, his body sagged. He leaned against the wall. Sweat broke out on his dark features. The guards seemed asleep standing up.

It was well past noon when the last petitioner left the room. My heart beat a bit more quickly as he departed. Now. Finally.

Then Agrippa called a recess. We would reconvene later in the afternoon. The guards led Elhrain out.

* * *

Baruch looked dispassionate and bored as he delivered his indictment. There was nothing unexpected. He began with an overview of the applicable laws of the land, borrowing freely from Asa's earlier exposition. Step by step he detailed Elhrain's violations. Only after he moved into his summary, painting his grim picture of Elhrain's threat to the order of the kingdom, did his delivery become at all impassioned. It was a feat accomplished. He played a rote game in it. When he sat down, Baruch looked thoroughly self-assured and pleased with himself.

I found myself wondering whether, if I were listening objectively to the recitation, I would side with him. My answer was—of course.

Theophilus, as appointed advocate for Elhrain, rose to plead his case. His face was grave. Surprise, complete surprise, replaced the look as Agrippa waved him down.

"With your indulgence, Advocate," he said, "I would like to question the prisoner myself."

Theophilus's voice was professional, atonal. "Certainly, Your Excellency." But when he sat next to me he shot me a look of utter bewilderment.

"Unshackle the prisoner and lead him forward," Agrippa ordered.

The guards hesitated, looked at Baruch, then quickly did so.

Elhrain walked slowly forward, pausing before Agrippa's raised chair. They seemed to study each other a long time, as if some unspoken contest of wills, or some unswerving searching of each other, was going on.

"Do you understand the charges against you?" Agrippa asked.

Baruch stirred uneasily. Understand the charges? That was not the prisoner's province.

"Yes, Your Excellency," Elhrain replied evenly.

"I am interested in your response. Baruch brings many charges. He understands them. I believe that I, having studied the customs and religious beliefs of these people, also understand them. I find them powerful charges, Elhrain. Now, I have appointed Theophilus as your advocate. A fair appointment, I believe, since he is a man who enjoys the eminent respect and the complete trust of his own people." He looked pointedly at Baruch. "A man," he continued, "who holds powerful social status and a position of inestimable prominence in this court. So, a worthy advocate.

"But, Elhrain, the charges against you, serious charges, depend upon your *willful* disobedience. You see my point? They assume you are a man of intelligence and free choice, yes?"

Elhrain hesitated, as if selecting his words carefully. "Any law that imposes rather than guides, that condemns rather than gives mercy, is suspect, Your Excellency. Yes, I have willfully disobeyed when the law imprisons the hearts of the people, persecutes the powerless, and exalts the authority of humans over God."

Baruch stood and shouted. "It is the law of God! This infidel denies God. You've heard it from his own lips, Your Excellency."

Agrippa glared at him. His voice was ice. "You've had your say. Please don't try to speak for me."

He turned to Elhrain. "Is this true? What the accuser says? That you deny God? For even though I do not hold belief in that same God, I do not deny their right to believe in their God. Think carefully, man."

"I do not deny God," Elhrain said evenly. "I deny humans who would take the place of God."

"Hmm. Well, that is the issue, isn't it? The Sanhedrin accuses you of such denial. If it is true, you are indeed a threat to their land. Now, I find here that Baruch," Agrippa reached over and took some notes from the scribe. "Yes, here. Baruch says you are a 'pagan king.' Bent on usurping the land and its laws. He says, furthermore, that you practice dark arts. A sorcerer or wizard. A 'Magus,' he calls it."

He dropped the notes. "Are you, Elhrain, a wizard? Or sorcerer? Do you hold common talk with demons?"

Chapter Twenty-Nine

"No."

"Would you define a *demon*?"

"Yes. One who lives without pity." Elhrain turned toward Baruch. "Look to the demons in your own hearts."

Agrippa spoke quickly. "Yes, yes. So, a demon is a human who doesn't behave as a human."

"No, that isn't what I said. Any person who has the opportunity to show grace, to give love, and fails to do so, who instead looks for ways to destroy, harbors a demon in his heart. He works for the Adversary to pervert truth and justice. He is a child of lies."

"So you do believe in supernatural presences. In evil, demonic presences in addition to presences of goodness—what, I believe, the people call angels."

"I do so believe."

"Then you see my difficulty." Agrippa paused a long time. "Who is to say which is which? How can a human determine these divine difficulties? And, oh yes, it is very much the issue. Many people in this land have been accused of demonic activity and executed by the authority of this court. By my own father, Elhrain. Did you know that? My father thought he was a god. The people encouraged it. But was he? Well, he was my father. Just an ordinary . . . no, I wouldn't even call him ordinary."

Agrippa's mind seemed to switch directions like a stream blocked in its course. He leaned forward, speaking in even tones.

"The request is for execution. The charges consist of certain crimes against the state, as stipulated in the record. These charges arise from violation of religious principles, practices and laws that bind the state. These charges are serious, for Rome by treaty and compact as well as a long interest in its provinces has permitted the state autonomy in its internal affairs. We are not a persecutory empire. We would rather have a people in alliance, a people free and self-identified who are loyal rather than mere puppets who are always abrasive and looking for the opportunity to undermine the empire."

Agrippa again paused. I shot a glance at Baruch, his face gone rigid with fury. His patience was stretched thin.

"Such an approach has served us well," Agrippa continued. "Our relations are good, conducive to our mutual interests. Without us, this land would not long survive. Any enemy knows that to attack this land is tantamount to attacking the empire of Rome itself. So it has proven a gracious, even glorious relationship.

"Now, then. When we face charges of villainy against the state, an undermining of its laws, rebellious acts, we take such charges seriously."

Baruch visibly relaxed. A small smile played over his tense lips.

"The state determines the crime; the empire executes the sentence. A serviceable arrangement. Some would say, a nearly perfect meeting of two different powers, a joining that produces inestimable convenience and clarity.

"We are the empire. We are responsible for civil order and public decorum. We will not shirk that responsibility."

He turned to Elhrain, looking him squarely in the eye. "The Empire, therefore, finds you guilty as accused."

Elhrain didn't flinch. I heard a long sigh from Baruch's direction. My fists clenched.

"Your sentence, to be enacted immediately, is"—the pause hung in the silent room—"the banishment of the prisoner now and forever from this land."

Baruch shouted something. Agrippa's retainers strode toward him. Agrippa motioned Theophilus forward, and I followed uneasily. Agrippa's voice was low and urgent.

"Will you see the prisoner from the court, Advocate? I am led to understand from my own sources that his family awaits him in the city of Faenza. You know the place?"

Theophilus nodded. Elhrain looked stunned, as if the news were too great to bear.

"North of Rome, Your Excellency," Theophilus said.

"Then make haste. Get him out of here and to the coast. He's on his own now."

*   *   *

We walked rapidly from the courtyard into the dusky light of late afternoon. A small retinue of legionnaires accompanied us, but once past the gates we would be alone, our only protection the authority of Rome, not its presence.

I glanced back and saw Baruch gesturing angrily in a circle of lawgivers.

"Quickly," Theophilus said. "There should be a wagon waiting with either Elihu or one of his men."

"A wagon waiting! You knew this would happen?"

"Not entirely. Not until Agrippa actually said it." He chuckled nervously. "He drew it out long enough."

Elhrain walked in the middle of us like a man dazed. He kept flicking nervous glances over his shoulder.

We stepped out into the street, the legionnaires coming to attention.

"There," Theophilus said, pointing. "Around the corner. There's the wagon."

We half-trotted from the protection of the soldiers, feeling terribly alone. We *were* on our own now, with one aim, to get Elhrain away from here as fast as possible. The driver sat sleepily in the seat, loosely holding the reins of the two-ox team. He started as we ran up.

I stopped in my tracks. Zophar!

The fat, white-bearded man grinned expansively. "So," he boomed.

"How did you—"

"I was in town," Zophar explained quickly. "And heading back to Noke. Who better? Elihu agreed. No secret boxes this time, I'm afraid."

Of course not. But we were out of sight of the lawgivers now. A loose pile of wood lay in the wagon with a bit of hay for the oxen and some blankets. Within seconds we had Elhrain stowed under them.

"Quickly," Theophilus said. "You have to be through the gate by dusk."

Zophar snapped the reins, and the oxen leaned into the yoke. The heavy wagon lumbered down the street.

"I'm going along," I said and started to run after it.

"No, not this time." Theophilus held a hand out to restrain me. "We can't risk it."

"Precisely." I broke free of his grasp. "That's why I'm going."

I caught up with the wagon, pulling myself into the seat as the startled Zophar looked at me in surprise. The wagon wheeled around the corner, leaving Theophilus in the distance.

"You don't know what you're doing, Doctor," Zophar said. "This isn't your place."

* * *

The oxen plodded on into the night, their hooves muffled in the dust of the road. Zophar was right. I didn't know what I was doing. What could I do if there was an attack? Wave a medical bag—which I didn't have along—at them and call for help?

The moon rose in the east like an orange blister, its face besmirched with clouds. Ground fog covered the road. The oxen moved sturdily. We passed through empty stretches, the road deserted.

Once I peeled back the blankets and looked at Elhrain. He was lost in the pure oblivion of exhaustion. The hazy moonlight made his gaunt features look like a weathered skull. I tucked the blankets back around him.

It had been a long day. I began to doze, slouched on the seat. Zophar seemed alert, wary. I thought of offering to relieve him, but exhaustion crept up on me.

* * *

The wagon lurched suddenly. I had the feeling that I was falling and started awake. No, we were heading uphill, no longer on the main road.

How long had I slept?

Trees hugged the path, branches slapping at us. Zophar snapped the reins, swearing now at the reluctant oxen.

"Where are we?" I asked.

"A place I know. We can hide there. Rest for the night."

The wagon swayed treacherously. We were high among the hills. The moon had paled, its light faint through the trees. I sensed more than saw a rider behind us; the oxen and the lumbering wagon were making so much noise I couldn't be sure.

"Where are we?" I insisted.

"Patience, Doctor."

"Patience, nothing! Stop. Turn us around."

"Can't turn around here."

The trees parted. To the right the road fell away precipitously. The valley was lost in fog and darkness. I turned and stared at Zophar.

His eyes reluctantly found mine. "A pity you had to come along, Doctor. I'll try to make sure you're safe."

I started climbing off the wagon seat. I would jump. I would run.

"Too late for that," Zophar said. "There are two of them behind us."

I peered into the gloom. It wasn't my imagination. I could see the

270

horsemen now.

"Think, Zophar," I shouted. "You can stop this."

He shook his head. "Not anymore. I sold my soul long ago."

The bumping of the road jarred Elhrain awake. He shoved the blankets aside and sat up groggily. He read the whole story instantly. When he spoke his voice was even. "How far do we have to go, Zophar?"

Zophar whirled, opened his mouth to speak, then clamped his jaws shut. He cracked the reins viciously. The wagon skidded dangerously on the hill path. The two horsemen closed the gap, riding directly behind the wagon now, guarding against escape.

*　*　*

The clearing, circled by trees and brush, was lit by a large fire. Shadow and light danced in tense warfare. Several horses were picketed in the clearing alongside a narrow, light wagon yoked to one ox. The animals pawed and snorted nervously as we drew near.

I looked desperately for a way to escape. Everything was shrouded in night fog, the light from the fire ahead turning rock and brush into orange shapes. One side of the road, lined by thick brush, fell away into darkness—a precipice. We were high in the hills. To that side lay certain death. The other side rose steeply in jagged rock. It might be possible to climb there, but it would be too slow. The guards would be on us in an instant. Past the clearing ahead the road dwindled to a narrow path disappearing among dark trees.

There was no way out.

The men warmed themselves around the fire. Dark and ill-clad, they were a rough company. Baruch stood with red firelight glowing against his black robe. Lit from the fire below, his grin was diabolical.

Had I been able, I would have fled, terrified, and run all night. Now I fought only to quiet the trembling. Beyond the men, a mound of dirt lay piled up. A pit gaped open, one end of a long beam shoved to its edge. I recognized it immediately—the post of a crucifix, crossed by twin stipes, one at the top, one about four feet from the bottom. Its significance was also immediate; the victim would be crucified head down.

The trailing horsemen dismounted beside our wagon. One hauled Elhrain out of the bed, flinging him bodily on the stony ground. The other seized my arm. I pulled back in recoil. He grabbed a handful of my cloak and wrenched me from the seat. He laughed as he held me at the end of his muscular arm, my toes barely touching the ground, the cloak knotted up around my throat, choking me. I kicked ineffectively.

"Put him down," ordered Baruch.

The man flung me sprawling to the edge of the flames.

"A pity you chose to come along, Doctor," Baruch rasped. "But, I suppose, appropriate to the occasion. After all, a physician is supposed to pronounce the death, even though it won't be a question in this case."

The men guffawed. One swaggered forward, kicking Elhrain's prone body. The blow sounded like striking wet wood. I tried to stand. Immediately a guard seized my arm, twisting it violently up behind my back. I screamed in pain. It felt like my shoulder was being ripped loose.

The men roared with laughter. Several walked over to Elhrain, ripping his garments from him, cursing and kicking.

"Easy," Baruch commanded. "I want him to know what's happening. I want the good physician to know what's happening." He turned to me and leered. "Your turn next, Doctor. We'll show you the proper sentence for all your sort. This is our land. *You* are the traitor.

"Do you recognize it, Doctor?" He glanced at the cross. "Head down, yes? If I remember right, you were there, weren't you? Years ago? When we hanged the madman? This is what it got him. What it got you, Doctor. Except we'll do you head down. You appreciate that, don't you, Doctor?" His face was malevolent, hideous. The green eyes glittered eagerly.

"The blood collects, pools, in your brain. As it does so, before you scream and scream with the pain, think of all the wrong choices you have made.

"Prepare the criminal for execution," he snapped.

I heard someone blubbering. Zophar.

Baruch looked past me. "What's that, fat man?" he shouted. "You wish to go now? Already?"

The guards hooted. Several of them dragged Elhrain, scraping his naked body over the rocks, toward the crosspiece.

"Zophar, you can't leave just yet, I'm afraid. No room to turn around. Stay and watch the show. We may have a third one yet tonight."

The guards cheered. I heard Zophar moaning. "It wasn't supposed to be like this," I thought I heard him say.

"Oh, Zophar," Baruch needled. "All the precious money you'd leave behind. And I know where every bit of it is, my fat friend. I will enjoy spending it with my friends here."

Elhrain was squirming against the wood. Several men held him down. His enervated body fought back with a will of its own. I heard him gasping for breath. One heavyset man knelt on Elhrain's crossed legs, weighing them down to the upper crossbeam.

A dull rumble of thunder seemed to roll in the distance, then disappear.

One man seized the heavy nail, holding it to Elhrain's crossed ankles. He was drunk and laughing. Another raised the hammer to slam the nail in. It slipped, the guard laughing uproariously. The hammer careened off Elhrain's ankle.

I had heard that sound before—that ominous but muted rumble of thunder. At the Master's crucifixion. The sky black. The earth shaking. The thunder had sounded like an army of horses then.

It grew now in volume. A guard looked up, startled. Several darted for weapons.

Horsemen came from two directions, up the road and blasting down from the hilltop into the clearing. The lead horse was as black as the night, its rider in the mail and flaring red tunic of a captain.

In one onslaught the charging horsemen scattered the guards, then leaped off their mounts to battle. Weapons glittered and clashed off each other.

A body slammed into me, knocking me to the ground. I tried to drag myself away. Feet tripped over me. A heavy body stumbled, falling heavily to the ground. He heaved himself to hands and knees, face wild, saliva dripping from his mouth.

I reached up and grabbed Zophar's cloak. He twisted, frantically trying to free himself from my grasp. His eyes were mad; he foamed and snarled. I let him go.

He stumbled clumsily into the brush by the side of the road, as if he had lost track of all direction. I shouted at him, a shout lost in the melee of battle. In his blind panic to escape, Zophar charged through the brush toward the precipice.

A sudden long scream rived the night; the sound diminished as he fell, then choked off suddenly.

I looked back at the clearing. Several guards lay sprawled on the ground. One groaned. Two others made no sound. The rest sat in a circle

273

surrounded by military men.

Baruch! He knelt before the fire, begging incoherently for mercy. Theophilus pushed back his visor, staring at the lawgiver before him. He looked at the cross, where two warriors were helping Elhrain to his feet, then back at Baruch.

"It would serve you right, lawgiver," he spat.

Baruch gibbered and moaned, bowing his face to the ground.

In utter disgust, Theophilus ordered, "Bind him. He will be returned to stand trial before Agrippa for crimes against the Roman Empire."

CHAPTER
THIRTY

Liske stirred for the first time in what seemed long hours. Evening light climbed through the open window like some fragrance, glowing in the spacious room at Theophilus's home. Through the window the western sky heaved bands of gold and crimson about the lowering sun.

We sat in the large room adjoining the garden. I had recently returned from one of my journeys and had come here now like one who called it home. From the kitchen I heard the sounds of Judith talking with her two little daughters—their laughter, the clatter of wooden spoons and cookware a sort of point-counterpoint to the tale I had been telling. The scent of bread floated from the kitchen.

As if mesmerized, Liske stirred slowly. He walked to the window. He was a tall, strong young man, his face and arms dark from long hours in the sun. One scarcely noticed that his left arm was slightly shorter than the other, the muscles thin and the shape a bit askew, the hand flexed rigidly. Liske himself was unaware of it. He loved the farm and was thoroughly capable of running it with his young wife, Sarah. His visit to the capital had ostensibly been to buy a load of lumber for reframing some of the ruined buildings. I am sure he had waited to make the trip until he knew that I was back.

I don't know if I will stay here long. I think perhaps I shall. Like another traveler I once knew, I am weary now with much voyaging. I would like,

I believe, to have a place to call home, to study these parchments, to add to them what is proper, necessary and fitting. Theophilus and Judith have offered me a room here. I'm not certain yet that I shall take it.

"I find it hard to take in," said Liske. "So much happened. So much. And you were once a part of it all."

I shook my head. "No, Liske. Not a part of it all. Elhrain was, in some ways, the most unusual man I have ever met. In other ways, at other times, he was just the most ordinary of men."

"Do you know what happened to him?"

I nodded, although Liske's back was to me. "Yes, I saw them all, just once. But it has been several years now. North of Rome is a city called Faenza. That is where Lycurgus held some land as a birthright. That's where they went. The region is famous, I understand, for its wine.

"When I saw him last," I added, "Elhrain was an old man. He was . . . dying."

Liske shot a glance at me.

"It comes to all of us, my son. I think Elhrain knew it. I am certain he has died by now."

"And Lycurgus?"

I chuckled. "As far as I know the old warrior still lives, although not fit for wars anymore, of course. Taletha and Doval run the household, but then they always did. Lycurgus spends much time with the boy."

"They are safe, then."

"Oh, to be sure, Liske. They are safe indeed. And busy. They are seldom alone and never lonely in their large house by the seacoast. The church in Rome is growing, even as the persecution intensifies. Why, when I left . . ."

But I stopped. That was not the story Liske wanted to hear. Suddenly I understood. "You're wondering if you're safe, Liske? You and Sarah?"

For a moment his face looked confused. Then, "Yes," he admitted. "I do worry. The farm—it's too much. More than I deserve. Maybe more than I can handle. And I am worried—"

"That someone will take it away?"

He nodded. Then he looked uncertain as I laughed.

"Liske, Elhrain may have seemed like a dreamer, a visionary, at times. He was also as shrewd and insightful as any human can be. His visions were tested in the practicalities of mere survival; his wisdom was tested in the cunning and intrigues of royal courts and military powers. No, he knew what he was doing.

"You see, I believe Elhrain knew what was coming, and he was prepared. And—yes, this too—he knew precisely what kind of person Zophar was. Shrewd, conniving, cunning as a hyena, but absolutely faithful to his own self-interests. And no interests were stronger than his family. It was part of his treasure."

"Most of that was seized," Liske murmured.

"Plenty was left," I said. "Tomit and Althea held the inn. There was enough to start over. Most of what was seized was illegal anyway."

"Such as?"

"Zophar was shrewd, Liske, but he didn't know exactly where a hard bargain became mercenary. He forgot the line where business had to be guided by mercy rather than money. For example, he loaned money to refugees escaping to the coast. A good thing. Except that he exacted interest that held them in bondage for years. He had a series of bondsmen along the coast supervising the operation. Other things. I won't go into them all. Especially the dealings with Jerusalem. It's not necessary.

"But Elhrain understood that Zophar was as utterly loyal to his own ends as he was utterly crafty in the means to get them. Yes, at the end he was in so deep that he couldn't get out. But Elhrain had Zophar draw up the papers so that the farm went to you and Sarah, and Sarah was, of course, the daughter of Zophar's only living relative, his niece, Althea.

"You can bet they were done properly. All taxes were covered for a certain number of years by accounts held in the capital, where the papers are filed. The lawgivers were dead wrong on that score. They tried to manipulate the civil tax records to make their case, but Theophilus's presence was too powerful for them to succeed. No. You have no need to worry, Liske."

"How did he know? I mean, did Elhrain know we would get married? That was years ago, when we were children. I never even found out about the farm until we were betrothed. Then this lawyer from the capital came and . . ."

I held up a hand. "Liske, that I don't know. Elhrain was a remarkable man. I don't pretend to know all his secrets, to understand the depths of his knowledge. Rest in the fact that he saw rightly. Enjoy it, Liske. Work the land, love your wife, care for your children if the Lord is so gracious as to grant them."

Through the window the evening sky had deepened to purple bands in the west. The sun had disappeared, flinging its afterglow through the skies. The room was in near darkness.

"May I ask one more question, sir?" Liske asked.

"Surely."

"Zophar. He's buried in Noke. Yet, if I understand correctly, he died that night."

I nodded. "He did. But Elhrain refused to leave until his body was recovered. Theophilus assigned a guard of two men to Elhrain, to continue to the coast by wagon.

"Baruch, by the way, was returned to the capital. Eventually, after holding him in the prison, Agrippa sent him to Rome for trial. I can only guess what happened to him there. He never returned.

"But Elhrain insisted upon recovering Zophar's body. Theophilus made Baruch's thugs, under the eyes of his own men, climb down through the brush and carry the body to a level place where it was loaded upon the wagon and brought to Noke. It was his nature, Liske. Elhrain had always loathed killing. He would rather die himself than see others suffer. He knew that there were those in Noke who, despite everything, still loved Zophar. I don't know what hold the lawgivers had over him, what extortion of payment was involved. I don't think I want to know. That died with his fall over the cliff. What survived, even in his death, were the memories that others had of him. These were what Elhrain honored."

"I see," Liske said. His eyes were puzzled. I don't know if he ever would sort it out, nor that I have. Words like *honor* and *loyalty* acquire meaning only in the deed, the living out of what they require in each person's life. For some it requires merely the fulfillment of each day's labor. No, that is not entirely true. Whatever the task, whatever the calling, loyalty and honor require grace.

I had Liske stay at the house that night. In the morning he left, and I began pondering the manuscripts that I had skimmed the day before.

* * *

No words, I understand, capture a life. Among the words might slip certain resonances—glimpses of insight—that begin to reveal the life forever shadowed by the words.

When I ponder these, what comes to mind first are the women—those fiercely loyal, heroic women. How does God send so much grace as a Taletha or a Doval into a person's life? There is a rare and glistening radiance about them that shines even through the dimness of recollection. Few people face the tests they did; yet, in a sense, each person does. The test is the mirroring of a character, and what shines in the mirror is a loyalty beyond hope or expectation.

They are the true warriors.

Elhrain was not. For he never wanted warfare, either of the spirit or of the body. That he did in fact accept the conflicts that reared before him, when he could have avoided them, is testament to his character. For he was a gentle man who longed more than anything for a sense of repose, to be at peace with the spirit and flesh.

Elhrain is the most complex man I have ever known—a man of consuming passions and terrible gentleness. I think that without Taletha's annealing touch, his life would lie in ruins. He was noble, but not good, if goodness is measured by absence of negative traits. Such goodness, the goodness of denial, is a cheap and easy trick, and Elhrain loathed it. Even as he battled against his own negative traits—his occasional arrogance, his uncertainty, his skepticism, his anger . . . the list goes on. He would be the first to assent to all of those traits.

I find his own words only limn the contours of that character I knew. He recorded the events, so very little of himself.

He was called Earth Master, and I believe, truly, he was. For the earth was created a harmony. This he sensed. And harmony he sought. But the earth as it now exists is distorted so that the vestiges of harmony must be sought and won at a price. His earth-mastery was the terrible knowledge of sacrifice.

No words can touch that spirit. For precisely that reason the spirit cannot be contained or extinguished. It is a light in the encroaching darkness. Others nurture its gleaming, and at times it grows to radiance.

It lives yet today, wherever people guess at its gleaming and respond to it. They may be crouched in dungeons; they may be huddled in homes. They may be in conflict where the light flashes like meteors against the darkness.

For most of us, I suspect, having caught a glimpse of its gleaming, this light of grace and harmony is nurtured in quiet ways. We return to it over and over again, and in our returning are nurtured by it.

The darkness does not understand this. The darkness cannot overpower this.

The light still shines in the darkness, its pale and pure gleaming a beacon even for hearts twisted by darkness. Still they come, and still they go forth, trailing lights upon whatever paths they take.

So I see Elhrain hunched over the desk, writing beside the oil lamp even as the darkness drew nigh. Or I see Taletha and Elhrain in the desert, nurturing the light from a handful of feeble twigs while the night ravens scour the skies and the jackals huddle watching. They rest before the fires, but the light is carried within them.

* * *

The wind murmurs among the leaves of the garden, and it seems to ask if it was all worth the effort.

I am not the one to answer. I have not paid a heavy price, borne a weighty enough burden, shared the most desperate of hardships. I have not walked in the valley of the shadows as these others have, that place where one fights for a glimpse of light. Although my own life has not been without event, I have had a different calling in the cause we all share. I have been the eyes and ears, the hand that records for some later generation that may wonder about the price others paid, the burden they bore, the hardships they endured.

The ones who have every right to answer are gone now. These words stand as evidence of the light, even when the shadows seem overpowering. So I let them stand.

So be it.

So let it be.